Praise for The Myth Adventure Series

"Asprin's major achievement as a writer—brisk pacing, wit, and a keen satirical eye. Breezy, pun-filled fantasy in the vein of Piers Anthony's *Xanth* series"—ALA *Booklist*

"A hilarious bit of froth and frolic. Asprin has a fine time with the story. So will the reader."—*Library Journal*

"Witty, humorous, a pleasant antidote to ponderous fantasy."— *Amazing*

"The novels by Asprin are loads of fun, extremely enjoyable humorous fantasy. We really like it."—*The Comic Buyers Guide*

"...an excellent, lighthearted fantasy series..."—*Epic Illustrated*

"An inspired series of magic and hilarity. It's a happy meeting of L. Sprague de Camp and the *Hitchhiker's Guide* trilogy."— *Burlington County Times*

"Humorous adventure fantasy at its rowdiest."—*Science Fiction Chronicle*

"Recommended."—*Fantasy Review*

"All the *Myth* books are hysterically funny."—*Analog*

"This is a fun read and series enthusiasts should enjoy it."— *Kliatt*

"Stuffed with Rowdy fun."—*Philadelphia Inquirer*

MYTH-GOTTEN
GAINS

Robert Asprin &
Jody Lynn Nye

Meisha Merlin Publishing, Inc.
Atlanta, GA

Myth-Gotten Gains Copyright © 2006 by Robert Lynn Asprin and Jody Lynn Nye

This book is printed on an acid-free and buffered paper that meets the NISO standard ANSI/NISO Z39.48-1992, Permanence of Paper for Publications and Documents in Libraries and Archives.

Myth-Gotten Gains

Published by Meisha Merlin Publishing, Inc.
PO Box 7
Decatur, GA   30031

Editing by Stephen Pagel
Copyediting and Proofreading by Easter Editing Services
Interior layout by Lynn Swetz
Cover art and interior illustrations by Phil Foglio
Cover design by Kevin Murphy

ISBN: Hard Cover 1-59222-104-1
ISBN13: Hard Cover 978-1-59222-104-2
ISBN: Soft Cover 1-59222-105-X
ISBN13: Soft Cover 978-1-59222-105-9

www.MeishaMerlin.com
First MM Publishing edition: September 2006

Printed in the Canada
0 9 8 7 6 5 4 3 2 1

MYTH-GOTTEN
GAINS

Robert Asprin &
Jody Lynn Nye

Chapter 1

"PSST! HEY, FRIEND! Yeah, you with the green scales! Buy me!"
I looked around.

I was browsing one of the myriad jumble sales that beckoned to me, not in the Bazaar, where the voice was probably that of the innocent-looking Deveel vendor behind the table, but on market day in the town square, in a dimension called Ittschalk. I'd stopped off on a tour of the provinces just for the hell of it, where the people were covered by masses of long, wavy hair like Rastafarians and the wide-open skies were greenish.

For the first time in years I wasn't dependent on anyone else for a ride to the next dimension—thanks to a gift from a friend. I was enjoying the novelty of being able to travel in my own company, staying as long as I pleased, where I pleased. If I felt like having a weeklong drunk in Pookipsie with the Pookas, I could do it. If I discovered the annual Broaching of the Casks festival in Harv was a bust, I could book out of there without having to wait around for a magician to give me a boost. Liberty was more of a kick than any champagne I'd ever drunk.

The Prounvip Annual Village Fair was a forest of tents set up in a wide-open square, amid the few scattered buildings on the dusty prairie plain. An oom-pa-pa band was tuning up under a conical, blue tent in the middle of the clearing. The savory smell of frying sausages and bubbling pots of spicy chili drew my nose's attention to the stringy-haired cooks laboring over pit stoves under an adjacent pavilion. Kids were having their long locks plaited into tiny dreads and tipped off with colored beads by nimble-fingered hairdressers, or sprayed in undulating patterns with glitter that their mothers were undoubtedly hoping would wash out easily later on.

Off to one side the hairy denizens were trying their luck at shying coconuts, trying to hit inflated colored bladders with darts, or attempting to knock down a pyramid of amphorae

with a stuffed cloth ball. Pretty primitive games, to my sophisticated Pervish eye, but the locals seemed to be having
fun trying their luck. I wasn't sucker enough to throw away
my coppers on the games, which were always rigged, at every fair in every dimension, or, from what I could see, on the
merchandise set out for sale on rackety tables arranged under the hot sun for my delectation. I surveyed it all with a
phlegmatic eye. Most of the stuff for sale was unmitigated
junk, but I was enjoying a look anyway before checking out
the quality of the local brew in the hostelry across the way.
Enough of the patrons were staggering out to give me a good
feeling about the place.

"Hey! Look down! Please, good fellow, get me out of here!"

I looked down. An eye peered up at me. It was reflected in
the inch or so of dull silver blade protruding from the worn
leather scabbard on the table. I glanced up. There was no one
nearby from whom it could be reflected. Intrigued, I grasped
the darkened brass hilt and pulled the sword out a few more
inches. A second eye appeared reflected in the blade. They
were long, steel-blue orbs outlined in black, keen and summing. I glanced up to see if it was the black-braided merchant
casting a spell on the blade to make it more appealing to passersby, but he was at the end, talking to an old lady covered by
long, silver hair about a flowered china chamber pot.

The voice murmured again. "Thank the Smith, I thought
you were never going to listen to me!"

"I heard you," I said, pleasantly. "Have a nice day."

I prepared to pass on to the next pile of goods.

The voice grew frantic. "Pray, friend, don't go! You may
hear something to your advantage!"

My ears pricked up. Pervish ears are well designed to hear
things to our advantage, being shaped not unlike those of bats,
who can hear noises up into the highest decibels. We can hear
sums well up into fifteen figures.

"What could you possibly do for me?" I asked, keeping
whatever interest I might have out of my voice.

"First, friend, cleanse me of the grime of this place."

"How?" I asked.

"If there be no enemy to strike, a sharp rap upon a stone will do it."

"Why not?" I said.

I don't carry weapons. Pervects like myself are well furnished by nature with defensive armaments, such as hide tough enough to turn a fairly sharp blade, yellow claws that could as readily disembowel an opponent as poke open a can of beer, and four-inch, pointed teeth capable of ripping into anything including the cheap steaks at a truck stop. Still, I know how they're used.

Scaring the pair of arachnoids next to me into dropping their egg sacs prematurely, I swept the sword up over my head and knocked the blade on the ground. It *hummed*. The corrosion just exploded off it. I covered my eyes to protect them from flying rust. When the dust storm ended, I found I was clasping a gleaming brand with a blade of white-hot silver and a hilt of chased gold studded with cabochon gems of the pure colors of ruby, amethyst, emerald and sapphire that made my palms itch with unrealized profits.

The eyes, now free of the film that had veiled them, were sharper than ever. I had seen eyes like that while playing Dragon Poker, over the top of a hand of cards, as my opponent wondered if I really held an Elf-high flush, or if I was bluffing. These made an intelligent search of my person from head to feet.

"A Pervert," it said. "I have both aided and killed your kind."

"It's Per*vect*, you hunk of tin," I snarled.

The eyes closed briefly as if the unseen being was bowing its head in apology. "As you will. Your people have attained a higher status, then, than they had when last I saw Perv. Pray, friend, buy me, and hastily. I would be away from this place. I will see to it that you will be reimbursed tenfold."

"Tenfold, eh?" Well, that was a pretty good return on an outlay. Still, I didn't have amniotic fluid clinging to me anywhere.

"In case you didn't know it, Skinny, you're a sword. Where are you going to get the money?"

"I will tell you my story, if only you will remove me from this locale. I fear that danger may lurk about us soon."

I observed just then that more people than I had taken notice of the transformation of the flea-market sword from letter opener to museum piece. I gave them a good glare and showed my teeth. They backed away, careful to keep their hands and feet far away from my mouth. I shoved the sword back into its shabby sheath and dragged it carelessly over through the dirt to the being who owned the stall.

"Ah, good...sir," the Ittschalkian said, turning his mass of braided fur my way. He eyed me nervously, but he wasn't about to drive away a potential sale. He peered at the weather-beaten tube of leather in my hand. I kept my fingers wrapped tightly around the hilt. "I see you have chosen one of my favorite artifacts. I am sure you appreciate its value."

"I sure do," I said. "Five gold pieces, and not a copper more."

"Five?!" the man asked, his face transforming spectacularly from oily accommodation to outrage. "How could you ask me to part with a family heirloom for a mere five coins, scaly sir? It's worth at least forty!"

I always thought it was amusing how a shopkeeper could set out a tableful of crap, ignore it unless it was being openly stolen, abuse it to his friends and family as the garbage it was, then instantly start spouting the woe-is-me-my-family-will-starve line. I'd heard the litany so often I could recite it along with him. If the guy's a good salesman, I will sometimes join in the banter just to enjoy the show, but this clown had no natural style. He was clearly one of the guys who'd bought the course advertised on the back of a magazine that was headlined, "If you can draw Sparky, you, too, can be a filthy huckster!" He just didn't have it in him. Besides, I wasn't in the mood.

"Too high an opener, brother," I said, shaking my head reprovingly. "A Deveel wouldn't have had the nerve to ask me for twenty for this pig sticker."

"Pig sticker!" echoed the voice in the scabbard. It was muffled, but there was nothing wrong with its hearing. "I'll have you know, varlet..."

"Shut up. Not you," I said to the merchant. "Five's my offer."

"Then I will say fifty!"

I sighed lustily. He had not seen the sword's transformation, and not only was I not going to tip him off about it, I gave a warning eye to everyone in the crowd gathering around us to make sure they didn't, either. "Six."

"Sixty!" the merchant responded.

"Seven."

"Seventy!"

"Four."

"E...what?" The runaway freight train just piled into a brick wall.

"You've just tripped into absurdity, brother. The price goes down from now on."

"Why, you can't do that!" His braids flapped with outrage.

I grinned, giving him the benefit of my last dental prophylaxis. He blanched at the sight of my Pervect smile.

"Sure I can. Do you want to make a sale or not?"

"That's the stuff, friend...!" the voice from my hand mumbled out.

"Shut up. Where were we? Four."

"Nay, good Pervect, I am worth at least a hundred times that!"

"Shut up!" I growled out of the corner of my mouth. "Do you want me to leave you here?"

"Nay, I beg you!"

"Then, zip it before someone hears you! Four," I repeated.

"No, sir, please!" The merchant was aghast. He wrung his hands together. "It cost me far more than that! I obtained it from a hairless, old soldier down on his luck."

"Probably out of drinking money," I said, coolly. I had the upper hand, and I wasn't letting it go.

"Give me twenty, at least."

"That's more like it," I said approvingly.

"Then you'll pay it?"

"No way. My original offer was five, and you're going to be lucky to get that."

"Fifteen, friend."

"Nope."

"Ten. That's just a single coin more than I paid for it. That's my last offer."

The truth rolls out if you give it time, and so does the local police force. I noticed a quartet of hairy pikemen trotting down the street towards us with purpose. Someone in the crowd must have decided that I looked dangerous. I could probably get away with stiffing the merchant at nine gold pieces, after his admission, but I didn't feel like tangling with the constabulary. This was supposed to be my vacation!

"Done." With an air of magnanimity I felt in a pocket for the right change and tossed the money onto the table. The coins rang as they clattered to a stop on a brass commemorative coronation platter. "Nice doing business with you."

I turned away nonchalantly, tucking the sword under my arm. In a cloud of hair, a bunch of people rushed toward the table to talk to the merchant, probably to tell him what a sucker he had been to sell a prize piece of cutlery like that at cut rates. I sauntered idly toward the inn.

"By heaven, friend, you are a frighteningly good businessman even for one of your kind."

Normally, flattery feels good, but it had just occurred to me that there was now a ten-coin-shaped hole in my purse that hadn't been there before. I snarled.

"Shut up. I just paid out good money for a sword that I don't need."

I needed a drink. I stalked into the inn, took sole possession of a corner table, planted myself with my back to the wall and my eye on both the front and back doors, and signaled to the barmaid, a fetching lass with long red hair all over her shapely form.

"Hey, babe! Whaddaya got on tap?"

A moment passed while I persuaded the girl that the egg-cups that Ittschalkians drank out of wasn't enough to keep a Pervect alive over lunchtime. By the time she reappeared with a hastily scrubbed bucket filled with beer, the sword could no longer restrain itself.

"By the Smith, it is good to be away from those pathetic artifacts and their master! Unsheath me, friend. I sense that we are in a reasonably defensive location with few potential foes nearby."

It was exactly the same assessment that I might have made of the situation. The main room of the inn was empty except for a few locals chatting earnestly over the long table right in front of the bar, and a couple of oldsters with thinning, gray locks playing a board game under the window on the opposite side of the room. I felt mellowed enough by the first mug of beer to indulge the sword's whim. I pulled it free of its case.

"What hight you, friend?" it inquired, giving me another one of those summing, X-ray looks.

"You mean you can't read it off my underwear band?" I countered. "Aahz is the name."

"Oz?"

"No relation."

"Ah. It was the green color that put me wrong. I hight Ersatz."

"Yeah, sure," I chuckled, taking a pull at the second bucket of beer. "So is every other talking sword in the dimensions, and most of the ones who can't talk."

"But I am THE Ersatz."

"That, my shiny friend, is what they all say." I looked down at the eyes. They were angry. "Okay, maybe the guy who forged you and set the intelligence spell in your metal told you your name was Ersatz, but I gotta tell you, you couldn't be the real one. *That* sword was made about ten thousand years ago. It fought in about a million battles..."

"One million, four hundred thousand, eight hundred and two—no, three. I have never been defeated."

"Listen, pal, you can spout off fake statistics until you're blue in the...er, steel, but there are hundreds or thousands like you."

The eyes blazed. "There is no one like me! I am unique! I, the leader of the Golden Hoard, am nothing like those hundreds or thousands who may have followed. They are named for me! I was at the side of the hero Tadetinko who saved Trollia from the blazing monsters from Lavandrome! I was in the hand of the conqueror who bested the usurper of the Deveel Corporation! I, and I alone, was the weapon who held back the gate that protected the capital of your very dimension and kept it from becoming a wholly-owned subsidiary of that very business concern. I am no imitation! I am the REAL Ersatz!"

At that moment I remembered where I had seen a sword that looked like Ersatz. It was woven into a tapestry that hung on the wall of the Perv Archaeological Museum in the city where I grew up. In particular, I had noticed the unusual pattern of jewels in the golden hilt. About two or three thousand years before I was born, a Pervect named Clonmason *had* defended the dimension against the invasion of Deveels that had attempted to occupy our main city. He drove them back to their infernal regions with a legendary sword named...

"Nah..." I breathed. "The Golden Hoard is a myth!"

"Indeed," said the sword, "we are not."

I sat back, forgetting even to drink my beer. The Golden Hoard had been renowned throughout the dimensions for thousands of years. It was a collection of fabulous animated treasures whose who seemed to find their way to people who were about to be heroic, so they could save the world from whatever peril had arisen at that time. I knew all about the Hoard. It consisted of all the traditional goodies, one of which some hapless knight comes across just when he was hoping to avoid a major conflict, and finds himself at the heart of a battle royal to save the world, turning up just in time to ransom a fair lady, or in the hands of a wet-behind-the-ears wizard enabling him or her to make the prophecy that saved a kingdom from certain disaster. They had all been around for thousands of years. I rarely feel awe for anyone living, and almost never for anything inanimate, but I had to admit I felt respect for the slip of steel in my hands. If it was the real Ersatz, it had led more generals than the hope for glory. It was worth a big chunk of change, making ten gold pieces a cheap investment against a potentially enormous return.

"So the crystal, the cup and the book...?"

"Aye, the ring, the flute and the endless purse of money also are members of our order. I am the eldest. The great shield is all to brast," the sword added. "He gave his all for the Liberation of Klahd, four thousand years past. The harp was crushed, stringless, in the rout that followed the Taming of the Centipede Giants. The Great Key was melted down in the fire that destroyed the treasure house at Nox. Yet, that is our fate. I have seen great treasures join us, only to depart this existence, yet satisfied that they had been crafted for just such a moment."

"Weren't there some more treasures?" I asked. "I heard about a golden mace some guy was hauling around some years back. It was supposed to be part of the Golden Hoard."

"We have an ongoing problem with wannabes," the sword said, with a sigh. "For a while, Heroic Treasures were coming out of the woodwork, so to speak. No mace was ever part of our number. There was a claim from the Bagpipes of Fear, but it turned out there was really nothing magikal about them. Their sound just naturally made anyone hearing them turn and flee, something any one of ten billion sets of bagpipes could do."

I shuddered at the thought of ten billion bagpipes. I examined the sword again.

"Looks like katae," I said, admiring the metal. It had been folded over itself again and again to make layers katae that were many times stronger and more flexible than any poured blade could be.

"Katae!" the blade shrieked. "My smith predated katae by ten thousand years! He devised and forgot about more techniques than any swordsmith since his day!"

"Don't get your quillons in a braid," I said, continuing my examination. The sword, "Ersatz," was once famed as the sharpest, most intelligent sword around, but so many fakes were made that the name became a byword for cheap and shoddy. "You look like you can still hack with the best of them."

"I'm still as sharp as I ever was," the sword insisted. "But I can't get anyone to believe it. YOU didn't believe it."

"The jury's still out, as far as I'm concerned," I said, but I was starting to take his word that he was what he said he was. "Where are the others?"

"I know not where most of my companions be," Ersatz admitted, the steel-blue eyes dropping slightly. "Many of us haven't seen one another in over a century. If truth be told, most of us don't care for each other. Kelsa—she is the great scrying crystal, the most accurate viewer of the future ever crafted, and she has never made a direct statement since the day she was carved. When time is of the essence, she cannot get to the point!"

"That's your specialty." I grinned.

"You have a sharp wit yourself, my friend."

"So, what am I supposed to do with you?" I asked. "I don't really need a trophy for my wall, especially not a talking trophy."

The blue eyes looked alarmed. "Nay, friend, I wouldn't want to be a fixture. For a time I was embedded in the wall of yonder eating establishment," the sword managed to glance in the direction of the street. Out the inn's door I could see a red-walled hut with customers emerging carrying flat, gooey comestibles that were this dimension's equivalent of pizza. "I lived side by side with a wain's worth of junk from all over this dimension. I was only freed from the endless chatter of 'tonight's specials' and 'two-for-one dinners' when the patrons finally decreed that they would no more sit at the table beneath my prisoning brackets. I think they did not like my comments upon the resemblance between their meals and the guts of enemies I have slain. That is when I was vended unceremoniously to yonder merchant."

"They just didn't appreciate good dinner conversation, I said, grinning. "I know a couple of pretty good swordsmen who would take care of you in your old age. Keep you all buffed up, listen to your stories."

The sword got huffy. "I do not need shielding! I need to be cast forth into fate's way once again, so that I may end up where I am needed next. Friend, you have proven to be an intelligent being who sees more than a few ducats at the end of the next trade."

"Who says?" I interrupted him.

"I need your help."

"Mine?"

"Aye, yours."

"Forget it, bud," I said. "I'm on vacation. I'll take you as far as the next war, then we part company."

For the first time the eyes bore an expression of appeal.

"Honorable master Pervect, I beseech you. Listen to my story. Then, if you must place me in the hand of some mudstained lad who is throwing himself into the battle, I will accept it."

"Fine. Suppose you can't buy me a drink." I glanced around for a likely spot.

"Nay, such is not my talent. I am sorry. I have been waiting for one such as you. I have heard word from a passing dagger that my fellow Hoard members are being *collected*. One greedy individual is gathering all of them up. This must not happen. We cannot gather dust upon a shelf for all eternity. We must be free to blow in Fate's wind."

I chugged the last of my second bucket and signed to the lass for a third one. She delivered it with some dispatch, and retreated. Guess that not many of her customers took a table for the purpose of talking to their weapons. "Sorry, skinny, but I stopped doing freebies, especially big, legendary freebies, not long after I stopped being an apprentice myself."

"Did I mention that one of our members is the Endless Purse of Money?" the sword asked, the reflected eyes gleaming.

I stopped in mid-gulp, entranced by the memory of that legend. There wasn't a Pervect child who heard it in school who didn't have itchy palms and avaricious dreams about it. "Well, yes..."

"Whatever you can get out of her, that shall be your reward."

"I've heard offers like that phrased before, and not just about money," I said. "Forget it."

The sword's eyes dipped with understanding. "Very well, I shall persuade her to give you whatever sum you require. On my honor, we will reward you more than adequately. Thousands of gold pieces shall be yours. Tens of thousands. But, first, we must find her."

The offer sounded better the longer I hesitated. "Well...all right. What do we do first?"

"You must take me to Kelsa. She is the only one of the Hoard whose location I know, and the only one who could tell us the location of the others. Then we will find each of them and free them from their captivity."

"Not part of the deal," I said, seeing visions of money bags winging away from me. "Forget it. I'm not going off on a quest just because you want to put the band back together. You wanted out of the flea market, and you're out. From my point of view you owe me a hundred gold pieces. That's all."

"But...care you nothing for the greater good?"

"Just because you and your buddies get cabin fever?" I snarled. "I don't think so. I'm just going to hang out here and have a little snack, then I'm..."

At that moment, the door burst inward. In a flurry of hair, the crowd from the square came rushing inside, the junk merchant at their head.

"There he is!" the Ittschalkian exclaimed. "The one who cheated me! We'll tear the hairless one apart!"

I had already sprung to my feet. Somehow the hilt of the sword sprang into my hand.

"Draw me, friend!" the sword shouted. "Let me drink of their blood. We will be victorious! Have at you, varlets!"

The mass of Ittschalkians was closing in. As a matter of course I have all the exits from a place scoped out in advance in case of just such a moment as this. I made for the rear of the establishment, only to come face to face with the local gendarmes bounding toward me with purpose in their eyes. One of them was raising a particularly nasty-looking magikal wand from its hip holster. I had no choice. I reached into my pocket for the D-hopper that had brought me there to Ittschalk, and hit RECALL.

BAMF!

Chapter 2

THE INN VANISHED. It was replaced in a magikal second by an equally dimly-lit room, but most of the occupants were already on the floor. Loud music filled the air, along with the indelible stink of stale ale mixed with vomit, fried food and unwashed bodies. The frat party I'd left behind in Bonhomme was still going on. I found myself straddling an upended beer stein and a purple banner reading "Vertebrates Rule!" A couple of the drunks on the carpet lifted their snakelike heads and tasted the air.

"Aahz!" one of them hissed. His black-bead eyes gleamed with pleasure. "You're back! Have another drink!"

"No, thanks, Sllisssiik," I said. "Just here to make a pit stop."

Sllisssiik aimed his tongue toward the doors at the rear of the room. "On the left, but watch your step. Tktktksssni went back to shed his skin and disgorged the prey he'd engulfed all over the floor."

"Poltroon," the sword said, sulkily. "Not one of those caitiffs back there was armed with anything sharper than a butter knife, and you whisk me away from the only good fight I have seen in ten years."

I glared. "Shut up, or I'll use you to shave with."

"Who's your friend?" asked Sllisssiik, blinking at the blue eye that stuck up over the torn edge of the leather scabbard.

"Ersatz am I," the sword said.

"Cool." The Bonhommey giggled and slid back to the floor.

The sword returned its keen gaze to me. "Well, friend Aahz, if you return to Ittschalk you will walk into a fight. I would gladly be at your side, but you say you care not for a hearty battle. Misadventure has thrown us together. What say we cast our lots into fate's wind?"

"The only 'lots' I'm interested in is the money you owe me," I pointed out.

The blue eyes were wistful. "Alas, I cannot repay my debt to you if you do not carry me to my friend Kelsa's side. If you'd lief not, I would understand, but we both feel strongly. I care not for being in debt, and you do not care to be owed. Indulge me yet one more time, friend Aahz. You will not regret it."

"I regret it already." My temper was up. I missed my snack, my third beer, and my quiet walk around the town. I wanted a vacation, and instead I got a sword that speaks fluent Forsooth. If I bent it into paperclips I couldn't get my ten gold pieces back. I stuck my finger at the blade between the eyes where its nose would be, if it had a nose. "All right, I'll give you one chance. How do I find your crystal friend?"

"She is in Ori."

BAMF!

It had been about twenty years since I last visited Ori. Nice enough dimension, but the rice beer didn't have the hit of good sake, and the women weren't interested in a guy with scales. Too bad, because they were a nice bunch of pussycats.

We appeared at the edge of Perrt, the second-largest town. Getting by the sentry box at the main gate took only a moment. The guards, who resembled enormous, sinewy black leopards, inspected my baggage, which consisted of one talkative sword, cash and the toothbrush in my pocket, and rubbed their jaws along my thigh, scent-marking me to indicate I'd passed inspection.

"Kelsa has spent the last hundred or so years counseling the great seer Ori Ella," Ersatz explained as I followed his directions through the maze of streets that wound in between the white painted plastered houses. "She is a great wisewoman, who has made good use of my friend's gifts."

I was a whole lot less interested in her gifts than I was in ridding myself of my talkative companion. We dodged a huge cart full of silver fish each the size of my torso, and the parade of Orion shoppers following behind it with an insane gleam in their eyes. I had the urge—resistible, fortunately—to yell "Here, kitty, kitty! Din-dins!" I quite rightly judged it would be the last thing I ever did. It would have picked the fight of a life-time with the locals, who were touchy about their resemblance to the small animal that was a house pet in over a hundred other dimensions. Ersatz would have been thrilled about it. While I walked he told me tales of his past derring-do, and he had a million of them, literally. Still, as I watched those long tails switching avidly on those furry behinds as they followed the fish cart, it would have been fun.

"...It was a sight you might have relished, friend Aahz. There they were before us, sixteen black-masked ruffians, each with six swords clutched in their many hands. They moved in upon us. I guided the hand of my young ward. Up, to guard in prime! Over hand, stabbing downward, into the vital midsec-tion of the first attacker. My blade passed right through the body and out the back into the lowest right wrist of another villein, severing the hand. Back out! My wielder drew me over his head in a two-handed stance and brought me down and around, spinning. I turned my blade so my sharpest edge was outward, and we severed the necks of three of them on the spot. Hah!"

I held up a hand to put an end to the spate. "Are we going the right way?" I asked.

The keen eyes surveyed the streets. "Aye. We are within a street's length. Do you turn left at the clock tower which yon felinoids are stropping their talons upon, and we will be upon Ella's doorstep in no more than a dozen paces."

I have good eyesight, but it took another hundred feet be-fore I focused on the shapes at the base of the tower. He was right. The clock tower looked like a popular meeting spot for the citizens of Perrt, a hundred or so of whom were spaced out around its square base, claws out and raking hard at the surface, which seemed to be made of a soft stone. From hun-dreds of years of wear it had been carved into long narrow ridges like corduroy. The Orions gossiped as they clawed, and came away from the walls with their fingernails honed to fine points and ears full of the latest news, the local variation on the old water cooler. I skirted them and counted twelve paces to the second doorstep.

"Mount here, good Aahz," Ersatz said. "Kelsa is within."

Ori Ella's tabby housemaid answered the door and left us in the hallway. I had given her my name, but told her I'd state my business to the mistress of the house. She took that without question. I would have bet that over 80% of visitors did the same thing. Either the seer would know all about us without having to be told, or she was a charlatan, and she'd get out of me what she could read from my body language when we met.

Apparently, Kelsa was good at choosing the company she kept. The arched door at the end of the hall burst open, and an Orion with pure white fur came bustling toward me, shimmering blue and green robes fluttering in her wake. She had huge blue-green eyes with vertical pupils that were open into wide ovals.

"Oh, Mr. Aahz, Kelsa has talked of nothing but you for the last two hours! Where is he? Oh, yes, I forgot!" She tittered, and put a coy paw to her breast. "You don't know me, and you don't trust me. I'm Ella. Welcome! Where is Ersatz?"

She was the real thing. I was impressed. In my experience, fortune tellers were either deluded sensitives who thought the voices in their head had some mystical significance, or scam artists who used a combination of psychology, body reading and shrewd guesses to tell the customers what they wanted to hear. I hadn't mentioned the sword's name since we hit the dimension, so she could not have heard it from an agent or a spy-eye. I hiked Ersatz a foot or so out of his scabbard. His eyes gleamed.

"Honored, my lady," the sword said.

"A pleasure," the seer replied, beaming down at him. "Both of you, come right this way! Oh, we have felt for weeks that monumental changes were upon us. I am only glad that you were able to get here so quickly. I've had a dreadful feeling that something was going to go *wrong*, but I'd rather be wrong about being wrong. Don't you agree?"

Still babbling, she swept around and led us toward the door from which she had emerged. I followed in her wake, rolling my eyes.

The house might have been a mansion, but the room she led us to could have been any gimcrack psychic's tent anywhere in the cosmos. The room was lit with candles in sconces. The wicks all smoked like sportscasters. The air was thick and tasted of cheap paraffin. All the furniture was covered with loud-colored silk throws, three or four to an item, so that a customer had to plant his feet firmly on the floor to keep from sliding off. There was lots of it. I had to watch my step in the dimness to avoid bumping into little tables filled with useless knickknacks that would have made any Victorian auntie beam with pride of ownership, like a clock shaped like a tarantula that told time with two of the arms, and a bronze ceramic vase so ugly I was surprised it hadn't scared the petals off the flowers in it. Amid the tables were four or five bureaus and a dozen upholstered chairs with stiffly upright backs. The portraits on the walls were of the Angry Ancestors school of art. I got glared at by assorted curmudgeonly Orions of both genders in various weird costumes, informing me that Ella wasn't the first one in her family to lack dress sense. I glared back.

All the kitschy décor faded into a dim setting as my eye was caught by a blaze of pure golden light. In the center of the room, on a little round table with a purple, star-spangled cloth, was a sphere. It was so perfectly shaped it reminded me of a soap bubble. It glowed like a movie sunrise. My feet started moving toward it under their own power. I hauled back, reminding my body to whom it belonged, but I kept my eyes on the gleaming orb.

"Kelsa!" Ersatz said.

"Ersatz!" the globe squealed. As I got closer I could see a face in the sphere, that of a female Orion wearing a turban adorned with a big gold aigrette and a backward-curving ostrich plume and jeweled spectacles whose corners angled upward. Her whiskers pricked out with delight. "The portents have come to pass. The energies have aligned themselves in the order I foretold as of old. I knew you were coming."

"Indeed she did," Ella said, gliding over and settling down on the ottoman beside the table. She gestured me to a small chair opposite her. "Why we have been talking about it for some time. I am pleased that you are here. Why, your exploits have absolutely thrilled me to the core of my soul!"

I preened. "Thanks, Ella. I don't talk about myself much, but it's nice to be appreciated."

"And, you, too, of course, Mr. Aahz," Ella added, with an apologetic inclination of her head. "Your past has been a *most* interesting tale. We didn't know until a very short time ago that you were the one who was going to convey the Great Sword Ersatz here to this place!"

I scowled. The face in the globe turned to face me, and became that of a female Pervect.

"Your fate has been foretold many times," Kelsa said, "and it changes as frequently as the weather. I believe that the Elements who govern chance send you to tumble like the dice they throw, yet you constantly turn up with a winning number. Oft and oft your future has altered. A benevolent power must be in your stars. How confusing it must be to constantly turn this way and that!"

"I take care of myself," I said curtly.

"I'm going to miss her so much," Ella said, stroking the crystal fondly with her paw. "We've had such marvelous times together! We've gotten to be good friends over these last few years, haven't we, dear?" She leaned fondly toward the globe, and the face within it became an Orion again. "And we've had our fun."

"Oh, we certainly have," Kelsa exclaimed. "Do you recall when the governor of Perrt came to ask—was it the first time, or the second time? No! It was the third visit after the great festival of Wheeleaf five years ago. Or was it six? About the three women he was keeping behind his wife's back?"

Ella tittered. "And one of them had sent a spy along in his entourage. How foolish of him to think he could come incognito to US. Why, you saw through her at once."

"Ah, yes," Kelsa said. "And he was having an affair with her, too. Silly girl. She didn't know whom she was going to betray first. Well, she DID, since she was there to betray the governor first, but then she was going to turn her coat on the mistress, but she wasn't sure in what order she was going to do the betraying!"

I began to see what Ersatz meant by Kelsa's inability to get to the point. Ella was a perfect match for her.

"Never mind that," I said, waving a hand to get their attention. "The sword here came for some advice. He wants to know the location the Endless Purse of Money. Give it to him so I can get out of here and get back to my vacation."

"Oh, your vacation!" Kelsa said, turning the Pervect face to me. She beamed, showing rows of razor-sharp teeth. "Why, you won't have to worry about your vacation. Not at all."

"Good," I said. "Okay, Ersatz, say your piece and let's get out of here."

"Fair Kelsa," Ersatz began, "I have suffered idleness for the last many months. I wish to return to battle in the hands of warriors, but I have also heard a disturbing rumor concerning the fate of our fellow Hoard members. Is it true?"

"But, *which* rumor, dear?" Kelsa asked, switching her attention to him. Her face changed from scales to steel, but the glasses were still in place on her now razor-sharp nose. "Did you hear the one about the Cup? He was said to have been offered as a prize in a school games day competition. That one is true. He was won by an eight-year-old Klahd for the twenty yard dash! Second place! He sits on a shelf between a collection of toy soldiers and a box of stale Milk-Duds. He's livid! What a comedown for the goblet that held the Wine of Peace between the Comdails and the Lenoils of Perosol!"

"Not that," Ersatz said.

"Or—here's one that made me laugh—I'm supposed to have been secretly transformed into a bowling ball in the Imper League Championships!" Kelsa let out a trill of laughter. "Picture me rolling down a lane toward a group of clueless pins to score a mere ten points."

"I can, no problem," I growled.

"About the rest of us, Kelsa," Ersatz urged. "I heard that the others are being stolen one by one, by a *collector*."

"Oh, *that*," Kelsa said. "That's not nearly so amusing as the one I picked up the other day from the ether. You just wouldn't believe it! I hear that the ring is living in..."

"That's the only one I want to hear about, Kelsa," Ersatz interrupted her.

"But it's so dreary!"

"Reveal it!"

The globe sighed, seeming to deflate slightly. The face inside stilled, and the eyelids dropped halfway over the round blue eyes. The turban on her head got fancier, and the stone in the aigrette started to glow bright gold. The eyes started to change size, one growing huge while the other shrank, then shrinking as the other bulged.

"The treasures of the ages shall reunite again," Kelsa intoned in a spooky voice that made the skin on my back crawl. "The seven golden ones shall be gathered again by a green hand. When allies stand at odds, fortune shall favor the one who casts them to the winds of chance. An enemy pursues closely, eager to foil happiness! The eternal dance must be set again in motion, led by a duo from two worlds. Ah! Lives may be lost! Fates will change! Disaster will fall upon the heads of the masses! Dentek up two, Porcom down a half, Scongreb unchanged in heavy trading..."

"A green hand! That must be you, Mr. Aahz," Ella said, beaming at me. "You are meant to put the Hoard together!"

"All right, that's it," I said, disentangling myself from the slippery cloths and scrambling to my feet. "I've had it. All I

promised to do was get Ersatz here together with his girl-
friend so I could get my money back. Forget it. I'll call it a
bad debt." My face felt hot. I needed to get out of there
before I trashed the place out of sheer temper. Ten gold pieces
lost! I smacked the scabbard down on the table and stalked
toward the door.

"Nay, Aahz," Ersatz protested.

Ella rushed to intercept me. She put a hand on my arm.
"Oh, won't you please reconsider, Mr. Aahz," she said, fluttering her large eyes at me. "It's not often that one is asked to
become an instrument of fate!"

"I don't care if you want me to be lead saxophone in a jazz
quartet," I snarled. "I'm outta here."

"...Lakers 32, Bulls 98...aaiiiieeee!"

"Stop her!" Ersatz's voice rang out.

Ella and I spun on our heels. It took me a moment to figure out what was wrong, since it seemed as though the lights
had gone out. The crystal was gone!

"After her!" Ersatz shouted. The blue eyes reflected in his
shimmering blade were wide with anger.

"How'd she get out of here?" I demanded.

"The green wench!"

"What green wench? Where'd she go? How'd she get out?"

"Up there, caitiff," Ersatz said. I followed the direction his
eyes were pointing, up the wall to the single window in the
room, twenty feet above the floor. Its small wing casements
were open, and the light muslin curtains fluttered in the breeze.
It didn't look big enough for anyone to have entered that way,
but clearly someone had. "She slipped down like a wraith. It
was the work of a moment to smother Kelsa in a cloth to still
her outburst, then up again, all without making a sound!"

I may not have my magik at the moment, but I can sense
when it's been used. This was not a hit and run. It was a surgi-
cal invasion, quick, precise and disturbing nothing more than
it had to. This was a professional theft.

"Is anything else missing?" I asked Ella.

"Well, I don't think so," the Orion said, peering around with her big, glowing eyes. "There shouldn't be. This is exactly what she predicted, after all."

"She did? She predicted this?"

"Oh, yes. She said she'd probably be stolen before she could finish telling you the prophecy about the Golden Hoard," Ella said. "And that's exactly what happened! I'm so pleased!"

She wasn't going to be any help. I ignored her and surveyed the room for clues.

"Did you leave that window open, Ella?" I asked.

"Why, no. It's so difficult to reach. I rarely use it. On the outside, it's a sheer drop of thirty feet to the ground. My goodness, this is exciting!"

"Exciting?" I asked.

"Was it locked?" Ersatz asked.

"Forget that," I told him. Any good thief worth his salt, or in this case, hers, wouldn't be stopped by a little latch. Come on." I grabbed him up and ran out. The chances of spotting the thief were vanishingly minute, but I had to try. Ella's voice rang behind me.

"Kelsa told me that there would be some slight hiccup when the two of you met again, but I had no idea it would be now!"

I jogged down the steps of the whitewashed house and around the corner into the alley that the window overlooked. As Ella has said, it was a steep wall with no handholds in sight. That would be no problem for a professional. Whoever it had been must have run off over the adjacent rooftops, which were so nearby that anyone could have made the jump unassisted by magik.

"Have after her at once, Aahz!" Ersatz demanded. "Wrest Kelsa from her grasp! I must know my fate!"

"Forget it, Bub," I said.

"What?"

I peered around, hoping to spot something that would give me a clue.

"I know a few professional second-story operators. They only work alone after dark. Usually during daylight they've got at least one lookout, maybe some hired muscle close by. I'm not going to dive into a trap. We're going to take this nice and easy."

"But she will be far away by now! Possibly in another dimension."

I met the sharp blue eyes on the blade. "If she could have magiked in and out without coming in the window, she would have. Nobody takes chances like that unnecessarily, and not for free, either. Speaking of which…" I opened my hand, as if about to let Ersatz fall in the gutter in front of Ella's house.

"Anything!" the sword said. "I will offer you a further reward, good Aahz."

I grinned. "Nice to see we're on the same page. All right. Let's see what we're dealing with. You're the sole eye-witness to the crime. Describe our perp. She's green. What else?"

"A well-shaped wench, or so many of my wielders would have described her. Tight garments, and yet they did not restrict the movement of her limbs, of which there were only four' two arms, affixed at shoulders to an upright torso on either side of the base of the neck, and two legs, affixed likewise, to the bottom of said torso. Musculature endoskeletal…"

"Cut to the chase! What dimension does she come from?"

"Oh, *that*. Well, then, good friend, she hails from that most fascinating of places, where dimorphism is of an extreme, in inverse character to many species for whom the female is the larger of the two in order to better conceive and carry offspring, a comparison that is something apposite in this case since the females are readily fond of mating…"

"What is she?" I bellowed, my voice ringing in the quiet street.

"A Trollop," Ersatz said. "A most limber one, like many of her species. A denizen of Trollia…why do you break into a smile? Is that good news?"

"Did I ever tell you," I said, unable to keep the glee off my face, "that I don't believe in coincidences?"

Chapter 3

IT TOOK A while to search out the local hostelries that served demons, but with a few threats and a couple of small coins to help spur memories, I got the names and locations of ones where a Trollop might hang out, if she had just finished a successful job and hadn't left Ori yet.

'Demon' doesn't mean 'terrifying monster from hell' as it does to races in backwater places where advanced magik and science are unknown—all right, it doesn't ALWAYS mean that. It's simply a shorthand way of saying 'dimensional traveler,' like myself and countless others who have the means of hopping in between locales at will. That's not to say that when we land in some places we're not considered to be terrifying monsters from hell. Some of the uncomplimentary descriptions I've heard of my kind have been enough at times to make me lose my temper, and anyone you ask will tell you that doesn't happen too often. That is, if they know what's good for them.

The inns where we tend to congregate have a few things in common, such as a magikal link to the Bank of Zoorik, off-dimension newspapers, a host of mercenaries and other beings-for-hire, and a hot grapevine where gossip, rumors and job offers are mixed up with the local news. They're not always friendly or comfortable places.

The first demon bar I visited had all the charm of the waiting room in the Bucharest airport. No one was there but a couple of loudly-dressed Imps hanging over a table in the corner drinking up the proceeds from the day's sale of snake oil to the locals. The second had just been raided by the Perrt Constabulary to haul away a drunken Ogre and the angry Salamander he'd ticked off. There wasn't anything left to sit on. All the furniture was smashed or burned, and the Orion proprietor was curled into a furry fetal ball in the corner behind the ruined counter.

We struck lucky, as I could have guessed, in hostelry number three. Even though the lights were pretty low I could see that the place was crowded. Hardly an Orion was in sight except for the bartender and the barmaids who swished their abundantly furry tails playfully around the patrons. Conversations, furtive or fueled by alcohol, were going on in every part of the big room. I walked in with Ersatz displayed in plain sight on my hip, golden hilt and gems glinting. I nodded to a couple of Deveels playing Dragon Poker, and cleared my throat.

"Yo, bartender," I called. "A table for me and my sword."

The elderly tabby Orion polishing bowls and glasses glanced around, then nodded toward a rickety two-top in the corner near the stairs. Every eye in the room followed me as I sauntered over and plopped myself down in a chair. Within moments, I felt a saucy tickle at the fringe of my right ear.

"Surprise," a voice breathed. "Is that a hand-and-a-half in that scabbard, or are you just glad to see me?"

A pair of lips planted themselves firmly on mine. When I could breathe again, I gasped out, "Tananda."

My old associate and even older friend backed away and smiled at me. "In the flesh, tiger."

"This is she," Ersatz said, "down to garments she was wearing when she sailed down the cord in Ella's study."

"How nice of you to notice," Tananda purred.

I let my eyes wander up and down Tananda's body. You can't say that female denizens of Trollia don't know the meaning of the word 'modesty,' but you might decide after having met a few that they have no use for it. Her attire was not only suitable for slipping in and out of small window casements, but for displaying those charms for which Trollops were so justly famous. Her tunic dove low at the top and reached high at the bottom, leaving just enough cloth in place over delectable flesh so as not to leave a trail of stunned males behind her as she walked down the street. Her skin was green, as were her tumbled locks of hair. It all made a very nice package.

"Fancy meeting you here," I said. "Have a seat, babe."

"I thought that was you I saw in the fortune-teller's," Tananda said. The lithe oozing movement that settled her into the chair opposite mine caused a dozen males in the bar to let out a breathy sigh. I gave them a glare, and they hastily went back to their drinks. "There aren't a lot of Pervects on Ori, and none I've seen with your dress sense. What are you doing here?"

"Trying to help a friend," I said. "What about you?"

"Oh," Tananda said, running her finger through a few drops of liquor on the tabletop, "I've got a little job."

"Lifting the crystal ball from a psychic isn't exactly your usual high-level handiwork," I said.

"Visiting one isn't usually on your calendar, either," Tanda countered, with a sweet smile. "Let's stop talking as if we don't know one another. That wasn't an ordinary crystal ball. I have information that says it's part of the Golden Hoard, along with a sword that looks a lot like the one you carried in here. So, let's talk."

I could tell by the look in the one eye visible over the torn scabbard that Ersatz was going to put his two cents in, so I flung up a hand to forestall him. "Let's not start spreading any rumors we can't squelch."

"Fine. I'll show me mine if you show me yours." Tananda grinned lazily at me.

"Promises, promises," I said, grinning back. "Excuse me while I whip this out." I slid the blade about a foot out of the sheath so both of the reflected eyes were visible. "Tanda, this is Ersatz, just like in the legend. Ersatz, this is Tananda."

"My pleasure, my lady," the sword said.

"Mine, too," Tananda replied, giving a little wave of her fingers. "So, what's going on?"

"We need that crystal ball back that you lifted. My friend here has business with it."

"You can't have it," another female voice said, in a strange accent. "It belongs to me, now."

I looked up. A lithe figure was suddenly standing next to Tanda. Where the Trollop was curvy, this girl was aerobics-instructor wiry. Where Tanda's hair fell enticingly all over her shoulders, the newcomer had her sleek black hair plastered down against her head and bullied into a shining knot at the nape of her neck. The rest of her face was a sharp, narrow beak, over which a pair of large, dark eyes regarded me. She looked a lot like a stork, or maybe an ostrich. She was wearing a tight tunic, abbreviated to show her navel, if one had been visible through the covering of feathers on her midsection, and loose trousers that cut off just below her knees.

"Who are you?" I growled. Instead of replying, the girl lifted her prominent proboscis proudly.

"Aahz, this is Calypsa," Tananda said. "My new partner. This place has a translation spell operating for demons."

"I heard what you said," Calypsa continued, her big, dark eyes gleaming. "That is Ersatz, the Great Sword."

"In the steel," I said.

"What do you want for it?"

"Not for sale, babe. He's an independent contractor. In fact, we're working together at the moment.

"But I must have it!" Her eyes flashed again. They were pretty nice eyes.

"No can do. The sword owes me money. We're together until he pays me off. You got a hundred gold pieces?" The girl's eyes fell. "I didn't think so."

The gaze lifted and battened onto mine. "You must understand. I must bring together the greatest treasures of the ages. I need them all!"

A little alarm bell went off in my mind. I met Ersatz's eyes, and I knew he was thinking the same thing I was. The rumor was true. Someone *was* collecting the Hoard. So, I asked the only practical question.

"Why?"

With the same kind of silken glide Tananda had used, Calypsa poured herself into the remaining chair. The movement looked totally different performed by the two women. Tananda seemed to be careless and sexy, but she had set herself up so she was on guard, ready to spring into action if there was trouble. Calypsa was focused, the energy of her motion aimed directly at me. If she'd been a missile I'd have been spattered all over the bar.

"It is my grandfather," she began. "The greatest dancer in any dimension, the great Calypso."

"What's he need with a sword and a crystal ball?" I asked. "I don't think there's a pair of shoes in the Golden Hoard."

"Once such footgear tried to join us," Ersatz began, "but we chivvied them hence. They were not so much of utility in the courtly art as they were mundane covering for the nether extremities, which the gold did not become…"

"Shut up," I interrupted, without taking my eyes off Calypsa. "Your grandfather did what?"

The proud head drooped. "I come from Walt. It is a peaceful dimension—or I should say, was."

"Yeah, Tootsie, I've been there. Peaceful to the point of boring!"

"Maybe before," Calypsa said. "That was before the evil Barrik arrived!"

"When was that?"

"Ten years ago. I live in a town called Pavan, at the curve of a major river just north of our largest port. At first we made no note of the castle being built on the hillside that overlooked the river. All of our lords like to have large domiciles so that they can host parties and dances. All Walts love to dance. It is in our blood. It is the source of our magik. In fact, a major rhythm was named for our dimension. Have you ever heard of Walts' Time?"

"In passing," I said. "Get on with it."

"We thought nothing of it when the castle grew to encompass the entire mountain top. It was made all of shiny black granite, which we considered an odd color choice, but we were more curious that we never saw anyone working on the building. We

believed the stones must be shifted at night by giant elves, or
something. It was a puzzle. I myself sneaked up there often
as a child, but always when I arrived, the elves had left the
building."

I groaned. She gave me a puzzled look, and explained.
"There was no one there. Yet the walls grew daily. At last, it
was finished. We of Pavan waited to be introduced to our new
neighbors, and hold a welcome dance in celebration. Weeks
went by. They never emerged. No one answered our knocks at
the great wooden doors. We left invitations on the step to our
own humble village dances. No replies. We began to think that
our neighbor was antisocial. But how antisocial we had no
idea! Henchmen like huge, evil birds began to emerge from
the castle. They swept down upon our humble homes and captured the finest dancers in the city. Sometimes we would find
them again, wandering lost and dazed in the fields, their feet
bloody. Barrik had commanded them to dance until they
dropped! Their choreography had been inexorably altered. They
were never able again to make the magik they had before, such
as the Dance of Sowing, so the crops would be healthy, or the
Dance of Precipitation to bring the rain. We were all fearful of
being swooped down upon and carried off.

"At last, his minions captured my grandfather, the greatest
dancer in the land. According to the other prisoners who were
set free, my grandfather refused Barrik's orders. He stood, unwilling to yield a single shuffle-ball-change. Barrik threatened
terrible torture, but my grandfather would not be treated like a
common entertainer. At last, the great Calypso performed the
Dance of Insult, fleering his defiance right in Barrik's face.
Barrik was furious!"

"Well, hurray for the old boy," I said. "How's this involve
us?"

"When Calypso did not emerge from the castle as the
others had, a huge group of us went and demanded to have
him set free. I stood before the doors, begging Barrik to deliver my grandfather. The next thing I knew, I was in a room

before a stone throne. The creature that sat upon it—too horrible to behold!"

I glanced at Tananda. "By the description he's a Dile," she said. "Green scales, long teeth."

"What's wrong with green scales and long teeth?" I demanded.

"Not everyone likes the overlapping shingle look, Aahz," Tanda said, patiently. "Now, I kind of like it, but you know what Troll men look like, so I'm not your most unbiased judge."

"Fine," I snarled. "Get past chapters twelve to forty-eight already. I want the upshot, now!"

Calypsa glared right back at me. "He told me the old man would die for the insult he had given him. I swore to do anything he wished, if only he would free my grandfather. I even promised to do the Dance of Lust for him, but he refused." Her eyes flashed again. "He said the only way I can regain my grandfather's life is to procure a great treasure for him. I must subdue and bring him all the members of the Golden Hoard. He has given me but thirty days to complete the task. Already ten of them have elapsed."

I shook my head. "Guy's a regular Wizard of Oz," I said. The girl looked at me blankly. "Forget it. Before your time."

"With the great crystal I have two of the treasures," the girl went on. "You would not consider helping me by giving me the sword, would you?"

"Au contraire," I snapped back. "I heard a prophecy that says that the Hoard should not be gathered together under any circumstances. Disaster will fall, and all the hokey words."

"But I must save my grandfather! The great Calypso must dance free!"

I looked at Tanda.

"Seems to me the best way is just to break the old man out of the shiny black castle on the hill," I said, reasonably.

"Impossible," Tananda said. "I've been over the place myself. This man takes his Evil-Overlording seriously. There isn't a weak spot anywhere where I could break in and make it all the way to the dungeons without being caught. His guards never sleep, and they're made of stone. Half of them are Gargoyles, half are Diles, and they don't like each other."

I moved on to the next practical consideration. "What about taking out the Dile himself? Remove the head and the body usually collapses."

"Never goes out without heavy-duty magikal shields and about a dozen guards. He's better protected than the next *Wizard School* novel."

"Hmm." Tananda knew her stuff. Second-story work was a sideline for her. She had been one of M.Y.T.H., Inc.'s greatest assets with her experience, brains and charm, but she had another sideline: assassination. If she couldn't close with a target, that was serious.

Tananda tried reason. "Perhaps we can work together."

"We are at cross-purposes here, Tanda. Ersatz doesn't want to be collected. All he wants is to have a conversation with Kelsa and we're out of here. I don't have any interest but getting my investment back. I'm on vacation. I'm sorry, kid," I told Calypsa. "Good luck, but you're going to be at least one gadget shy."

"No!" Calypsa protested. Before I could move, she had swooped down and seized Ersatz from where he lay on the table.

I made a grab for her, but she zipped out of reach again.

"How'd she do that?" I sputtered, staring at my empty hands. "I couldn't follow her on a broomstick!"

"The Dance of Speed," Tananda said, amused. "Her family's famous for it."

"Whew! I have never seen a dance that was practical for anything but seduction before."

"Well, get used to it," Tananda said. "She's got a bundle of them. You should have seen her up on that roof. I'm an old hand at second-story work, but that Dance of Balance of hers had her tippy-toeing along the eaves like an Orion."

I eyed the girl, and she eyed me back. Fancy footwork was one thing, but low-down cunning was another. She didn't have any of that. If she was hanging on to Ersatz, she couldn't have Kelsa in her immediate possession.

"Kelsa!" I shouted. "Where are you? Ersatz needs to talk to you!" My voice echoed off the rafters. Everyone in the room turned to stare.

No answering voice replied, but I noticed that the dimness was beginning to lighten. Within moments a golden glow lit the cobwebbed space under the stairs. I could see what looked like a clump of undistinguished rags become incandescent, then blinding.

I grinned at the girls. "Can't talk, but there are other ways of communicating." I got up to retrieve the crystal.

Before I took two steps, Calypsa was in front of me, her narrow chest heaving, one feathered hand held over her head in a flourish. "You shall not pass."

"Don't try me, kid," I said. I stepped around her. She appeared in front of me in the proverbial twinkling, but I was never one to hold with proverbs.

She was fast. But she was light. I picked her up by the elbows and moved her out of my way. She eeled in front of me again. I moved her. I heard a titter of laughter from the rest of the room. I gave the onlookers a snarl. By the time I turned back, Calypsa was halfway up the stairs, the glowing bundle in her arms with Ersatz balanced across it.

"You shall not trick me again, Pervert."

I fumed. Tananda chuckled.

"Give it back to him, Cally," she said to the young woman, who clutched the sword to her breast like the heroine in a bad novel. Tananda couldn't stop grinning. I snarled. "We want his cooperation. Aahz could be your best friend, but taking his toys away from him just makes him bad-tempered."

Eying me distrustfully, Calypsa stepped daintily down the stairs. I snatched Ersatz from her hand and slipped him halfway out of the sheath.

"You all right in there?"

"Si," he replied.

"All right," I said, smacking the hilt home against the worn leather. "I'm walking out of here right now. Good luck, kid. I mean that. No hard feelings," I told Tananda. "I'll figure out some other way of getting paid back."

"Look, Aahz," the Trollop said, winding herself around me in the way of a very old friend and whispering in my ear. "We both have something the other wants. What'll it take to make a deal here?"

"There isn't room for compromise," I said. "You want Ersatz. He's a free agent here. He doesn't want to be collected."

"But we have something *you* want: information from Kelsa. Couldn't you...come along with us for a while, in exchange for that information? Maybe Barrik will be satisfied having all the Golden Hoard assembled in one place for a moment. Then you and he can go off again."

I eyed her. "You're not going to tell me you believe he will trade the old man for a collection of legendary junk, do you?"

"Friend Aahz!" Ersatz burst out.

"No offense meant," I said smoothly. "Come on, Tanda. You weren't born yesterday."

"Certainly not," Tanda said, tossing back her head full of wavy green hair. "I'd use it as a ploy to get into the castle. I think it will be a lot easier to get a shot at him and save Calypsa's grandfather if we show up carrying what he wants."

"Nay," protested a muffled voice. I pulled Ersatz free. The sharp, dark eyes reflected in the shining blade were alarmed. "Nay, good Aahz. It would be a fearsome thing to assemble the Hoard. Why do you think it has not been done in all these centuries?"

"I'm with him," I said. "I don't invite disaster without a reason."

"Then why did Kelsa say they would be reunited?" Tanda asked, reasonably. "I could hear everything hanging upside down from the window-frame. A green hand—that could be either you or me."

"Or Barrik," Calypsa said, faintly. "He is green, too."

"There," Tananda said, beaming. "So, shouldn't we find out more from Kelsa what she meant?"

"She will not explain properly," Ersatz said. "She has never been able to keep to a narrative."

"We'll get it out of her," I said. I smacked the table with a palm. "Put 'er there."

Very reluctantly, Calypsa unfolded the cloth that contained the crystal ball. The second the folds fell away, we could hear what had probably been an uninterrupted stream-of-consciousness, if you could call that babble consciousness.

"...this has all been very exciting, you know. I haven't been carried off in many years! Well, not since I was staying with a Rhinoid fortune teller, and her neighbors stampeded, taking the entire tent with them on the tips of their horns as they thundered across the plains. What a ride that was! I haven't been so bobbled in..." The turbaned head turned around in a circle, and the eyes behind the diamante glasses blinked at all of us. "There you are! My goodness, I wondered why no one answered me. It was dark in there!"

"And she's a seer?" I asked, with a groan.

"She is clueless regarding her own circumstances," Ersatz said, resignedly. "It was ever thus."

"Hi, er, Kelsa," Tananda said, tapping the crystal ball to get her attention. The head turned to look at her. Kelsa beamed.

"Oh, yes, you're the one who stole me! Very deft, you know, very deft. Why, I would think that you're the smoothest thief ever to remove me in...oh, six centuries!"

"Thanks," Tananda said. "Look, do you know why I took you?"

The eyes blinked. "Why, of course I do, dear. You want to reunite the Golden Hoard!"

"Can you tell us why you think it might be a bad idea?"

"It depends, dear. What do you consider a bad idea?" Kelsa asked. "Explosions? War? Fire? Cannibalism?"

Tananda blinked a couple of times. "Yes, those would qualify in my book as bad ideas."

"Of course you do! I can tell just by looking into your soul." Kelsa nodded knowingly.

"Tell us why it's going to happen, then."

"Well, because it is! I told you all before."

"No, it is not, Kelsa," Ersatz said. "Have you no memory? Don't you recall the last time we were all together? What a terrible time that was?"

The large eyes clouded for a moment, then looked alarmed. "It wasn't that bad, dear. Not really."

"Indeed it was, Kelsa," the sword insisted. "I will not co-operate with this. Neither will my friend Aahz."

"Wait!" Calypsa pleaded, leaning toward me. "Is there nothing that you would take to let me have this sword and complete my quest, Aahz? Do you have no heart's desire that I can fulfill?"

"Nothing." I crossed my arms firmly. "One hundred gold pieces, and I'm out of here. That's all I want."

"Oh, that's easy," Kelsa said, interrupting my protest. Her eyes had gone all unfocused again. "He wants his magikal powers restored."

"No!" I bellowed. "Not a single thing! Not a...*what?*"

"His powers are gone," Kelsa went on telling Calypsa, as if I hadn't spoken. "He's been without them a while now, though he's done well enough by his cunning. Don't discount his brains, dear, in spite of his looks. A foolish trick by a trusted friend, now dead. A joke, but with serious consequences."

"Can it be undone?" Calypsa asked.

"Oh, of course!" Kelsa said. "Why..."

I leaned forward, interested in spite of myself.

"No!" Ersatz exclaimed. "We seek only to locate Chin-Hwag. She can help me to pay my debt. Then we will go. Can you tell me where to find her?"

"Now, wait a moment," I said, holding up a hand to fore-stall him. "It couldn't hurt to ask the lady. What would it take to get my powers back?"

"Well," Kelsa said, turning her Pervect-face to me. "It might be that the Cup can help. Or perhaps the Ring. The

Book would have all that information at his fingertips, so to
speak, since all he has is pages. He's full of useful spells. He is,
after all, the Ultimate Grimoire."

"Really?" I asked. The possibility of having my powers restored again had never occurred to me. I had been so relieved to
be able to wander the dimensions freely with the help of the D-
hopper that my imagination hadn't taken me any further—not
yet, anyhow. That imagination was operating at full throttle now.
I could be a full magician again? Never again to be taken advantage of by some two-bit huckster who had picked up half a
spell from the back of a box of Witch Crunchies cereal? Not to
set off magikal boobytraps because I couldn't feel the force
lines leading into it from sky or earth? "How do I find them?
What do I need to do to get my powers back?"

I ignored the cat-ate-canary grin on Tanda's face as she sat
back in the chair and swung her boots up on the table top. I
was just gathering facts, that was all.

Kelsa squeezed her eyes shut and concentrated. "Hmm.
The possibilities are most intriguing. Plenty of scope. You need
scope."

"Keep the personal remarks to yourself," I growled. "Just
read me the small print, willya?"

"Just a moment, Aahz," Ersatz said, the sharp eyes showing panic. "You cannot agree with their insane plan? It will be
a disaster."

"Just considering it," I said, casually. "It doesn't do any
harm to hear what she's got to say, does it?"

"No...I...of course it does! Harden your resolve, friend!"

My resolve was already working on a list of people who
had interfered with my life over the past few years while I had
been powerless. It was compiling a compendium of ways both
subtle and nasty for getting even with them, all the while keeping
the connection with me out of the picture. I had no wish to
spend a single moment involved with any correctional institution, when I was only righting the balance of justice in my
favor. Let's see, there was the Geek, and...

"Aahz!"

"What?" I snarled, coming out of a blissful daydream of the whole Merchants Association of the Bazaar offering me a percentage of their profits to avoid having me make information about their business dealings public—all legal and aboveboard, though underhanded. I liked the mental picture of all of them, hands trembling, handing over bags of gold so big they needed wheels to move. It'd take a while, though to get together enough dirt to make all the Association cave at once, but as soon as I had my magik back...

Ersatz's keen eyes fixed upon mine. "Aahz, listen to me. I have told you of the danger. I, who have fought in hundreds of thousands of battles, have no fear of ordinary war, but I tell you that what these women propose is dangerous beyond recall!"

"Uh-huh," I said, absently. "So, Kelsa, baby, what have you got?"

"Well, Aahz—I can call you Aahz, can't I?" She blinked at me coyly.

"If you get on with it!"

"The path to regaining your powers is fraught with peril. No sure way exists to restoration without redemption. Friendship stands beside you but also in your way. Do not destroy that which is, to gain that which may not yet be."

I wasn't starting to lose patience with her circumlocutions, I was in the next county already. "Get to the point!"

She tilted her head quizzically. "But, that is the point, dear Aahz. All of this is important."

"I'm listening. Which one of the Hoard can restore my powers?"

"Well, I am not yet sure," Kelsa said. "This is what I see at the moment. Look deep!"

I leaned forward and gazed into the crystal ball. The face under the turban vanished. In its place was a dimly lit room with stone walls. No clue there' I'd been in houses, castles, museums and dungeons with the same décor. I saw myself standing on a dais. My image raised a huge golden cup to its lips and drank. As the reflection of me lowered the cup, I saw a huge grin on my face. I knew I echoed the expression as I sat back in the wooden chair. "All right, I'm on board."

"Thank you, Mr. Aahz!" Calypsa leaped forward and wrapped her feathery arms around me. For such a lightweight, she had a good grip.

"But I am not!" Ersatz said. "If you try to involve me in this, Aahz, then know me for your mortal enemy! Our deal is off. I shall not persuade the Purse to reimburse you for my rescue."

"Oh, yes, you will," I said. "You still owe me the cash."

"Oh, no, I won't." His eyebrows telegraphed danger. "You cannot make me."

"Oh, yes, you will."

"Oh, no, I won't."

I draped the silencing cloth over the blade and let him continue his protests in silence. Tananda protested.

"Aahz!"

I shrugged. "What's he going to do? Walk out of here?"

"Oh, but I don't want him to be angry!" Calypsa dropped gracefully to her knees beside the sword and plucked the cloth away. She gazed into the steely orbs glaring out of the blade. "Please, Ersatz, won't you reconsider? I need your help. My grandfather is the mainstay of our family. He is in terrible danger, and only the full Hoard will be able to ransom him free. I know from Kelsa that you are the head of the order. You can persuade the others to cooperate. Please. I need your help."

Her big brown eyes had tears in them. I cleared my throat of a sudden hoarseness. I could tell Ersatz was moved, too. The harsh gaze softened.

"Child, your story touches me. I must continue to warn you that what you seek to do will rock the very foundations of the universe!"

"Please, sir, I love my grandfather," Calypsa begged. "He is a proud man. I know that this time he went too far and got himself into danger. You cannot say no. You just can't!"

Ersatz sighed. "You are courting disaster," he said, then raised the sharp eyebrows to forestall another outburst. "BUT I will aid you. My steel is at your service."

"Oh, thank you!" Calypsa said, joining her palms together in a gesture of thanks. "You will never know what this means to me!"

"Alas, child, you may find out, to your cost."

"Good," I said, slapping my hands together and rubbing them. I could almost feel the lines of force tingling through my hands again. "We're all on board. Where do we start?"

Chapter 4

"THEY ARE ALL looking at us," Calypsa said nervously. "They are so strange looking!"

I grumbled under my breath. "This would all have been a lot easier if you had let me and Tananda go in alone."

"Nothing doing," the girl said, holding the bundle containing Kelsa protectively to her narrow chest. "I go where you go. I do not want you to slip away inconveniently. My grandfather's life is in danger."

"Then, shut up," I said, with a glare I hoped would seal her lips for the time being. "You don't speak the local lingo, and I don't want anyone to misconstrue what they think you said." I grinned affably at a man who was watching us talk. "Nice spring day, isn't it, friend!"

The people of Mernge watched us out of the corners of their eyes as we went down the street. The trouble with Klahds is their dimension is almost bereft of magik, and equally devoid of technology. As a result, very few of them are familiar with either, so the appearance of anything strange is met with the utmost suspicion. Without the aid of complex mechanical or magikal means of assistance, Klahds have to rely on animal power, either their own or another animal's, to get around. Hence, they don't travel much, so visitors are more rare than in other dimensions. When roused, Klahds tend to break out in deadly and punitive force. Sophistication and smooth talking are no match for a rope, an ax or a torch. I've been on the business end of all three of those unfriendly greetings more times on Klah than I feel comfortable thinking about. How they would have reacted to a Pervect, a Trollop and a storklike Walt I could just imagine, and it wouldn't be pretty.

So you're asking yourself, why weren't they reacting to the sight of a Pervect, a Trollop and a Walt? In the interests of self-preservation, I had Tananda put a disguise spell on the three of us. If I had had my powers, I could have done it in a wink, no problem, but I had to admit Tananda had done a pretty good job. I was used to delegating jobs like that now, not a bad skill to have learned, though I wasn't crazy about the condition that had forced me to learn it. Still, we were attracting attention anyhow, because we were clearly not locals.

I always said that the best way to go into any situation was as if you belonged there. In the guise of a wealthy merchant, I swaggered down the street, accompanied by my two female associates. Tananda, in her dress and kirtle, undulated, but she'd exude sex appeal if she was disguised as a raccoon in bloomers. Klahdish males gawked after her, some with open mouths.

After a few false starts we'd disguised Calypsa as a school-marm. With her posture it was either that or a sergeant-major, and I didn't want people to think that the military was invading their little hamlet. No, I had come up with a stratagem to separate an eight-year-old boy from his sports trophy. Not that I had any qualms about getting it away from him; the trick was to do it so we could remove it and ourselves from the arena without causing the town elders to examine our credentials too closely. I could *bamf* us out of the place if we failed in our attempt, but rumors of that kind of thing has a way of getting around, and I did not want attention drawn to this little corner of Klah. I rarely paid any attention to the provinces, except when their existence impacted my earning potential or well-being in some way. In my experience, most city-dwellers feel the same as I do. Anyone who lives within smelling distance of cows is less important than anyone who lives within nose-range of exhaust fumes.

At any rate, we couldn't help but have to march through town like a trio of traveling players. Kelsa had been pretty obtuse about finding the boy, but she let us know by telling us 'hot' or 'cold' whether we were walking in the correct direction or no. Unfortunately, she didn't know the meaning of the

word "undertone." Every pronouncement was made at the top
of her ringing voice. Since we couldn't muffle her and still
figure out where we were going, Tanda had to cover every
outburst with meaningless chatter.

"Left here!" Kelsa announced.

"My goodness," Tananda exclaimed loudly, for the benefit
of the crowd following us. She veered in that direction, talking loudly over the crystal ball's continuing babble, something
about the cobblestones being the bumps in the gods' thought
process. "What a fine butcher shop window! Isn't that the best
display of cow hooves you have ever seen?"

I stumped along behind her and took a brief gander at the
meat display. The Klahd behind the counter glared at the trio
of strangers. He had the same poleaxed expression as the car-
cass hanging on the hook behind him. He brought his cleaver
down with a thunk! Bone chips flew in every direction. Tananda
gave him a winning smile, and sauntered, seemingly at ran-
dom, down the little lane beside the shop. We had left Ersatz
out of town, concealed in the trunk of a hollow tree. He had
had second thoughts about the hunt, in spite of all Calypsa's
heart-wrenching pleas, and had spent plenty of time trying to
talk us out of it. We just couldn't afford to have two disembodied voices drawing the crowd's attention.

"So, watcha doing in Mernge?" a boy asked, running alongside me. He had red hair, freckles and eyes the same color as
pond silt.

"Minding my own business," I snapped.

"That sounds boring!"

"Aahz!" Tananda said, pointedly. She dropped an arm
around the brat's shoulders. "We're scribes from the Margrave's
castle. We're here to get an important story about a boy who
took part in a race."

"I ran a race," the boy said, eagerly. "I won the race in
front of our whole school!"

"Not you," Tananda said. "It's another boy who ran that
we're interested in."

"But I won!"

"That's not as interesting to the Margrave as the boy who tried hard, but didn't succeed," Tananda said. It sounded lame even to me.

I took charge of the conversation. "Bug off, kid. You don't want to get involved in Margrave's business, do you?"

The kid's face screwed up, making him uglier than ever. He kicked my shin. "I'll tell my dad on you! He's the mayor! He'll make you interview me!" I made to grab him, but he ran away. I added him to the list of people I was going to 'chat with' when I got my powers back. He needed to learn some manners, one way or another.

"Are you sure this is the best way?" Calypsa asked, with dismay. "The open approach, in the middle of the day? Why could we not make a secret visit, perhaps in the night?"

"Right turn, no, left. Left!" Kelsa's voice echoed in the narrow alley. Tananda gave an apologetic smile to the crowd following us.

"It wouldn't be secret with our own personal foghorn letting off like that," I said. If the crowd was growing suspicious of the disembodied voice, the swiftly spreading rumor of the Margrave's involvement kept them from getting too curious about our strange behavior. I began to get nervous about the formidability of the local laird, and wished we'd done a little more investigation before we marched into town. Too late, I thought, squaring my shoulders. Just keep going.

"That's it!" Kelsa screeched happily as we arrived in front of a house. The garden gate was painted white, and young shoots of climbing flowers were just twining their way up the arch. The house beyond was pretty good sized. We were dealing with a merchant or better. I sized up the amount of gold I still had in my pocket, and wondered if I might have to slip the dad a bribe.

"My goodness, Lord Wordsmith," Tananda said, flourishing her hand at the door. "Is this not a fine place?"

"Could use a coat of paint or two."

"Well, I like it," Tananda said, pouting prettily for the crowd. I spotted some movement behind the curtains. The family must have been tipped off we were heading in this direction, because they came boiling out of the door like a horde of puppies that had heard the words, "Chow time!" The Klahds, two girls, a boy, a man and a woman, were dressed in their best clothes. All I could say was that in my experience only one person had had taste that bad, and he had been taught better. The woman beamed at me out from under a tall, conical green hat tied onto her head with a bright yellow scarf. Around her shoulders was a shawl of blue and red, over a brown dress and white apron. The man must have been at the same sale of clown-clothes. His parti-colored tunic of brown and green was topped with a purple hood. He looked uncomfortable, as if he was not responsible for the choices, yet had no option but to appear in what he was given. It was a good thing I wasn't there to write an article praising their garments, because it was going to be hard enough to keep a straight face.

"May I help you, sir and ladies?" the man asked.

"Good afternoon, sir," I said, heading straight for him with my hand out. "I am Lord Wordsmith. The Margrave has commanded me to record instances of great importance and record them for the kingdom archives. He has sent me here today because of an accomplishment in your own family. May I have all of your names. For the record, of course?"

The man looked nervous. "The Margrave is interested in us?"

"That's right," I said. "He was pretty impressed. He sent us to get an interview that will become part of the permanent record."

"Oh." He looked a little less nervous. "Was it my scholarly takeover of the gristmill in Fleben?"

"Why, no, though that was a masterful stroke," I said, though I had no idea what he was talking about. He preened.

"Maybe the embroidery exhibition that my wife and her sisters put on at the village hall? The Margrave must have heard that she made over thirty-five different kinds of antimacassar!"

"No! I mean, no." I softened my tone as they backed up a pace in alarm. "We're here to talk to your son about the race he ran at school. We understand that he came in second."

I turned to the boy. He was a stocky lad of twelve or so summers, just the age when a young man's heart turns to petty vandalism and wondering why the girl next door seemed to be growing into such a different shape than his. "How about it, son? Why don't we go inside and talk about it a little?"

"Oh, yeah!" the boy crowed. "That'd be terrific!"

"Well," the woman said. "I hope you'll excuse the house. I didn't know you were coming here today, you see. The place is a mess!"

I put on my most sincere smile. "I'm sure it's fine." I nodded to Tananda. As soon as we crossed the threshold she was casing the joint. I love working with professionals.

"Imagine, us Skivers in the royal archives!" the woman said. "Oh, I'm Melangelie. This is my husband, Feothor. My son, Imgam. My daughters, Vencie and Ludanna."

"Pleased to meet you," I said.

"Oh, the honor is all ours! Please come in!" She showed us into the small sitting room, still fluttering. Her husband and children followed. She plunked embroidered cushions down behind Calypsa's upright back, pressed a few around Tananda, and hovered around my elbow until I finally lifted it so she could put a ruffled pillow beneath it.

"May I offer you some tea?"

I didn't gag out loud. Tea's all right if there isn't any other water to wash in, but I don't make a habit of drinking it.

"No, thanks," I said. "I'm hoping this won't take too long." That was Tananda's cue.

She made an apologetic noise to Melangelie. "Could you tell me where the, uh…?"

"Down the hall to the left, last door," the hostess said, with a smile, but her attention was fixed on me. "Is there anything else I can get for you? Cookies? Biscuits? Pie? I don't have any more coffee cake, but perhaps I can go borrow some from the neighbor?"

"No, thanks. Please sit down. You're making me nervous." Melangelie dithered for a moment more. "Sit!"

She sat.

"That's better." I made a big deal out of taking a roll of parchment and a pencil out of my bag and handing them off to Calypsa. "Miss Ermintrude here will take notes for us."

The girls sat on either side of Calypsa, and watched her hands. I leaned toward the kid. I didn't know how much time Tananda would need, but I was going to give her every opportunity. The house wasn't that big, and Kelsa had assured us that the cup was on an open shelf.

"Give us your impression about the contest."

"Ah, it was just a fifty-yard dash," the boy said, waving a hand to make me think it was no big deal.

"Now, just a moment, son," Feothor said, holding up a hand. "Not another word."

I narrowed my eyes at him.

"Why not?" I asked.

He turned an oily smile my way. "Well, I don't mind having his memoir become part of the public record, of course, but I want to make sure that all of his rights are preserved. You understand, don't you?"

"I understand." I sighed. "You're a lawyer, aren't you."

He put an innocent hand on his ill-clad chest. "Just a friendly defender of the public welfare. And that includes my son, of course."

"Of course," I said. It was an effort to be patient, but I made it. "What's the deal?"

"Well," Feothor said, taking a sheet of parchment and the pencil out of Calypsa's hand. Instead of making notes, he started to write sentences—long sentences—right off the top of his head. "Before my son makes any kind of a statement, I'd like you to sign this."

"Sign what?" I was definitely beginning not to like him. He offered me a bland look.

"This waiver. It will grant the Margrave permission only to place Imgam's story in the national archives. My son, his heirs and assigns, will retain the rights to all proceeds, royalties, future income arising from the publication of his memoirs, allowing him rights to his own story, should he choose to publish further writing in the future." He whipped off a pageful of paragraphs and reached for another piece of parchment with an air of efficiency that gave me the uncomfortable feeling I was back with the minister who had made my life so miserable in the court of Possiltum with his regulations and rules.

I peered at the Klahd's face. "You aren't related to JR Grimble, are you?"

"Grimbles? They're uneducated trash," the Klahd said, sneering. He went on writing. "We Skivers have been students of law since the first written word!"

That I could well believe. I leaned forward.

"Look, we're not here to cheat your boy out of his future rights. All we want is to hear what he has to say. He can tell it again to anyone he wants, from now on until the end of time, for all we care. Come on, we don't have all day."

Feothor didn't even look up. The pencil point flew. "Just another few paragraphs."

"Dad!" Imgam protested. "When do I get to talk?"

"Almost finished," the Klahd said.

I was beginning to lose my temper. "This isn't the formula for cold fusion we're talking about here," I snarled. "The boy and I are just going to have a conversation. You can listen to the whole interview. I'm not trying to get him to betray state secrets."

"See here, Lord Wordsmith," Skiver said, pointing the pencil at me. I barely restrained myself from leaning forward and biting it off at the elbow. "I'm just trying to protect my child. You would do the same thing to safeguard your own offspring from having someone cheat him, wouldn't you?"

"Not to the extent of preventing him doing what he wants to do," I said. "All we want is enough for a simple article. Nothing fancy. In fact, it'll be shorter than what you've turned out already. Do you want me to go back to the Margrave and tell him you wouldn't let Imgam here give us the details he asked for?"

I glanced out of the window. On the lawn, the crowd was growing, as more ambitious parents turned up with their off-spring. With my keen hearing, I could eavesdrop on their conversation, which amounted to a question as to why the entire athletics program of the local school wasn't going into the archives, winners AND losers, as befit their precious children's activities. And so on. I was beginning to regret my choice of approach. We might have to make a run for it, and soon.

"One more moment, my lord, one more moment. Hmmm, hm hm, hmmm."

Calypsa gave me a worried look. I signed to her not to worry. I didn't mind signing his waiver. It would have all the legal standing of anything else that was signed with a phony name by an extradimensional being wearing a disguise spell. I invited him to catch me later for breach of contract if he could. I fingered the D-hopper in my pocket.

"Look," I said, rising from my seat. "We came as we were instructed to do. We can't get you to tell us what you don't want to. We'll just have to go back to the castle and tell them we failed."

"Not completely," Tananda said, with a sweet smile, ap-pearing at my side. She tipped me a small wink. "We won't have our story, but we will have an interesting tale to tell the Margrave. He will be most interested to hear about your lack of cooperation. We should go, Master Wordsmith."

"But how can you go until you hear my story?" the boy said, springing to his feet indignantly.

"How can you leave until you sign the contract?" Feothor asked.

"How can we go without the Cup?" Calypsa demanded, gawking at me.

The others all gawked at me, too. The Walt language isn't very much like Klahd, but they have some sounds in common. Unfortunately, 'cup' was one of them.

"Cup? What cup?" Feothor asked.

"Nothing," I said, grabbing the Walt by the arm and hauling her toward the door. Tananda was right behind me. "Miss Ermintrude just wants a cup of tea. That's all. We can't wait around for it. We'll have to get refreshments back at the Margravery. Thanks for your time. Too bad it didn't work out."

Imgam was much smarter than the average Klahd.

"Cup?" he exclaimed. He jumped up and ran out of the room. "It's gone! My trophy is gone!" He pointed a finger at Tananda. "She stole it!"

"Nonsense, kid," I said, yanking open the door. "You must have left it somewhere. Nice to meet you folks. Goodbye."

I attempted to step outside.

Unfortunately, when I opened the door, a dozen people fell in on top of me. The neighbors, who had been gathering in force, started protesting even before they managed to get back to their feet.

"My son is the best archer in town!"

"My daughter collects spiders! All kinds! You should write about her!"

"I need to talk to you about my twins." A crude hand drawing of two moppets with golden pigtails was shoved in my face. "Aren't they gorgeous?"

"Stop them!" Skiver yelled. "They're thieves!"

Looks of shock, disbelief, and outrage—in that order— came over the faces of the townsfolk. I started tossing Klahds over my shoulder in an attempt to get outside, to a place where I could employ the D-hopper, but there were just too many of them. A dozen or so stood or lay on each of my limbs to hold me down.

"Pay close attention, thief," a red-haired townsman said, glaring down at me as an equally roseate-polled younger male went to work with a long strand of rope around my hands and feet. "My son won awards for knot tying."

I groaned and let my head fall back. I knew I should have stuck to my guns and kept out of this scavenger hunt.

Chapter 5

THE MARGRAVE WAS typical of embedded public officials, in my experience. He wore an air of menace that went poorly with his unimpressive physique. Fiftyish, plump, black hair slicked back over an egg-shaped skull, he was shorter than an average Klahd. I could look him square in the eye as he went up and down the line, glaring at the three of us.

"This is an outrage," I said, jangling the manacles on my wrists so the rusty yard of chain rang..

I was keeping up an air of official grief to throw him off balance. The gyves were attached to irons around my ankles by links of sturdy chain with links as thick as my thumb. My leg irons were connected to Tanda's on my left and Calypsa's on my right. We had been hauled up by rings around our necks so I was perching on tiptoes. The whole contraption was fastened high on the stone wall behind us with a staple that could have held the entire text of the Tax Code. I was grateful that Tananda's disguise spell had held, or we'd probably have wound up tied neck to heels, if not worse. It was uncomfortable, to say the least, especially after we had been kicked and beaten by the crowd and dragged along the cobblestoned streets the entire four miles to the castle behind a pair of yoked pigs. My clothes were smeared with droppings, along with everything else that Merngeans threw out into the streets and hadn't washed away since the last rain. I could hardly stand my own smell. To add to the ambience, rats and bugs, most of them sizeable, were starting to crawl out of the walls, attracted by the scent of strangers.

"Release us. You have no idea whom you're dealing with." I use 'whom' when I'm really torqued.

"You are charged," he boomed, in an impressive-sounding voice, "of impersonating officials of the crown, theft, wasting time by deception, fraud, corruption of the young..."

"Of *what?*" I burst out, not believing my handsome, bat-wing ears.

The Margrave leveled a beady black eye on me. "The boy whom you tempted into surrendering his personal reminiscences."

"We didn't get a thing out of him, if you ask your eye-witnesses."

"You admit it!"

He spun on his heel and walked to the table where all the contents of our pockets, shoulder bags, boot tops, as well as the various unmentionable places where Tanda tended to conceal things. (Even though the muscular guardswoman had been pretty thorough in her search I was certain that there were still more weapons and tools hidden about Tanda's sumptuous person. She had been doing this a lot of years.)

"What is this?" the Margrave demanded, waving the D-hopper at me. I cringed inwardly, hoping he wouldn't drop it. The technology to build them had been long lost, and though sturdy enough to withstand dimensional travel, they got goofed up when they hit stone floors. I didn't want to lose it.

"Massage stick," I said. "Good for easing those tight muscles."

I leered, letting him think worse thoughts. He blanched and put it down hastily. I grinned. He had a dirty mind.

"Why do you have this?" He held up Kelsa.

The crystal ball was empty, the beturbaned head nowhere in sight. We had instructed her over and over again not to talk to anyone but us. I was glad she had paid attention, because all we needed was her unfocused chatter to make matters worse.

"It's a family heirloom," I said. "I travel everywhere with it."

"Are you a witch?"

"Do I look like a witch?" I countered.

The Margrave sneered. "You look like a charlatan. Something is wrong with you. My soldiers say that your flesh feels coarser than it appears."

"Skin condition," I shrugged. "Had it since I was born. Are you going to prosecute me for that?"

"I intend to prosecute you for something," the Margrave said, lowering his eyebrows. I'm sure he'd made strong men cringe with that expression, but I'd had meaner teachers in Pervish primary school.

"It seems we got off on the wrong foot here, Lord Margrave," I said, my voice a low purr. "I told the Skivers that we had come from your castle, but it was a lie."

"You admit it!" Seemed to be his favorite phrase. I relaxed slightly.

"Sure I do. My true mission was a secret. I have been under sealed orders, until now. I have no choice but to reveal to you my actual purpose for being in Mernge."

"Well?" The Margrave looked suspicious but very curious as did Calypsa and Tanda behind him. I gave them a nod to assure them I had this whole thing under control. "What IS your mission?"

"Gathering information," I said.

"What kind of information? Surely not statistics on school athletics!"

"Kingdom security," I said, lowering my voice. "Sealed orders from Her Majesty." The Margrave had to lean closer to hear me, then jumped back in case I was going to take a swing at him. I almost wished I had been able to.

"The queen sent you?" he exclaimed.

"Shh!" I looked at the guards in pretended alarm. "All right, the secret's out. You blew it. Just wait until I tell her."

"You're frauds. I don't suppose you even know the name of the duke of this province."

"Spruesel," I said at once. "That's his private name. His official name is Congreave, but his mom used to call him Spruey. He's a couple inches taller than you, brown hair receding around a widow's peak and squinty hazel eyes, and favors red flannel combination underwear...but I probably shouldn't say anything about that even to you. On behalf of her serene majesty, Queen Hemlock, he sent us to get the full story on the boy, Imgam."

The Margrave narrowed his eyes again. I had made him re-evaluate us, and he didn't like that.

The royals in this country had birth names, but took a new name when they ascended the throne. I happened to know because I'd had all the archives of the Possiltum court at my fingertips, which included information, maps and portraits from spies and cartographers visiting the neighboring countries, plus some very confidential data from diplomatic diaries.

When he was still prince of his country, before it had been absorbed by Possiltum, Congreave had proposed to Queen, then Princess, Hemlock more than once. She had never taken the proposals seriously, since she thought that Congreave's nickname and underwear were both hilarious. She probably wouldn't have been as thrilled if she knew the nicknames that her brother monarchs had for her.

I pressed my advantage, and shook my manacles.

"Now, look, Highboy, Duke Spruesel is not gonna be happy that you locked up three of his favorite courtiers in chains over a stupid little misunderstanding, is he?"

"It's Highperin," the Margrave said, automatically. He looked less certain than he had before, then he recovered himself. This was still his ball field, whatever kind of sneaky base-stealing I had just done. He came up, kicking aside a rat, and glared me straight in the eye. "You will call me Lord Margrave!"

I was casual. "Whatever you like. You can call me Lord Fistula."

"Never heard of you." He hoped I was lying. I smirked.

"The duke has. I am his good right hand."

"Not so good, if you are capable of starting a near riot through your ineptitude. The Skivers..."

"You oughta be proud of the Skivers," I interrupted him. "Holding up the honor of the province like that. They weren't willing to blab a syllable to a stranger without making sure it was going to hold the people, and hence, its ruler, in the best possible light. I call that pretty impressive. Right off the bat, they were trying to do things right. I have to hand it to them. It's going to go in my report."

Highperin stroked his fat chin. "I see…"

I built on my theme. "His grace will be glad he sent us. I'll get it all down on parchment. Just as soon as you unclip the iron jewelry. It doesn't go with the rest of the outfit." I jingled my gyves again.

"Well, Fistula, if that IS your name, if the king is so impressed by security, then he will not be displeased with me."

I held out my wrists, but he waved them away.

"I'm not going to take you at your word. You will remain here, without food or drink, until my messenger gets back from the capital. That should take," he gazed at us, enjoying our dismay, "about three days. Each way. If you are whom you say you are, then I shall apologize and make amends for detaining the Duke's archivist and his minions. If not, then I shall devise a very public punishment for the three of you. I have plenty of scope for my imagination, as you can see." He waved a hand at the wall.

I had already been admiring Highperin's collection of nasty torture devices, most of which would delight a socially-deficient crowd like the one that had dragged us here through the streets. They were, one and all, the kind of objects capable of doing things to a body that you hope never happen to yours. Hovering beside them like museum docents eager to show off their display of impaled butterflies was a handful of professional torturers, complete with black hoods and oiled bodies naked to the waist.

Pervects could take a lot of punishment, but Trollops had less stamina than we did, and Walts were more fragile yet. A session with any of the devices would probably ensure that none of us would ever play the piano again. I vowed to the God of Second Chances if we got away unscathed I would start taking lessons immediately.

I glanced at Tananda to see if we had a hope of magikal escape. She gave a little shake of her head, and I realized that she was stretched to the limit maintaining our disguise spells. I was afraid her powers were stretched as far as they'd go. She could do smallish spells, mostly connected with her many professions. The padlocks securing our chains were old and probably somewhat corroded. I glanced meaningfully at the cup. If I'd been motivated before to get my powers back, I was rarin' to go now. It was our last chance.

"So, you see, Lord Fistula," Highperin said, with a smile, "we are very security-minded here. See you in six days." He started toward the door. His torturers, with a backwards look of regret toward their working tools, set down their irons and followed him.

"I salute you, Margrave," I called after him. "In fact, I want to offer my respects."

Curious, he turned back to me. "And how would you do that?"

"Let me drink a toast to you. What would it matter if our six-day fast starts now, or in a minute?"

"Are you thirsty, Lord Fistula?" Highperin said, returning to me with a gloating look spread across his plump little face. "Why not use the object of your most convoluted theft?"

As I hoped he would do, he snatched the Cup off the table and waved it in my face. The dented, time-dulled goblet didn't look like much, but I recalled how miserable Ersatz had seemed until I knocked the tarnish off him. The Cup was similarly disguised. No Klahd would look twice at it. Unlike Pervects, they can't smell gold. We can.

I sneered at the goblet, trying to let none of the eagerness I was feeling show on my face. "You really don't expect me to drink out of something that tacky."

"If you consider it beneath your notice, perhaps you will tell me why you wanted a boy's cheap trophy?" the Margrave asked. "I don't see anything special about it."

"My associate probably wanted me to see it," I said, shrugging as best I could with the weight of the chains. "We were interviewing the kid about the race he ran to win it, after all."

"Fine, then," the Margrave said, waving his hand impatiently. "Drink my health. I don't see why not, since you're all going to die in this cell, once His Grace confirms that you are all frauds. In celebration of your last moments of daylight, go ahead."

One of the guards poured the cup full of murky water from a rain barrel next to the window. I guessed that it was used to quench irons used for torture. "What, not even wine?" I asked, aggrievedly.

"You're lucky to get that, you criminal," the guard said haughtily.

I shrugged. "I can put up with water once in a while. I just don't overdo."

"I almost salute you, Lord Fistula," the Margrave said. "Showing such nonchalance in the face of doom."

"Suave's my middle name," I said.

The guard held it out to me. I reached for it. He tilted it and deliberately let the water splash to the floor. I stifled an outburst and glanced at the Margrave. The big cheese was getting a kick out of this. I couldn't wait to get my powers back. I'd give *him* a kick he'd remember the rest of his soon-to-be-shortened life. At his employer's nod, the guard dredged up another cupful and handed it to me.

My hands trembled as I took the cup. The anticipation was nearly killing me. I was seconds from getting my powers back, after all these years. I was almost floating. In the vision I had quaffed the whole cupful. The water smelled unappetizing, and there was a dead bug floating on the surface, but anyone who'd ever eaten Pervish food had had worse.

What to do first when the joke powder had been flushed out of my system? Should I just get us the heck out of there, or should I bounce the arrogant SOB all over the walls? Should I tear him into little pieces and rearrange them? I thought I'd begin by making the chains float in the air like clouds, then drop them on the Margrave's round little head.

I raised the cup high. "Your very good health, Margrave. You're the epitome of a government official, and I mean that from the bottom of my heart."

I drained the cup in a single gulp. Well-being flooded through me. I felt stronger than I had in years. Every bruise and bump that I had gotten from the mob who had jumped us and dragged us here faded away. My eyesight seemed clearer. I could hear birds twittering miles away outside the window. I felt connected to the world in a way I hadn't been in a long, long time. "Ah!" I patted my chest and stretched my arms. Look out, world, here I come!

The Margrave gestured impatiently to a guard to take the cup away from me.

"There, you've drunk my health. Does that make you feel better?"

I grinned. "As a matter of fact, Highboy, I feel great. Now, let me show you a little trick."

I took a deep breath, balancing myself on the balls of my feet. I pushed back the manacles so my hands were clear, wound up, and threw my hands toward the Margrave. Maybe I had put a little too much body English into it, but it was worth it. I opened my eyes.

Nothing happened.

I stared at my hands. What went wrong? I reached far down inside me and hoisted up all the energy I could, drew back, and threw it at the Margrave.

"And what am I supposed to see?" Highperin asked, one eyebrow most of the way toward his thin hairline.

"Uh."

He should have blasted apart into six pieces, by light- ning that ought to be *still* ricocheting around the room! I felt around for the force lines. There ought to be plenty of power in reach, since Tananda was still using it to maintain our disguises. I reached deeper and came up as embarrassed as a diner who'd forgotten his wallet. There was nothing there. The rush of power that had gone through me had left me feeling absolutely terrific, but I was still bereft of magik. My shoulders sagged.

"I see," the Margrave said, flicking his fingers derisively at us. "You're just wasting my time. See you in six days. I don't know precisely what I will have done to the three of you, but I promise you, it will be humiliating."

It couldn't be any more humiliating than the way I felt at that moment.

Chapter 6

THE HUGE IRON door slammed shut behind him. The noise echoed in the stone room, battering at my ears. I hung from my manacles, too brought down even to stand up under my own power.

"Slick," Tananda said.

"Shut up," I growled, not bothering to look up. "That should have worked."

"Diplomacy's not an exact art." Tananda was being nice to me. I couldn't stand it. "What's he going to do when he finds out there's no Lord Fistula?"

"There is one," I said, swaying mournfully from my chains. The cockroaches and rats swarmed out of the walls and began to circle our feet. "The trouble we're going to have is when he finds out that the real one is still at court, or was, last time I heard."

"What's the penalty for impersonating a favorite of the local duke?"

"Same as always, death." I stood up and tried the chains again to see if I could dislodge them from the wall. No, the staple had to have been driven in at least a foot. The force required was beyond even that of a Pervect in good shape. I doubted anything short of a Troll could have yanked them free.

"Are you sure?" Tanda gulped.

"Klahds just aren't that imaginative, Tananda," I said. "They like torture and killing. Most of their hobbies revolve around one or the other. Hunting. Cockfighting. Football. Skeeve's a peace freak compared with his fellow demons."

Calypsa looked even more taken aback. "This is my fault. I apologize. If I had not thought out loud, we would not be in this sorry predicament."

"I wouldn't have called it thinking, girly," I said, grumpily. "I don't know how you lived to the age you are without having someone strangle you for blurting out whatever comes into your head. Look at what they did to my clothes. This jacket came from Bond of Savylle. I haven't had shoulders fit this well in thirty years."

"Woe is me," Calypsa said, enlarging upon her theme of self pity. She clasped her hands together and jangled her manacles as she beseeched the sky. "Now I *and* my champions are locked up in a foul dungeon, and my poor grandfather languishes without a hope of rescue." A bug touched her foot and she recoiled on tiptoe. "Eek!"

"Shut up!" I boomed. "I'm trying to think!"

"But the Margrave will kill us when he discovers your subterfuge! The fate of the family of Calypso is doom! Why are you not frightened?" She kicked away more insects.

"We've been in tighter situations," I said, trying to get back to the fly in the ointment. I mused aloud. "That should have worked. It shouldn't have mattered what I drank from that cup. I felt the power. My powers should have been restored instantly. Why weren't they? What in the nine Netherhells is wrong with that cockamamie cup?"

"Well, perhaps if you had told me what you needed me to cure. I could have told you that it wouldn't work," the Cup said suddenly, in perfect Walt. "Silly Pervert."

"Pervect," I corrected automatically, then did a double-take.

"My apologies. All the people from your dimension I have known were such lowlifes that "Pervert" comes automatically to my lips."

We all gazed at the golden goblet.

"It talks!" Calypsa said, starting forward. The chains jerked her back.

"All of the Golden Hoard can talk," Tananda said. "You know that."

"But it did not say anything before!" Calypsa said.

"I didn't have to defend myself until that Pervert maligned my talents," the Cup said in a ringing contralto female voice. The two rubies facing us were sharp with reproof.

"That's *Pervect!* I may have swallowed your potion, but I don't have to swallow insults. What if I stomp you into a solid gold floor tile?"

"Nonsense," she said. The engraving around the bottom of the bowl curved upward into a grin. "You can't reach me from there, and we both know it."

"Besides, it was Kelsa who said you would be able to restore his powers," Calypsa said.

"Did she?" the Cup asked. "She sees accurately, but I wouldn't give you dregs for any of her interpretations."

"Fair cup, then what is it that Aahz felt when he drank from you?"

"My name is Asti, you polite child," the Cup said. "I have a lot of talents. I can cure poison. I heal. I nourish—and by the way, I can tell from here you're not getting enough vitamin C. You'll get rickets in those long legs of yours. I create harmony between parties, weddings and peace treaties a specialty. And I brew some dandy hooch. Catch me in a good mood some evening when the moon is shining over my bowl. How'd you lose your powers, Per*vect*?"

"Joke powder."

"From the Bazaar at Deva?"

"Yeah." I had no wish to go further into my misadventures.

"Ah," Asti said, knowingly. I could imagine her nodding her head, if she had one. "Sorry. Not in my playbook. Ask the Book or the Ring. That's more up their street."

"What DID you do to me? I thought I felt my powers return!"

"Oh, that's just general purpose healing," Asti said. "You have fifty-five bones that have been broken at least once each over the course of your life, including all of your fingers and toes. You had Scarolzzi fever, can't say when, messed up part of your circulatory system. You're lucky it's not contagious any longer. You had lost about 30% of your hearing, normal wear and tear for someone your age. Your liver has been run over by some pretty bad booze, lots of it. There were a dozen or more other minor conditions I won't bother to name. All that's gone. You've got a clean slate, but I suppose you'll just go back to your bad habits again. I can only cure. I can't make you stay healed."

"I like my bad habits," I said, sulkily.

I glanced sideways at Tanda, who was grinning at the long list of ailments as Asti reeled them off. I didn't like the cup mentioning the Scarolzzi fever. It was a little condition I'd picked up on Zimwod from a female there who'd been very friendly, and not at all forthcoming about her past...but I digress.

"Everyone does," Asti said, with a sigh. "I never deny healing to anyone who needs it, but I often regret that my talents are wasted on some people."

"So," I summed up, "I'm perfectly healthy, but I still have no magik."

"That's my diagnosis. You can thank me at your leisure." Asti's mouth settled back into a line of tarnished engraving. I snorted and began to pick at the locks with a talon.

"Then, we are trapped here," Calypsa wailed. "Trapped here until that horrible man chooses to come back and torture us! To death! No food, no water, no comfort! And all this vermin!" She began to drum her toes on the insects milling around us, only scoring on two or three out of every hundred.

"C'mon, cupcake," I chided her. "That's no way to stamp out roaches. You need to do it like *this*." I brought the flat of my foot down on the nearest cluster of wildlife, smashing it flat. "Put some body English into it." I kicked away a few more rats. One of them took a nip out of my left foot, and I launched the critter into the water barrel. It surfaced, gasping, and slunk over the side toward the hole in the base of the wall.

"But we are prisoners! Prisoners!" Calypsa exclaimed.

"Maybe...not...for long," Tananda panted. I glanced her way, and my jaw dropped. You think you know someone, then, even after more than a hundred years they can surprise you. She had bent one of her legs up behind her, and was pulling her pointed toe upward toward between her shoulder blades, a feat of elasticity that I didn't think even a Trollop was capable of. With both thumbs she peeled back the tip of her boot. Holding the foot steady with one hand, she pulled a long, skinny pick out from between the upper and shin of her boot. Triumphantly, she let her leg drop and brandished the shaft of metal at me.

"I can't get it out by reaching forward," she explained. "That's how it goes undetected if I'm ever searched."

"Tanda," I said, grinning, "you're the best."

"That's why they pay me the gold pieces," she said. "Give me a moment. These old locks are stiff."

Tanda bent her head over the chain on her left wrist. I heard rather than saw the noise of the pick scratching away at years of rust and who knew what else caking up the mechanism of the fist-sized locks. I kept my eye on the door. Groans, shrieks and wails for mercy the guards would ignore. The sounds of an attempted escape were more likely to attract their attention. My keen ears, made more keen than I could recall in a lot of years by Asti's charm, were open to the noise of returning footsteps.

While Calypsa and I watched in fascination, Tananda popped the hasp of the first lock. The thick wristlet sagged open with the creaking sigh of a disappointed torturer. She let the chain down very gently so it did no more than jingle against her skirt hem as she started in on the other chain. The tip of her tongue stuck out between her teeth as she probed around in the keyhole. The pick scratched less certainly here. Tananda's forehead creased.

"Would an anti-rust cantrip help?" I asked. It's impossible not to kibbitz when you're watching an expert at work.

She shook her head. "The lock's bespelled," she said. "I'd have to drop the disguise spell to absorb enough power from the force lines."

I glanced at the door. "Do it," I advised. "I don't want Highboy coming back and deciding he wants to get a head start on his torture program."

The fetching form of a female Klahd vanished, and the familiar shape of Tananda in her working clothes emerged.

"Ahhh!" Tananda shook out her hand and held it over the recalcitrant lock. It started quivering, not an uncommon reaction when Tanda gets close.

"What's the problem?"

"This is an old spell," she said. "They don't get wizards around here much, but this one—whew! He knew his torture devices."

"I bet he was fun at parties," I said, keeping my ear open for any interest by the guards. My keen Pervish hearing picked up conversation beyond the door about the latest serving wench and who was likely to get between her plackets first.

"Darn!" Tananda whispered.

The pick jumped out of her fingers. She made a swipe for it, but the point bounced off her fingertips. It tinkled on the floor and rolled, sounding louder than an electric guitar in the silence of the dungeon. On the other side of the door, footsteps hustled in our direction. The door sprang open.

"Hey, fellahs, we were just gettin' lonely," I said. They gasped. Our disguise-free state evidently turned them off.

"Monsters!" one of the guards exclaimed.

"Kill them!" the captain of the guard bellowed.

"Now, come on, fellows," I said, spreading out my hands with a friendly grin on my face. The guards blanched. They leveled their crossbows at us and prepared to fire.

"La di dah! La di dee! La de da daddle daddle dah!" a soft voice began to croon by my right ear. I turned to gawk. How could Calypsa think about singing at a moment like this?

She wasn't just singing. I don't know how she was doing what she was doing, but her long, skinny body undulated back and forth, setting a fascinating tempo. Her arms lifted and began to weave backwards and forwards. I found myself taking a

helpless step in her direction. Her long neck curved bewitch-
ingly from side to side. I felt transfixed but divinely happy, like
a fly caught in a jar of grape jelly. How come I hadn't noticed
before how large and lustrous her eyes were? The fans of thick,
black-and-white fluffy plumes spread between her arms and
the sides of her body concealed and revealed, leaving me gasping for another glimpse of her half-smile. The guards were
similarly agog. Their crossbows drooped toward the ground
like...crossbows drooping. In no time at all they had forgotten
that we were demons, dangerous prisoners of their employer.
All they could see was Calypsa.

She lifted her chin and nodded in the direction of the fallen
lock pick. I snapped out of the half-trance, but not as fast as
Tananda, who flicked a finger at the length of steel. It leaped
up into her hand, summoned by a burst of 'come-hither' magik.
I forced my eyes toward her. The guards never turned to look.
Tanda scraped at the wards of her lock. With a screech, it
popped open. She dumped it on the floor. She bent and unfas-
tened the chains around her feet, then sprang over to free me.
The guards weren't about to interrupt her. They couldn't take
their eyes off Calypsa. I had to work hard to avoid falling into
the spell again.

Tananda undulated toward the Walt, steering the pick
through the air with a tickle of magik. It nosed into the keyholes of the locks on Calypsa's wrists and ankles, until the
chains fell to the floor with a THUNK! The slender girl
whirled in place, her hands flashing. Tananda and I hurried
to stuff our possessions back into our pockets and other hiding places, and to gather up the Cup and the wrapped crystal
ball.

"Talented girl," Asti stated, one of her jeweled eyes watching her critically over my shoulder.

"Shut up," I growled, shoving my purse back into my
pocket. Good thing I never carried a credit card. In an effort to
stave off fraud, the modern ones issued by the Gnomes of
Zoorik bore the owner's picture. If Highboy'd had any brains,

he would have realized the coins were just as much a give-away that neither I nor my companions were from around there.

"How are you going to extract her from here? If she stops dancing, they'll snap out of it."

"No problem," I said. I edged around behind the fasci-nated chief guard and lifted the heavy ring of keys out of his belt. He never budged. "Hey, doll," I called to Calypsa. "Let's play peek-a-boo with your new admirers."

She looked a question at me, so I jerked my head toward the heavy dungeon door. She nodded, and worked the gesture into a sexy spin. The girl was brighter than I had given her credit for. Tananda might be right about the promise she showed. Too bad about her impulse control problems, but most of that would probably work out over time. If we all lived that long.

Tananda had already caught on to my idea. With the light-ness of someone who was accustomed to moving in and out of a location undetected, she had edged past the guards and backed up the stairs. In one hand she had a dagger by the point; in the other she cradled the muffled form of Kelsa. I didn't need any other armament than I had been furnished by nature, but I was hampered with Asti, who, being made of solid gold, was a heck of a lot heavier she looked, and squealed whenever she was tipped sideways. How no one in that pa-thetic little town had failed to cotton on to the metal, let alone the quality of her workmanship, made me despair of Klahds ever entering seriously into the realm of advanced commerce. I stuffed her into one of our carry sacks and ignored her com-plaints. Too bad we didn't have a second silence scarf like the one around Kelsa.

As Calypsa undulated around her admirers, I edged out of the dungeon. Except for Tananda, I couldn't hear anyone else breathing within about twenty yards. I recalled that the door through which we had been hauled wasn't far from the dun-geon—all the easier to make deliveries. I could smell fresh air, or what passed for it around here, redolent of cow manure and kitchen garbage.

The Walt wriggled her way up each of the stone stairs. The guards followed her, tongues hanging out. She stopped to pirouette on the top step, with a cute little boom-sha movement that would have been worth its weight in gold pieces at any of the quality strip clubs on Perv, like Gawker's or Irv's Red Hotsies, and gave them a little toss of her head as if to say "here's one for the boys in the back row." When she got in range, I snaked my arm in, yanked her out, and slammed the door.

It took a moment for the spell to break. By the time the guards realized they'd been tricked, I'd locked the big door on them. Tananda beckoned over her shoulder and fled into the dark hallway. I hauled Calypsa along behind me.

"But I was not finished!" she protested. The guards started pounding on the door and yelling, from frustration or anger, I couldn't tell.

"We don't hang around for curtain calls," I snarled, hustling her toward the disappearing green figure of the Trollop. "What *was* that?"

"The Dance of Fascination," Calypsa said, tossing her head proudly. "My great-great aunt, the dancer Rumba, was the first to perform it."

Chapter 7

I WISHED WE could have used the D-hopper and *bamfed* out without all the fancy footwork, but we still had to retrieve Ersatz. I was regretting leaving him behind in the woods, but it was better to have to backtrack and get him than to have to search the castle for whatever armory in which Highboy would have stashed an obviously valuable sword after he confiscated it from us. I didn't know whether Calypsa's hips would have held out for that long.

We paused at the door while Tananda whipped us up a new disguise spell, then plunged out of the castle, disguised as Highboy and two generic soldiers. The guards on duty outside threw me a grand salute, which I returned, looking harried. Not a bad imitation, if I do say so myself.

Ersatz spotted us long before we could see him. He was hidden at just above eye level in a hollow branch of a big tree overhanging the forest path.

"Well, friend?" the sardonic voice asked. "Is all well? Are your powers restored to you?"

"Don't ask," I grunted, as I yanked him out of his post.

"Have you the old beaker with you? She has not yet poisoned you, at any rate."

"I would know that rusty garden gate of a voice across the universe," Asti shrilled. "Let me out of this rag bag at once!"

I looked around to make sure no one was coming, then I brought Asti out of my rucksack. The jeweled eyes and the reflected ones regarded each other with expressions of mutual dislike.

"So, there you are, you cake spatula," Asti said. "The last time I saw you, you ruined a perfectly good peace accord I was overseeing on Jahk!"

"An assassin of the Bruhns bid fair to stab the ambassador of the Bhuls in the back!" Ersatz replied. "A good peace accord signifies that all have agreed to down weapons, not plunge them into the other party's representatives."

"And no one would have, if you hadn't bellowed out, 'Ware assassins!' Suddenly both armies whipped out knives, knouts, brass knuckles—you name it—and the table went over as the Bruhns shoved it onto the Bhuls' ambassador's toe. In no time the place was a shambles. That's where I got this dent," she added, the ruby eyes rolling up toward a bulge at the rim.

"And added more since," Ersatz said, with less tact than I would have expected out of him. "You look rather the worse for wear."

"No thanks to you! No one even thought of tapping it out. My beautiful roundness, marred, and it's all your fault!"

"Wait a minute," I said, raising my hands. "How long ago was this?"

"Five hundred twenty years, nine months and three days," they said in virtual unison.

"And four days," Kelsa piped up, as Calypsa unwrapped her. The face appeared in the ball. "You forget about universal drift and daylight savings time!"

"Be quiet," Ersatz said. "You were not there."

"I don't have to be, my dear," Kelsa reminded him. "I know all, see all, remember!"

"You told them I could bring back his powers!" Asti burst out.

Kelsa's face changed until she looked like a goblet herself, but with the turban and glasses over a couple of jewels shaped like eyes.

"Why, I never did. I only told them what I saw."

"Aha. And you believed her?" the cup asked me, shocked. "When she hasn't had a clearheaded moment in centuries?"

"Clearheaded?" Kelsa asked, the image thinning in the golden crystal until it was almost transparent with fury. "I am always clearheaded. Look at me? Why shouldn't they believe me! I told them the future! Everything I said came to pass. They didn't interpret it correctly."

"And you didn't interpret it for them?"

"My dear, my job is to predict! If I was known for interpretation, there would be many more usurpers taken to the block and many more crowned heads safe on their pillows at night. Fewer little girls would take chancy trips through the woods unescorted, and the divorce courts would be full since no cheaters could possibly go undetected. My facts are undisputed to the open mind. You're the one who's full of alcohol all the time!"

"Not all the time," Asti said, sulkily. "I make other potions than alcohol. All kinds. Anything that purports to 'know all,' should know that."

"Why, Asti, I didn't say you couldn't. I simply inferred that you *didn't*," Kelsa said. She looked smug.

"You silicon implant, you have no right to blare people's private business all over the cosmos!"

"Certainly I do. My job is to predict, inform, provide light in the darkness, give a head's up to my possessor as to events which will shape his future and that of the rest of the dimensions. By the way, dear," she said, turning to me and winking an eye, "you might want to pick your feet up. There's a hunting party on the way. Horses, lots of sharp, pointy objects. Ersatz can't possibly take them on all by himself."

"Who says that I cannot, wench?" the sword fumed.

"Knock it off!" I said, not wanting to deal with his ego at the moment. "Who is it?"

"Lord Highperin, his chief huntsman, three sergeants-at-arms, fifteen men-at-arms, a pack of hounds…"

A loud bay confirmed at least part of her statement. I glanced at Tananda.

"Where to?" she asked.

"Anywhere but here," I said. I grabbed Asti and started to shove her back into my rucksack.

"Just a moment!" she said, sounding horrified. "You're not putting me back in that wretched rag again, are you?"

"You bet I am, sister," I said.

"Over my bent stem, you are," Asti retorted.

Out of her bowl, sour-smelling red liquid began to pour, then spray upward in an increasing fountain like a fire hose. I held her away from my face. The liquid was wine, a crummy vintage that I wouldn't have used for insecticide. The spray rose higher. In a moment it would rise higher than the trees. Highperin wouldn't need the dogs to trace us.

"Turn it off!" I shouted. "What do you want?"

"I thought you might see reason. After all, you want your reward, don't you?" The stream cut off between one drop and another. The ruby eyes regarded me with a pleased expression. "I just want a case that befits my status, Mr. Aahz. I am one of the most important members of the Golden Hoard. You can't just wrap me in rags and expect me to be happy about it."

"A *case?*" I asked, dumbfounded.

"You always possessed delusions of grandeur," Ersatz said. "You will not give in to her petty blackmail, will you?"

"Oh, yes, he will," Asti said, confidently. "Well?"

"Not a chance," I said, with my teeth gritted.

Wine began to flow over my hand again.

"All right, all right!" I shouted. "We'll get you a case."

"A nice one," Asti said. "One with a decent silk lining, tooled leather, and my name written in jewels. Those don't have to be as nice as my own, of course," she added. "Gold clasps would be acceptable, and padded with the best cashmere. Dyed purple, I think. It sets off my patina so well."

I started to growl, "Over my dead body," but Calypsa put her hand on my arm.

"Asti is an ancient treasure, and we do need her help," she said. "The purse will surely reimburse you for any outlay you make. I would feel better if she was made the most comfortable."

The cup beamed. "I like this girl. She *knows* how to treat an artifact!"

Tananda and I looked at each other.

"Deva," she said.

If you're one of the non-dimension-hopping rubes who have never been to the Bazaar at Deva, picture the biggest shopping arena you know of.

Now, double it.

Now, double it again.

Just keep on doubling it until you run out of numbers.

The Bazaar is well known throughout the dimensions as the go-to place for almost kind of merchandise. If it can be bought, sold, traded, stolen and sold again, it's for sale in one of the tents, booths, open-air rings, tables and even cloths spread on the ground in its dirty, crowded, noisy, hot lanes. You can get a tattoo anywhere on your body, including the inside. You can, as I know to my everlasting regret, buy a live dragon here. (If you have any sense at all, you won't.)

You can find restaurants serving food from countless lands, including one of the only Pervish restaurants I have ever found ex-dimension. Most other races don't want to serve Pervish food, because it tends to be ambulatory, and it has a pretty strong aroma—make that stench. No item or ingredient is so exotic that money won't bring it to your table, unless it's sentient. Even the locals aren't that sick.

The local species, who run most of the establishments, are known as Deveels. In appearance they're similar to the beings of Klahdish nightmares, with dark red skin, little horns on either side of their foreheads, and lower limbs that end in hooves. To deal with a Deveel, you had better be a savvy trader or be willing to lose whatever you're carrying on you. There's no truth in the rumor that you can lose your soul to one of the merchants in the Bazaar, unless you were foolish enough to put it on the table in the first place. In other words, you need to understand what you have agreed to, and make certain that there are no handy loopholes in your verbal contract, or the shopkeeper will wriggle out of fulfilling his end of the bargain if he can find any way at all to do so.

They are the slickest businesspeople in the universe, and they can sense the presence of money. Being cheated by a Deveel is a normal event in the Bazaar, but if you can keep your head, you can find goods of surprising quality among the acres and acres of *dreck*. Some of the finest craftspeople of all races have shops there. The chances were also pretty good that if any of the other treasures of the Golden Hoard were presently for sale, they might be kicking around here. I thought it was worth taking a look.

The Bazaar was also the site of the former offices of M.Y.T.H., Inc., the operation that had been headed up by my old partner, Skeeve, with me as his advisor. The tent, which was, to quote another dimensional traveler, was substantially bigger on the inside than it was on the outside because of a common trick used in the Bazaar and elsewhere, of setting only the front door, and maybe the anteroom, of a building in a particular dimension, and carving the rest of the space out of a neighboring dimension by means of a spell. Our tent backed onto a dimension called Limbo, which even the Deveels were loath to visit. The main race there was vampires, with werewolves and a few other children of the night thrown in for makeweight, or make-wight, if you like. It had explained why our tent had been priced so reasonably even though it was located on a main thoroughfare. Skeeve insisted that the Limboans were as afraid of us as we were of them, but the place gave me the creeps. Still, I used it as my pied-à-terre — you can't argue with the fact that it was already paid for. A few of the gang came and went as business brought them to Deva, but it wasn't like the old days.

Even though most people would hesitate to tangle with a Pervect, especially a notable like myself, I felt very uncomfortable carrying three very valuable pieces of magikal hardware through the Bazaar. The pickpockets and thieves that roamed the lanes could smell gold through ten layers of bespelled safe-satchels, let alone buried in the middle of ancient sacks that we'd lifted from a nearby potato field in Klah.

Ersatz we couldn't hide at all, except to cover his hilt with an old sack. Bumping along on Calypsa's narrow shoulder, he was getting a lot of attention from the shopkeepers we passed. I kept a hand on the D-hopper in my pocket. It was an ancient artifact, and there weren't many around. No way after all this time was I losing my ride.

"I don't see why you have to have a special carrying case," I told Asti sourly. "That kid who had you on his shelf sure didn't have a fancy set up for you, especially not one with jewels and tooled leather."

"I don't expect dancing girls and acolytes, Mr. Aahz," Asti said, smugly, now that she knew she was getting her way.

"It's just Aahz," I said.

"As you wish. I liked Imgam. In every way that counted, that simple setting was a shrine. Imgam gave me the very best he had. He set me on a plinth of wood he cut with his own hands. He polished me with the finest cloth in the house, a piece of silk his mother got as a wedding present. It was cheap by comparison with most of the polishing cloths I've had over the years, but there was none better to be had. He handled me with love and the deepest respect." She sighed. "Outside of the Temple of Shamus, I have never had such worship. I really enjoyed it. You had better have removed me from his care for a very important reason indeed, and not just to restore powers to a Pervert."

Calypsa opened her mouth to speak, but I held up a hand to shush her. "Not here," I said. "We'll get you your case, then go to someplace where it's less likely we'll be bugged."

"My goodness, what an interesting place," Kelsa said, from Tananda's shoulder bag. She had insisted that we not use the silencing cloth, and she had babbled nonstop since we *bamfed* in. "Did that Deveel really just take that Imper for the last silver piece he had? And all because he was palming the bean that should have been under at least one of those shells?"

Her shrill voice was plenty audible enough so that the Imp in question heard it. He glared at the Deveel, who glared in *our* direction. The Imp demanded a refund. The Deveel, no surprise, refused. That started an argument with the huckster that drew an audience from the surrounding booths. I put a hand into Calypsa's back and hustled her out of the way of the brawl that was going to start in, oh, ten seconds.

Nine. Eight. Seven. Six.

"You cheated me, you scarlet shyster! Give me back my money, or I'll blow your head off!"

Oh, well, a little ahead of schedule.

The Deveel behind the leatherwork counter listened as Calypsa recited the details of the case Asti wanted. We all thought it would be better if none of the Golden Hoard said anything. The last thing I needed was a rumor going around that they were in the dimension. It would start a gold rush the likes of which hadn't been seen in a century.

"...And cashmere lining. Purple," Calypsa said. "Good enough to last for a hundred years."

"Uh-huh," said Stankel, noting down the information on a scrap of leftover parchment. "Not the usual stuff I do for you, pretty girl," he said, patting Tanda on the bottom. She smiled at him with such concentrated sweetness that he moved his hand back in alarm. I grinned.

"Just give me the estimate," I said.

"Well, it's custom work," he began, ticking off the items on the list. "Rush job, you said. Special dyes. It'll have to be clegborn beetle wing dye for the lining—it's the best. Doesn't run, won't fade. Tooling on the leather representing water flowing up out of a fountain, waves crashing on the shore, that kind of thing. If you don't mind magikal carving, I can do anything you want. Saves time. The name on the top is Asti, you said?"

He glanced up at me with a gleam in his eye. I was afraid that he'd catch on. Deveels didn't get to be the most feared traders in a hundred dimensions by missing implications, and they never forgot any detail that might be worth a copper to them.

"Yeah." I leaned close. "I wouldn't want it to get around. We're running an...operation. You understand. Set a fraud to catch a fraud, you know. Not like we've got the *real* Asti."

"I see," Stankel said, licking the end of his pencil and scrawling a final note. "No, I get it. Where would *you* get a Hoard treasure, Aahz?" He laughed.

I resented his implication, but I didn't want to start a fight. Not yet, anyhow.

"*How* much?" I asked.

"Oh, well, seeing as how you're an old friend, and Tanda here's a regular customer...half a gold piece."

"How much?" I asked.

"Half a gold piece. And I'm taking bread out of my children's mouths to give you a price that low."

"Your children are in their sixties," I pointed out. "If you're still feeding them, you're as crummy a parent as you are a businessman. This might be good work, but I could get Steger to whip out the same for a tenth."

"A tenth! You're out of your mind!"

I smiled. Now things were beginning to move. "Not so crazy as you are."

"How could you even think of offering me such a pathetic sum for my quality leather goods?" He appealed to passersby. "This stinking Pervert thinks he can ask the craftsman Stankel for custom work for a rotten tenth of a gold piece! Four tenths, or I'll throw you out of this booth on your scaly bottom!"

"That's Pervect," I bellowed, "and I'd like to see you try it! Two tenths!"

It was past lunch time, so the crowd that gathered to listen to us haggle wasn't as large as it might be, which suited me just fine. I didn't want anyone reading over Stankel's shoulder. Tananda was used to the custom of bargaining in the Bazaar, but Calypsa was beginning to shy backwards, away from our voices. I couldn't take the time out to let her know this was normal. Suddenly, I saw the gleam of Ersatz's eyes peeking out of the wrapping over her shoulder. Gradually, the Walt stopped trembling. After a while, she looked as if she was actually enjoying the show. When we finally finished haggling and agreed on a quarter gold piece, she joined in the applause. I thought it had been a pretty good show, myself.

After letting Stankel take measurements of Asti, we left him to work. He wasn't too impressed with the pathetically banged-up cup for which we were buying a fancy box, but had bought the story we were using it to run some kind of elaborate scam. He knew, as any Deveel would from birth, that it was solid gold, but I had chosen Stankel on purpose because he was almost as magik-blind as I was at the moment. He couldn't feel the mystical wallop she and the other two packed.

"Give me a couple of hours," Stankel said. "I should be able to whip something together by then."

Chapter 8

I SWAGGERED AS I led the others out of the booth, leading them deftly through a party of drunken Vikings negotiating for hide-covered shields. We shoved past an Imp buying yard goods in colors nature never intended, and swung wide around a party of gaping Kobolds taking snapshots of an eight-armed juggler, whose partner was picking their pockets. As we went past a cross street Calypsa went weak at the knees.

"What is that stink?" she gasped, staggering. I caught a strong, malodorous whiff that made me smile.

"Pervish cooking," I said. "The restaurant's not far away."

"No," Tananda said firmly. "Hasn't she been through enough in the last few days? There's no reason to subject her to your kind of food."

I lowered my eyebrows. It had been a while since I had tasted home cooking. Tananda gave me one of those looks that meant business, as in we were engaged in business, and pleasure would have to wait. I thought about it. We could split up, but that only meant double the chances that some of the free-lance brigands that shopped the Bazaar could get a crack at the goods we were carrying. I sighed.

Instead, I headed for the Yellow Crescent Inn, where my buddy Gus the Gargoyle pulled strawberry milkshakes for those discerning customers who could use a little privacy when they ate lunch The Yellow Crescent's food was bland, because the diners liked it that way. I could eat it, but I considered it no more than fodder.

To my relief, the other patrons who were in the Inn were all strangers. We didn't have any trouble taking possession of a corner booth, where both Tanda and I could have our backs to the wall. Gus waved to us with a broad stone hand, then came around the counter to greet us.

"Hey, Aahz, long time no see!" he said, extending bone-crushing handgrips with us. "You been away? Hey, Tananda. You look lovely, as usual."

"Hi, Gus," she said, warmly.

"The usual?"

She nodded. I grunted. "Yeah."

Gus turned to Calypsa.

"How about you, honey? You're a Walt, ain't you? Don't get a lot of your kind here on Deva. What'll it be? Milkshake on the house for a friend of my pal here."

Calypsa looked confused, so I shook my head.

"Let the kid here see the menu, Gus, and make sure no one interrupts us, okay? We've got a little business to discuss."

"No problem," Gus said. He left a greasy parchment by Calypsa and went back to the counter.

"Okay, Asti," I said, plunking the cup on the table. In her sorry condition no one in the room paid much attention to her. The toys that came with the kids' meals looked more impressive than she did. "Let's talk. There's a few things you gotta understand."

"Oh, I understand," Asti said blithely. "You and this green floozy…"

"Trollop, please," Tananda said, with some asperity.

"As you please…you are a pair of hired hands. Have I got that wrong? If not, then I suggest you listen to this lass. She's your employer, isn't she? She has persuaded you to join her on a mission that tugs at the heartstrings' to save her beloved grandfather. I look forward to hearing the whole tale later, naturally. I love a good tearjerker. And she wants to treat me with the honor that I must inform you I am due. I suggest you listen to her. Obviously, she knows her history. I have anointed kings and queens, blessed babies, cured poison, elicited truth, sealed oaths, toasted dynastic marriages…I'm the stuff of legends, baby, and don't you forget it!"

"So, what if we do find you a different container. Is that going to make you cooperate? No more floods?"

"Possibly," Asti said, the line on her bowl curving upward.

I heard some hubbub coming from Calypsa's side of the table. Muffled exclamations were coming from the disguised sword. Alarmed, the girl hoisted him off her back and put him on the table, blade half out of his scabbard.

"Friend Aahz," Ersatz said. I could see the one baleful eye looking out of the torn leather at me. "At least I counted you friend! Until now."

"What's the matter with *you?*" I asked.

The eye blazed. "You have promised good gold for a polished and bejeweled husk to carry this wretched, leaky vessel in state—and you have not extended the same to me!"

"What?" I demanded.

"Aye, and I had come to believe that you had respect for me. You, who recognized my quality. You, who bought me out of *tchochke*dom and who are bearing me forward into an honorable destiny. You, who know my history, back as far as the mysterious fires that gave me birth. You who know the battles I have fought. YOU—would let me go on in this worn and limp scabbard while Asti has a new case to contain her pathetically beaten form?"

"Oh, yes," Asti piped up. "And I want you to find a goldsmith to tap me out again. No sense in continuing to look like the last target on the fence. Oh, and you might see if he can find me a replacement for the oval chalcedony on my foot. I noticed a chip out of it, just at the base..."

I glanced from her back to Ersatz. "No."

"No, what?" Asti asked.

"No to a polish job, and no to a brand new scabbard. And no," I added, as Kelsa started protesting from Tananda's substantial purse, "to a monogrammed miniature bowling bag to contain the world's most talkative crystal ball!"

They all burst out talking at once.

"Quiet," I shouted.

They quieted. I leaned toward Asti, making sure she got a good look at my bared teeth.

"First of all, dixie-cup, I may have taken on a job and need your cooperation to complete it, but you never call my friend Tananda names again. Do you understand? You may be an immortal treasure and have a hundred songs sung about your exploits, but you're still a piece of metal. I can flatten you and use you for a bookmark in my copy of the *Perva Sutra*. Got that? Second, just because we are working for Calypsa, the arrangement is temporary. When it's over, I'll be a private citizen again, so don't treat me like the help. When she's done with you, you'll be out of immunity cards. Get me?"

"My goodness, he can be touchy, can't he?" Asti appealed to Tananda. "Very well. I apologize for assuming you have no morals. But look at the way you dress!"

"What, this old thing?" Tananda asked, tugging at her neckline so that her assets jiggled fetchingly. "You should see me when I want to attract attention."

"The fact remains," Ersatz said, regaining the floor, "that I, too, merit presentation in a more fitting sheath."

"I thought that one fit fine," I said, but he didn't give me any credit for my wit. Trust a straight sword not to have a sense of humor. He carried on without changing expression.

"This slip is not meet, nor spruce, nor any of the things that I could wish. It protects my edge and, yea, provides me with some anonymity, but as you can see, friend Aahz, it is falling apart! Surely your leather-working associate back there can fashion something in which I will not be ashamed to be seen?"

"Be fair, Aahz," Calypsa said, batting those long black lashes of hers.

"And who is going to pay for this meet sheath?" I countered.

"Well," the Walt said, lowering her head in embarrassment. "You are."

"To fit me out sweetly, I am certain that Chin-Hwag will add the price to your fee," Ersatz said, "with an emolument for making the outlay, of course. She and I were always well disposed to one another."

"Oh, that's it!" Asti said. "You promised him a big reward from the Endless Purse as well as restoring his powers! My goodness, I thought you were assisting this girl for the sake of her grandfather! I wish I could give you Scarolzzi fever again, you...you Pervert!"

"That's Pervect!" I growled.

Her accusation stung, but it was the truth. Why hide from it? I was doing Calypsa a favor. So what if I got something in exchange for my help? I wanted my powers back. If I could get them by collecting the whole set of Franklin Talkative Treasures, then I'd do it. I've done worse.

"If we wish to discuss greed, what about you?" Ersatz said, turning to Asti. "You are a member of the Golden Hoard! You are supposed to assist those in need without consideration for material return! The makers who set us on our path would be horrified that you put your base needs in the way of our mission."

"Hmph! I notice that you're dipping into fashion yourself at the moment," Asti said, a superior look on her bowl. "A new scabbard. I suppose you want jade plates carved with the tales of your exploits sewn to it."

"I had already sworn my allegiance to this child and her companions," Ersatz countered. "I had no idea that they would neglect me and my offer of service in their haste to pander to you."

"It's only because she threatened to drown them in bad wine," Kelsa pointed out, cheerfully. "That upchucking trick's always been one of her favorites. Why, I was looking in once when she washed away an entire garrison..."

"You're no better, blinding people or misleading them," Asti said, the line of her mouth drawn into a sneer. "I'm surprised you haven't already asked for a multi-sided box lined with mirrors so you can watch yourself from all angles."

"Why, what a lovely idea!" Kelsa said, beaming. "Although I was very much taken with Aahz's suggestion of a bowling bag. Very compact and cosy. I don't need mirrors to see myself, dear. Besides, if I rolled into one and broke it, I'd probably end up like you, seven years bad luck—or seven hundred. Wasn't that when you first got banged up?"

"Will you stop harping on that?" Asti asked. "Do you think I like looking like this? It throws off my flow."

"Yes, I saw how you got that big thumbprint in your stem. But who knew that curing that Troll of Gnrshkt poison was going to bring his strength back all at once? Well, I did, but I wasn't there. I wish you could have heard me. I was shouting my head off, telling him to let go. Of course, I was ten dimensions away at the time. It was quite a shock to the Kobold I was working for. He nearly forgot to invent the magikal superconductor!"

"That cursed Troll only made it worse when he tried to fix it," Asti said, aggrievedly. "I thought every jewel was going to pop out of its socket."

"Take your dents as hallmarks of your experience," Ersatz said.

"Oh, I suppose you let little nicks in your blade go by, do you?"

"Nicks interfere with my function. I don't see that dents prevented you from causing an unnecessary flood of wine in that forest!"

"Now, now, what do mere appearances have to do with your eternal quest to aid and assist those in danger?" Kelsa asked.

Both of the others rounded on her, united in a common enemy.

"Be quiet!"

"I was only pointing out the obvious!"

"That's all you can do, isn't it? Nothing useful, like cure poison," said Asti.

"Or slay enemies," added Ersatz.

"That's not all there is in life," Kelsa said, imperturbably. That provoked the other two into another tirade.

"They hate each other!" Calypsa wailed. "They will never cooperate, and my grandfather's life will be forfeit!"

"It's worse than that," Tananda said, leaning close to me. "They're causing a buildup of force, right here in the restaurant."

"They're what?" I asked.

"You can almost see it," she said. "I'm not much of a magician, but even I can feel an influx that large. In a minute, there's going to be an explosion if they don't stop drawing in power!"

I put my hands on the tabletop' it was starting to vibrate. Tanda was right. If the Hoard was the source of the disturbance, we were in trouble.

"All right," I said. I turned to the three artifacts, who were bringing up each other's shortcomings dating back at least a thousand years.

"And you predicted that those Imps would create a device so powerful that it would destroy a world!"

"I was right! Three-card monte was the cause of the first decline of the Zoorik economy!"

"What about your poisoning the Gnome Princess on her wedding night?"

"It wasn't poison, you idiot! It was a nerve tonic. So she drank too much. So she fell asleep for three years. What about *you*...?"

The table-shaking was achieving the proportions of a fraudulent séance. I slammed my hand in between them.

"All right. ALL RIGHT! SHUT UP! KNOCK IT *OFF*!"

The rafters rang, but it got their attention. The vibration slowed. It didn't cease.

"Why the shouting, friend Aahz?" Ersatz asked mildly. Evidently his beef with me was forgotten.

"Take a look at the atmosphere around us. Magik is piling up in here like dung in a stockyard, and you three have to be the cause. This place can't take it. Can you let the magik out without blowing up the inn?"

Kelsa closed her eyes behind the diamante spectacles. Her face disappeared for a moment, and was replaced by the image of a horrifying explosion that sent a curling fireball into the sky. "Good heavens, this isn't like me!"

"I warned you, Aahz," Ersatz said. "You asked why the Golden Hoard never assembles in any one place for long."

"We'd better get out of here," I said, rising hastily.

"Too late," said Tananda.

She was right. Rumbling began throughout the tent. The ground shook. The pillars holding up the roof started to sway. Around us, the diners held onto their tables. Suddenly, milkshakes began to fountain upward. I got hit by a cold shower of sticky brown liquid. Calypsa disappeared in a hail of fried potatoes. I grabbed a handful of paper towels and sponged cola out of my eyes.

"If you're doing that, stop it," I ordered Asti.

"Good heavens, why do you think it's me?" she asked, innocently. A blob of strawberry milkshake came down with a *splat!* and landed in her bowl. "Say, that's good! Will your friend give me the recipe?"

I ignored her. The other patrons were regarding us with distrust and concern. One Deveel had thrown himself across his tray to prevent his food from taking off. Sandwiches flew around the room like Frisbees.

"We're going to have to take the food to go, Gus," I called. "Magikal emergency. You know."

"Sure do, Aahz," he said. He turned to load the paper-wrapped food into a white paper sack. I slipped some money over the counter and hoisted the bag into my free arm. "Always good to see you guys."

"Same here," I assured him, hustling the others out the door.

"Where are we going?" Asti asked. "We haven't picked up my case yet."

"We'd better get out of Deva," I said. "I have no intention of paying for damages the Deveels dream up if you three cause an explosion in one of the tents." The reason that insurance never caught on here is that the Deveels started to plan fires and disasters to consume unwanted or unsold merchandise and collect substantial loss reimbursement. It would take a master magician or a master strategist to figure out what had actually been in the tents at the time of the catastrophe.

"What about my case?"

"And my scabbard?"

"And my...whatever I'm going to be dressed in?" Kelsa asked.

"Forget about them. We have to get out of here." I was ticked off because my lunch was going to be delayed by three pieces of ancient bric-a-brac who didn't know how to control themselves in public.

Calypsa laid a feathered hand on my arm and opened large dark eyes at me. "We must keep our promises to them, dear Aahz."

"Look around you, sweetheart," I snarled. "This may look like friendly territory, but if the rumor gets out that we're carrying three members of the Hoard around, we're going to run into trouble. None of us has the firepower to deal with a thousand Deveel merchants all wanting to get a piece of us. Come on."

"Oh, no, not back into the rag bag again!" Asti wailed. "I'll have revenge on you...murfle murfle Perfle."

I wound the bag shut and turned to Tanda. "The tent's bespelled against magikal firepower. Let's duck in there. We can figure out where we're going after that."

Chapter 9

"ANYONE HOME?" TANANDA called, as we shut the door of the tent behind us. No one answered her. "I thought Guido and Nunzio were around, but Don Bruce must have them out on a job."

"Just as well," I said.

I didn't feel like saying hello to anyone. I was regretting that I ever got involved with Calypsa and her little mission. Twice while we were crossing the short distance from the Yellow Crescent Inn to our front door, Tananda had signaled me that the magikal buildup was starting again.

I had hustled us past the dragon pen, crowded us to the far side of the street away from the magik mirror shop, and avoided eye contact with a few Deveels I knew who were big noises in the enchanted weapons line. Luckily, they were arguing with an Imp who was trying to sell them a carriage-mounted rail gun he must have lifted from one of the high-technology dimensions. No matter how legendary or magikal, a sword just didn't have the drawing power of ten megatons with computerized three-dimensional targeting.

"Why, it's bigger on the inside…" Calypsa began, staring around her with wide eyes.

"Yeah, yeah," I interrupted her. I plopped Asti onto the table just inside the door and took a quick look around.

It was one of the narrowest and most humble-looking properties on the crowded lane, but the inside was luxurious. I had called it home for a long while.

"Very nice," Kelsa said, once we got her out of her cone of silence. "Quiet, though. Not what I expected."

Inside her globe was an image of the room, but as it had been months ago, with the whole of M.Y.T.H., Inc., running around in there, working on an assignment, checking in with each other, minding each other's business, feeding or avoiding the dragon. You could almost hear the voices' Guido's growl, Nunzio's nasal alto, Skeeve's tenor, Chumley's cultured voice belying the colossal fur mattress it was coming from, my own dulcet speech, and Bunny's high-pitched tones cutting through with a reminder to keep expenses down. I caught myself staring and yanked my gaze away. I had to admit I missed those days, but they were past.

A fountain burbled away in the atrium that was lit by a shaft of sunlight from a magikally warded skylight in the roof. Yes, I said roof. Once beyond the door, we weren't in Deva any longer, and unbound, as I mentioned before, by the square footage suggested by the cloth-and-stick enclosure that was our front door. We were safe here…I hoped.

"Where are we going next?" I asked Calypsa.

"You ought to be going back to Stankel's booth," Asti said. "I'm sure my case is ready by now."

"No. Where's the next treasure?" I asked, paying no attention to the cup. Out of the corner of my eye I could see the cheeks of her cup turning bronze with annoyance. "Any of them here in Deva?"

Calypsa turned to the crystal ball, whose face had already vanished in a swirl of clouds and sparkles. "No, not here," Kelsa said, after a moment's contemplation. "My goodness. There certainly is a lot of magikal interference. I can't get through…yes, I can. Ha, you can't keep me down for long! Aaaah, ooooh, aaaah."

"What are you seeing, Kelsa?" Calypsa asked, running to kneel down beside the table like a swan gliding onto a lake. I shook my head to clear it. The Dance of Fascination must have some residual effect. If I started thinking skinny feathered babes were appealing, then I needed a shrink.

"You see the Purse yet?" I asked. The sooner I could get paid and out of there, the better.

"I can't see Chin-Hwag at all—my guess is that it's not time for us to find her. The Book is keeping himself hidden. Not surprising; he always hated the hustle-bustle of the Hoard.

The Ring is in a dark place. I hear gurgles, like sewer pipes, and music. I haven't got a clue as to what *that* means. Yet. Give me time, dear. As for the Flute..."

"Where is he?" I asked.

"I see bright lights," Kelsa said, her voice becoming dreamy. "Loud noise—applause. Thousands, no—millions are hanging on the melody. There's such a mood of peace over the entire crowd, even the cutpurses are apologetic. Yes, I see the landmarks. I know the dimension..."

"Well?"

Kelsa's face reappeared in the globe, a Pervect wearing a turban and diamante glasses. She smiled sweetly at me. "...which I'll tell you just as soon as you buy me a lovely carrying case. I agree with Calypsa' you should keep your promises to us, you know. It's bad karma otherwise!"

"Careful! I don't want my case touching hers," Asti protested, as I stalked through the streets of Haze, a town in the dimension of Elb.

We were disguised as members of the local species, a narrow-faced, skinny race whose fur came in varying shades of pink, from light shell to shocking neon. Neither Tanda nor I had been here before, so we didn't know if the particular colors indicated status, so I had her deck us out in three different shades. I was the darkest pink, but the others were bright enough to short out my retinas. I swung the purple container to my other shoulder, away from Tananda, feeling as though I was floating through a psychedelic nightmare.

"Well, you don't think I want more contact with you than I can help," Kelsa said, through the isinglass window of her pumpkin-colored tote bag. "Your aura is very confused at the moment. I never noticed that, at several dimensions remove, and believe me, I think I would have preferred you stay at that distance. You're interfering with my reception."

"As if you get anything except hallucinations and infomercials," Asti said, with a skeptical laugh.

"Be silent, the both of you," Ersatz commanded.

His dark blue eyes reflected off the length of blade that could be seen through a convenient hatch that opened in his new scabbard, dyed gunmetal blue and studded with cabochon diamonds, which complimented the gems in his golden hilt. It was fancy but not gaudy, and the stones wouldn't notch his blade if he came in contact with them.

"Who died and left you Ka-Khan?"

"I AM the leader of this group!"

I ignored them. My coin purse was a good deal lighter than it had been three hours before. I was in a pretty bad mood over having been railroaded into making two more purchases.

Tananda kept trying to tell me it wasn't as bad as it could have been. Stankel hadn't had to make Kelsa's carrier from scratch, except to put in a window so she could see out. Not that I had let him hear her babble' after a big-eyed appeal from Calypsa, I took down a list of the crystal ball's yens and put them before the Deveel leather-worker. Stankel had given me a broad wink, as if he got the idea that he was part of a big scheme I was pulling. There were times when having a reputation for shaving the truth close enough for the silk veil test had its advantages. Nor had he had to do more than edit a stock scabbard a little to fit Ersatz's length and breadth, and add a few baubles. We haggled out the price until *he* was green in the face and *I* was turning red, but we left the shop with the three required containers. Each of us took one, since the Hoard treasures decided they were entitled to an exclusive bearer apiece. Three of them, three of us. It was no skin off my nose, just one more inconvenience I had to suffer. Ensconced in their new finery, they ceased griping, for at least twenty yards.

Then it began again.

"Friend Aahz, I have just counted the number of gems Asti has adorning her new domicile. I do not wish to be a constant complainer…"

"Then, don't," I said, cutting him off.

The master cutter didn't take the hint. "I think you should have made certain we were equal in all ways."

"You should have said something at the time, then," I said.

"You told me that if I spoke again you would twist me into a knot. And Kelsa you would use as a ball-bearing in a dung-wagon. And Asti you would use as a chamber pot."

"Yeah, yeah," I said, absently. "And I should have, too."

"Is that any way to speak to heroes of history?" Asti asked, putting in her two copper pieces.

"Yes. Where are we going?" I asked Kelsa, for the 45th time.

"What?" she asked, in a dazed voice.

I took the orange case away from Tananda and stuck my face in the little window. "Where...are...we...going...now?"

"Oh, isn't this nice?" she said, the green face spinning dizzily in the globe. "I haven't had as attractive a reticule like this since, oh, two thousand three hundred years ago. Since then, it's been patch, patch, patch! Or sitting on a table under a cloth. I don't mind that, because you're not getting bumped around, actually, but you understand, when you're on the move, it makes all the difference to be really *comfortable*...!"

I groaned.

It had taken some serious persuasion to get Kelsa's attention away from her fancy new surroundings before she came up with the name of the dimension where we could find Buirnie, the magik Flute' Elb. Then I had to make sure she was directing us toward the part of Elb where we could locate it. I considered this particular treasure a waste of time, from my point of view, since the Flute couldn't help me regain my magik, nor could it repay what was turning into a substantial debt. The sooner we could get him and get on to the next treasure, the better.

I didn't worry whether the notoriously flaky Crystal Ball had given us a wrong steer. From the looks of things, the fourth member of the Hoard didn't bother trying to conceal his presence; in fact, just the opposite.

Close to the center of town, we started seeing posters plastered to the side of buildings advertising a concert. "Buirnie! Playing All Week! Tickets from Three Silver Pieces! The Elb Arena!" At the bottom, superimposed over the image of an impressive building, was a hand-drawn illumination of a golden flute studded with gems and surrounded by a halo of light.

"Guess we found him," I said.

"Do you think he might be in the Arena now?" Tananda asked.

"Oh, yes," Kelsa assured us. "He likes to warm up before playing. Loosens all his valves, he says. Sometimes I just tune in to him to listen. He's really very good…"

"Why is that a surprise?" Asti asked. "Of course he's good! He's one of us!"

"Why are you defending the noisemaker?" Ersatz asked. "You never cared about him before this."

"You never tried to defend him yourself," Asti pointed out. "You always told him to shut up because his playing was making your metal bend."

I tuned out the babble.

Locating the Elb Arena was easy. Over the top of the shops and houses, I could see the cupola that had been pictured on the poster. I led us through the narrow alleyways and through streets crowded with donkey wagons and foot traffic.

The Arena stood in the center of a square filled with museums, galleries and public sculpture, a hulk of a building constructed of greenish stone and decorated in a local style that approximated rococo but with extra flourishes. The entrance was an archway of fancifully twisted and carved stone depicting flowers, hairy nymphs, fish and birds, all gilded and painted as if there had been a special running on loud colors at the home-decorating store.

Finding the back-stage door was easier yet. At the center of the rear wall was a smaller version of the grand entrance, nymphs and all, but in miniature.

Trying to get through said back door was a different question.

"Come on," I told the two heavily-armed Trolls lounging against the wall as if they were holding it up, "we're friends of the band. Buirnie will be ticked off if you don't tell him we have come to see him. We came all the way from another dimension to visit him."

"Dey all say dat," the first Troll opined.

"Take off," the second Troll said, not troubling to take a toothpick, the size of a belaying pin, out from between an incisor and a bicuspid.

"Look," I said, leaning toward them confidentially. "We've come a long way to see Buirnie. We're not from this dimension."

I nodded to Tananda, who took the disguise spell off. The Trolls stood upright.

"See? We brought a few special guests with us. If you don't believe me, take the names in to the Flute, and see what he says. If he tells you to toss us out, then do it. What have you got to lose?"

"Don't like to interrupt Mr. Buirnie," the first Troll said, letting his lower lip hang loose.

But I could see that he was eying Tananda. A Trollop like her wouldn't be fooled by the dense act that the males of Trollia put on when they were in other dimensions. Her brother Chumley, a large, purple-furred Troll, concealed his intellectual qualities so he could get work as a bodyguard, under the *nom de guerre* Big Crunch. I figured these two were also pulling down decent salaries by concealing their IQ points.

"Oh, come on," Tananda said, sidling in between them. She put an arm around each, running her hands up and down their furry backs. I know what kind of effect she has on other species; to her own kind that touch must be electrifying. The big lugs practically started purring. "One of you can just run inside and ask Buirnie if he'll see some old friends, can't you? For me?"

The two Trolls eyed one another.

"You go," the first Troll said.

"No. Me like it here. You go."

"I senior. You go."

"Now, boys," Tananda said, keeping her personal magik going as her fingers flew along their spines. "We'll *all* go."

Before we went inside, she restored the disguise spell. Just in time, too, because the theater was bustling. Backstage bosses in purple coveralls were yelling at the crews, who carried pieces of sets and rolled racks of costumes past us. Calypsa followed, her beak agape with astonishment. I brought up the rear, making sure no one followed us down the corridor.

"I don't see how you are earning any part of your reward today, Aahz," Asti said. "You botched the negotiations. Your Trollop closed the deal, and neatly, I might add. Nothing to do with you at all!"

"Shut up," I snarled. I had just been admiring Tanda's technique, and the goblet's remarks drained all the joy out of it like a hole in a wine keg. "We got in, didn't we? I don't care what works as long as something did. If she hadn't persuaded them, I would have found another way. I didn't have to. End of story."

"Ah, well, you have an excuse for everything," Asti said, in a dismissive tone, as we passed through a felt-covered door. "I suppose you have to, with your lack of success."

"What do you mean, my lack of success?" I bellowed.

"Shh!" one of the Trolls hissed, distracted away from Tananda's ministrations. "Buirnie doesn't like nobody's loud noises but his own."

"What's allthe racket going on out there?" demanded a shrill voice that filled the short hallway. "I can't hear myself whistle!"

The Trolls held open a set of double doors adorned with huge gold stars and escorted us through them. There was no doubt we were entering an audience chamber. The room was crowded with furniture and people, but I had no trouble picking out Buirnie himself. For one thing, he was the only gold flute in the room, arranged upon an emerald green velvet pillow, and for another, a spotlight shone down on him. The glare off his golden carapace was almost blinding. It cast everything else in shadow. I squinted and got a better look at him. Buirnie wasn't exactly a flute. He was in the flute family, but he was one of its smallest members. He was a fife.

"Who's there?" he demanded. "Come on, who has come to visit Buirnie of the Golden Voice?"

"Buirnie of the Colossal Ego, you mean," Asti said, in a long-suffering voice.

"Asti? Asti, is that you? I thought I felt a disturbance in the Force. How the *peep* are you?"

"And me, dear," Kelsa spoke up. "And Ersatz."

Little round emeralds at the top of the Flute above the embouchure widened into large emeralds. "Well, this IS a surprise! I thought that the next time we all met would be one of the signs of the Final Apocalypse!"

"Nothing that spectacular, I hope," Asti said.

"Tell me all about it! I love surprises, especially when they aren't fatal ones!" Buirnie let out a high pitched chuckle.

This was some kind of signal, because the Elbans in the room broke out into hysterical giggles. He let out a sharp whistle, and they stopped, all glancing at one another nervously. Hangers on. Sycophants.

"Not fatal, you silly bird-call, but important."

"Can we talk in private?" I said, trying to wrest control of the conversation back from the Cup.

"Clear the way, folks, clear the way!" Buirnie exclaimed. "Make way for my oldest and dearest friends! And a few new ones," he said, eying Tananda, Calypsa and me warily. "Sit down, sit down. The rest of you come back when I whistle!"

The Elban attendants hustled out, but the two Trolls remained. They stepped forward to flank the velvet pillow. When everyone else was gone, the emeralds turned toward me.

"So, the band is getting back together!" Buirnie said, with a jovial, easy attitude that I didn't buy for one minute. "You have a masterful air about you, big fellah. You tell me what's going on. To what do I owe the honor of this visit? Do I owe any of you money?" Buirnie broke into nervous laughter. The drum on the floor next to him rolled a rim shot. "Hey, thanks, Zildie!"

"I'm just the brains of this operation, but the one I want you to listen to is the skinny girl back there." I aimed a thumb at the disguised Walt behind me. "Calypsa's got a story to tell you."

"Sit down, lovely child," Buirnie said hospitably. She looked at me for clarification. I signed to her to sit down on the hassock beside the raised cushion. "Klik, widen the beam so it illuminates both of us, will you?"

"Gotcha, boss!" A voice came from overhead. I glanced upward. The brilliant light which was focused upon the Flute hopped from one part of the ceiling to another, and the glare increased. "How's that?"

"Great!" Buirnie said. "Calypsa, is it? You're a pretty little gal, aren't you? Will you have some wine?" He let out a sharp whistle, three brief blasts. A tall Elban female came rushing in with a tray, smiling shyly at us. "Now, what can Buirnie the Great do for you?"

"Tell him your story," I said.

Calypsa took a deep breath. "It all began ten years ago...."

"How about some sweetmeats?" Buirnie hadn't listened to a word. He tootled a trill. Another Elban hurried behind her, pushing a wheeled tray. "These are the best cocoriddle waffles in the city. Or so I'm told. I don't eat them myself, of course."

"No, thanks," I said. I turned both females around and hustled them back out, and locked the door behind them to prevent any more interruptions. I signed to Tananda. Our disguises dropped. The Fife's emerald eyes went wider than before.

"You're not from around here, are you? A Trollop, a Walt and a Per...Pervect. Don't hurt me, please. I give pleasure to millions!"

The Trolls stepped closer, folding their meaty arms across their chests.

"We're not here to hurt you," I said. "We need your help. Okay, kid," I told Calypsa. "Talk."

She tried. Buirnie was too nervous to be a good listener. He kept interrupting with offers of hospitality, comments on the weather, compliments to us, and musical interludes. In the end she got it all out.

"So I appeal to you," she concluded, "honored Buirnie. Join me and help set my grandfather free of the terrible wizard's chains before the time runs out!"

"What an awful situation! I can see why my brother and sister Hoarders are involved. And these fine people are helping you, too? That's very noble of them," the Flute said.

"Not so noble," Asti burst out. "*Rewards* are involved."

"That's not uncommon," Buirnie chided her. "They're only mortal, after all. No offense!" he added, as I rose from my seat with intent.

"Let's get to the point," I said. "She needs the entire Golden Hoard, and that means you, too. What about it? We've got three more treasures to look up after you."

The Fife turned to Calypsa. "Little gal, I feel for you. I know how much your grandfather means to you, but I really have too much to do to come on another quest at the moment."

"Buirnie!" Ersatz chided him.

"Ersatz, I am serious. You wouldn't kick loose from the middle of a war to go bounding off to another battle, would you?"

"No..."

"Then you will understand why I can't leave. I have obligations here. Very important ones."

"Ones that make *you* feel important, you mean," Kelsa said.

"Naturally, sweet thing!" Buirnie said.

"But my grandfather's life is at stake here!" Calypsa said, wringing her hands together. "This is important."

Buirnie let out a whistling sigh. "That, little lady, is what they all say. Sorry."

"I'll do anything if you will come with me!"

"Anything?" Buirnie asked, on a rising note of interest.

"Within reason," I said, firmly. "You're not going to pull any funny business on this girl."

"You bet. I would never ask this little lady to do anything that might make her uncomfortable. Let's make it a fair contest," Buirnie said, clearly not liking the expression on my face. "Well, then, I've got a proposition for you. I'm sponsoring a contest in which I am looking for the very best singer on Elb."

"What's it called?" Calypsa asked eagerly.

"It's called *The Very Best Singer on Elb*. I named it myself," Buirnie said proudly. "I host it every year, in several different dimensions. Maybe you've seen me on the crystal network?"

"Oh, I have," Kelsa said. "The last one on Calliope who won, I thought she wasn't quite as good as the second place, though somehow the audience voted for her..."

"Not now," I said, cutting her off. "We're talking business."

"Oh, very well, but she wasn't as good!" Kelsa subsided, blinking at me from behind her glasses.

"Nobody cares," I said, curtly. I turned back to the Flute. "What's this proposition?"

"It's perfectly simple," Buirnie said. "I'll play you for my cooperation."

"But that isn't fair," Calypsa said. "I am a dancer, not a singer."

Buirnie shuddered. "Neither are most of the people who enter the contest. But, it's my challenge. If you really want my help, you'll rise to the occasion. Come up on stage with me tonight. If you enter the contest—and you win—I'll come with you now, and abandon my other obligations to help save your grandfather. What do you say?"

What choice did we have?

Buirnie had the Trolls escort us out of his dressing room and down under the stage into a huge chamber that had all the charm of the dungeon in Mernge. Its rough stone walls had been lined with mirrors and clothes racks where all the other contestants were getting ready for the contest. I had Tananda restore our disguises. I didn't want to scare the locals. Besides, Calypsa was so nervous that her feet did the flamenco all the way down the stairs.

"I don't even speak the language!" Calypsa wailed. "How can I please such an audience? Woe to the House of Calypso, that it should be reduced to a *singing* contest to save itself!"

"Since when did you ever have stage fright?" I asked her.

"Fear not, child," Ersatz said, soothingly. "Be valiant and do your best. All will come out well."

"Can you give her a potion to calm her down?" I asked Asti.

"Oh, no artificial stimulants permitted!" Kelsa shrilled. "She would be disqualified."

"Maybe that would be best," Tananda said. "She's too nervous to compete."

"You stay here," I said to Tananda. "I'll scope out the competition."

Buirnie was right' most of them weren't good. That was our best hope, that whatever peep Calypsa could let out in front of the audience would sound better than the rest of them.

"Aaaahhh hohhhh! Ah hah hah hah! Ah hee hee hee hee hee!"

I narrowed my eyes. That sounded suspiciously like opera, and pretty professional, too. I shoved through the crowd of wannabes looking for the source of the sound.

At the very back of the big dressing room, a huge female Elban was warming up. Her voice was so loud it rang off the rafters and the stone walls. Most of the contestants near her had edged as far away as the crowd permitted. I grabbed a powder puff off the nearest dressing table, tore it in half, and shoved it into my ears. If the Elbans near me noticed a discrepancy between the apparent size of my ears and the amount of fluffy wool I could stuff into them, they were in too much misery to say so. Not that I would have cared; it was a matter of survival.

The female, a bright pink like I was supposed to be, tipped me a wink, laid a delicate hand across her ample chest, and burst into song. My heart sank. Calypsa was right. We didn't have a chance. I went back to my companions to wait out the inevitable and work on a Plan B.

Chapter 10

THE EXCITEMENT IN the wings of the immense theater was palpable, but I knew we were fighting a hopeless cause. Tananda and I had helped Calypsa go over every song she knew to pick out one that would please the audience and the Flute, who had avoided all contact with us from the moment we'd been ushered out of his dressing room. It didn't help that the opera singer had been as good as she had sounded warming up, but even the bad singers were better than our candidate. The producer, a stout male with a pale coat, kept shushing us. I felt like tearing his head off, but that wouldn't have made Calypsa's singing any better. I don't think anything could have.

"I don't know why we didn't just pick him up and *bamf* out when we had the chance," I grumbled, not for the first time.

"It is fair for him to set such a contest," Ersatz said. "Why, I mind me of a time when I was rammed into a stone by a wizard, to seek him who should be king of the land."

"Don't tell me—a twelve-year-old boy drew you."

"Nay, of course not," Ersatz said. "It was a great lug of a man with all the brains of a slime-mold, but he had the muscle to overcome the objections of his peers. In the end he was no worse a king than anyone else might have been."

"Shhh!"

At that moment, Buirnie was out on stage with the ever-present spotlight, Klik, shining down on him, showing him off in the best possible light. Petite Elbans with aprons came out and polished him in between acts, dusting off minute motes. The Fife was fussier than any ten divas I had ever met. He certainly looked good in comparison with his hapless contestants. And sounded better. I had cotton stuffed in my ears to protect them, though it didn't block out all the noise.

At intermission, I went out to get a drink—Crom knew I deserved one—and started sidling up to people in the bar and in the lobby. Since it was audience's choice who won, a little persuasion, threat or bribery might help our candidate to the finish line.

"Vote for Calypsa," I told a big Elban with a white mustache in the middle of his light pink face. "She's the best."

"Someone's got to be," the male said, with a grimace that told me he was enjoying the contest about as much as I was.

"Vote for Calypsa," I suggested to a tableful of matronly looking females seated at a table in the back of the bar. "She's an orphan, and she could really use the break."

"Awwww." The women put their heads together. I went after a cluster of young Elbans giggling in front of a poster of Buirnie.

"Vote for Calypsa. She's a personal friend of his, ya know."

"Really?" one of the females asked, her eyes wide. I tapped the side of my nose with my forefinger, and the kids went into a huddle. I cornered a couple of big males by the men's room.

"If you know what's good for you, you'll vote for Calypsa."

They backed away from me. "All right! All right! Take a pill, man!"

After a few more swings as good-will ambassador, I went backstage again. I had done all I could to stuff the ballot box.

In the wings, Calypsa was pacing up and back, fluttering her arms in agitation.

"What are you so nervous about?" I asked her, more than once. "You don't have stage fright. I don't see that you are afraid of much at all. You danced in front of the crowd in the bar. You're good. I've never seen a pip with more pizazz! You stood up to an evil wizard. You've even faced me down. What's the problem?"

"I am not dancing for these people!" she said, her Elban-disguised face long with despair. "I am *singing*. The Walts do not sing, they dance. You will see. I will fail."

"Nonsense," Ersatz said, as Calypsa handed him off to Tananda. "You will do well. Stout heart! You are of the great clan of Calypso! Never forget your honored heritage."

She gave him a faint smile.

"Calypsa!" A faded, middle-aged Elban bustled up to us and hung a numbered tag around her neck. "You're on." He shoved her out of the wings and into the glowing spotlight.

"Break a leg, kid," I said.

She might have gotten better reviews if she had.

She was terrible. I mean, beyond terrible. She was so scared her whole body trembled visibly.

"Oh, the pretty little flowers, how fair their faces in the sun," she warbled uneasily. "The rain rains down, the clouds are blown, and spring is here for everyone…" Her voice went off key every other word. I winced at the horrible rhymes, but it was the best we were able to do in a hurry to render the lyrics of the folk song from Walt to Elban. You know there are phrases that lose something in translation. This was not only lost, it was beyond retrieval.

The audience had responded to good candidates with whistling and applause. The mediocre ones got a mix of clapping and booing. The awful ones fled the stage to a medley of jeers and derisive laughter. Calypsa's effort was rewarded with total silence. No, not quite total. Far away in the dark a single set of hands was clapping.

A stagehand peeked out through the curtains. "That's old man Dovacek. He's tone deaf. He likes everything."

"She's dying out there," Tananda said, sympathetically.

"Who says Calypsa is dying?" Ersatz exclaimed. "She shall not die alone! Get me to her hand! I will save her."

"Not literally dying, you letter-opener," I snapped. "She's just going to lose. I wonder if it's possible to come in farther back than last. She's just got to relax. There's nothing to it."

"If it's so easy," Asti said, from the pouch under my arm, "then you go out there."

I ignored her. We had bigger problems.

"We're going to lose this round," Tanda whispered to me. "Buirnie said he'd only come along if we won. Wonder if I can find a talking recorder out there I can paint gold."

"No," I said. "A fake won't fool a real wizard. If this Barrik's worth any of his reputation, he'll see through it, and her grand-father will be toast."

"It could with a good enough illusion spell. If we have all the other treasures, maybe he won't pay too close attention."

"It's worth a try," I said, thoughtfully.

"You won't have to do that," Asti said, from the pouch under my arm. "Get out there and win this contest yourself!"

"What?" I yelped. The stagehands all glared at me.

"That child can't succeed. You haven't done a thing to earn your keep today, you worthless sack of scaly skin. Go!"

I looked out at the vast bowl of the theater.

"Not a chance," I said. "Buirnie set her the challenge, not us."

"You said you would help her, and by the Singing Bowls of Aphis, she needs your help now! Go!"

Suddenly, I felt something warm dribble down onto my right foot. It started burning. I hopped onto the other foot and clutched my toes. The liquid stung my hand, too.

"Acid!" I jumped back to avoid it.

I held the case out at arm's length, but she had burned a hole in the leather at the top. A spray narrowly missed me. I dropped her and dodged the next fountain of pain. The next thing I knew, I was under a hot white light.

"Whee-eet!" Buirnie whistled in surprise. "Well, then, this is an unexpected pleasure! Thank you, Calypsa! Welcome our next contestant, Aahz!"

"Now, sing, you ugly lizard!" Asti's voice rang through the arena, louder than the opera singer had been. A titter ran through the audience. I snarled. No one laughs at me!

"Go ahead, Aahz," Buirnie said, encouragingly. "Wow us!"

I couldn't really see the audience past the first few rows, but I knew there were over ten thousand spectators watch-ing me. Well, they were in for a treat. On Perv I was con-sidered to have a pretty decent voice—no, a great voice. All I had to do was decide what I was going to sing. I knew thousands of songs, ranging from drinking songs to lieder to Broadway show tunes, from hundreds of dimensions. I went through my memory for the best one to show off my range.

It was blank. My mind could not recall a single song. I gritted my teeth in frustration. Come on! I chided myself. Me, Aahz, with *stage fright?*

Somewhere in the darkness, a high voice tittered. A few guffaws joined it. I gritted my teeth. I was going to get my powers back, and I would come back here and knit their fuzzy coats together in a giant afghan.

In the meantime, the show must go on. Finally, a tune came back to me. One that would knock them all out.

"Hail, Perv!" I burst out. "We're green and scaly. We mean business. ..."

Before I knew it, I had launched into the national anthem of Perv. Written about three thousand years ago, it describes how we came to be an independent, united dimension, by defeating our enemies. The first verse is the usual bluster, albeit true, how great Pervects are. The second goes on to list our conquests of other dimensions. Subsequent verses are about maiming and torturing our enemies, all in the name of freedom, going into exquisite detail, including how my ancient ancestors had their way with the captured women, to further our chosen way of life. It had eighteen verses, fifteen of which I hadn't sung since school. Once I could remember the first line of the next stanza, it came rolling out like I was back in Miss Grimnatz's primary school class. I started to relax, belting out the high notes, and rumbling the low ones like threats.

After verse two, the members of the audience in the first few rows, which was as far as I could see with the spotlights in my eyes, looked uneasy. After verse four, some of them started to get up and edge toward the doors. The sixth verse, which features a pretty good description of hot irons and whips, made them run for the doors. Wimps, I thought.

I finished the song without blowing a single line. At the end, I held out my arms for applause. Instead of the expected roar of approbation, it was tentative and faint.

"Hey, there," Buirnie said, when I glared out over the footlights at the unseen audience, "sympathy applause is better than no applause at all, eh?"

The drum beat a rim shot.

"Thank you, thank you," Buirnie said, modestly. "Now, the voting! Everyone hand in their ballots. He peered into the darkness of the audience. "Is *anyone* out there?"

The Trolls lumbered off the stage. They were back in a moment. One of them brandished a sheet of paper. "Here's duh vote," he said.

"One vote?" Buirnie asked, astonished.

"There's only one guy out there." The Troll pretended to count on his fingers. "Yeah."

"Just one," the second Troll confirmed. "Dat old pink guy. Don't hear so good."

"Well, all right," Buirnie said, faintly. "Who won?"

The Troll pointed at me. "He did."

"I did?" I said, doing a double-take. Then I straightened up. "I mean, I won! Yeah. Well, did anyone doubt it for a minute?"

Tananda zoomed in and gave me a passionate kiss of congratulations. "Never, handsome."

"My hero!" Calypsa declared, running out and hanging on my arm.

"You sounded like an alligator gargling ball bearings," Asti said. "But you did it. Well done. The drinks are on me."

"Never mind that," I said, uncharacteristically putting liquor behind duty. I turned to Buirnie. The golden Flute looked up uneasily at me from his cushion. "All right, I won your cockamamie contest. You got a suitcase you want to use?"

The Flute regarded me with some confusion.

"Er, what for?"

"You're coming with us, aren't you?"

"Well, no. I can't."

"No?" I bellowed. "After I stood up and sang? You bet you're coming."

"You made a bargain, Buirnie," Ersatz said severely.

Buirnie turned to his fellow Hoard members. "You know, I never liked any of you. Bringing a Perv...Perv...*Pervert* into MY theater!"

I couldn't help myself. "That's Per-VECT!"

I reached out to yank his little ferrules off. The Trolls grabbed me and twisted my arms behind my back.

Buirnie gulped. "Not so fast, not so fast, er, Pervect! I was just jerking your chain. I just wanted to see how badly you wanted my help. You would not believe how many untalented fame-seekers come looking for me, hoping to make a fast buck in the troubadour world. Of *course* I will help you. I am a member of the Golden Hoard, after all! Our job is to fight for right. I'll join you...."

"Good." I relaxed, and the Trolls let me go. "Let's pack you up and get out of here. We've got three more treasures to find before we can get Calypsa's grandfather out of hock."

Buirnie tootled a protest.

"Not so fast! I will join you *in six months*, when my current tour ends."

"Six months!"

Calypsa sank down beside him.

"But I need you now! My grandfather has only a couple of weeks before Barrik will kill him! I do not know how he survives in the terrible dungeons of the evil Barrik, eating perhaps who knows what awful food, and subjected to frightening tortures!"

Buirnie turned large, sympathetic emeralds toward her. "Well, little lady, I am sorry. This program that I'm working on boosts the self-esteem of thousands of would-be performers of many races. The needs of the many, you understand, outweigh the life of one, no matter how devoted, fan. How bad could prison food be? And torture—let me tell you about torture! I have to listen to thousands of untrained singers just to find a few who can get up on stage and belt it out! I have another week here, then I go to Imper, then Zoorik, then Chimer, so, it was nice seeing all of you, but unless you want tickets, there's nothing more I can do for you."

"This is important!"

"So is this, little lady."

"To your ego, perhaps, mighty fife," Ersatz said.

The Flute let out a blast that made my teeth curl. "It's not just my ego! If you knew how many lives were being changed here, you wouldn't be so dismissive. Sure I get some ego-boo out of it. This is a battle for the fine arts, for the souls of these people. There's a harmonic convergence on the way that will join together force lines in six dimensions. Peace will flow among these races. It'll be the greatest thing to happen since...well, since *never*. Well, it was nice to see you. I hope it never happens again. Maybe by the time my tour ends you'll figure out some other way to rescue Calypsa's grandfather. Bye!"

I shook my head with a sigh. "You know the trouble with you, pal, is that you protest a lot, but you've got one big weakness."

"What's that?"

"You're portable." I reached for him.

"No! Don't touch me!" He let out a tremendous shriek. The sound went right through my sensitive ear drums and into my brain, but I couldn't move my hands to protect my ears. Suddenly, the tune changed. One of my feet lifted and set down again. Then, the other one rose and fell. My arms developed their own personality, something they were channeling from an insane disco dancer. They waved and flailed as gracelessly as drunks at a wedding, but that was nothing compared with what my feet were doing. Hop-hop-hop, slide, hop-hop-hop, slide, kick, kick. The music was irresistible. I couldn't stop moving.

"Aahz!" Tananda shouted, twirling like a Dervish in drag. "Do something!"

"I am," I growled, through gritted teeth. "I'm doing the Spanish Panic."

The obvious solution was to get Buirnie to stop playing. Fighting my disco-infected feet, I struggled to move toward him. I felt as though I was swimming upstream. The harder I fought to control myself, the more frenziedly I danced. Calypsa whirled and pirouetted around us like a ballet dancer caught in the spin cycle of a tumble dryer. I got within a couple of feet of the Flute, but I couldn't force myself any closer.

"Stop the music," I ordered Buirnie.

"No!" he said. The music continued even while he was talking. Evidently he was an expert at multi-tasking. "Not until you agree to go away and leave me alone. I'm happy here."

"Since when," Ersatz asked, jouncing along on Calypsa's back, "were you or any of us meant to be happy?"

"Well, I admit that I came to it late in life, old pal, but it's really nice. You should try it!"

"I have no intention of 'trying it.' My joy lies in service to others. You cannot keep these people dancing forever."

"Don't have to," Buirnie said. "My Trolls will throw you out into the street, and that'll be that."

"They're stuck in your musical spell, too," I pointed out. "If you let them go, we're free, too."

Buirnie looked past me. The two Trolls were slam-dancing. All around us, the stage hands had broken into a boogie. The Flute's personal assistants danced the hora in a circle in the wings.

"Oh," he said. "I forgot. Well, if you promise to go away, I'll stop playing."

"You made *me* a promise," Calypsa said. "You will come with me now."

"You can't make me, little lady," the Fife said, with smug satisfaction.

"I can!" Calypsa said, throwing back her head easily. Her feet flew. "You do not trifle with the line of Calypso! Music will not stop me!"

With that, she began double-stepping the music, adding flourishes and twists. Her nostrils flared, and her hands rose over her head, fingers clicking together to the drum beat. She twirled from toe to toe, moving ever closer to Buirnie. She was dancing as I had never seen anyone dance before. I was so fascinated I forgot my feet were prisoners. Buirnie upped the tempo, driving her back, but Calypsa wasn't pushed far. She stayed right with him. When he piped staccato, she drummed her heels on the floor. When he whistled a tarantella, she kicked and frolicked along. He tried hot jazz. Her big eyes flashed as she leaped in the air and came down in a split, then bounded up again and rolled over backwards to come up on one foot like an ice skater. The Flute's jeweled eyes followed her, glowing with fascination. I was fascinated, too, but I wasn't about to show it. As far as I was concerned, I wanted him to think this was a walk in the park for Calypsa.

"You can see she can take anything you throw at her," I panted. "You give up yet?"

"Never!" Buirnie said. He switched tempos, going to a broken beat. Calypsa didn't even blink. She added whirls and leaps to her footwork, clicking her fingers together. She fixed her luminous eyes on him. Buirnie's music hesitated. I could tell Calypsa had him now. She circled in on him, slowing. The music slowed down in response. My feet stopped pounding the stage like telegraph keys and settled into a two-step so I could keep an eye on them. She picked up the Flute from his pillow and held it aloft in triumph.

"Will you yield to me now?" she demanded.

"You bet, little lady!"

Chapter 11

"ATTA GIRL," I said, smirking. "Well, flute, you've been out-classed, outsung and outdanced. What do you say?"

"I think I'm in love," Buirnie said, the emeralds turning heart-shaped. "Little lady, I'll go anywhere you want me to!"

"Er...I...well, all right," Calypsa said, a little uncertainly. I shook my head. She was going to have to learn to handle her successes with more confidence.

The tootling concluded in an exhausted coda that I'd describe as 'shave and a haircut, two bits' with extreme prejudice. I whirled to a halt, gasping for breath. Tananda spun in against me. I caught her before she fell over.

"I feel sick," Asti said, from my side pocket.

"You and me both," I said. "You got anything in the way of motion sickness potions?"

"Coming right up," she said. Pale pink liquid flooded the bowl of the goblet. The level immediately sank by a couple of inches. She sighed. "Ah, that's better." I tipped her up and glugged down a hefty swig of what was left. It tasted of peppermint and the hair of the dog, but I felt the vertigo recede immediately. I passed it off to Tananda, who gulped the rest of the potion gratefully. Calypsa didn't need it. She didn't even look winded. Buirnie was delighted. He never stopped talking.

"You're *more* than worthy to have me serve you, lovely lady! I can't wait to meet your grandfather. If you're anything like him, he must be extraordinary! When I think how long it's been since anyone could keep up with me...I can't even tell you, but it wasn't in THIS century! How'd you like to be my protégé? We'll make beautiful music together—that is, I'll make the music, and you'll perform to it. Wow, no one's ever done such original interpretation of my polka ballet! I can't wait to play you some more of my compositions. I've got thousands that no one has ever heard, let alone danced to!"

"Back off!" Ersatz thundered from his scabbard. "I have first call upon this wench's education!"

"You? What can a sword teach a little gal like this one? She's none of your warrior stock! Look at those legs! Look at those graceful arms."

"I see great promise in this child, and she will not be well served by such a frivolous tootler as yourself!"

"Frivolous! Who are you calling frivolous? Swords are like dress clothes—you only need them once in a while, then you stick them in the closet until the next time! Music is for every day!"

"That is why you must not waste her time, with your everyday *pipings*," Ersatz said severely. "Such a talent is not to be expended on trivia."

"Who do you think you are?" Ersatz asked, magnificent in his dudgeon. I see promise in this girl, the likes of which I have not seen since the great Marisu! It should not be wasted on such nonsense as tootling!"

Buirnie wasn't going to let the matter drop. "Well, you *got* Marisu. You ought to let this child work with me! She's got a musical bent. She belongs with me."

"My goodness, Marisu! I haven't thought of her in years!" Kelsa said.

"Who's Marisu?" I asked.

"A protégé of the greatest possible promise," Ersatz said with a sigh. "She might have accomplished anything, any goal she chose to strive for. I was sorely grieved to lose her."

Tananda's face softened. "What happened to her?"

"She got married to a handsome prince," Kelsa said.

"And lived happily ever after," Ersatz added, glumly.

"I suppose that is a tragedy if you're a war-sword," Tananda said, trying not to laugh.

"Ah, fair lady, you have no notion of how great a tragedy it is!" He glanced at Calypsa. "It would be an honor to teach you my craft, if you would care to learn."

"How about mine?" Buirnie asked. "Music is a lot closer to her natural talent than hacking and slashing!"

"Hold it right there," I said, getting between them. "What makes you think you have ANY authority over Calypsa at all?"

That stopped the two of them dead. They glared at one another, then Ersatz turned to me.

"Forgive me, Aahz," the Sword said, apologetically. "If I have stepped upon your purview. I did not realize you had taken her on as your protégé."

"Well, how could you...WHAT?"

"I presume that, like my companions and me, you have discerned the depths of this youngling's talents," Ersatz said, his steel-blue eyes understanding. "I assume that your interruption of our discussion means that you have staked a claim. I would never seek to interfere with that, friend Aahz. If you wish to be her teacher, then I defer in your favor."

"NO! I don't need any more apprentices," I said, maybe a little more harshly than I intended. At the sound of my voice, the stage hands had all fled for the far end of the stage. I noticed that Calypsa looked a little hurt. Ersatz didn't take offense.

"All is well, then. If you don't mind, then I shall put myself forward as her instructor. I believe that it will benefit us all to have this child trained in the martial arts. What do you say, lass?"

"I..." The Walt hesitated. "I had not thought about it. I am concerned with my grandfather's safety."

"Then, think," Ersatz said, kindly. "You are wise. Any such engagement requires due thought."

I walked away. What was I thinking? I didn't feel the need to train anyone else, in magic or anything. My last apprentice had become a huge success, then walked away from it all. Like any other teacher, I couldn't really take credit for all his accomplishments. I'd just recognized a talent and set him going on the path he was going to follow, with or without my help. He just progressed a lot farther and faster than he would have alone. Calypsa might need the same kind of steering. She had nerves, brains and talent, three attributes that would make an excellent student, regardless of her field of study. Skeeve wasn't the only person I had ever trained. So, why was I reluctant to put someone else in his place? Not that that had been my intention when I joined up with Tanda and Calypsa. I had never volunteered to teach the kid anything. My arrangement with her was strictly business.

It was a subject I really didn't feel like dealing with at the moment.

"We can talk about this on the road," I said, abruptly. "We have three more treasures to find. Let's get a move on."

"Wait a minute, wait just a minute!" the producer came waddling up to us. His feet looked sore, which was no surprise, since he had been doing a clog dance all by himself in a corner. "You can't leave! What about your contract?"

"What about it?" Buirnie asked, blithely. "The contest is over."

The hefty Elban fumbled with a clipboard, then thrust it at us. "Here's your print," he said, pointing to a round mark in ink on the bottom line. "You agreed to stay for an entire season!"

"The season's up, my good man," the Flute said. "Isn't that what it means when you run a contest and declare a winner? We have a winner!"

The manager eyed me uneasily. "But we...well, we hoped that the winner would be an Elban."

I shoved up to him. "Are you saying you're prejudiced against Pervects?"

"Well, no...but Buirnie, baby, you can't leave without saying goodbye to your fans! I could have ten thousand of them here by midnight! At ten gold pieces a ticket...I mean, it's the least you can do, leaving me with an empty theater for the rest of the year! I mean, how can I find another musician of your caliber with such short notice? I mean, it's late, baby! You're not going to start out on a quest at THIS hour, are you?"

The emeralds rolled toward me, then back to the manager, then over to Calypsa. "Well...one teeny little blowout of a farewell extravaganza wouldn't hurt, would it?"

"But what about my grandfather!" Calypsa protested.

"One more night in captivity won't be any worse than he's already suffered, little lady," Buirnie said smoothly. He started oozing gentle music that wove in and out of our consciousness. "How about it? It'll do you all some good to get a nice rest overnight here. I know how tired mortals get after dancing..."

"Do not pay attention to his blandishments," Ersatz said, his voice piercing the air. I rattled my head, shaking off the spell of the Flute's voice. "He only seeks to delay for his own ego's sake."

The producer and I exchanged glances. "Why not let him have a curtain call?" I asked, seeing a few dollar signs of my own in the offing. "You know the old saying. Always leave 'em wanting more."

The next morning, I was feeling refreshed. The Flute's fame was such that even though the going away party wasn't announced until evening, in two hours flat, the place was packed with fans, cheering, weeping, screaming. Buirnie played a medley of his greatest hits, music created in a few dozen dimensions over an equal number of centuries. I could see why the producer didn't want to let go of such a guaranteed moneymaker. I had taken him aside and negotiated a cut of the proceeds, based upon my forbearance in not removing his star from the premises the moment Buirnie had made his farewell announcement. The producer wasn't happy about it, but he coughed up. The small bulge the 'honorarium' made in my purse didn't come close to the output I had made already on Calypsa's behalf, but I didn't see any point in having an opportunity go by. The deal gave me something to enjoy in the party that followed.

The others didn't mind the delay. Kelsa had a ball, so to speak, telling fortunes all night in the corner. With several free hours ahead of her, Asti didn't waste a moment talking Buirnie into lending her his metal-work crew. She went in for the full treatment. Afterwards, I hardly recognized her. All the dents had been beaten out of her. Every inch of her had been polished to a blinding gleam. She was in such a good mood that she woke us all up before dawn and made espresso for everyone, laced with something that took care of the hangover I was nursing from drinking a case or two of the cheap red wine the caterers had supplied. A couple of the stage hands packed up what was left of the hors d'oeuvres from the canapé tables for me. It was hardly enough for a Pervish-size snack, but it would do until I found somewhere to get elevenses. The Golden Hoard had been tucked into their cases. The only thing I needed now was directions.

"All right," I said, clapping my hands together. "Let's get this show on the road. Where are we going?" I asked Kelsa. "I am only going to ask that question one time, and one time only, and that's because I am in such a good mood."

"No problem!" Kelsa assured me. "I will prognosticate… could you pipe down!"

This was addressed to Buirnie, who was carrying on about something or other. His entourage was fussing over him so much that I couldn't understand what he was saying.

"Well, at least let the little lady carry me. She can give Ersatz to one of the other two," Buirnie suggested.

"Unthinkable!" Ersatz roared.

"I will carry both of you," Calypsa said.

"But we cannot touch one another. I can't stand his emanations."

"I don't like your vibes, either," Buirnie said.

"Good," I said, with relief. "She can put one of you on each shoulder. Let's go."

The Flute let out a warning whistle.

"Not so fast! I can't go without my entourage."

"What?" I asked. "You're out of your mind!"

Buirnie looked indignant. "You're not seriously thinking that I am going with you tucked in your breast pocket like a fountain pen, do you? I have luggage! Do you have mules?"

"Nope." I was firm.

"A truck?"

"No."

"How about a wagon train? Eight carts ought to do it."

I folded my arms. "You get one bag for yourself. If you don't want to share it with anyone, then they'll have to come separately. Calypsa isn't going to carry anything but you."

"Oh, that's no problem," Buirnie said, his embouchure quirking into a smile. "Klik!"

Out of the rafters the light came sailing down toward us. "Zildie!"

The snare drum waddled over to us. I could see that it stood on three feet made of bent wire about half an inch in diameter.

"Let's see…Buffanda, where are you, darling?"

"Coming, Fifie!" a playful voice called from the wings. An animated polishing cloth flew out and curled itself around the Flute's skinny body. "The other girls are folding themselves. Give us a moment. Do you want the brushes, too?"

"Sure!" Buirnie said. "I need to look my best on the road!"

"You are not taking all that with you," Ersatz said.

"Why not?" Buirnie replied. "They're my buds. They help me stay inspired."

"This is not fit. You should be complete in and of yourself."

"Get with the current century, brother! Don't you ever feel like you want a cheering section? Pepping up?"

"Of course not," Ersatz said. "That would look foolish on the battlefield! Should you require 'pepping up,' as you call it, ought you not sing yourself a rousing air and raise your spirits in that fashion?"

"Nope. I prefer applause. There's just something in the sound of hands clapping that I can't resist. It just feels great."

"Dilettante."

"Bore."

"Lightweight."

"Tone-deaf!"

"Loudmouth!"

"Unworthy impostor! The Harp had a far greater heart than you will ever have!"

"Oh, so that's it!" the Flute exclaimed. "You still think he should be here, not me! Well, brother, so sorry that I didn't tear myself to pieces on the battlefield! I've saved plenty of lives in my time, as well as enriching the culture of dimensions I've passed through. I doubt you could say the same!"

The other two treasures added their own two cents, until all of them were haranguing one another. The ground started rumbling.

"Aahz," Tananda said, alarmed. "The magik's gathering again."

"Stop it," I ordered them. "Hey! You're going to cause another explosion! STOP IT!!!"

They all looked at me.

"My apologies, good Aahz," Ersatz said. "It has been so long since we were together that even I forget the disasters that we can cause."

"Good," I said. "Let's get out of here. Exit. Stage left."

Chapter 12

"I KNOW THE Book is not far away," Kelsa said, as we came
to a crossroads. "I can feel it. But he's hedged himself around
with spells. I can't tell you exactly where. He has the wisdom
of the ages written in his pages, and his magik would fool all
the sages. Oh, I made a rhyme!" She giggled insanely. Buirnie
played a flourish, accompanied by a roll from Zildie, the snare
drum, to drown her out. He was still sulking about having to
share Calypsa with Ersatz, but since he didn't want to scare
off a potential apprentice, he was annoying on a minor scale,
so to speak.

I let it pass.

I surveyed the terrain. It had plenty of hedges. And bushes.
And trees. Not a lot more. We had been walking more than a
day already. According to the signpost, we were just outside
Pikerel, population 80. Pikini, the dimension we were in, bore
no interesting features I could see, except the locals' skill at
brewing beer, which we discovered at a series of small road-
side hostelries, and the Book, which always seemed to be another few hours' walk away. According to Tananda, few power
lines arched overhead, but little technology had evolved in its
place. Hence, the dimension's denizens, the Pikinise, got by
on muscle power, theirs or their beasts of burden. We were
disguised as black-furred Pikinise to avoid trouble.

"Why would a hot magik item hide himself away in a nowhere burg like this?" I asked.

"We all have our tasks, Aahz," Ersatz said, reprovingly.
"We do not seek to place ourselves in the midst of excitement. Where we wind up is a matter of fate."

"Fine. Where exactly did fate drop the Book?" I asked.

"Hmm...I don't believe he is between assignments," Kelsa
said. Her eyes began to bulge and shrink again. "He is out at the
end of the...longest path...nice little place, all modern conve-

niences, four bedrooms, outhouse handy out the back, kitchen, workshop, dining room, property taxes for the current year thirty-five gold pieces, good school but a very long commute…"

"*Where?*" I demanded. "I'm getting tired of guessing."

She blinked at me. "Location IS the most important thing, isn't it?"

I tried again. "What kind of workshop?"

"Mixed use," Kelsa said. "I see leather-working tools, carpentry tools, a small forge, some candle molds…"

"Sounds like a boutique in New England," I commented. "Can you steer us toward it?"

"I can't give you a path to follow. I can only tell you if you're going hot or cold."

"Fine," I said, in exasperation. "What about this way?"

"Warm," said Kelsa. I turned to my right. "Hot." I stepped out, opening my stride. The others fell in alongside me. The surface of the road was pitted and torn up by cart tracks, but it was better than walking along the sides, which were knee-deep in mud. We stepped up over a hill and headed toward a solid line of trees.

"Do you mind if I whistle while we walk?" Buirnie asked. "I always feel it helps to pass the time."

"Keep it down, okay? I don't want to annoy the locals."

"How can you say it will annoy them? I know plenty of Pikinise music. They'll LOVE it."

"Well, I would appreciate it if you would not sing, Buirnie," Ersatz said, sounding weary. "We have heard far too much of your voice over the last several hours, and I for one would prefer the sounds of nature."

"All right, I'll take a vote," the Flute said, imperturbably. "All those in favor of lovely, wonderful music, a round of applause, please!"

The drum, which waddled behind us on little metal legs, produced a sharp roll.

"Thank you, thank you! For my first number, I would like to render my version of the Flight of the Bumblebee, with a jazz variation that I cooked up for the Crown Prince of Whelven..."

"Be quiet," Asti snapped.

"But I thought you liked my music!"

"For once I agree with Ersatz," she said. "Give us *all* a rest."

"A quarter rest, a half rest or an eighth rest?" Buirnie asked.

"A *whole* rest," I said. "And I'll tell you when it's over."

Buirnie let out a breathy sigh. "I should have known you weren't music lovers. Except for Miss Calypsa here. Why are you traveling with such unappreciative characters, little lady, when you could be traveling with someone fascinating like me?"

"La la la! You sure do love the sound of your own voice," Asti said.

"Well, since you sound like a burp in an air pocket," Buirnie began.

"How did the Golden Hoard get started?" Tananda asked, interrupting the eternal argument.

"Oh, it is an interesting story," Buirnie said, pleased to be asked a question. "I wrote a song about it. It has eight thousand verses. Would you like to hear it? It would help to pass the time! You'll like the chorus. It goes, 'Once upon a time there was a Hoard...'"

"No!" I roared.

Birds and small animals erupted out of the bushes and fled in all directions.

"My goodness, big fellah, you sure can project when you have to," Buirnie said. "I could play some instrumental music, so the little lady can dance!" His emerald eyes twinkled up at the Walt. She looked like a shy girl at a dance being annoyed by a couple of nerds. I put my foot down.

"No songs," I said. "No epics. No poems. No katas. No dances."

The Fife pouted. "You're no fun. How about a joke? Hey, Calypsa gal, I know some jokes about dancers. Guy walks into a barre, goes up to another guy and says, 'Say, do you dance here often?' The other guy says, 'No, but my kids plié around here.' Get it? Barre? Plie?"

Calypsa laughed. "I have not heard that one before."

"Thank you, thank you, I'll be here all week. Don't forget to tip your waiter."

"That's how you entertained kings and emperors?" I asked. "I'm not impressed."

"Perhaps the joke was above your comprehension, Pervect," Buirnie said. "I'll talk slower next time."

"Perhaps *I* will tell it," Ersatz said. "I can cut things short when required."

"Bravo, Ersatz!" Buirnie exclaimed. The drum rolled a rim-shot. "You're a laugh a minute! Not!"

"Did I say something funny?" the sword asked.

"Didn't you say it on purpose?" Buirnie asked. "Cut? Short? Get it? He's got no sense of humor."

"The Hoard," Ersatz said, raising his voice over the soprano pipe of the Fife, "formed almost by accident. It happened in the great dimension of Valhal."

"Valhal?" I asked. I searched my memory. "Never heard of it."

Ersatz let out a singing noise like a sigh. "Not surprising, for it is no more. I will tell you what came to pass. Thousands of years ago, there was a terrible war between four factions, the nations of Thorness, Odinsk, Freyaburg and Heimdale, each led by rulers who were eager to capture the whole of a most fertile and rich continent."

"It's starting to sound familiar," I said.

"They were famous in their day. Naturally, they have since passed into legend. Four armies, each legends of power and prowess, each carrying one of us."

"Not me, of course," Kelsa said. "I wasn't there. Yet."

"Nay," Ersatz said. "It was I and Asti, Chin-Hwag and Pilius, the Great Spear. Each of us was at the height of our powers. I had been brought to Valhal in that very year by a traveling Deveel salesman whom the Emperor of Thorness chose to arm him for the coming battle. The armies met on the field of honor. They battled one another bravely, using our abilities and talents, as well as those of mere spear-carriers..."

"You should excuse the expression," Kelsa added. "There was only one spear who *really* mattered."

"...The mortal soldiers," Ersatz continued, with a long-suffering glance at her. "Yet, they came to a standstill, all four facing one another over a square portion of territory that came to be known as "No-Val's-Land." None could penetrate the others' lines. When sally after sally produced no movement, it behooved our leaders to attempt to end the war through negotiation. Such was my counsel, at any rate."

"Mine, too," Asti said. "I was getting tired of healing sword slashes and mace blows, and all for nothing!"

I nodded. "Stands to reason. That's what I would do."

"Aye. It was a demonstration of the greatest futility of war, the slaying of pawns, yet not gaining another inch for all the pain. They came to a halt around a small vale, where lay a vaulted hall, long abandoned, but still large enough for the four leaders and their advisors to use as a meeting place. It was a historical moment when we were all brought together by the four leaders as they attempted to hammer out a peace accord. Beer flowed freely. In fact, we were all inundated in it!"

"It was my best beer," Asti sighed. "A very special recipe I came up with for the occasion."

"Sounds like a great party," I said.

"In the presence of that catalyst, we felt ourselves changed. Our auras overlapped, and an alteration came to pass."

"I've been at parties like that," Tananda said, with a reminiscent smile.

"That is not what I meant," Ersatz said sternly.

"That's what YOU think."

"We had become sentient, and aware of the others. We were greater than our creators had made us. We had purpose.

That which was lacking in each of us had been awakened by the others."

"Sounds like some kind of mutual admiration society," I said.

"Not really," Asti said. "All I knew was I was no longer the only magik item. I was used to sharing, but not the attention paid to me. I didn't like it."

Ersatz eyed her. "None of us did. We were accustomed to being individuals. Yet there was no denying that we were equals, each with superior skills that the others could not duplicate. Perforce, we came to a mutual respect. When the room filled with our power, all the mortals presence realized they were in the presence of greatness, yet they knew not the source. The Wizard Looki discovered that it was we who were the fount of it, decided to pool together their resources to make one nation greater than any that had come before it, and stave off the barbarian hordes that nibbled at the boundaries of the lands. We made a vow among ourselves, the immortals among the temporal ephemerae, to fight thereafter for those who were in true need of our services."

"The *really* epic battles that needed to be won," Asti said. "Not these petty border skirmishes, fighting for an inch or two of land, or the hand of a wench. Just those that would end oppression, free the enslaved and preserve the environment."

"That is so heroic of you!" Calypsa said, clasping her feathered hands in admiration. Ersatz looked pleased.

"Aye. Since we refused our services to settle petty border disputes, nor would raise shield against one another..."

"So to speak," Asti added.

"...the masters of the realm were forced to employ diplomacy. When we did step in, all could tell that the matter was serious. Our reputations alone caused many an uprising to be quelled on the rumor of our involvement, so less blood was shed than ever before. Peace reigned. The four rulers sat side by side on thrones in a grand palace constructed on the site of the vaulted hall. It was a golden time," Ersatz added, with a sigh. "We enjoyed a truly pleasing life for a time. We were much celebrated for our wisdom and generosity. A grand Treasury was constructed to hold us, where we could be consulted by the high and low alike. We posed for an artist, who created decks of cards bearing our likenesses, the Taro, because the cards themselves were made of the fiber of that ubiquitous root. Four suits, for we four treasures. They were used for divination as well as gambling, the first pasteboard oracle."

"I've seen those," Tananda said. "But I thought that the fourth suit consisted of coins. Shouldn't it be a picture of the Purse?"

Ersatz and Asti exchanged glances. The Cup *hemmed*, a little uneasily.

"Well, when you meet her you'll see that Chin-Hwag isn't very…"

"Photogenic," Kelsa supplied. "They won't say it, but I will. She's ugly. Talented, but ugly. It doesn't matter! It's what's inside that counts. That's what I always say!"

"As long as what's inside is gold coins, I don't care what she looks like," I said.

"Those were the very words of King Brotmo," Ersatz said. "He whose realm Odinsk stood to the north of Thorness. He bore the great spear into battle. His people were very poor, so the wealth given to them by Chin-Hwag by the grace of the Lords of Freyaburg eased the poverty there. He bore the great spear into battle against the Wlaflings, the wolf-kind who poured out of the hills and harried the Thornessians. Everyone helped one another.

"But Valhal was not content to be the home of only four treasures of renown. The four rulers sought to set themselves apart from the others. First there was the escalation of thrones. All the leaders tried to have the highest. It only ceased when the Lady of Heimdale actually fell out of hers and plunged sixty feet to her death."

"Hard luck," I said.

Ersatz grunted. "Hard, indeed, especially the landing. Then the richness of regalia. Then the size of retinue. Shortages of space and resources became the cause for much in-fighting, and rules had to be reestablished as to how many attendants each monarch may have when he or she was in council with the other three. So, each secretly sent out mes-sengers to attempt to find another epic treasure to add to the Hoard, who would wield more power in his or her name.

"More and more treasures were brought in. As soon as these came in contact with us, they awoke to knowledge of their power. Some of them we accepted into the Hoard. Others were not worthy to be in our company. In the end, only twelve of us were of sufficient quality. Much jeal-ousy arose, as is to be expected, but we had to have stan-dards of excellence. No one may rest upon his reputation alone, though as you may judge, good Aahz, it helps to stave off futile exercises if one's opponent is in awe of what he has heard."

"True," I said. "In our organization, M.Y.T.H., Inc., we had standards like that. It helps if there's general agreement that everyone who is there belongs there."

"Oh?" Asti asked. "So you *had* a fellowship. Not with this child, surely, but with the green wench. I can tell that you two know one another well. You do not always communicate with words."

"Yeah, we had an association," I said. "It was a damned fine one, too. When we had to, we could kick epic butt."

"Aye, mortals often believe that they can achieve frater-nity as we did," Ersatz said, with a nostalgic sigh. "It was such a friendship as has never been seen in any time before or since. We were truly happy in one another's company. You don't know what it is like to be part of a group, each expert in its own field, respectful of one another's talents, able to defeat all com-ers, always knowing that one's back is defended as well as if one had been multiplied into an army."

"Sure, I do," I said. "Why, in M.Y.T.H...."

"Oh, there's no mortal equivalent," Buirnie interrupted, dismissively. "Never has been, never could be. You couldn't possibly know what it is to be a member of a fellowship like ours. It was unique!"

"What the hell do you know about it?" I demanded. I was beginning to get an inferiority complex from the constant hammering from the eternal treasures of the Hoard. As if I didn't know what a fellowship was!

"Nor would your petty band have taken on missions that would change the future of an entire race," Asti said.

I am a patient man, but I was beginning to lose my temper. "You're out of your mind, sister. I'd have staked M.Y.T.H., Inc. against any bunch of adventurers in the land, mercenaries, legendary heroes, mortal or immortal—whatever you had, we had it better. What we do...*did* was vital! I remember a time when our gang teamed up to put an end to the gang war that was brewing in the Bazaar...."

"Perhaps it was important as you mortals count it," Kelsa said, blinking at me. "But it wasn't important on a cosmic level, as our adventures were, dear."

"In your humble opinion," I snapped.

"I only tell the truth! I know all, see all!"

"Blow all," I said. "You're so terrific that you end up in flea markets and fortune teller's parlors. That's where the great Golden Hoard has gotten to, right?"

"Good Aahz, we have offended you," Ersatz said, apologetically. "Perhaps I will cease my narration. I have carried on nearly as long as that penny whistle over there."

"Hey, who are you calling a penny whistle?" Buirnie said. "I've never charged a penny for my music in my life! I do it all for love."

"No," Tananda said. "You're not offending us at all, Ersatz." She shot a reproving look at me, and drew a long finger down the blade. "I want to hear the rest. You're *so* good at telling stories."

Ersatz's eyes closed. He almost seemed to be purring. "You have your own magik, mistress, surely."

"Go on," she said, in a caressing voice. "So, how did you end up in the flea market?"

"Alas," Ersatz sighed. "Change of fortune, and change again. Ah, me, those were the days. While we were in Valhal, peace existed between us all. There is not much more to tell. Sadly, our utopia was all temporary. So many of us could not exist in one another's company. Each of us must be supreme. The power we generated together began to build up. The first explosion destroyed the treasury, but left us all unscathed.

"Not the Drum, dear," Kelsa said. "His head was torn right across."

"But his frame remained sound. Heads are easily replaced. It was determined that we should be divided before we fractured the realm once again. The warning came too late. They had brought too many of us together. We began to argue about the best way to safeguard our realm. We could not agree. The power built and built. Looki, always a most observant man, attempted to warn the leaders of the four realms to depart before a disaster came. They wouldn't listen. None would depart and leave the field to the others, or so they perceived. Such thinking proved to be catastrophic."

"The explosion, when it came, blew up the entire dimension of Valhal," Asti said. "It killed everyone, and scattered us all to the four winds. We turned up in some of the most unexpected places. When the dust settled, I was in a housewares display in a department store in Imper."

"I was the aggie in a game of marbles on Titania," Kelsa said. "Most exciting!"

"I blew right into the hands of a jazz musician in Nola," Buirnie said. "My first taste of stardom!"

"And I was cutting salamis in Trollia," Ersatz said, heavily. "I have sought for traces of our long-ago home, but it seems to have been severed from the dimensions, if it exists at all."

"Well, we were better than that," I said smugly. "I mean, we never blew up a whole dimension."

"If you are so superior," Asti said, "then why are you not together any longer?"

Ersatz answered before *I* could blow up.

"It seems that there are flaws in all of us. Since then, I have put myself into the hands of those who are about to fight epic battles. How about your fellowship?

"I don't want to talk about it," I said. "It's gone now. Maybe good things aren't meant to last forever."

"Nonsense," Asti said. "Look at us! We ARE meant to last forever. Durable, that's the way it ought to be. We seldom come together, but we are never really apart."

I felt a pang. I resented it.

"I don't believe that is to what he refers, Asti," Ersatz said, sternly.

"How do *you* know what he is talking about? Your authoritarianism just twists my stem sometimes," the Cup said, rolling her rubies scornfully.

"He and his companions *may* have aspired to such a fellowship as ours."

"Oh, *please*, don't try to convince me he is anything but a greedy egotist."

"All right," I snarled, "I won't."

"I wrote a song about us," Buirnie said, interrupting the argument with one final attempt either to make peace or show off, I wasn't sure which. "Now that you know the backstory, it will be much more interesting. 'Once upon a time there was a Hoard...'"

"NO!" I bellowed. The ground almost shook at the sound of my voice. Buirnie looked taken aback.

"A simple 'thanks but no thanks' would have done the trick," he said, reproachfully.

"I know your company must have been special to you," Calypsa said. "But Ersatz has lived so many thousands of years, and done so many important things. I know you must feel small next to the Hoard. I know that I do."

"Child, never lose your sense of self worth," the Sword said, kindly. "Your adventure is just beginning. Someday you will realize that meeting us is the most important thing that will ever happen to you."

I opened my mouth, then snapped it shut. I realized I was never going to be able to convince them of the quality of what I'd had and lost. Tananda gave me a sympathetic look and a gesture to let it go. Well, if she could, I could. Let it never be said that I let my memories affect my mood.

"Look," I said. "There's someone we can ask for directions."

Chapter 13

THE BLEAK, OPEN landscape let us spot the carter more
than half an hour before we reached him. The black-furred
Pikinise studied us curiously but with no fear. He stopped his
cart as I called out a greeting, and leaned his elbow onto his
homespun-clad knee.

"Heading for Pikerel?" I asked, trying not to show the impatience that I felt.

"About," he replied. "Come from there?"

That was a safe bet, since the road we were standing on
led directly back to the small hamlet.

"Yeah," I said shortly. "I wonder if you can help us. We're
looking for someone."

"And you found him," the carter said, leaning back and
looking pleased.

"Not you."

"Well, then, you ain't found him yet," the carter opined. I
reached up and took him by the bib of his overalls.

"I've been walking for two days, and I'm not in the mood
for yokel humor."

The Pikinise brushed my hands away and sat back.

"There's no need to get ugly," he said. "I thought it'd make you
happy to get done what you're aimin' to do. Who you lookin' for?"

"He's right, friend Aahz," Ersatz said. "Perhaps if you'd
been more specific…"

"Shut up," I said. "I don't do everything perfect like you
four." I turned back to the local. "I'm trying to find a guy who
lives out in this direction. He lives out in the middle of nowhere. He studies all the time. He's got books."

In no hurry, the carter scratched at the fur on his shoulder
with a meditative hand.

"Seems to me," he said, "you might want one of the folks
who lives out on the wild heath. The happy floormaker is

somewhere out there. Very artistic fellah. He searches the mud puddles and hollows of the marshes and fields for found materials and clay and just other little mineral treasures to make the blocks and artistic mosaics that he takes such joy in. He takes folks in who just want a quiet place to stay. That's his territory." The carter waved a hand out vaguely behind him.

"I see," I observed, "so that's the Merry Tiler Moor."

I looked at the man for applause. I shouldn't have bothered. I had never seen such a blank look in my life.

"Wal, you might phrase it that way, stranger. Follow the wild beast trails. Ain't no road to his place. Good luck."

"What did he say?" Calypsa demanded, following closely on my heels as I looked for another person to ask for directions. "And what did you say before that? Why did he look so puzzled?"

"All right," I said, rounding on her. "This is turning into a regular liability. I can disguise you as a local. I can guide you through a hundred dimensions and locate the treasures of the ages, but I don't have time to give you language lessons! If you don't understand something, stow it. I'll tell you if it's important. I've got enough problems to concentrate on."

The Walt quailed. "I am sorry, Aahz, but I only wish to know what is going on so I can help…"

"Well, you're *not* helping," I said. "Just shut up. I'll tell you when there's something you really need to know."

"Isn't that just a typical Pervect?" Asti said, through the leather of her case. "Temper, temper, temper, and never a thought for anyone else's feelings."

I rattled her case. "The 'shut up' goes for you, too, sister. You're always riding me, and I don't deserve all the abuse you are handing out. I'm doing what I can. Sorry if I would rather accomplish her mission than provide the Cook's tour to dimensions we're passing through."

"I know all tongues from the lands through which I have passed in my years," Ersatz said. "I would be pleased to help Calypsa with interpretation."

"But you might not be with her everywhere she goes," Kelsa said. In her depths was a picture of Calypsa passing through a door with the outline of a woman on it.

"Oh, I can fix her," Asti said. "Take me out of here, Pervect. I don't like messing up my case." As soon as she was clear of her carrier, her bowl filled up with a bright green liquid. "Drink this, child. All of it."

Calypsa looked nervous. "What will it do to me?"

"Do? It'll make you the superior of these two in languages. You will understand all tongues, of every creature that walks the dimensions."

"Dial that back," I said. "If she starts talking to fish and trees, someone's going to think she's insane."

"Why not?" Asti said. "You talk to goblets and swords. Go on, Calypsa."

The Walt lifted the goblet in quaking hands. With a nervous glance at Tananda and me, she dipped her beak in the liquid, and tilted her head back so it ran down her throat. She coughed violently.

"Ugh! It is disgusting!"

"I didn't say it wouldn't be," Asti said. "You are tasting the tongues of a thousand dimensions. Of course there's bound to be a little halitosis here and there."

Calypsa held the goblet away from her. "Tongues!" She looked as though she was going to be sick.

"Drink it anyhow, child. Pinch your nose...ah, you don't have one. Pretend it's medicine. It is, in a way. It will cure you of non-understanding."

"Drink it, dear," Kelsa said. "Then you will be able to understand what Aahz has been muttering about you beneath his breath."

"He is *what?*" The Walt looked at me accusingly. She seized the Cup in both hands and bent her beak to the foaming liquid.

"What muttering?" I asked, suspiciously.

"Dear me, did I say that out loud?" Kelsa asked, but the eyes behind her glasses twinkled.

"Drink, drink, drink, Arvernians…" Buirnie burst into song. "Come on, Calypsa! Don't think, just drink!"

"Chug, chug, chug, chug!" Ersatz chanted. Calypsa made a face, but went for a second mouthful.

It took a lot of encouragement, and more bobbing and tilting, but pretty soon the goblet was empty. It fell from Calypsa's nerveless hands. I just barely caught Asti before she hit the ground. Tananda caught Calypsa.

"Are you all right?" she asked.

"That was horrible," Calypsa said. She looked shaken. Her normally high-pitched voice wandered all over the octaves. "I feel funny."

Tananda and I grinned at each other.

"What are you smiling at?" she asked.

"You just said that in perfect Troll," I said.

"I don't speak Troll!"

"You do now," I said. "And Pervect. Now, come on, we've got ground to cover."

Tananda entertained herself for a while trying out Calypsa's new talent by talking to her in languages she had picked up over the years. I tuned them all out. I preferred to be alone with my thoughts. I was envious that the Hoard had given Calypsa a great gift like that, when I'd had to pick up my fluency the hard way. Still, I had to agree that we really didn't have the time for her to learn anything, and it was a pain translating everything we heard, then explaining the cultural references that went with them. This girl was so-oo-oo young. I knew I had never been that green. So to speak. No one I knew ever was…no, that's not true. I was pretty sure that Asti would give both me and Tananda the potion, too, if we asked, but I would rather have my scales peeled off with a paint scraper than ask. She already had the wrong impression about my sense of fairness regarding compensation, and I was not going to give her more ammunition. I already was tired of listening to the litany of my shortcomings, in her immortal opinion.

"Hot," Kelsa said, as we came to a crossroads.

"Which way?" I asked.

"Left, I think. It's a pity we are looking for the Book instead of traveling with him, because he has all the addresses in the world in his index. Absolutely anyone who's anyone! Of course, we don't know the name of the person with whom he is staying…it's such a muddle. The being's head is just full of names, I can't pick out his own!"

Tuning out the babble, I turned left. "Still hot?"

"Yes! Hot."

I strode along the narrow path behind Tananda. It was just a track that local ruminants must have made. My feet slipped on the ground. The mud was compacted to a rubbery surface with just enough dew on the surface to make it slick going. I kept my eyes just ahead of my feet to keep from tripping on exposed roots.

"…Hot…hot…hot…cold!"

"Cold? I thought you said it was hot!" Tananda said.

"Well, it will be cold, if you go through that bush just ahead," Kelsa said, blinking up at her, transformed into a very sexy Trollop with diamond-studded spectacles. "The bridge is out."

"Say, I know a song about a bridge!" Buirnie volunteered. "It's a tragic dirge. You'll love it. It's just the kind of thing to make our hike go faster."

I ignored him.

"This way," I said, as we crested yet another muddy hummock, early on the third day of our trek. "I hear hammering."

"Well done, Aahz!" Kelsa crowed. "Yes, I was just going to say…There it is. Off to the right, just past that stand of hawberry trees."

I led the way. As we got closer, the mud-colored building on the other side of the copse started to take shape. One fat oval story sat on top of a lower level that spread out in all directions, looking as if it had been built up over centuries. As an inhabitant decided he needed another room, he just broke a hole in the wall and built alongside it. Smoke was coming from several of the dozens of chimneys sticking up from the tiled roof. We halted about ten yards away.

"Turn off the music," I told Buirnie. "This has to be the place."

"Oh, thank the Choreographers!" Calypsa exclaimed. She headed for the front door.

I pulled her back.

"Not so fast! What do you think you're doing?"

"Going inside?" Calypsa said. She looked from one to the other of us, puzzled. "Or should we not use the door?"

"It might not be as easy as it looks," I said.

"Well, of course it is," she said, eyes wide. "You lift the latch, then push it open...what am I missing?"

I groaned. She was SO young.

"Guile," Ersatz said. "Dear child, this is an extremely isolated location. If you lived here, away from aid, would you not have concerns for your safety from passersby? You would set up some manner of defense."

Calypsa looked abashed. "I've always lived in the village," she said.

"Houses about ten feet apart, right?" I said. She nodded. "When the neighbor has Limburger, you hold your nose?"

"What's Limburger?

"Forget it," I snapped. "Kelsa, is this place booby-trapped?"

"No, it's not, but there's one detail that might be of interest to you, not that *all* the details of this quest aren't *interesting*, they'll make good telling in the saga that Buirnie is going to write one day, but..."

"I am?" the Flute asked brightly. "Wow! Will it become world famous?"

"Of course, dear," Kelsa said. "Don't all of your songs? But, Aahz..."

"Can it. Tanda, let's look like the locals. I don't want to spook this guy. I just want to be one of the brotherhood. Savvy?"

"One disguise spell, coming up," Tananda said, closing her eyes to concentrate.

"Amazing!" Calypsa said, as soon as the spell took effect. She had been transformed into a slender, black-furred beauty, if you could call the locals beautiful. "You are even more ugly than usual!"

"Thanks a heap," I grunted.

Ersatz had said that Payge was a completely interactive grimoire, so the chances were that we were dealing with a magician of some kind. Tanda made me into a fellow master magician of the local species, formidable yet approachable. I'd suggest a trade, or barring that, a contest to win the Book from him. I was prepared to cheat my way to success under any circumstances. She and Calypsa were dressed as a couple of attractive acolytes carrying my magikal impedimenta, namely the Golden Hoard. I hoped that we could make some sort of peaceful arrangement. We had little more than a week left, and Calypsa was getting antsier by the day.

I rapped on the door with a stick I had picked up from the woodpile, now doing double-duty as a wizard's staff.

"Anyone home?" I asked.

No answer. I realized the door was ajar. That was never a good sign. That could mean anything from a bucket of water to a thermonuclear grenade armed to go off when we passed over the threshold.

"Oh, Aahz," Kelsa said. "One thing you really should know…"

"Not now," I said. "Stand back."

I stepped around to one side of the frame, and shoved the door open with the end of my staff. The hinges protested like a dozen banshees with hangovers, and the door slammed against the inner wall.

Tortured souls poured out of the house in a cloud of chartreuse smoke. They screamed woe and sorrow, pointing bony fingers at us. Their empty eye sockets gleamed red as they swooped down at us. Mouths opened on multiple sets of fangs.

Calypsa screamed. I grabbed her hand and towed her behind me, her toes scraping the ground. As soon as she got her wits moving, she shook loose from my grip, and took off ahead of us like an Olympic sprinter. Tananda wasn't too far behind her. That left me in the rear. The ghouls flowed after me in a wave. I kept glancing back at them over my shoulder. What could I do? I didn't have any magik to dispell them. They were catching up. The ghouls grinned. Their claws were inches from scalp. They could tear me apart. I put on a burst of speed.

The going on the marshy path was heavy. I felt something grab my foot. I saw the root as I went flying. I rolled over, claws and teeth pointing upward, ready to fight to the death.

The cloud of ghouls kept flowing past me, wailing and screaming. They paid no attention to me. Within a few yards, they dissipated into a haze of burnt yellow smoke.

"Party howlers," I said, with disgust. I got to my feet and brushed myself off. "Pretty tasteless color combination, too."

"That was one undignified sprawl," Asti observed, from her case. I retrieved her from where she'd fallen in a swampy pool at the path's edge. "Ugh! And all over my nice leather, too. Make sure you get all the dirt off, Pervect. I can't believe you fell for that!"

"Zip it," I told her. I started trudging toward where the rest of my party had disappeared.

At that moment, Tananda came rushing back over the crest of the hill, knives drawn in each hand. I suspected, but couldn't see, that at least one of them was enchanted against magikal attack. Behind her, Calypsa came up holding Ersatz, drawn, in both hands. They saw me standing there, unhurt but muddy. I waved a hand.

"I appreciate the effort," I said. "It was nothing. Party favors. Our friend in there has a sense of humor. I'll remember that when we negotiate with him." I bent down to peer eye to eye with Kelsa. "I thought you said the house wasn't booby-trapped. I could have broken my neck trying to get away from those cartoon ghosts!"

"Oh, well, I'd put that little outburst in the same category with practical jokes," she said. "Booby-traps are usually meant to be fatal, you see. At least, that is my understanding…"

"Never mind," I said, cutting her off. "Come on. If that's the worst he's going to throw at unexpected visitors, then he's a pushover. Let's get the book and get out of here."

I retrieved my staff from where I had thrown it, and poked it in the front door. I waggled it around, checking for electric eyes, tripwires, or deadfalls. Nothing else happened. Cautiously, I peered around the doorpost. The front room was empty.

I went in for a closer look. The room seemed to have been abandoned recently. I could see dust on the floor that outlined a bedstead, a chest, and four small squares which were probably the feet of a table. Similar lines on the shelves built into the wall suggested the room's owner had had a substantial library, which had also gone. A handful of papers were scattered on the floor. I picked one up. It was a past due bill from a stationer's store.

BANG! A smashing sound somewhere in the house grabbed my attention. It was followed by a string of colorful phrases, none of which I could really call invective, but still showed some imagination in expressing frustration. I wondered if our quarry hadn't quite made good on his getaway. I signed to Tananda to go out and around. We could catch him in a pincer movement, unless he dimension-hopped away from us. Tanda nodded to me, and ducked out of the door.

"Anyone home?" I called.

"Back here!" a hearty voice shouted back.

"Let me do the talking," I said, pushing ahead.

With me in the lead, Calypsa and I sidled through the overgrown cottage. It had been divided a few rooms at a time into several living spaces, each decorated in very different tastes. After the empty front quarters lay the diggings of a herbalist who slept in her shop and had entertaining taste in undergarments, several of which were drying on racks alongside snozzwort and hipporemus root. Beyond that was a small room used by a student of mathematics, to judge from the formulae scrawled in chalk on the walls and floor around the shabby rope bed. The slamming and thumping noises came from the next set of rooms, where a brawny male in an apron was smacking dusty forms down on a broad wooden worktable.

He looked up with a grin that shrank just a little when he saw the formidable shape I was wearing. This was the happy tiler. Then his native optimism took over, and he came around to greet me. Tananda appeared behind him, and shrugged.

"Hail, friend!" he said. "What can I do for you?"

"I seek a great treasure," I said.

"Well, I've got a bunch of them here you might like," the tiler said, pleasantly. "Just finished a batch of Flornezian interlocks with real gold in the glaze. Nice enough for an audience chamber, if that be what you're interested in. I can give you very attractive terms on financing..."

"No, it's a book we want," Calypsa said. "We're looking for a big book. With a gold cover. Maybe some jewels embedded in it. And I think it talks."

"Ah!" the Pikinise said, rocking back on his heels. "You're looking for the wizard Froome, then."

"Is he here?" I asked, after giving Calypsa an exasperated look.

"Sorry, no," he said. Since we weren't customers, he went back to loosening his wares from the frames in which they had hardened. "He came through here with that big book of his, muttering, 'they're here.' Must be you he meant."

"And where did he go?" I asked.

"Ah, couldn't tell you that," the tiler said, with a grin. "He just disappeared. Right there," he gestured with a table scraper. "Like magik, it was."

"Why didn't you tell me the Book was gone?" I snarled at the Crystal Ball, as I stalked out of the cottage.

"Well, I did try to," Kelsa simpered up at me. "You told me to be quiet. Now, I do try to comply with your wishes—that's a measure of my growing regard for you, dear—but..."

"But?" I interrupted again.

"Well, it just happened! That moment! Just before we went inside. He must have been reading about our progress in the Book. Payge does keep up on current events, you know."

I groaned and rolled my eyes. "So this whole three-day trek was pointless!"

"Three days of my grandfather's incarceration?" Calypsa echoed.

Kelsa blinked, transforming from Pervect to Walt and back again.

"Oh, not at all! He wouldn't have gone away if we hadn't come here. The thing to do is go where he has gone now."

"And where is that?" I asked, through clenched teeth.

She brightened, literally, glowing like a beer sign. "Vaygus!"

Chapter 14

"STICK WITH ME!" Buirnie exclaimed, as we made our way down the teeming streets. Customers from every race in every dimension walked in and out of the brightly-colored buildings. Many of them had that world-weary look of the hardcore gambler, but most of them wore a look of open astonishment at the attractions on offer: dancers, gambling, stage show extravaganzas, you name it. It was like a Bazaar for the entertainment industry. It was night in Vaygus, but, then, it had always seemed to be night when I had visited there in the past. Flick, the Flute's spotlight, turned an actinic glare on us that lit us better than the road under our feet. I kept bumping into people who were blinded by the light. "I know this place like the back of my hand." Zildie, the snare drum, rolled out a rim shot.

"You don't have any hands," Calypsa said, looking confused. Ersatz was on her back with a cloth hiding everything except his eyes. The local laws against carrying weapons, especially potent magikal ones, were pretty strict, as they would be anywhere there was a lot of money changing hands. I figured we wouldn't be stopped. Law enforcement always had too much to do around here with real crime, as drunks staggered out of the hotels with money from the tables. In any case, he was wearing a disguise spell that made him look like a set of glitter-covered twirling batons. Nobody would steal those. The other Hoard members were similarly disguised, except Buirnie. I figured there was no harm in carrying a musical instrument. In any case, there was no way to disguise his entourage.

"Well, if I had a hand, I'd know it as well as I know Vaygus," the Flute confided. "Look around you! It's a wonder of magik and technology! I had a theater here for ten years, right up the street, over there. Full orchestra, show girls, the works!"

"Seems like a great life," Tananda said. "Why'd you give it up?"

"Well, a war started, the One-Armed Bandits versus the Crap-Shooters. It got ugly, I can tell you! The Bandits enlisted me on their side. I thought they fought a little cleaner. I wrote them some pretty terrific war music! It was a lengthy battle. We practically lost our sponsors, it took so long. At least twelve seasons, with summer reruns. We won, of course, and peace was restored, but there was terrible damage. The Strip was stripped bare, not that stripping doesn't still go on." The emeralds rolled from side to side roguishly. Tananda laughed. Calypsa just looked confused, as usual.

We strode down the broad avenue. According to Kelsa's directions, we were looking for the Lion's Head Casino. I was in a bad mood. This wizard Froome obviously didn't want to let go of his Hoard treasure, and who could blame him? I don't know why I didn't just blow out of there. It was a nice evening. You could hear the ka-ching! of the gambling machines over the cacophony of voices and music. I liked visiting Vaygus once in a while. The brilliant orange bulk of the Fountainshow Casino, ablaze in its own spotlights, lay just across the street. I could go in there, ask the maitre d' for my usual table next to the stage in the Gambler's Theater, and lay back. Hot-and-cold running babes danced by in skimpy outfits, and the drinks were served in Pervect-sized containers, as long as you kept on rolling the dice. I could almost feel the stack of chips in my hand. I bet that Barrik would be happy with the four we had. He probably doubted that Calypsa would ever come back with one, let alone within the deadline. But, no, we have to chase a recalcitrant wizard toting an oversized gazetteer through the Million Gambler March.

"How do we keep Froome from blowing out of town before we catch up with him again?" I asked Kelsa.

"At the moment he doesn't know that we're here," Kelsa said, beaming up at me from Tananda's shoulder bag. She'd been disguised as a large goldfish in a bowl, but nothing could conceal the diamante glasses. "He's very relieved to have gotten away before our arrival. My goodness, I love doing these up-to-the-minute bulletins!"

"Well, look a little further ahead," I said. "I want to know where we get the Book, not just what he is thinking at this moment. Use your talent."

"I predict..." the eyes swam in the depths of the glossy orb. "I predict that he will not be able to escape you once you are...surrounded by...his kind..." She blinked, and her face came back into focus. "Did I say anything interesting?"

"His kind?" Tananda asked. "Are there any other Pikinise here?"

"Oh, of course! There's Malkin, from Brumtown, and the entire Skruse family..."

"Not that kind," I said, snapping my fingers. "He's at the Magicians' Club."

"Why there?" Tanda asked.

"Where else? It's the one place where nobody will ask awkward questions. He's hauling a huge book with a solid gold cover. This city is full of pickpockets and muggers. There's security out the wazoo inside the casinos, but anything that happens outside is no one's business. Nobody wants to know if you got rolled or mugged or grifted. It's bad for publicity. Whatever happens to you in Vaygus will be disavowed by the secretary, the mayor, the police and the press. The club the perfect place where a big-time magik item like the Book will be safe."

"That sounds like sense, good Aahz," Ersatz said.

Even Asti couldn't find anything sarcastic to say. I smirked.

"Of course it does. Let's go."

I felt smug as I headed down the strip with the others in my wake. It felt good to be in charge again.

"Are you sure you don't want a guided tour while you're here?" Buirnie piped up, desperate to regain leadership of the group. "I know absolutely everyone! I can get us in backstage to all the shows! The city council owes me a bunch of favors for writing theme songs for their advertisements."

"Maybe another time," I said, pulling a step or two ahead of Calypsa to get away from his voice. "In case you have forgotten, we're on a time limit."

"You are useless here, Buirnie," Ersatz said. "As you are everywhere."

"Me?" the Flute squealed, making everyone within fifteen feet clap their hands to their ears. "What about a sword? How many showgirls and gamblers do you think we will need to slay in pursuit of the wizard who has Payge?"

"Don't waste your time," Asti said. She looked like a tin camping canteen in a canvas case, nothing worth stealing, a lowly disguise that made her cranky. "Let the mortal try and earn his keep. He's done little enough so far."

I shook her container. "Listen, sister, I'd trade you in for a leaky bucket if the kid here didn't want to keep you. In fact, I might just sling you out in the desert for a while. Let a bunch of thirsty camels play kick the can with you."

"You wouldn't!"

"He might," Tananda said sweetly, with a wink at me. "You know what Pervects are like."

"Per*verts!*" Asti exclaimed in alarm.

Calypsa looked from the Sword to the Cup. "I think Aahz and Tananda are doing a fine job," she said. "I would never have found all of you without them. Especially not so swiftly. You must have served with some very impressive heroes if everyone was able to do things more efficiently than they!"

I preened. "All in a day's work, kid," I said. Maybe I was teaching her something after all, in spite of my refusal to undertake her formal education. At least she appreciated me.

I strode on with a spring in my step.

"Hmmph!" the Goblet snorted. "Laying balm on wounded nerves is usually my task."

The Magicians' Club didn't advertise its presence. By their nature, the shows in Vaygus used a lot of magikal practitioners, everything from illusionists to major transformers, using every gizmo from trick cabinets up to complex special effects that would make motion picture producers wet themselves in envy. It was a great place to kick back in between shows and complain about the casino bosses and the customers, without a chance that anything one said would ever be heard by another living creature. The place was shielded with some of the most sophisticated spells out there, plus a few guardian critters like dragons and weresnakes that had a taste for trespassers.

I had joined the club on my first visit, years ago when I was fresh out of school. I had a membership card and a signet ring, neither of them with me, and I'd sworn the oath of secrecy which said, among other things, that we were never to reveal the secrets of our brother and sister magicians. That promise often concealed the fact that half the magikal workings in Vaygus weren't magik at all, but complex technical effects that a Klahd could do with one finger up his nose and the other on a button. The best thing about the club was the professional seminars. Presentation was everything, so they taught a lot about showmanship. I'd done a series of lectures myself here, years back. I knew the other guys would be glad to see me. They ought to help me deal with our runaway wizard.

The building was down a surprisingly dark alley in between two of the biggest theaters. Klik was the only light for a hundred yards in any direction. I sidled up to the well-concealed doorway and gave the membership knock.

Rap rap rap, dadadadada, rap rap rap. Boom boom boom. Rap rap rap rap rap. Tap tap!

A round porthole appeared in the center of the door. "Who seeks admittance?" asked a hoarse voice.

"A fellow seeker," I replied.

"By what right do you seek admittance here?" the voice continued.

"By common interests and brotherhood," I said. "Look, can we skip the rest of the litany? I don't have twenty minutes to waste tonight."

The voice got haughty. "We have standards to maintain! To continue' what brought you to this place?"

It was question three of fifty-one. I sighed. "The search for wisdom."

"...And what is the name of the seeker who seeks admittance, under the bylaws and statutes of this august institution?" the voice finally asked, almost an hour later. The others had waited behind me, out of earshot, since the whole password thing was supposed to be a secret. I could hear Asti and Buirnie giggling. I had felt that humiliated in my life, but not recently. I gritted out the last answer.

"Aahz. Aahzmandius. Now, open the damned door already!"

"Aahzmandius...let me check the records. Yes, membership dues paid up to date. Come in, seeker, and be welcome!"

The eye slot slammed shut. I stood back. Most of the wall opened up to reveal double doors of solid gold inlaid with impressive jade sigils. Most of them were jokes that only other magicians would get, like the one on my left as I strode in that said, "Eat at Joe's," in a remote, ancient dialect of Imp. Another was a complex recipe for seaweed stew.

As I entered, two scantily-clad females in pink and blue sequins flanking the doorway threw up their gloved hands and posed.

"Ta-daaaaa!" they chorused.

Tananda pussyfooted her way inside, as one who always felt at ease no matter where she was, but Calypsa was openbeaked, gawking at everything like the most backwoods country rube.

I had to admit that the place had its impressive elements. Illusions of trapeze artists swung around the chandeliered ceiling in between the triple images of fire-breathing dragons. I realized I was wrong—the one in the middle really *was* a dragon, part of the club's security system, since even advanced magicians generally needed a specialized control device to keep from getting eaten by a dragon that they had not personally impressed. This one, a brick-colored monstrosity with five heads, clung to a protruberance like an upside-down Christmas tree. It lowered one head to sniff at us as we came in. I signed to the others to hold still for the pat-down as the monster nose ran us up one side and down the other. Fortunately, I had encountered this one before. Dragons never forgot a scent, of people to whom they were indifferent, and people they hated. They rarely, if ever, liked a nondragon. Gleep, Skeeve's smelly pest—I mean, pet—was a notable exception. Tananda winked at it as it drew away, which startled it into letting out a puff of sulfur-scented smoke.

I felt right at home. Magicians from a hundred dimensions hung out there alone or in small groups, absorbing alcohol and other intoxicants. Just to my right, one stout Kobold was demonstrating to a goggle-eyed Vulpine how to breathe out a stream of fire. Beyond them, a big group of Imp magicians in gaudy outfits only Imps would think were stylish were engaged in a loud discussion about cabinets. Same old, same old.

"Bar's over there," said the haughty voice, only minimally warmer. It turned out to be coming from a sawed-off little squirt of a guy with a long, thin nose and large, limpid eyes. "We had to move it from the original location while the new library was being installed. Half the books kept absorbing the alcohol. Although you can still have a drink in there. Some of the members need it while they're reading."

"Thanks," I said. "Say, can you tell me if one of my buddies came in in the last couple of hours? He's a Pikinise. He's got a book he said I could borrow."

"Oh, him! Yes, he's in the library." Squirt pointed us toward the huge oil painting of a room full of leather-bound books on carved wooden shelves. It was a magikal illusion that covered the doorway. Another couple of stage assistants stood by to acclaim anyone who came or went through it. "Guy sure can drink. Not much for talking."

"Thanks." I started in the direction he indicated.

"Come on," I said to Tananda and Calypsa. "The library's filled with tall shelves. We can surround him and sneak up on him."

"I fear not, good Aahz," Ersatz whispered to me from inside his illusory disguise as a set of twirling batons. "I can sense Payge, therefore he can sense us. He may alert Froome. We must hurry."

"Right." I sauntered faster. "Move it."

Five feet from the oil painting, we bounced off an invisible barrier. I shoved at it, but it seemed to stretch out in every direction. I stormed back to the concierge's desk.

"What's the idea?" I demanded.

"Sorry," Squirt said. He blinked at us. "Are your two very fetching assistants fully qualified magicians? Because if they're not, they can't go in. Sorry for the inconvenience, ladies. Rules of the house. You know that. Chapter 18 of the Magicians' Club Guidelines and Grimoire."

I shrugged to the others. That caveat had slipped my mind. The big reception room and the bar were the only parts of the club that strangers, that was to say, nonmembers, could enter. Which was a shame, since it was a pretty interesting building, with its own handsomely-appointed, plush theater for club-only performances where magicians tried out their new acts for one another, private rooms for banquets and business meetings, repair facilities for magikal items, a wine cellar that would astonish maitre d's at the hotels around us.

"That's all right," Tananda said, sauntering toward the deep, velvet-covered couches and divans that were arranged in cosy conversation groups all over the vast room. "We'll just make ourselves comfortable."

"Say, Bub," I said, drawing the sawn-off doorwarden aside. "Is there any way I could arrange for a private conference with my friend in there? I don't want to disturb anyone else, but we've got to have a major professional conversation."

The Squirt eyed me. "You know the rules about ruining the décor. No incendiary magik, no summoning elementals, no ordnance except what's specified in the Magus Convention."

I held up an innocent palm. "If anyone rips the wallpaper, it isn't going to be me," I promised him.

"All right. I'll have a word with the others and see if they'll give you a little privacy. Come with me."

I trailed him to the library door. He stepped through and turned to give me a harried look.

"Well? I haven't got all night."

I rammed into the invisible barrier. I pounded on it with my palms, then my fists. It didn't make a sound, but I couldn't move any farther forward. "What the hell is going on here? I'm a member in good standing."

"Hmmm." The Squirt came over to me, then held up his palms and walked all the way around me. He frowned. He did the hand test again. Then he beckoned. From amidst the trapeze show on the ceiling swooped a gray-skinned, winged and fanged hulk in a tuxedo. I recognized him as Savona, a Scourge, denizen of a dimension I didn't visit very often, partly because the locals make me think of vampires on steroids. Villagers with torches and pitchforks don't run after them, they run away. Scourges were very long-lived, very smart, and very tough. The Club had employed them for millenia. I suspected that the current employees might even be the originals. They have senses not unlike those of bats, including hearing that make Pervects seem as deaf as elderly Klahds. If you whisper a drink order anywhere in the club, the Scourge behind the bar will make it for you and send it to your table on a wisp of force. They believe in good service, but they still give me the creeps. Having one show up when you aren't expecting him is a good way to get a cardiovascular workout while sitting down.

"How may I serve, Mr. Polka?" this one asked, very politely.

"Test him, Mr. Savona," the Squirt said.

The Scourge's left eyebrow went up. "But, this is Mr. Aahzmandius."

"That's what he says. Test him. Something's wrong. Why can't he go through the members-only barrier?"

Savona fixed his gaze upon me. The large black eyes seemed as though they were looking right through to my backbone. He lowered his voice.

"Mr. Aahzmandius can't pass the barrier because his ties to the force lines are broken."

"He has no magik?" Polka asked. "Then, why did the main door let him through? Even if a stranger answers all the questions, it doesn't mean the portal recognizes him."

"He is carrying a very powerful magik item in the bag over his shoulder," Savona said, aiming a talon-like fingernail at Asti's bag. "No doubt the door thought it was coming from him. The same for the ladies in his company." He bowed to Tananda and Calypsa. Tanda wiggled a couple of fingers at him and smiled invitingly. Savona's complexion turned a deeper gray. Even Scourges weren't immune to Trollops' charms.

"Items? What kind of items?"

"All right!" I said, slapping Polka heartily on the back. "You got me! It worked!"

"What worked?" Polka asked, his little face wrinkling in concentration.

I leaned forward confidentially. "The board of directors didn't want it known yet, but they wanted to check the security systems here in the club to make sure they are working. They've sent in several other members over the last month—maybe you've noticed a few of them? They seem perfectly normal, but there's something a little off about them?"

Polka looked astonished, but Savona cleared his throat gently. "Like the Deveel that had been multiplied into triplets? He only had one membership card, but he requested admission for all three of his simulacra, sir."

"I remember. We let him in. I wasn't happy about it, but his was the face on the card. However, we did not allow him to buy three drinks for the price of one."

"Yes, that's right," I said. "You handled that one just right, too."

Polka frowned.

"So let me get this straight—you let the Board remove your powers temporarily so you could trigger the 'members-only' barriers?"

"Yup. And to see if I could get you to let me into the rest of the club premises even though I don't qualify." I laughed heartily. "But you stuck to procedure. They're gonna be really pleased with you, lemme tell you!"

Polka looked horrified. "Why would anyone do that? Leaving yourself...helpless!"

"Well," I said, looking modest. "Sometimes you've just got to take one for the club, you know? Rule 46: a member must keep the well-being of his fellows uppermost in his mind at all times."

"That's Rule 47," Polka said, peevishly. "

Savona cleared his throat again. The soft sound had menace behind it. His fangs gleamed.

"He's lying, Mr. Polka."

"No, I'm not," I said, heartily. "I'm just a good guy helping out."

"This is the first that I have heard of a test of the security system. I have been in charge of that department for 1,043 years. The Board has never shown any signs of being discontented with my work or that of my colleagues. There have been no significant breaches that would provoke them to undertake such a test. I believe he must have lost his powers under some other circumstances. I am afraid, though, that such a loss does constitute grounds for dismissal from the membership."

"Hold it, hold it!" I said. "I'm still a magician. Of course. It takes more than power to qualify. You know that. There's prestidigitation, misdirection, illusion, none of which requires magik."

"That's very true." Polka snapped his fingers, and a pink sequined top hat appeared in his hands. He thrust it at me. "If you are still a magician, then pull a rabbit out of this hat."

Now, everyone was looking. Tananda started to make motions. She was going to try and raise a rabbit for me behind everyone's back. Of all the gin joints in every dimension, this was the wrong one. Everyone in the lounge turned to stare at her.

"Yipe!"

Savona aimed a talon, and she and Calypsa were both wrapped up in a cocoon of ribbons from shoulder to hip.

"I am terribly sorry," he said. "No outside interference is permitted. Pray proceed."

I was on my own.

"Well?" Polka asked. I grinned painfully.

"C'mon, I don't do rabbits," I said. "That's small-time stuff."

"Small-time?" A tall, thin, blue-skinned magician rose up in indignation. He was about three feet taller than I was. He loomed down at me. "Pulling rabbits from hats small-time? I'll have you know I have wowed them at the Borean Palace for over fifty years with rabbits!"

"Look, I'm not trying to offend you," I said, reaching up with some difficulty to slap the Bore on the back. "I'm just into bigger effects, that's all."

"Then produce one," Polka said. "Not with the help of your assistants. Not with the help of those fancy gizmos you have with you. Just you. Wow us."

I'm famous for thinking on my feet, but there's times when not even slick talking will help.

"Look," I said, leaning closer to the Squirt and grinning companionably. He leaned away. "You wouldn't embarrass an old member, would you? Down on his luck, and all. I'll get 'em back one of these days. In fact, that's what I came to talk to my buddy about' restoring my powers. You wouldn't want to get in the way of that? I've been a member in good standing for decades. Don't I get a little leeway?"

"Well..." Polka's expression softened slightly, but Savona's didn't.

"I would like to point out that the monitors have detected the character of the items concealed about the persons of Mr. Aahzmandius and his colleagues. They are *Prohibited*, sir."

Even I could hear the capital P. By now we were attracting attention. I tried jollying him. "It's just part of the test, Savona. C'mon."

"I am very sorry, sir, but there are no bylaws under which you may carry into these premises either a magikal sword, especially not one of such intrinsic power…"

"A sword?" Polka squeaked, but Savona wasn't finished.

"…or a device for prognostication. In fact, the latter would be banned anywhere in the city. It could predict the outcome of bets, possibly resulting in the loss of millions at the tables. The accuracy readings are off the charts."

"Hmm," I said. "I never thought of that." Kelsa might have some uses after all. But Polka wasn't up for speculation.

"Where is it?" he asked, shaking with rage.

Savona pointed at Tananda. "That young lady has it in her possession. She is the architect of an illusion spell that is keeping the normal appearance of all the items concealed."

"You were planning to cheat the casinos?" Polka demanded, breasting up to me. "Using the club as a base? That's outrageous!"

"No, that's not why we're here," I protested. "Look, all I want to do is talk to my friend in the library, okay?"

"We only have your word on that, sir," the enormous Scourge said. He lowered the crossbow so the point of the quarrel was aimed directly between my eyes.

"I am afraid, Mr. Aahzmandius," Polka said, with dignity, "that I must ask you to leave."

"Leave?" I said, desperately looking at the library door. Behind it, the Book was waiting. If I could just…reach…it…. I shouldered into the invisible barrier again. "Why should I leave? I belong here!"

"Well, you're not a member any longer, not until you regain your powers, since they were the source of your qualifications. Otherwise you would not have gained access, you know. Where's your membership card?"

The entire room was definitely looking at me now. I mumbled, "Deva."

The Squirt clapped his hands together, and a rectangular wallet card suddenly lay in his outstretched palm. The fancy Magicians' Club logo was embossed in baby blue on the left. My moving picture had been applied to the right half, over my signature. The youthful me in the image was grinning like an idiot. The mouth was moving. I had been talking to the magician taking the magikal photo. I snarled at that callow youngster, who couldn't do a damned thing to help. Polka tsk-tsked. He flicked his other fingers at the card, and it burst into flames. The Pervect in the picture yelled silently, then crumbled into ashes.

"You can't do that to me!" I bellowed.

"It is my duty," Polka said. He didn't have to look so pleased about it. "You have broken several of our bylaws. You have committed fraudulent use of membership, failing to inform the committee about a change of circumstances, carrying prohibited magikal items into the club, attempted assault of another member, and finally, disturbing the calm of the Magicians' Club, which has been famous as an oasis of peace and quiet for our brethren and sisteren for over seven thousand years! See him out, Mr. Savona," the Squirt concluded, with a majestic wave of his skinny little hand. "If they try to get back in, you have my permission to use scorn as well as deadly force."

"Hey, wait a minute!" I said.

"I'm afraid I must fling you out into the street, Mr. Aahzmandius," Savona said, with what looked like genuine regret. I tried to sidestep him, but it's not easy to get out of the reach of a guy with wings. In a flutter, he had the back of my neck clamped with his talons, and my right arm bent up behind my back.

"No, you don't," I said, trying to get out of his grasp, as he propelled me inexorably toward the front door. "C'mon, you don't have to make it look so real. Check with the Board. They'll tell you…"

"Ta-daaaaa!" sang the stage assistants, arms up, as the door whisked open.

By that time I was airborne. I landed about thirty feet down the alley. Two pairs of feet appeared before my eyes as I was picking myself up.

"What happened to the ribbons?" I growled up at Tananda and Calypsa.

"Savona cut them off," Tananda said, with a little smile. She gave me a hand and heaved. I popped up. Sometimes I forget how strong she is. "With one swipe of that talon! I like a man who has a decent manicure. He gave me his number. We've got a date if I ever get back this way again."

Chapter 15

"WELL, THAT WAS an appalling screwup," Asti said, as I dusted myself off. "Badly handled. Not only did you not secure Payge, but Froome has escaped again."

"I suppose you could have done better, sister?" I asked. I glanced back. The doorway had vanished, replaced once again by an eye-level slit.

"Of course I could! Your story was weak from the beginning. Telling them you're a secret investigator. Hah!"

"It almost worked!" I said, defensively.

"*Almost* is the operative word," Asti said. "Pitiful."

"Pitiful!" I bellowed.

Tananda put a sympathetic hand on my shoulder. I shrugged it off.

"Inept, then. Do you like that better?" the Cup asked.

"For your information, honey, I was doing pretty well, until I rammed into that wall. I should have seen that coming."

"How could you see an invisible wall?" Calypsa asked.

I shook my head. "I should have asked to see Froome in public, gotten Polka to bring him out where we could jump him."

The Cup rolled her engraved eyes. "Hah! Then he would have cried for help. While you were dealing with the enforcers, he would have run back into the safety of the members' rooms, where you couldn't follow. Still a failure. Utter lack of preparation, and in a locale that you claimed to know well. You should have recalled that there would be protective spells. You could have come up with a much better cover story. They could tell right away you didn't have any magik, apart from us and that ancient bauble in your pocket. You could have come up with a much better story. I could have come up with one in my sleep!"

"Then why didn't you, sister?" I snarled, holding her up eye to eye with me. "You're so free and easy with the criticism. I thought you were in on this mission. But you'd rather carp at me than help!"

Asti's engraving looked as if it was etched into granite instead of gold. "Mortal, you fail or succeed on your own. You can ask us for help, but we're not going to jump in and rescue you from your pathetic lack of strategy. Buirnie offered to be of assistance, but you turned him down. Under those circumstances, I felt no need to offer."

"I thought that his approach was the correct one," Ersatz put in.

"Thanks," I said.

The Sword wasn't finished critiquing me. "But even so, you did not push hard enough. You have a forceful personality; why did you not use it?"

"Or charm!" Buirnie said. "A little more friendliness would have helped."

"All right, that's it," I said, cutting them off with one hand. "I've had enough of you riding me. I don't have to justify my actions to you. So this attempt failed. We're not dead yet, and neither is Calypso. Unless I want your input, keep your comments to yourself. I'm going back in there if I have to take on the whole room. I'm going to get Froome." I cracked my knuckles. "Come on."

"No point," Kelsa said cheerfully. "He's gone. He blinked out when the argument started."

I gawked. "Why didn't you say something?"

"Well, you get so cross when I interrupt you, but I do think, dear Aahz, you ought to relax that stricture, since it often runs counter to what you need to know at certain psychological moments…"

"Never mind," I snarled.

"Do you see?" Asti said. "Calypsa, child, in future be guided by us. We have millennia more experience to draw upon. This Pervert has led you astray over and over. There is little time left. Do not waste any more of it."

"That's it," I said. "I can take it when you four argue among yourselves, but I am tired of being needled when I'm doing my best. Forget it. I don't want any part of you, except Kelsa."

The Crystal Ball blinked huge yellow eyes. "I'm honored!"

"Don't be. If you weren't useful I wouldn't bother with any of you." I swapped the case containing Asti with Tananda for Kelsa's bowling bag. I'm going after Froome on my own without you. I'll meet you back in the inn on Ori," I told Tananda.

She tucked her hand into my arm and eased close to me. I eyed her with suspicion. I had a good mad on now, and I didn't want to waste it.

"You can't go, Aahz," she said.

"Yes, I can," I said. "I've got the D-hopper. All I need is a guide to catch up with this guy. I work better alone." I yanked the device out of my pocket.

"No, you haven't," Tananda said.

"What?" I bellowed. "I've *always* worked alone."

"But not better," she said, with a little smile quirking the corners of her mouth. She took Kelsa away from me and handed her off to Calypsa, who stood in the blaze of Klik's spotlight. Tananda drew me aside.

"This isn't just about how much nagging you've been getting from the Hoard, is it?" she said in a low voice. "I miss Skeeve, too. But I never saw you think harder or work more effectively than when you were trying to live up to the image he has of you in his mind."

"Dragon dung," I snarled. "Maybe I'm just fed up with having everything I do being criticized. Women always have to have a deeper explanation for things."

The smile became a broad grin. "Maybe. Dragon dung is real, and so is what I'm saying. You know why he went back to Klah."

"He got tired of us," I said, tossing a hand casually. "I know how he feels. I got claustrophobia working too closely with everyone. I'm not used to it. He probably felt like he couldn't take the pressure any more. I'm feeling like that now."

She shook her head. "You don't have to lie to *me*. He went back so he could work on becoming worthy of hanging

out with us. As if we could live up to *his* standards. Admit it'
Skeeve makes you feel proud and small at the same time.
He's more of a realist than I ever would have thought, after
that first moment in the Bazaar, when I could have stolen
the bones out of his body without him catching on, but he
has this shining image of us as the ultimate companions. Partners. That word has a special meaning for me, now. Except
for Chumley I hardly ever trusted anyone I work with, but I
learned to trust all of you, and I learned that you were worth
trusting, because Skeeve opened my eyes. You don't even
believe you're trustworthy, because you keep going back to
how greedy you are. Asti's playing on that, and it stings,
doesn't it? But it's natural for Pervects, nothing to be ashamed
of. Skeeve took that into consideration, and so do I. You're
pushing us away, even though we're perfectly good companions, because if you think Skeeve told us to take a hike, then
no one is worth hanging around with. But he didn't. He told
himself to leave. I think he hoped the rest of us would stay
together, but, admit it, Aahz, he was the glue. In my business
you can't get too attached to anyone, but I'm attached to
him. He's family, and so are you. So, cousin, are you going to
reopen your brain and take us with you, or are you going to
march in there alone?"

I don't like having my private feelings dredged up and
smashed into my face like wedding cake, but as Tananda said,
she's an old friend who knows me pretty damned well. It had
bugged me when Ersatz implied no mortals could have a fellowship as good as theirs—which didn't seem so terrific to
me, the way they fought all the time.

"All right," I said, keeping up the show of reluctance. "But
if you're coming with me, no screwing up."

"I'll try." She grabbed my ears and planted a solid kiss on
my lips. "Attaboy, Aahz," she said. "Come on, Calypsa, we've
got to get moving!"

BAMF!

The contrast between Vaygus and Tomburg was so marked that I thought we had jumped from a color set to black-and-white. Where neon had decorated not only the buildings but the clothes of the people of Vaygus, those of Tomburg's denizens I could see hunched over reading at desks in cubicles around me were dressed in drab, natural colors, matching the musty-smelling books on nearby shelves. We were in pretty close quarters. Tanda and Calypsa were jammed in tight.

"Where is he?" I asked Kelsa.

"Shh!" A round face was thrust into mine, a finger held vertical against its lips. I jumped back.

Only long experience kept me from smashing the face in with my fist in surprise, but I felt like doing it anyhow once I had my bearings. I didn't think that round a face could compress into that many wrinkles of disapproval. The guy behind it was cylindrical in shape, with at least nine pairs of arms and legs running down his body.

"What the hell is your problem, Bub?" I snarled.

The forefinger moved away from the fat little face, and pointed at a sign on a pillar between two tall cabinets filled with books.

SILENCE, it said. The forefinger stabbed toward it several times for good measure.

"What is this, a monastery?"

The chubby being shook its head at me. I took a good look around. The shelves of books behind me weren't the only ones. In fact, they seemed to stretch away down the aisle in which we were standing, almost to infinity. Once I tamped down my temper enough to listen, I heard dozens of unseen beings breathing and the rustle of pages turning, scholars sitting in unseen carrels bent over their books. We were in a library. I turned to Tananda and Calypsa.

"Of all the…"

"Shh!"

I scowled at the librarian, but lowered my voice. "Of all the sneaky tricks!"

"It's just what I told you," Kelsa said, for once moderating her shrill tones. "You will find Payge here among his fellow books!"

"That isn't what you said," I reminded her.

"Oh, it was something like that. What does it matter? He is here. All you have to do is catch him. I have foreseen it!"

"You foresee a lot of things," I commented. The bookworm behind me shushed me once more. "All right," I breathed. "I'll whisper!"

He nodded, then inched off, I supposed, to harass another visitor.

"Where, exactly, is he?" I asked Kelsa. "No, don't talk. Show me."

The Crystal Ball fogged up, then cleared. In its depths I saw another rank of bookshelves, identical to the ones that were around us.

"That does not help," Calypsa whispered. "They all look alike."

"Not completely," Tananda whispered back. "Look! He's standing under a sign that says "Fe-Fi." Maybe he likes being near his initials."

I grinned. "Well, let's go and Fo-Fum this Froome. I'm tired of playing catch up all across the dimensions. We'll split up and surround him." I glanced up. The local species, who resembled big bookworms, didn't just travel the floor of the aisles. I saw them clinging to the sides of shelves, even the ceiling, as they perused a row of covers.

"Can you climb up there, too?" I asked Tananda.

"Piece of cake," she said. With a supple movement, she clambered up the nearest tier, and vanished over the top.

"Then, you jump him from above. I'll go around to the right. Calypsa, you take the left." I leaned down and stuck a forefinger in Buirnie's face. "One peep out of you, and I'll use you for a U-bend under my bathroom sink, holes or no holes. Savvy?"

"Oh, very well," he said. "I will be pianissimo piano."

"No kind of piano. Not a note of music until we're out in the street. I'm not taking any chances on getting thrown out of here. Let's move.

"I can put everyone in the library to sleep," Asti suggested, as I tiptoed past "Do-Du." "I've got a wonderful soporific gas that will drop every breathing being in its tracks."

"No, thanks," I said. "I don't want anything like that circulating while Tananda's on the ceiling. If we can get close enough, you can zap him. Just try and keep me out of the fallout, all right?"

"Aahz, I have millennia of experience at this!"

"Give me a lucky beginner over an experienced veteran every time," I said.

There's something about a library that always makes me want to go to sleep. Not only is there the gentle sound of shushing in the air, but the air itself seems to be as still as glass. With sun pouring through the windows, the building was comfortably warm, and the scent of old books just acts like a sedative on my system. I felt like slapping myself in the face to keep awake.

I got some annoyed glances and a few surprised ones as I plowed my way toward the F's. They didn't show any nervousness about Pervects, which I believe to be a sign of intelligence. We usually only attack when provoked. Or offended. Or hungry.

My keen hearing informed me that Tananda was doing her best to keep Kelsa quiet as she clambered over the tops of the stacks. Ersatz was giving Calypsa whispers of advice as she took the right flank around Froome, through the G's and H's.

I edged along cautiously, watching out for that first glimpse of black fur. I had never gotten a good look at our quarry in either of the two dimensions through which we had just chased him, but the odds of another Pikinise being here in the public library on Tomburg were between slim and none.

The readers and browsers around me inhaled and exhaled softly, with the exception of one older bookworm in the corner, who was panting. I grinned at him as I went by. He was reading a racy novel with his eyes bugged out on stalks. Once I had tuned him out, I started to become aware of one more respiration apparatus in operation. This one was wheezing, not in lust, but in fear. That had to be our boy. I tiptoed faster.

I slipped around the next bank of books. There he was! Like his tiler friend back home, he had an inverted triangle for a face covered with black hair, but he was dressed in a long brown robe, belted around the middle, and a pair of boots far more suited to hanging around in bars than hiking. His back was pressed hard against the shelves as he looked left and right. Over his left shoulder he had a huge satchel, just the kind of bag suitable for hauling around a precious tome made of solid gold. I eased back before he saw me.

In the shadows I considered my options. I had no means of disguising myself as a local. If I came around the corner at him, he would just run off in the other direction. I couldn't hear Ersatz, so Calypsa wasn't in place yet. I looked overhead for Tananda. Depending on the traffic on top of the shelves, it could take her a moment or so to get here.

I had a bright idea. I slid into the aisle behind him and made my way to the opposite side of the bank of shelves. If I plunged forward at just the right moment, I could grab him from behind and hang onto him until the cavalry finally made it up the hill. I peered through at the back of his head, crouched, and prepared to spring.

"May I help you?" a pleasant voice asked me. A female bookworm sidled up beside me.

"Quiet!" Asti commanded. "He is attempting an ambush."

"Thanks for nothing!" I said. The sound of our voices had alerted Froome. I caught a glimpse of terrified eyes just before he dashed away to the right. I shoved the helpful aide to one side and set out in pursuit. "What did you say that for?"

"Well, we didn't need her help, did we?" Asti asked, just as annoyed with me. "She might have alerted him as to our presence!"

"So you did it for me? Thanks a heap."

"Shh!" hissed several of the bookworms clinging to the walls. I stepped up my pace.

In the silence, the Pikinise's footsteps were perfectly audible. He turned and turned again, hoping to throw me off his trail, but that was pretty well unlikely.

A shape whisked overhead like a squirrel leaping from tree to tree as I crossed an aisle. Tananda gave me a wink and gestured to the left. I went right. We had to corner Froome before he got out the door.

Suddenly, the footsteps stopped. I halted in the middle of a long corridor filled with dusty, brown books each three inches thick on one side, and windows on the other. A glance told me that we were on the second floor above the street. Tananda went overhead again, and the footsteps doubled back. I spun and went in pursuit.

I raced into the nearest intersection. A small party of bookworms stood in the center, holding a book the size of a bed. Froome came charging out of the corridor just opposite me. His eyes went huge, and he dashed to the left. I had to dive over the open book to follow.

"Aaggh!" Asti protested, as I bounded to my feet. "Watch the judo rolls, will you?"

"Unless you've got a flying potion, I've got to go with regular locomotion, babe," I said.

"I'll make one, I'll make one," she said. "Just stop jostling me!"

The head start Froome had gotten helped him to lose me, but not Tanda. I whistled, and a shrill blast came back to me, from about five rows over. I jogged in that direction, dodging in between browsers and students. Tananda whistled again. The sound was closer. I looked up.

"Where'd he go?" I asked.

"Shhh!" the readers chorused.

At that moment, a black-and-brown blur zipped past us through the nearest cross row. We looked at each other, then rushed after him. Where was Calypsa?

Ahead, I could see a sign with the zig-zag pattern that was the universal symbol for stairs. He was making for the ground floor. I put on a burst of speed. I didn't want to have to deal with security, if this place had any. He was pretty quick on his feet. He managed to outdistance me in seconds.

The stacks suddenly opened out to an open area, with a railed staircase at the far end of it. I saw Froome, bookbag and all, racing ahead of me. Suddenly, he pinwheeled to a stop, with his hands raised. I hurried to catch up. Tananda leaped down from the shelves ran after me.

Chapter 16

AS SOON AS I drew level with him, I could see why he had
stopped. Calypsa stood at the top of the staircase. She had
Ersatz drawn and leveled under his trembling chin. Froome
looked from her to me and back again.

"Please! Please don't hurt me!" he begged.

"Steady does it, child," Ersatz said. Calypsa looked as
frightened as the Pikinise did, but she clutched the Sword with
both hands. "He is no threat to you. He won't flee. Use me as
a deterrent, not a weapon. Do not lean forward or you will spit
him through the windpipe."

"Ulp!" said Froome. Under his fur, his skin turned
greenish.

"I am trying," Calypsa said, but she was as nervous as our
quarry. The Sword's point wobbled up and down. I put a finger
underneath it and lifted it up out of the way.

"Ah, there you are, friend Aahz!" Ersatz said.

"How did you know where he'd be?" I asked.

"Ersatz figured it out," Calypsa said. "He made me take
him to a chart of the floor. After only one look, he said that
Froome would probably flee to this point. And he has. I used
my Dance of Speed to bring us here ahead of Froome. I have
so much to learn from Ersatz!" She fixed an expression of
worship on the blade. The dark blue eyes dipped modestly.

"I offer my small skills for what they're worth."

"Nice work," I said. I turned to the cowering Pikinise. "We
came for Payge. Give him to us. Now."

It's hard to look scared and defiant at the same time, but
Froome managed. He stuck out his pointy chin. "Y-y-you can't
have him."

"Look," I snarled. "I have not chased you across three dimensions to have you say no to me. I might have been inclined
to negotiate about three days ago, maybe give you something

for your trouble, but not any more. You've got him. We need him. Gimme the bag." I held out my hand.

More than reluctantly, he slid the thick strap off his shoulder and handed the bag over. I grabbed it from him.

"You have no right to do this," he said. "I'm entitled to my source material. You're interfering with my job!"

"Yeah?" I asked, glaring him in the eye. "Well, you're interfering with the life of that young lady's grandfather. I'd say that that trumps your career."

"His life?" Froome said, looking less annoyed and terrified, and more interested. "Tell me more."

Calypsa never needed more than a single word of encouragement to open the floodgates.

"Well, you see, my grandfather is the great Calypso..."

I opened the bag and pulled out the book I found inside.

"There," I gloated, shoving it in Asti's field of view. "Think I'm a screwup now?"

"'Mud and Malarkey, The Account of My Years as A Village Idiot in the Kingdom of Ruizmotto,'" Asti read off the spine. "Yes, I agree, it *could* be your life story. That's not Payge."

"What?" I said. I looked at the book.

"Besides, he has a solid gold cover," Asti reminded me. "This is morocco calfskin in a disgusting shade of green. Published about fifty years ago, I'd say by the smell."

"I've been to Ruismotto," Buirnie said. "I know a song about the queen who ruled fifty years ago. She had a very big nose. Want to hear it?"

"No!" I said.

"...And the wizard Barrik turned out to be a bad neighbor, a very tyrant who terrorized us..."

I stuck my hand in again. Sure enough, there was another "This thing is more roomy than it looks." I decanted that volume. On a shiny black leather cover in silver were the words "Volume III."

"Not right."

I kept removing books from the bookbag. It seemed to have an infinite capacity, all of it filled with lengthy personal accounts, histories, collections of poems, legends and urban myths. Then I remembered the dusty shelves in his study on Pikini. I glared at Froome. "You had to bring the whole collection with you?" I asked.

"I…" the guy swallowed. I realized he was fairly young. "The account of your conquests in the Golden Book was fearsome. I didn't think I would be safe to return. Are you going to pull out my guts and tie them in knots?"

"Only if I don't find what I'm looking for, PDQ," I said. I had run out of room on the desk, and was stacking books on the floor. "Where is it?"

"It's not here," Kelsa said.

"How do you know?" I demanded, hauling out an entire set of encyclopaedia, one fat volume at a time. It was followed by The Complete Little Nemo, books of Pervish cartoons, a Dragonette cookbook, and at least fifteen books on how to write stories.

"My dear Aahz! All of these are ordinary books. Not a single magikal text in here. They're all storybooks. Novels."

"You are putting me on!" I shook Froome. "Where is it?"

"I'll never tell you where I have hidden the Golden Book," he said, throwing his head back defiantly. "I would rather die."

I shoved my face close to his.

"That can be arranged."

"Gold? Oh, I saw that," Tananda said. "That was Payge?" She hurried back to the last standing shelf and climbed up to the second highest tier. Froome's face fell.

Tananda braced herself, and clamped her hand around one volume. Now that I was looking in the right direction, I could just see a glimpse of gold.

"What's the matter?" I asked.

"I can't get it out!"

"What do you mean, you can't get it out? It's probably just too heavy to pull with one hand."

"I mean, it's not moving at all."

"There they are!" a soft voice declared.

A bookworm slunk up the stairs and reared his upper body to point in our direction. Several other bookworms, dressed in uniforms with gold braid on their peaked caps, came swarming up around him. They surrounded us. A whole coterie inched up around Tananda, heading her off before she could clamber to the top of the stacks.

"All right," the leader whispered, as he rose up to stare me straight in the face. "You are disturbing the peace of this establishment. You must go."

"We can't go yet," I said. "I need a book!"

"It looks like you've got all the books you need," he said. "When you have finished with those, come back. But quietly! In the meanwhile, please leave, or we will have to use force."

"At least let us take a look at the book on that shelf," I said. These characters didn't look that strong. I figured once we got it down, we could make a break for it with the D-hopper.

"Absolutely not," the library clerk said, as clerks shoveled Froome's collection back into his satchel of holding. "All books on our shelves become part of our permanent collection. They are accessible only to card holders! Take them out of here," he instructed the guards.

I had been given the bum's rush more than once while working for Calypsa, and I wasn't about to let it happen again. I shook off all the little hands and marched down the stairs with dignity ahead of the bookworms.

"You're making a mistake," I said. "We have permission to be here. We're making a documentary about this place. You've just earned a role as the designated villain. You've got one chance to make us change our minds."

"Shh!" the guards hissed in unison.

"You have to let me get that book!" Calypsa pleaded, as they hustled her out. They got us into the foyer. Long lines of bookworms were waiting at the desk to check out their choices.

"If you do not listen to me, I will dance until you do!" She threw up her arm.

I grabbed it. "Save it for outside!" I said. I tilted my head toward the door. Her eyes widened, but she nodded and relaxed.

They marched us out into the street, then left us, dusting their hands together. Froome stumbled into the gutter, clutching his bag to his chest. A vehicle shaped like a bowl on wheels with three Bookworms in it screeched to a halt and sounded a horn at him that sounded like an indignant canary. Froome scrambled back onto the pavement and headed for the entrance.

"I'm going back for Payge," he said. "I'll explain it's all a mistake. You can't stop me!"

"Says who?" I demanded, making a beeline for him. "I'm going back for it! I'll toss you over the next building!"

"In front of all of these people?" Froome said. "They'll jump you before you can hit me twice. This is a very law-abiding civilization. I'm going to take back my book!" He turned back to open the door. I dodged in front of him. He tried to get past me. I put a vise grip around his wrist.

"Shall we dance?" I asked. "Buirnie, hit it!"

A blast from the Flute caused everyone, including Froome, to turn and look. Klik, the spotlight, flew about twenty feet into the air and beamed its brightest light down on Calypsa. The drum swung into a sexy rhythm.

"Give it all you've got, girl!" I said.

Calypsa started whirling, waving her arms up and down to the music. In no time, her Dance of Fascination had captured the attention of passersby. Plump, round-faced Bookworms were crowding and shoving to get an unobstructed view of her. The bowl-shaped vehicles stopped where they were. The occupants slithered out to join the growing throng. Bookworms climbed walls and light posts to take a gander at Calypsa.

For her part, the Walt was making the best use of her audience. She flirted with the guys in the front row, tickling under their chins with her feathered hands as she stepped and sashayed. She brought Ersatz into the act, spinning the gleaming blade over her head, then bringing it down and caressing it. Children were agog until their outraged mothers covered their eyes with one hand. I gawked, enjoying the show. Nothing seemed as important as what the slender Walt would do next.

Suddenly, a finger hooked itself in the corner of my mouth and turned my head. I found myself looking into Tananda's eyes. She shook her head.

"Can't ignore a pretty girl, can you?"

"Thanks," I said.

"Don't mention it. She's good, isn't she?"

The effect on Froome was just as good as I had hoped. The Pikinise wizard stopped trying to pull away from me. He stared at Calypsa with his jaw hanging open. I let go of him, and tipped her a wink, careful not to watch her movements too closely.

"Keep him there until I come back," I told Tananda. "I have an idea."

"You have an idea?" Asti said, as I pushed open the door. "That's worth a headline."

"Shut up," I said, with great pleasure. "We *are* entering a library."

I swaggered up to the desk. If the Tomburgian male behind it was surprised to have a Pervect addressing him, he hid it well. I gave him my most affable smile.

"Afternoon," I said, calmly. "I'd like to apply for a library card."

Applause and gasps of admiration came in through the open door from the street. The librarian behind the desk straightened his goggle-thick glasses on his big nose and peered over my shoulder. "What is going on out there?"

"Who knows?" I said. "May I have the application, please?"

In no time at all, I was the proud possessor of a card for the Main Library System of Tomburg. Two minutes later, I was on the landing where Froome had stowed the Book. It slid off the shelf into my hands without a catch or a fuss. Two minutes after that I was standing in line at the desk. The same librarian who had given me my card stamped it out.

"You can keep it as long as you need it," he said. "If there's an interlibrary request for it, we can use our crystal ball to find you."

"You do that," I said, blithely. "Have a nice day."

I sauntered out into the street with the Book under my arm. I waved over the heads of the crowd to Calypsa and Tananda.

"Got it!" I called.

With one final spin, Calypsa sheathed the Sword and stopped dancing.

"Awwwww!" The crowd let out a wail of disappointment. Bookworms glanced sheepishly at one another, then scattered about their business. Within moments, the sidewalk was clear of all but a few passersby.

Froome blinked a few times, then came to himself. He saw the Book, and made a grab for it. I stiff-armed him. He was taller than I was, but as weak as a strip club martini.

"Sorry. He's coming with us, now."

"You'll never get away with it," he gasped.

"I just did."

"But, what will I do without him?" Froome said. "He gave me so many ideas!"

"Ideas?" It was my turn to blink. "You're a magician. Use the force lines, like everybody else."

"Magician?" he said, puzzled. "I'm not a magician. I'm a storyteller."

"You're a what?" I asked, taken aback. "We thought you were using Payge as a grimoire. You're a member of the Magicians' Club."

"No, no!" Froome said. "I do sleight of hand. It makes my live performances more interesting. Payge taught me to dimension-hop. It's so easy anyone can do it."

"Not everyone," I growled.

Froome didn't seem to notice. "Payge is a great teacher. He is far more than a grimoire! He's full of amazing stories, dating back millennia. Some really astounding tales. A lot of them have to do with the Golden Hoard." He stared at Ersatz and Kelsa. "These are some of the treasures, aren't they? I recognize them from his descriptions. Are they really as marvelous as the legends say?"

"Shhh!" I growled, looking around at the foot traffic passing us on both sides. "Yes, they are. Don't make headlines out of it."

"Amazing." Froome simply looked fascinated. "I have always lived a very quiet life. All I do is sit in a small room and craft stories, which I sell to make my living. Nothing ever happens to me. One day, I went to a cave, to inspire myself to write a story about underground terrors, and found him there on a shelf, gleaming like a..."

"Like a beacon in the night?" I supplied.

"Yes! You should be a writer. Payge has been my best source material, better than any other book I've ever read. I've been so productive with him critiquing my writing. When I read in his archives that you were coming, I just panicked! I packed up everything I had and fled. He's more than a treasure, he's my friend, my mentor! Are you sure you won't just...give him back to me?"

"Sorry, kid. Win some, lose some."

Froome was forlorn. "How can I go to the Saylemanor Festival without him?"

"If leading us on a chase across the dimensions hasn't given you the material for a terrific epic," Tananda said, "then you can't be much of a storyteller."

"Not to mention Calypsa's tale of woe," I said. "And you just met four of the other members of the Golden Hoard. That was Ersatz, the great Sword, at your throat up there in the library."

"I..." Froome looked at each of us, enlightenment dawning. "It was? Why, I DID have an adventure of my own, didn't I?"

"You certainly did," Tananda said, giving him one of her killer smiles as she sidled up to him. "And you can tell your listeners that you went up against the mighty Aahz, one of the toughest and smartest guys ever to come out of Perv, and that you beat him two times out of three."

"Hey, wait a minute!" I said. "Who's telling this, anyway?"

"Why, Froome will be," Tananda said, giving me a wink. She ran her fingers up the sleeve of his robe. "Won't you?"

He seemed to be afflicted with a terrible case of dry-mouth. "Why, I...how can I resist it? Yes, it'll make wonderful telling! I'll be the hit of the festival. What...what's your name, beautiful green lady?"

"Tananda," the Trollop said. "Make sure you spell it right."

The Pikinise was already mining through his capacious satchel for a quill and a notebook. "And just what was it that you did to make me stop in my tracks, Miss Calypsa?" he asked.

"The Dance of Fascination," she said.

"It was...it was fantastic," he said, with an admiring glance. "Good luck in freeing your grandfather."

"Thank you," she said, modestly. "You are very kind to let me take Payge."

"You're welcome," he said. "All I ask in return is that you let me know how it all comes out. And then, look out, Morigrim Festival of Champion Storytellers. Here I come!"

He blinked out of sight.

BAMF!

Chapter 17

"WELL DONE," ASTI said, grudgingly. "That was almost brilliant."

I swaggered along the main street of Tomburg, looking for a handy alley that we could slip into, to avoid jumping dimensions in front of the crowd. Froome might have been into public displays of magik, but I wasn't.

"It was pretty clever, now that I think about it," I said.

"On a scale of stupid to stellar, I'd give you a six."

I bared my teeth.

"Give it a rest, sister! Who else could have helped put together five of you Hoard in a matter of twenty days?"

"Twenty-one," the Book under my arm suddenly spoke up.

"Well, another delegate heard from," I said. I turned the book over so I could see the cover. Jewels and jade formed the picture of a grand landscape framing the image of a big, cushy chair with a reading lamp shining over it. I turned it one more time, to look at the spine. Where other books had a colophon at the top, Payge had a little face, with sapphire eyes and a wry mouth shaped like a dingbat. "Why didn't you say something to Froome before he left?"

"I hate goodbyes," Payge said. "I prefer happy endings."

"Who says this isn't going to have a happy ending?"

"Payge has never liked confrontations of any kind," Ersatz said. "It is most annoying. He will not even defend himself in an argument."

"Froome does not need me," Payge said. "I will not be able to teach him more magik, alas, but he will be the greatest storyteller of this age. I have confirmation in my own future annals. See page 2,398, and also pages 3,567 to 3,582, inclusive. I am sorry I will not be with him to witness his success, but I shall know of it just the same."

Kelsa, who looked like the Reader's Digest myopia edition in her diamante glasses, went hazy for a moment. "Oh, yes, dear. Very successful. Take a look!"

I flipped the book over and thumbed through it until I came to the first reference. Sure enough, an illustration of Froome's cheerful face, somewhat grayer than I had just seen him. He sat on a cushion in the middle of a sea of admirers. The image topped an article entitled "Word Magik." Below was a fairly comprehensive biography. I caught sight of my name in the middle of the text. I paged ahead to the second section, which was a collection of what would one day be Froome's most famous stories.

"Not a bad life," I commented.

"If it comes true," the Book said. "There is the remote possibility it will not come to pass, but I would say his chances of success are over 98%. See my section on Statistics, chapter 2, pages 6,104 to 6,106."

The logo of Payge's face appeared at the bottom of every page. I addressed the one on page 3,570.

"You have *all* of history written there?"

"Oh, yes, I keep the records of every civilization at hand since I was first bound, even the ones that no longer exist."

"So, you're annal-retentive, huh?" I asked. Everyone looked at me blankly except Tananda. "Forget it. Do you have anything about Calypsa here rescuing her grandfather?"

"I have an infinite number of possible outcomes of that quest," Payge said. "See page 4,000 for the branching chart, a fold-out supplement. Too many variables still remain for me to have a definitive opinion in print."

"Your pages change all the time?"

"Naturally."

"You know what we're trying to do?"

"Indeed, I do. I was following Calypsa's account as she narrated it to Froome. I must say, she does not deviate by so much as a comma, from telling to telling. I could scarcely have done better myself."

"Thank you," Calypsa said.

"You are welcome. That is not to say, it becomes tedious on hearing it retold time and again," Payge continued. "In my chapter on Compelling Narratives, I suggest varying the pace and perhaps the details of your account once in a while—not sacrificing accuracy, mind you, but omitting certain facts and stressing others depending upon one's audience. In Froome's case, you were fortunate, since he wants ALL details. That made him a most apt pupil. I can't hope to find one so promising this century. Unless," he eyed Calypsa, "you have a good ear, you are loquacious, and you're certainly trainable. Are you interested in applying yourself to an advanced degree in literature?"

"Back off, book. She is my protégé," Ersatz said.

"Ah." Payge paused. "Yes, it is so written, in the Current Events section between pages 300-600. Alas. I did not expect to succeed, but there are still branches left in the tree of events. I need to study. I need peace and quiet!"

"Look, are you going to cooperate with us, or not?" I said. "You've wasted almost five days of our time. If we don't get out there and find the Purse and the Ring in the next few days, Calypsa's granddad is history."

"I am so sorry," the Book said. "I am simply suffering from information overload. Sometimes I just can't keep up with it. I promise, I will cooperate. Very well, I am at your service. I confess myself terrified. I know too well what Perverts are capable of doing. My pages are full of accounts containing page-curling details."

I snorted. "You shouldn't believe everything you read, chum," I said. "I've never tortured a book that didn't deserve it."

"If I have gotten my facts wrong, I wish to correct them. We are going up against Barrik, who has imprisoned Calypso against his will? That has not changed?"

"It hasn't," Calypsa said.

"What is the plan? I haven't found one among the information I have been accumulating about you three and my old colleagues."

"There is no plan," I said, firmly. "We're gathering you all together. We take you to Barrik. He frees Calypso. End of story."

"But…you are gathering the finest force the universe has ever known, to be bartered as if we were a set of the Encyclopedia Gnomica?"

"Not my deal, Bub. I'm just doing what the little lady here wants."

The sapphire eyes slewed wildly to Calypsa and back to me.

"But advise her differently! Are you prepared for the consequences of what will occur if we are put into the hands of a tyrant?"

"Oh, he'll be out of there like a shot once the deal is done," Asti said. "He won't stay around to see the results of his action. The girl is *paying* him, Payge. Actually, it's Ersatz's fault. What was the debt you incurred?"

"One hundred to set me free from the merchant who held me," Ersatz recited. "Then there is reimbursement for the outlay for the cases…"

I was tired of hearing that litany.

"What's wrong with a straightforward transaction?" I demanded. "You wanted a fancy slipcover to work with us. You got it. I'm waiting for my payoff." I turned to the book.

"Kelsa said you know all the spells in the universe."

"If it has been written, then I know it," the book said, without a trace of modesty. "At the moment you are my master, since you extracted me from the library. What spell is it you wish to know?"

I hated saying it out loud again, but this was one of the two treasures that Kelsa had promised could help. "I lost my powers. I want them back. What's the spell to restore them?"

"Not so fast, not so fast!" The Book rustled his pages. "That's not as simple as it sounds! I will need to know all there is to know about the circumstances regarding the loss of your powers. Then I can search through my indices to find

the appropriate incantation, and lists of the ingredients for
potions and so on that will effect the cure. You can tell me
all as we travel, for I see within my annals that Kelsa is about
to give us direction to find our next colleague."

"Why, you almost sound prescient, dear!" the Crystal Ball
exclaimed. "You're right, of course. I keep forgetting that the
depths of your scholarship reach into the future as well as the
past. It's not as good as actually being a seer, of course, but
you make such educated-sounding guesses…"

"Don't you have the whole story somewhere in you?" I
asked, interrupting Kelsa's inevitable flow. Payge's dingbat
turned upside down into the semblance of a frown.

"I have a brief retelling, but I need every detail that you
can recall, scents, lighting, impressions, all in your own words,
of course."

"Go ahead, Aahz," Tananda said, encouragingly. "What's
the harm in telling it one more time? This could be the last."

I disliked going over the circumstances that had lost me
my powers, but it sounded like I had no choice. Giving Tanda
a quelling glance, I took a deep breath, and began.

"Up until that day I'd always liked Garkin. He had the
same kind of sense of humor I had…"

Chapter 18

"ALMS, MISTER, ALMS!" Another one of the skinny, ruddy, toadlike people grabbed for my ankle. He was wearing only a loincloth and a headcloth. His bulgy eyes rolled up at me appealingly. I growled.

"Just kick him off," Kelsa advised. "They expect it."

I had already done so.

"I don't need you to tell me that." I looked around me. "What a dump."

The city of Sri Port, largest population center in the dimension of Toa, stretched out in all directions except up. Most of the mud-and-straw buildings, once painted in bright colors and now faded by the sun, were less than three stories, and most of them were in conditions so wretched that no one would want to live in them unless they had absolutely no choice. From the look of the locals, they *had* no choice. I couldn't estimate the population, but I had to guess it was in the millions or tens of millions of hairless, froglike individuals, who shared their homes with skinny ruminants that chewed on the weeds that grew in the mud. Sri Port looked like the summer home of at least two of the Four Horsemen of the Apocalypse. The sun beat down through a haze of humidity thick enough to swim in. I glanced back at Calypsa, who was picking her way daintily through the piles of garbage, dung and broken bricks that obstructed the narrow path between buildings. Behind her, Tananda kept an eye on anyone who might be following us. She was fondling the blade of a knife with a deliberate thumb. The Toadies standing in doorways or stumping through the narrow alleyways glanced at her and hastily away again. I grinned. She could look plenty formidable when she chose.

Strings of laundry swung over our head, flapping in the hot breeze. Noise battered at our eardrums, smells clawed at our nostrils, and the locals bumped into us at every possible turning. The streets and alleyways were far too narrow for the crowds. Following Kelsa's directions, I led the way, shouldering through locals arguing with one another, bargaining, wooing, bullying, child-disciplining, praying, playing, begging, gossiping, and more bargaining.

Allowing for the difference in the physical form of the locals, Sri Port looked precisely like the Bazaar at Deva, if you sucked out all of the money from the latter.

"A donation, good sir, a donation for the poor and blind child of leprous drunkard!" A skinny, purple, clawlike hand reached up to me from a collection of filthy rags.

"He's lying," Kelsa said, cheerfully. "He's not blind, of course, and neither parent has leprosy. Actually, his mother has a degree in dental hygenics from the University of Sri Port, but they are having trouble keeping up with the mortgage on their little apartment. No cost of living increase this year, or for the last three years, for that matter. The dentist can't afford to give her one. He's having trouble with HIS mortgage, by the way. Shagul, here, begs after school, but he really should be home doing his book report. It's due tomorrow morning."

A pair of goggling eyes glared hatred out of the folds of cloth. "The curse of the Thousand Gods be upon you!"

"Go do your homework," I snarled, lunging toward him. He crabwalked hastily backwards away from me, scrambled to his feet, and ran.

"Now, this one *is* poor," Kelsa went on, as we walked by a female dressed in a swathe of patched but clean cloth. "You've got a small silver piece in your purse. Drop it on the melon-seller's wagon as we go by. She'll pick it up."

I didn't like having anyone dictate what I did with my money, and I'd spent plenty already in the service of the Golden Hoard. Besides, I already had a coin in my hand I'd been planning to drop in the shabby female's way. I'm not a total miser, no matter what you might have heard about me before. I brushed my hand over the rail of the cart, leaving the donation on the splintery plank. I didn't look behind me, and I wouldn't meet Tananda's eye. I could tell she was grinning. I cursed all magikal treasures and Trollops.

"This is it!" Kelsa announced, as we shoved through the throng into yet another crumbling city square. The buildings here were just as dilapidated as the others, but the people here, by and large, were smiling. A lot of them squatted in the dirt in front of a low, more-or-less whitewashed building with big holes in the walls and a holey pink curtain for a door. "That's the place."

"You could buy the whole house for a Devan nickel," Tananda said, letting out a low whistle.

"The Purse is *there*?" Calypsa asked, in disbelief. "The source of unending wealth is in that hovel?"

"That's what we're going to find out," I said. "Either the person who's got it doesn't know how to use it, or it's a fake. We've got to check it out."

Tananda grabbed my arm. "Aahz, if that's their source of income, we can't just march in there and take it away from them. Look at the condition of this city!"

"I'll make up my mind when I see it. Come on."

When we started to cross the square, the Toadies hanging out in front of the white building sprang up. Three of the biggest breasted up to us. They stood maybe as high as my collar bone.

"Who do you think you are? We were here first! Wait your turn!"

"Who do you think YOU are?" I demanded. "I'm a peaceable kind of guy, so get out of my way before I stomp you into the dirt!"

"Please, please," a low, musical voice said from the doorway. "No fighting here! This is a place of peace. Raniti, how rude you are! Can't you see that these are guests? All who come here are welcome."

The crowd, which had clearly been spoiling for a good fight, all settled down into their crouches once again, grumbling under their breath. The speaker came out and took my hand. She was a very short, very wrinkled, old Toady in a swath of much-mended cloth and a head veil. She didn't seem particularly special to look at, with an unusually wide mouth and a flat nose, but there was fire in those bulgy eyes. I was impressed in spite of myself.

"Come in, come in," she said. "I am Sister Hylida, abbess of the Toa Ddhole Mission. Welcome, welcome!" She gestured toward the door.

There seemed to be as much deconstructed architecture inside as out, but it was arranged better. Two bricks propped up a vase with a broken foot. A shrine at one end had been put together out of pieces of carved marble, detritus from a number of different temples, each with its own idea of ornamentation.

"Ugh, what a stench! They're using dung fires," Calypsa said, in a low voice.

"I think it's the food," Tananda whispered back.

"Reminds me of Pervish cooking," I said. The smell was making me hungry.

A couple of skinny Toadies in loincloths hurried to spread out a few straw mats over the packed dirt floor for us to sit on.

"May I offer you cool water and a cloth to wash your hands?" Sister Hylida asked. The toadies hurried over with a chipped ewer and mismatched clay cups. I held mine in both hands, keenly aware of the solid gold, gem encrusted, magikal goblet in the custom-made carrying case next to me on the mat.

The toadies hunkered down near the far wall as Sister Hylida squatted down with us. I heard curious whispers and giggles, and realized that faces were peering in the door and through the holes in the wall.

"Our business is private," I said.

"You will find that privacy is rare here," Hylida said. "But we can try to find some." She waved away the eavesdroppers with a little smile. The faces behind the wall retreated a few feet. I hoped they didn't have as keen hearing as Pervects did.

She glanced at the sword lying half-sheathed across Calypsa's knees. "You won't need that here. What a beautiful weapon it is, though."

Pervects are not normally concerned with the concept of 'an embarrassment of riches.' I don't usually have quibbles with who owns what. If I want something that belongs to someone else, sooner or later I'll figure out a way to get it. But this entire city seemed to be dirt poor, and here we had come clanking in with enough wealth to buy the whole place, mineral rights and all, looking for probably the only thing of value remaining. I felt like a rat as I cleared my throat.

"Look, we're not from around here," I began. "We're on a mission..."

"You are? Blessings be upon you from the Thousand Gods!" The little sister jumped up from her cloth and ran to the altar. She lit a stick of incense at the small tin brazier and stuck it in a dish full of sand in front of a tattered poster containing a myriad of images, no doubt her thousand gods, and chanted a tuneless wail that went up and down the scales like a cat's love song. Two of the acolytes ran in and began shaking sistrums and banging tambourines. My eardrums twisted at the noise. Hylida concluded her prayer and sat down again. "I am so happy to hear that. Most outworlders who find their way here are lost. How may I serve you upon this mission?"

It was an unmistakable opening, but I couldn't take it. I opened my mouth. Nothing came out.

Ersatz jumped in. "My good friend Aahz wishes to tell you that he requires you to give us the Purse of Endless Wealth, which we judge to be in your possession. That is the sum of our task in this place."

"How can you just blurt that out?" Tananda asked him. The steel-gray eyes rolled toward her on the visible portion of the blade.

"It is the next step in our task to save Calypsa's grandfather, is it not?" Ersatz asked, reasonably. "Mistress Hylida asked us, and since friend Aahz appears to be tongue-tied, I have taken the step of saying the words for him. That is what you wish, isn't it?"

"Not very subtle, are you?"

"Subtlety wastes time," Ersatz said, unperturbed. The eyes turned to our hostess. "Well, mistress? Do we seek the Purse here in vain?"

Hylida clapped her hands. "I have seen a wonder today! A sword that talks! Is that your request, green-scaled one?"

I felt doubly stupid, now. "Uh…yeah. That is it."

"Then I am happy to tell you you have succeeded! Chin-Hwag *is* here."

"Oh, yes, Aahz," Kelsa said. "I told you I saw her. Would I lie?"

"Lie, no," Asti said, exasperatedly. "Be mistaken, constantly."

"I always see true! Much better than someone who poisons people by accident!"

"If you don't mind," the Book said, aheming for attention, "but I have a record of *all* of your errors over the centuries…"

"More wonders!" Hylida said, happily. "A Book that talks! Brothers and sisters, we must celebrate!"

The Toadies jumped up again, and began dancing, more vigorously than before. The people outside rose and started shouting. They banged pots and pans together, shook maracas, and danced all around the square.

Bam! Boom! Zing! Bom!

"Stop it!" I shouted. No one paid any attention to me.

"Hey, this is fun!" Buirnie said, through his little window. "Mind if I join in? Zildie, from the top! A-one, a-two, a-three…"

The spotlight hit his case. The nimble leg of the drum flicked it open, and the Flute joined in the chanting on the backbeat. The people stared at the solid-gold Fife for one moment, then accepted it as yet another miracle to celebrate. He led them in singing a rondo with a catchy rhythm. I sat with my arms folded, waiting for it all to blow over, but Calypsa started to get into it. She sprang up and started to dance, kicking and twirling. The locals grabbed her hands and swung her into their circle. The noise reached epic levels.

"Enough, already!" I bellowed.

Buirnie's playing died away with a whine.

The crowd paused to stare at me.

I glared at Sister Hylida. "If this is what you call private, then I want to see what you call an open town meeting!"

"Oh, it is an event of even *greater* enjoyment," the Toady nun said. She signed to her people to sit down. They groaned their disappointment, but they sat. Buirnie glared at me from underneath his spotlight. "But you were asking about Chin-Hwag. She has been my companion for several years now, and a great help to me in my mission. We help the poor and serve the hungry here. You see?"

She waved toward another ragged curtain. Beyond it was a room larger than the one we sat in. Several Toadies stirred huge, dented kettles over glowing embers. Steam rose from the pots. The aroma we had noticed on the way in came from there.

"We share good fortune as well as bad here," Hylida said, placidly. "But do not worry. No one will speak of what they see and hear in this place."

I didn't believe that, but I didn't have time to argue. We had business to accomplish and a road to hit. I cleared my throat.

"Abbess, we want to be fair. What will you take for the Purse?"

At my question, protests rose from the Toadies squatting in the house and outside the broken walls.

"Sell Chin-Hwag? I could never sell her!" Sister Hylida rose and removed a slab of plaster from the wall next to the altar. Behind it was a small alcove. I nodded approval. It would be hidden from potential thieves—who would suspect that the greatest fortune in any dimension might be concealed in those crumbling walls?—but easy to grab if the sister had to evacuate her soup-kitchen in a hurry. "You must see her, of course. Here she is."

I expected a kind of shapeless bag, but the Endless Purse of Money was an inch-thick octagon of leather about six inches across, stitched together from strips of a very smooth hide that had been dyed ochre. A good deal of the surface was covered with silk embroidery so fine that it would take a magnifying glass to admire the detail. It wasn't pretty, but it was intricate. I realized that it was studying me as keenly as I was studying it. Just like the other treasures, Chin-Hwag's intelligence was out there where anyone could see it. A couple of embroidered horizontal ovals above the pull-strings around the mouth narrowed, and the purse-strings moved.

"By all that jingles, a Pervert! You keep your scaly hands off me, greenboy!"

Hylida looked scandalized.

"Watch your language, Chin-Hwag, he is a visitor!"

The embroidered eyes shifted.

"I can see what he is—a member of one of the greediest races in all the dimensions, after Deveels and a few other born felons. Find out what he wants, then send him away, swiftly."

"You misunderstand him," Calypsa said. "Aahz is most kindly helping me. He has no thoughts of wealth on his own behalf."

"Oh, don't listen to her," Asti interrupted. "He *is* out for money."

"Only what he is owed, by a debt of honor which I incurred," Ersatz said. "On behalf of our employer, whom you will come to know as a worthy being."

"Thanks a lot," I said.

The embroidered eyes moved around. "By clink and clank, Ersatz! I thought I felt my insides twisting! How many of you are here?"

"Five of us," Kelsa said. "Almost all of us who still exist."

"How peculiar and unwelcome a notion!" Chin-Hwag said.

"That is not very charitable," Sister Hylida said, shaking a finger at the Purse. The embroidered eyes turned toward her.

"You are not worldly, Hylida. You don't know what these other objects are like," Chin-Hwag said, the mouth drawing tighter. "In a crisis, they do too much when a little will do."

"They are still our guests today," the little nun said. She turned to me. "You must join us for our meal."

"If you don't mind," Tananda said, with a look at Calypsa's face. It was almost as green as hers. I think the smell must have been getting to her. "Maybe we can take the Purse and go. We don't want to impose."

The nun's kindly face fell. "I am afraid that I cannot let you take her just yet. Tax day approaches. The Majaranarana's collectors will be coming by to assess each of the people you see out there, and take money from them according to each assessment. They do not have it, so Chin-Hwag must give it to them. Tomorrow, please, or the day after."

We looked at Calypsa. In spite of her nausea, she was sympathetic.

"What do you say, kid? There's only three days left on your deadline."

"Of course we must allow you to help them," the Walt said. "I couldn't let anyone get into trouble. We are so close. Surely we will find the Ring in good time."

I didn't like cutting our fudge factor, but I shrugged. "It's your show. Besides, I could use a square meal."

"Good!" Hylida said. "Then let us have food." She clapped her hands.

"Who's the Majaranarana?" I asked.

"Oh, he is the absolute monarch of our land," Hylida said, as the Toadies ran around and laid out huge bowls and spoons at each place. This looked promising, since we hadn't eaten much in the last few days. "Our land produces much wealth' crops, minerals, silk, machinery, but very little of it benefits us. All of our profits are taxed heavily."

"Are you at war?" Ersatz asked, with a expert's eye on her.

"No! But our neighbors look at us greedily. The Majaranarana has been using all the money to pay off the other rulers, to keep them from thinking about invading." She sighed. "It might have been better to have raised an army when he could afford one. Now he wrings all he can out of the people. We cannot go on much longer in this fashion."

In the meantime, one of the servers set a big kettle of stew down next to me. I inhaled appreciatively. It tasted like *farkasht* fritters, a dish that my grandmother used to make, except none of the components wriggled. Too bad. It was the closest I'd found to Pervish cooking in a hundred dimensions. I scooped the contents into my bowl and started eating.

"All right, everyone, dinner is served!" Hylida said.

Pointed silence descended. I glanced up from my meal.

"What?" I asked.

Tananda tilted her head meaningfully toward the bowl in front of her. Another server had ladled some of the stew into it, about enough to cover my palm. I looked at Calypsa's bowl. In it was also a single, meager scoop of food. If I judged by proportion, the pot I had just emptied was supposed to have fed about a hundred people. I felt like an idiot. Why did these people use such huge dishes if they weren't going to fill them?

"Uh, sorry."

"What an appetite!" Hylida said. She looked pleased.

"Like feeding a garbage disposal," Asti exclaimed.

"Nothing would surprise me about Perverts," Chin-Hwag agreed.

"I have records of feasts where they've eaten whole villages!" Payge said. He turned terrified blue jewel eyes toward me. "I mean, the contents of their larders and their animal pens, not the people. I...please don't tear my pages out."

"Knock it off!" I said. I turned to Hylida. "Sorry for the inconvenience .I'll make it up to you."

The nun smiled. "I do not mind. You were so appreciative of the flavor of our cooking. I do not see that very often. Usually my clients are just grateful to have the food, they do not care what it tastes like. It is charity, but they still complain."

"There, you see? He didn't even wait to see what it tasted like." Asti snorted.

"All right," I snarled, glaring down on her. "Knock it off! I deserve this one, but I'm fed up with getting *tsuris* from you on preventable faux pas. Why didn't you warn me?"

"Not my job," Asti said, smugly. "Why didn't the Dumbstone do it? She's the one who sees the future."

"Because he was meant to do it," Kelsa said. "He was hungry! You ought to be more compassionate about that. How can you think clearly on an empty stomach?"

"Thanks a bunch, Kelsa." I wasn't that grateful. I was smarting at the humiliation. The Toadies in the wall were staring at me in open admiration.

"He ought to live more in the life of the mind," Payge said.

"If I was made of paper, that would be easy," I grumbled.

"What can we do about the people who are waiting to eat?" Calypsa asked, politely.

"We're not here to solve all their problems," I said.

"But that *is* what we do," Kelsa said.

"Not today."

"Oh, but, Aahz, we must!" Calypsa pleaded.

I gave in.

"Can I get raw materials from somewhere else?" I asked Hylida.

She spread her hands sadly. "There are no other supplies, I am afraid. The crops have been bad, and we have few farmers who bring their surplus into the city."

Now I felt really bad. I got up, reaching for the D-hopper in my pocket. "I know. There's a good pizza place in the Bazaar. They deliver. They can be here in half an hour. I'll be back. What do you think, about a hundred pies?"

"My goodness, a Pervect who sees beyond his own needs!" Chin-Hwag exclaimed. "Do you actually feel shame? I am impressed."

"Shut up, sister," I said. "I may need your help, but you don't get to slam my character."

"Forgive me! I have never before met a Pervect who had one!"

I turned my back on her and set the D-hopper for Deva.

"Don't go," Asti said, just before I hit the button. "I'll feed them. Let them drink from me. They will find enough sustenance to strengthen them for a week."

Hylida bowed deeply to the shining goblet. "That will help us mightily. We usually cannot afford more than basic needs."

"That doesn't make sense," I said. "If you have Chin-Hwag, and she'll cough up whatever you need, then why are you so desperate?"

Hylida smiled. It was a saint's smile. I could see why the people around there worshiped her. "It is not money we need here, but heart. The people here are poor. They can't afford new clothes, or household goods, or even wigs."

"Wigs?"

"Oh, yes. They are a status symbol in Toa. We cannot ask Chin-Hwag for these things. A sudden influx of too much money would only cause confusion and break down the bounds of the current society, with nothing to replace it. In measured amounts, they still strive to care for themselves. It is a matter of pride."

Asti seemed to square her shoulders.

"Let's get this over with," she said. "I haven't had to pitch in like this since the cooks burned the Grand Trompier's wedding feast in the palace of Belaj."

But before the soup-line could begin, the jingle of metal and the thundering of hoofbeats made the Toadies leap up.

"Run away!" they shouted.

"What's the problem?" I asked. Hylida looked grave.

"The tax collectors are here," she said.

Chapter 19

INTO THE SUDDENLY-CLEARED square galloped a troop of riders. The steeds, pulling to a halt in a cloud of dust, looked like giant blue newts, saddled and bridled with scaly leather trimmed with gold. The barding protecting their soft underbellies was studded with hooked spikes. The armored and helmeted Toadies mounted on their backs brandished spears with hooks on the ends like the canes vaudeville theater owners used to yank unsuccessful acts off stage. One of them caught a little Toady woman in pink by the neck. They hauled her in.

"Tax time!" he shouted gleefully.

"I don't have any money!" the woman protested. "Please let me go!"

I started outside. I was twice the size of any of the soldiers. I could get her free. Hylida grabbed my arm with a virtually weightless claw.

"Do not interfere," she said. "It only makes it worse."

The guards dragged their prisoner before the most elaborately-dressed Toady, one wearing a huge blond wig that stuck out from underneath his helmet like a cloud of steel wool.

"Name?"

"Ranax, sir," the woman sobbed.

The captain took a small plastic tablet from his saddlebag and jabbed at the screen with a stylus. It hummed and clicked, and a plastic strip rolled out of the top.

"Ranax. Your family owes six silver pieces!" The tablet chittered, and the strip grew to about three inches. He tore it off and thrust it toward her. The little female took it in trembling hands.

"I...I will have to go home for the money, sir!"

The captain aimed a finger, and the guards dropped her from the hook. The Toady woman waddled out of the square as fast as her thick little legs would carry her. The guards went after an elderly male.

I heard a minor hubbub behind me. Ranax wriggled in through one of the large holes in the wall, and was kneeling before Sister Hylida and Chin-Hwag. She must have gone around the corner and come back through the rat's maze of alleys.

"Let me see, six silver pieces, at the current rate of exchange…" the Purse said, clicking the beads on her strings together like an abacus. "*Hack!* Ugh! There you are." She opened her mouth and spat a tiny gold coin into Ranax's outstretched hand. "Don't drop it!"

"No, I will not. Thank you, sister!" Ranax left the way she came. As she exited, two more of the tax-collectors' victims squirmed inside. For the next few hours, Chin-Hwag coughed up a mix of small coins to satisfy the demands. The captain read off his demands from the little screen in silver, but the Purse produced only gold coins, some so small they could get lost underneath my fingernails. The Toadies clutched them and ran out to pay.

"How long does this go on?" I asked.

"Until they have checked off everyone on the list," Hylida said. Her eyes widened. "Oh, hide!" she said, suddenly. "They are coming this way!"

The Toadies still in the room dove for one of the exits. Tananda, Calypsa and I grabbed up the Hoard and followed them, but we weren't fast enough. The armored newts spotted us. They bellowed. Their riders turned to see what they were looking at.

"Strangers!"

"Take them!" the captain shouted.

Waving their hooks, a couple of the biggest Toadies turned their newts toward me. I ducked as they galloped past. When I sprang up again, I saw they had hooked one another. I grinned, but it didn't last for long. Another soldier came thundering my way, spear at the ready.

"Oil, fast," I ordered Asti. "Make it slippery."

"What? All right." The Cup filled with a viscous green liquid. I tossed it out under the feet of the onrushing lizard. Its beady eyes widened, but it was too late to backpedal. Its front feet slid forward, with the back feet still windmilling. It did a respectable death spiral, whirling with its head between its feet. I would have awarded them six points, but the rider went flying into the nearest tent. It collapsed under him.

"Next time keep your knees clenched!" I jeered at him.

I felt a poking sensation at my back. I turned to see a dozen other soldiers, still securely in their saddles, pointing spears at my back. Slowly, I lifted my hands in surrender.

They had already rounded up Calypsa and Tananda. I clutched Asti, hoping that she would have the sense to keep her lip zipped. All I needed was to have the treasures confiscated when we were so close to having collected the whole set.

"How dare you assault my officers?" the captain asked, staring down at me. "I am Captain Horunkus of the Royal Collection Agency!"

"Well, Horunkus, if someone told you that wig made you look like Shirley Temple, you ought to sue them," I advised. "I am Aahz, Royal Magician of the Palace of Vaudeville!"

"A royal wizard," he said, but he didn't sound too impressed. His eyes were pinned on Asti and Payge. "You are strangers! *Rich* strangers."

"What about it?" I snarled, flexing a claw or two. "Try and take these, and we'll make your lives miserable. Didn't you see how we bested half a dozen of your best men?"

"I did notice…Er, did you not know that to visit this esteemed city of Sri Port, you must pay a visitor tax? You must have a tourist visa to be here!"

"No one sold us one at the gates," I said. That was true, after all.

I could see him making a mental note that the excise officers manning the gates were to be awarded one horse-whipping each, or whatever penalty they used around there. Horunkus curled his upper lip.

"Well, then, I will collect it, so you do not have to go to the trouble of returning to the gate where you entered." He wrote energetically on the electronic tablet in his hands. "Yes. Half a gold piece each, please."

The 'please' was punctuated with a jab from the spears.

"Watch it, buddy!" I snarled. "I can't reach my wallet if you're poking me." I hastily stuffed Asti back in her bag, and tucked Payge under my arm. I tried to be discreet about the contents of my purse, but this Toady must have had some Deveel blood in him. At the chink of coin, he perked up still further.

"You are also carrying goods of more than five gold pieces in value. Those artifacts in your possession are worth more than that, are they not?"

"What if they are?" I asked.

"Please submit an estimate of their current market value."

"Why, they are priceless!" Calypsa said. "Do you not know that this is the great sword..."

"Hsst!" I hissed at her. "Ix-nay on the eech-spay!"

Her potion-based language talent struggled for a moment, but enlightenment finally dawned upon her face. "I am so sorry, Aahz!" she said. "I wished but to extol the virtues..."

"Don't extol. Don't talk. They're gold-plated goodies, Horunk," I said. "Street value, about five gold pieces each. The sword's just a letter opener. Nothing special. In the markets of Bupkis, you can find stuff like this in every stall."

"Lying to me will cause the items to be confiscated at once!" Horunkus boomed, as much as an overgrown toad can boom.

"You try and take them," I said, showing all my teeth. The soldiers holding the spears on me backed up a pace.

"You're the ones who are armed," the captain roared at them. "Keep him under guard!"

"I swear on my mother's grave, Horunk, these are junk!" I said.

"Who are you calling junk?" Ersatz boomed.

"Who said that?" the captain demanded, looking around.

"She did," I said, pointing at Tananda. "She's a ventriloquist. She's an entertainer who travels with me to amuse me."

"Take the goods into safe-keeping," Horunkus said. "If they lack value, as you say they do, then they will fail the standard assay test."

"You can't take them!" Calypsa brayed.

"Why not?" Horunkus asked.

"I thought I told you to zip it!" I whispered to her. "Now, captain," I said, my voice at its most silky, "you wouldn't want it getting around that Sri Port's officers rob travelers under the guise of determining the value of the goods they're carrying, do you? That'd dry up your import stream in a matter of weeks."

I didn't think I had come across the only honest politician I had ever met. He had almost certainly been on the edge of doing exactly that. I wanted him to know that I knew, and that unless he locked me and my friends up, we'd certainly spread the word. Horunkus didn't want to be responsible for losing any part of the revenue coming in, if Hylida's description was accurate. Horunkus's warty brow drew down under the ridiculous blond wig.

"Of course we are honest with travelers!" Horunkus protested, a little too readily. "I will estimate the market value myself, then. Five gold pieces each, times five items." The tape rolled up and curled over the top of the tablet. "And you say that they come from this Bum-kiss?"

"Bupkis," I corrected him. "But for you, Bum-kiss is appropriate."

He didn't get the insult. "Then you are also subject to import tax. That is another seventeen percent. Payable on demand." He tapped some more numbers into his machine. "And there will be a transportation tax of four gold pieces each…"

"We *walked*."

"Hmm. Road use tax. You used the roads, I assume?" He peered at me over the top of his tablet.

"We're magicians! We came in by magik!"

"Right here? To this space?"

"I saw them come through the market," a small Toady said, running up to Horunkus's stirrup. He made a face at me and stuck out my tongue. It was Shagul, the kid Kelsa had pointed out to me. If I could have reached the little brat at that moment, I would have wrung his neck, but two of the soldiers poked me in the neck with their spears. "One of them's a soothsayer! She told me to go and do my homework!"

"I see," Horunkus said, and pursed his mouth. "Well, then, you will need a permit for fortunetelling."

"We're not opening up shop here!"

"But it sounds like you have already delved into other people's business here."

"It was just a passing remark."

"And penalty for humil...I mean, assaulting the guard. Unless you would rather serve time in the Royal Penitentiary instead?"

The guy had absolutely no sense of humor. "Aw, come on, it was just a little rough-housing!"

"Disturbing the peace," Horunkus said, writing more on the tablet in his hands. I was getting more and more torqued off as the strip on the top of the tablet grew longer.

"That comes to a total of thirty gold pieces, eight silver. Payable upon demand." He tore off the strip and handed it to me.

"You're out of your mind," I informed him, looking over the list of charges.

"Insults! Do you wish me to add another penalty, for insulting one of His Lofty Monarch's officers?"

Tananda and Calypsa looked at me. It was hard to argue that he had caught us red, or rather, gold-handed, since we were standing there holding the equivalent of an emperor's annual wages. I could have gotten out of there with the D-hopper, and Tananda had enough magik to travel the dimensions herself, but we would have had to leave Calypsa by herself in the middle of a troop of unfriendlies. As much as the alternative pained me, I couldn't do that. I reached for my wallet. Horunkus's flunky stuck out his palm.

Every coin I had to part with was a death knell to my heart. Every shining little disk seemed to cry out to me, "Don't send me away!" I gritted my teeth, because hesitating seemed to bring me out in a rash of jab marks from the guards' swords. One by one, I counted out the coins. Some of them had been handsomely milled and beautifully struck; others were more timeworn, but precious for their experience in the universe. It was more painful than I could stand.

"That's thirty," the captain said. "Eight silver pieces."

I felt around in my scrip. I had four silver pieces and a handful of coppers. I balanced them in my hand against the one remaining gold piece I had.

"Would you take an IOU?" I asked hopefully.

"I will take cash!"

Very reluctantly, I held out the 31st gold piece. The captain snatched it from me and dumped all the coins into a heavy leather pouch at his saddlebow.

"Thank you, stranger," Horunkus said, signing to his men to lower their spears. "Welcome to Sri Port. I hope you enjoy your stay here."

"Hey, wait a minute, what about my change?"

Horunkus gave me an 'are you out of your mind?' look. "I could add on a 'Questioning the authority of the Majaranarana' tax," he said, smugly.

"That's it," I breathed, my ire rising. This guy was due for a clobbering, no matter what it cost me later.

"Yes, that is it," the nun said, stepping in between us and holding out a minuscule handful of coins. "Here is the mission's tax payment for the week. Thank you, gentlemen." She turned me away from the soldiers and hurried us inside.

"Well, he squeezed us for everything we had," I said, feeling glum.

"I've still got a handful of silver. That ought to hold us for a while," Tananda said.

"I don't like going out without walking-around money," I retorted, peevishly.

"At least the Hoard is safe," Calypsa said. She hugged Ersatz.

"Really, wench," the Sword said, sounding embarrassed.

"Safe for now," I said, with a look over my shoulder at the departing troops. "I doubt that's the end of it. Horunkus is going to go back and report what he saw. I'll bet you my two front teeth that before we get out of here there'll be an attack by 'footpads,' not affiliated with the government, of course. The longer we stay here, the more likely the Hoard's going to be in the Majaranarana's treasury sooner or later."

"We'd better get out of here, then," Tananda said. "This place is indefensible."

"Ah, me," Sister Hylida said. "This never happened when I was at the Abbey of the Shaor Ming. Because we prayed for anyone who needed us, we were never asked for taxes or other fees."

"So nobody is supposed to squeeze the Shaor Ming?" I asked.

"Yes," Hylida said, surprised. "How did you know?"

"Lucky guess," I said. I jingled my wallet grimly. It was too light. I felt like I had just lost my oldest friends—thirty-one of them.

"Well, I would say it's just about time for you to ask Chin-Hwag for your fee," Asti's voice broke into my thoughts.

Her taunting tone was just what it took to raise my dudgeon to its highest setting. I turned to the Purse, cradled protectively in the Abbess's arms. Everyone was watching me. I took in a deep breath, but it whooshed out of me like the air from a punctured balloon. I just couldn't do it, not in the face of the shocking poverty surrounding me. Besides, I wanted to negotiate in private.

"Fee?" The Purse's mouth moved, the drawstrings wagging like skinny mustaches. "I have no objection. If my friend

Ersatz has agreed on a fee, I will pay it, but not a dust mote more. How much was it?"

I had a figure in mind, but I wasn't going to announce it until the Sword and I had a chance to confer.

"This job ain't over yet," I said, sidestepping briskly. "You saw what just happened. I don't know how many more expenses I'm going to incur."

The Abbess seemed to read my mind.

"I see. You need to take Chin-Hwag with you. That is fine. I have all that I need. Take her. Now. It is all right."

"But the tax collector just took everything you had," I said. "You're flat broke."

Hylida gave me a serene smile.

"I managed to get along before she was here. I'll get along after she is gone. She has been a wonderful help."

"I have been glad to help one who is a true saint in her time," Chin-Hwag said. "You are so unselfish. Never did you ask for anything for yourself. I feel honored to have been in your service."

Hylida, very moved, came up to touch the Purse.

"You have been a good friend to me and my flock," she said. "Thank you for giving me confidence when my faith was waning."

"Your faith was what made me happy to contribute to your cause," Chin-Hwag said. "I wish more of my protégés were so generous with themselves and their efforts. How often people forget that material things are not what is truly important in this world."

The mutual-admiration society meeting was beginning to get on my nerves. The more the Abbess and the Purse praised each other for selflessness, the stronger the feeling I got that maybe, just maybe, my personal priorities were the ones that needed changing. It's not really like I needed the money. The fact that I didn't have any with me didn't mean I was tapped out, not by a long chalk. It'd been forever since a hundred gold pieces changed the decimal place in my bank account. One

thing working with Skeeve had done was to make me and all
the other members of M.Y.T.H., Inc. very rich. Not disgust-
ingly, mind-blowingly, fountains of gold rich, but plenty
wealthy enough to buy the hotel if the waiter won't mix your
drink the way you want it.

Hylida turned her brilliant gaze to me.

"I am sure you will be moderate in your requests of my
dear friend. You strike me as a good person, in spite of your
bluster. Take good care of her."

"Uh...thanks," I said. I accepted the Purse, who looked
up at me skeptically. "We'll do the right thing with her."

"We shall all seek to live up to your example," Ersatz said,
dipping his eyes. "Noble lady, I feel enriched for having met
you."

"Your name is written in gold in my annals," Payge said.
"In future I will advise readers who need a moral lesson to
peruse your story."

Buirnie let out a blast that drew attention to him. His personal spotlight set him in the most favorable light. "I'll write a
song about you. All royalties will benefit your mission."

"Why, thank you," Hylida said. "That is very generous of
you."

I started to say something sarcastic, but Tananda cleared
her throat.

"Now, if there's no more interference," Asti said, "I have
some people to feed. Do you mind making them all line up?"

Calypsa and I were both champing at the bit to get out, but
every time I thought of interrupting Asti's soup line, I found I
just couldn't do it. Hungry Toadies came from everywhere to
join the line. Whatever the Cup was serving must have been
pretty good, because none of them wanted to let go of her
even when the bowl was empty.

"All right," the Cup said, faintly, as the last of the Toadies
staggered out of the door into the night, replete. "Let's go."

"Right," I said. I glanced down at Chin-Hwag. "You have any
special implements, gizmos or containers you need us to pack?"

"No," she said cheerfully. "Just stick me in your knapsack anywhere. Not in your belt. I do not wish to be seen by the locals. It might tempt them too much. They have been good so far. As long as all of them are poor, then no one is above anyone else."

Buirnie let out a whistle of protest. "You deserve something, even a bag."

"Pah. I am already a bag. You don't put a bag in a bag. I don't need anything. I have lived in behind a broken plaster wall for thirty years."

"You can share my satchel," the Book said.

The embroidery rolled in his direction. "That's nice of you, but it doesn't look like there is much room."

"It is kind of snug," the Book agreed. "But I would be honored if you would like to room with me."

"Or me!" Buirnie said. "Why, I have lots of luggage. You can have whatever bag you choose!"

"No, thank you. I think I will fit in Aahz's purse."

"Fine," I said. "Let's just get out of here, all right?" I pulled open my poke and extracted the tax collector's ticket from it. "C'mon."

"Do not touch me with that," Chin-Hwag said, alarmed. "I am allergic to plastic."

"You have an *allergy*?" I asked in disbelief.

"There was no plastic in the time that I was made. Nor several other modern materials, either. That is why I have been glad to be here in this humble place."

"Suit yourself," I said, tossing the ticket into a trash barrel next to the food preparation area. "Everyone ready?"

A ragged Toady came running into the mission. He collapsed at Hylida's feet.

"The Majaranarana's men are coming back!"

Chapter 20

THE ARMED NEWTS came galumphing into the shabby square.

"There are a lot more of them than before," Tananda said, peering over my shoulder. She was holding Kelsa's bag and Buirnie's case. "We need to *bamf* out of here ASAP. Calypsa, hurry!"

"You!" Horunkus shouted, spotting me in the doorway. "Halt! Stay where you are!"

I sprang back into the mission, glancing around for Calypsa. She was there, but she'd picked up a few friends. A number of the tax collector's men had sneaked in through the holes in the wall. They surrounded the Walt with lowered spears. Another bunch had rounded up Hylida and her worshipers. Two of the armored Toadies came up to take Tananda by the elbows.

Horunkus swung down from his mount and swaggered over to me. I stuck the purse in my belt to disguise it.

"Nobody open your mouth," I warned them, hoping the Majaranarana's men hadn't noticed the animated drum stand or the flying light. "Let me do the talking." I gave the captain my most ingratiating smile. "Long time no see! What can we do for you, gentlemen?"

The blond bewigged official puffed himself up.

"I have come to collect the taxes. There are more fees you visitors must pay. Many more fees."

I had just about reached the limit of emotional range I could handle, almost being ashamed of being greedy in the face of the selflessness of this dimension's own Mother Teresa, and having my butt kicked around the block by the Hoard over my shortcomings, on top of already almost emptying my pockets for this blowhard. I leaned toward him, my teeth gritted.

"Forget it," I said. "I've already coughed up enough."

"Then we start confiscating things." He eyed the treasures distributed among us. "I think I'll start with that flute."

"Oh, yeah?" I asked. "Confiscate this!"

I hauled off and socked him in the jaw. Horunkus went flying, but he had brought plenty of backup.

Before I even dropped my fist, I had five hulking Toadies on my back. They were more unwieldy than heavy. I bent my knees and flipped two of them off over my head. They landed on their backs with a crash. Three to go.

Twenty or thirty of Hylida's flock jumped in and started hitting the fallen with bowls, rocks, anything they could pick up.

"Please!" the little Abbess cried, surrounded by four or five newtsmen, who were in turn surrounded by more worshipers trying to get her free. "Violence never solved anything!"

"It's sure a handy timesaver, sister!" I shouted.

I swung in a circle. Two of the Toadies stumbled off. I backed the other three into the wall. Half the plaster crumbled off on their heads. One of them tried pounding on my head. I grabbed his wrist and flipped him overhand. He went sailing through the air.

SPLASH!

The Toady guard landed in the pot of boiling stew.

"Auggh!" he shouted, surfacing. He leaped out and dashed out the door.

"Waste of good food," I commented.

Tananda was engaged in a tug of war. Two teams of Toady guards were pulling at her shoulder bags from either side. She was stretched between them like a prisoner about to be torn apart by wild horses. Buirnie's drummer and lighting guy kicked and battered at the guards trying to steal their boss. The Fife himself was shrieking with fear.

"Don't let them touch me! Roadies! Help!"

"Help!" Kelsa shouted. "These beasts have bad karma!"

I grabbed up a handy bowl and heaved it. It hit the lead guard on the Buirnie side smack in the face. He dropped like a stone. With expressions that said that the following action was against their better judgment, a dozen more lowered their spears and charged at me.

"What do you have that they don't like?" I asked Asti.

"I've barely recovered from feeding the five thousand!" she protested.

"Save the blather!"

"Oh, very well!"

A blue liquid bubbled out of her bowl and dribbled onto the floor. It smelled like industrial-grade soap. I brandished it at the charging guards. The leaders windmilled to a stop, and fell back on the spears of their comrades. I sloshed more of the blue stuff toward them. They shrieked and ran in the opposite direction.

"Thanks!" Tananda said, rubbing her shoulders. "My goodness, I haven't had to deal with so many aggressive males since Frat Night in Imper."

"Slumming again?" I said dryly. She winked. "What was that stuff?" I asked Asti.

"Commercial dessicant," Asti said, as the liquid immediately dried to a crust on the floor. "These creatures need their skins to stay very moist, or it cracks."

I grinned. "No wonder they don't appreciate the beauty of scales like mine."

"NOBODY appreciates beauty like yours except those who are totally blind!"

Tanda went on guard.

"Look out!"

The warning was unnecessary. I knew that at least eight of the guards were within a few feet of me.

I spun, brandishing Asti.

"You guys really have to oil your armor if you want to sneak up on someone," I suggested, sloshing them with the contents of Asti's bowl. They batted at the stuff with both hands, then looked at their hands in horror. The webs between their fingers shrank noticeably.

"Agh! Dry skin! Dry skin!"

They backed away from me. I followed, still flinging sludge. They fled, calling for help. I laughed at them and shouldered aside the curtain leading to the courtyard.

My eyes widened. The entire square was full of soldiers. At the rear was a gigantic carriage drawn by four matched newts. In it, a scrawny little guy wearing a rusty red wig bigger than his whole body.

"What is wrong with you?" the wizened little guy yelled at the soldiers. "Take them! Bring me the treasures!"

Hylida dropped to her knees. Most of her flock followed suit. "That's the Majaranarana!"

"Yield to me!" he shrieked, whipping his newts until they charged us. "I want the gold!"

The soldiers shouted. "For the Majaranarana!"

Buirnie outshouted them. The Fife let out a deafening trill that turned my ears inside out. The noise set the newts bucking and tossing their heads. Riders were thrown off their backs, including the Majaranarana, whose carriage flipped wheels-up as the four beasts tried to flee in several directions at once. The riders tried to grab their mounts, but the panicked lizards fled out of the square.

Klik, the spotlight, flew up out of reach and shone a blinding beam down on his boss, as Zildie started beating a martial rhythm. Buirnie blasted out a war song.

I kept spattering soldiers with Asti's special brew. Tananda flitted from guard, deftly kicking the spears out of their hands or knocking them flying with a stewpot on a chain she had picked up from Hylida's kitchen.

Our defiance of the tax authority had awoken something in the Toadies of the Abbey. They were fighting back, to the astonishment of the soldiers, who obviously were used to bullying them whenever they felt like it. The armored males defended themselves at bay or cowered with their hands over their heads as gangs of the neighborhood poor battered at them with pots, pans, rocks, unripe fruit, spoiled food and garbage. The soldiers might have been better armed, but they were vastly outnumbered. It looked like a cross between a soccer riot and the great pie fight. Poor Hylida stood huddled against the front wall of her mission, shouting at people to calm down and stop fighting. It was no use. Her followers were fed up with their treatment, and were taking probably their one and only opportunity in their lives to fight back. I tried to get to her, but I spotted Calypsa in the middle of a ring of soldiers who were still trying to follow their master's orders and seize the Hoard. She looked terrified. I started throwing guards out of my way to get to her.

"Draw me!" Ersatz bellowed at her. "Come on, lass! Defend yourself! Draw me!"

Almost in a trance, Calypsa dragged the brand over her head. "Now what?"

"Wield me, lass!" he exclaimed. "I will guide you! Your dancer's wiles are better than a trained fencer's. Forward with right foot! Bring me around, cut upward! Slash right! Good, lass!" he called out, as the lead guard's head went bounding across the floor. "Quick, two-step to the right, *plunge* me behind your back! No, POINT first. *Point first!*"

"Ugggh!"

Calypsa turned gracefully on the tip of one toe and found herself staring at the biggest of the thugs, arms crossed over a belly-wound that I could tell was fatal.

"She doesn't need you," Asti said.

Ersatz shouted orders, and Calypsa followed them. She swung and danced, and the long, blue blade flashed in the sun like a pinwheel. To my surprise, the guards began to fall back.

"You're right," I said. "I'll be dipped in…"

"Help, aid, assistance!" Payge's soft voice suddenly exclaimed, from my other side.

I felt something tugging at the straps of the shoulder bag. I tugged back, and found myself looking into the beady eyes of the Majaranarana.

"Give that to me, or die," he said, showing his rows of jagged little teeth. At his back were thirty soldiers, most of them looking pretty beaten up. Still, I couldn't take on thirty of them. Very slowly, I extended the book bag to him.

"That's better," the scrawny ruler said, flipping open the top and fondling Payge's spine. Did I imagine it, or did the Book shudder? "Horunkus, give him the demand."

The captain cleared his throat importantly and raised his electronic tablet. "You underquoted the value of the goods which you brought into the Imperial city of Sri Port, and must pay five thousand gold coins per item that you undervalued."

"Five tho—Not a chance!" I snarled.

Horunkus grinned evilly. "Furthermore, there is a penalty of seven hundred gold coins per item for lying to officials. Or, if you cannot produce the cash," he leered at me over the keypad, "you can surrender said goods into the hands of the tax authority of the Majaranarana Taricho. Immediately." With a flourish, he tore off the length of plastic tape and handed it to me. The soldiers loomed closer in anticipation.

"You want gold?" I asked. "I'll give you gold."

I grinned at the Toady, then took the Purse out of my belt and very deliberately stuck the ticket he had given me in Chin-Hwah's mouth.

The Purse protested.

"No, don't you dare, you Perv—BLEAAAAAAGHH!"

A fountain of coins spurted up out of the pouch sitting on my palm. The Majaranarana's eyes widened, and he threw himself at the growing river of coins. Horunkus, less of a fool than his master, made a grab for the Purse itself. I slugged him with a kidney punch. He turned, weakly, torn between the lust for revenge or greed. Greed won. He started trying to catch coins as they fell from the sky. The plume of glittering gold rose higher. Soldiers dropped their weapons and joined in the coin-catch. I turned and shielded my head so I didn't get a faceful of hard little disks. The roar of the fountain grew louder and louder.

After what seemed like an hour, the deafening rain of coins came to a halt.

"I feel unwell," Chin-Hwag announced weakly.

I looked around. The square had fallen silent. I couldn't see the Majaranarana or any of his men anywhere. Calypsa stood over a couple of bodies, covered with blood. Ersatz was clutched in both of her hands. I grabbed her elbow and hauled her into the doorway of the mission. She looked dazed.

"I defeated two guards!" Calypsa said, over and over again. Tananda jumped down from a rooftop and piled in after us.

"Nice work, too," Tanda said, wiping the Walt girl's face with a rag. "None of this blood is yours. You were terrific! I'd never have dreamed you have never held a sword before."

"I never lose," Ersatz said, with no attempt at modesty, as Tananda rubbed him down and restored him to the scabbard on the unprotesting Walt's back. "But the lass has innate talent. Had she been trained since birth there'd be no army could stand against her, outnumbered or no. Ah, once we can begin training you, you will be legendary. Let us continue against the foe. They shall not take us by force!"

"Forget it," I interrupted them. I stood aside and held open the curtain so they could see. "It's over."

Chin-Hwag's gold eruption had buried half the square. Hylida's parishioners stood flattened against the crumbling walls of the surrounding buildings. Except for our breathing, the whole square was quiet as a tomb.

I stared at the heap of coins, piled higher than my head. I had never seen so much money in all my life. *No* king had a treasury like that. It was astonishing. It was *unreal.*

"That," I said hoarsely, "is the most beautiful thing I have ever seen in my life."

Everyone gazed at it, their shoulders heaving, eyes gleaming.

"Now, let us behave with moderation," Hylida said, addressing her flock with her hands raised. "Please, show restraint..."

The townsfolk stared at the pile of gold for perhaps three seconds, then they dove at it, grabbing coins off the heap, stuffing them into their pockets, purses, bras, hats, whatever would hold anything, and making off with it before anyone stopped them. Not that there was anyone to stop them at the moment. The guards were all gone.

The Abbess shook her head sadly. "After all my work. The Majaranarana's going to be angry."

"Afraid not," I said. I pointed. The swiftly-diminishing pile of coins in the center had melted away to the point where the bodies buried underneath it were visible. Hylida came to see. She gasped.

"The Majaranarana! We...we killed him!"

A couple of the Toadies gawked up at her.

"She's the one! She is responsible!"

The crowd surged around her, shouting and waving their arms. A few of the guards, who had sneaked back into the square to collect some of the gold and looked shocked to see their monarch flattened on the ground, drew their swords and homed in on the little abbess.

"Save her," Calypsa begged, as I pulled back toward the shelter of the mission.

"It'll should all right," Chin-Hwag said. "This has been coming for a long time. The city could descend into anarchy, but it has been trending that way for a long while. There might be a few guilty consciences, but Hylida is innocent. They shouldn't harm her. I am *fairly* certain." The Purse sounded uncertain.

"Hmmm." I pushed my way into the middle of the crowd and held Hylida's hand up over her head like a championship boxer.

"She's the one! She caused the miracle! She brought the shower of gold to punish the greedy despot!"

"Huh?"

I scooped up the hairpiece that had fallen off the deceased monarch, and plunked it on the head of the confused Sister Hylida. "What you need is the hair of the frog that fit you," I said. I turned to the crowd. "She freed you from the tyrant!"

The Toadies swarmed forward, chanting. At the sight of the wig on her head, even the guards joined in the jubilation.

"Hylida saved us from the tyrant! Hy-li-da! Hy-li-da! She saved us from poverty. Hy-li-da! Hy-li-da!"

The little Abbess shouted protests, but the crowd surged in around us. They hoisted her to their shoulders and marched out of the square, still chanting. I watched them go.

"Let's get out of here," I said to the others.

"Where?" Tananda asked.

"Anywhere but here. I need a good night's sleep, and I won't get it if any of them decides they want us in on the coronation ceremony, or whatever they're going to do once they reach the palace."

"But what about poor Hylida!" Calypsa said. "They will tear her apart."

"No, kid," I said. "She's just become a legendary hero. Unless you want to be one, too, minus one grandfather, we've got to move. The crowd looks ready for a celebration that will last a week, minimum."

"Are you sure?"

"I am," Kelsa and the book said at once.

"Look here," Kelsa and the book said at the same time. They glared at each other.

"They're carrying her, and the crowds are enormous, and you can't believe...!"

"The fated day has come to pass...!"

"*One* of you tell it," I said. "Payge, talk."

"I don't talk, I narrate," Payge said sourly. "Turn to page 836, and see. I have just felt an illumination sprout. I think it will tell you all you need to know."

I hauled the heavy cover over and thumbed through the heavily-illustrated pages until I found the indicated folio. On a page that began with an ornate capital I, for "In the heretofore blighted city of Sri Port, the reign of the tyrant Majaranarana Taricho came to pass, in the sacred enclosure of the mission of the Banana God Frojti. Grave was the suffering of the

people of Toa, eased only by the Lady High Lida, whose kindness was as fragrant as the flowers."

"You need an editor," I groaned.

"No commentary, please," Payge said. "I record the ver-
nacular."

I continued reading. "The Majaranarana threatened the Lady
High Lida with imprisonment and torture to endure seven years
if she did not give him treasure. Three strangers appeared from
nowhere to her aid. A mighty battle was fought between the
two sides. At the end of this battle, the Majaranarana was
buried in a shower of gold. The holy mother superior High
Lida flew overhead to reassure the masses that all would be
well. She was acclaimed ruler of the region, and reigned for
forty years in peace with her people and her neighbors."

"And she lived happily ever after," Calypsa said, with a
happy sigh. "I am glad."

"There they are!" a voice cried. "The holy ones who helped
our Hylida defeat the tyrant!"

A crowd of Toadies came running back into the square,
beaming. They held dozens of flower garlands, and looked as
though they intended to festoon us thoroughly. Tananda threw
her arms around me. I grabbed Calypsa by the shoulder and
thumbed the stud on the D-hopper.

Chapter 21

"WHERE ARE WE?" Calypsa asked, looking around at the foul-smelling room. "Who are they?" She asked, pointing at the reptilian bodies on the floor. "Are they all right? What are we doing here?"

"Bonhomme," I replied, curtly. "Bonhomies. Yes. Drunk is just about their natural state of being. They're friendly, and this is a safe place to get some rest and work out what we're doing next. Any other questions on this test?"

She recoiled slightly then held her chin up proudly. "That is all I require to know for the moment, thank you."

"Good," I said.

"I have a bone to pick with you, Pervert," Chin-Hwag said. "What gave you the idea to thrust the plastic ticket down my throat?"

"I've been around a while," I said modestly. "There are a lot of dimensions that use a new gizmo that originated in Zoorik, I said, modestly. "You stick a plastic card in this hole in the wall, and it spews out cash. It just made sense."

"This is quite modern?" Chin-Hwag asked.

"Pretty much."

"Hmm. Then someone in the past must have seen me suffering my malady. You must promise me not to do that again!"

"If you cough up—excuse the expression—what the Hoard owes me, then I won't have to."

"I have already said I will make good on my fellow Hoarder's debt," Chin-Hwag said, her embroidery contracting into a sour expression.

"The overthrow of that miserable Toady might well have happened years before, if you had acted in a more assertive fashion," Ersatz said critically. "Why didn't you?"

"You question me?" Chin-Hwag said, slitting her eyes in annoyance. But she answered in a civil fashion. "She did not want me to. I have been trying years to persuade her that she was in a position to take over and rule as a benevolent queen. It was your precipitate arrival, and your sickening behavior."

"I am not the one who made you suck plastic," Ersatz said.

"You told him my weakness!"

"You told me yourself," I snapped. "Some of us mortals are capable of putting two and two together, you know."

"So they keep telling me," Chin-Hwag said, with a weary sigh. "Sums are only one of the things that all of you keep getting wrong."

Now, there's about three dozen rooms in this place. Find one that's empty and get a little shut-eye. The food's mostly processed carbohydrates, but there's a lot of it, and no one will mind if you help yourself. The booze is community property, but I paid for plenty of it when I was here last."

"But, Aahz, we cannot rest now!" Calypsa said. "With Chin-Hwag, we lack only one of the great treasures."

"Aren't you tired?" Tananda asked her, in a soothing voice. She wrapped an arm around the girl's shoulders. "Tell her, Ersatz. A warrior is only as good as her preparation."

"Indeed, yes, wench," the Sword said. "Come, let us find a place where you may settle down and clean my blade, and I shall tell you the story of the battle of Corepos."

"And I will give you a potion in case that boring old saga doesn't manage to put you to sleep," Asti promised.

"But there's a great party going on here!" Buirnie exclaimed.

"Knock yourself out," I said. "I'm going to bed."

A warm presence wrapped itself around me and intruded itself into my dreams.

"Aahz," a soft voice said.

"Mmph."

"Aahz. Get up. You'll want to get in this."

"Too tired," I said. "Maybe later, sweetheart." Fingers played with my left ear. I smiled. The fingers took a firmer hold, then twisted firmly. I sat bolt upright, outraged. "What's going on here?"

Tananda sat up, looking pleased. "There, I said you weren't too hung over to wake up."

"Said who?"

"Come on. I think Calypsa's getting confused."

"What now?"

I followed Tananda's curves as they undulated through knots of Bonhomies blinking against the invasion of daylight. Drinking was on again, as the sun had hoisted its bleary red self over the yard arm.

"What time is it?"

"Noonish," Tananda said. "Hurry. I'm not making much headway with them."

"With who?"

In the small room behind the frat bar that Calypsa had chosen as her dormitory for the night, some kind of meeting was going on. The members of the Golden Hoard were arranged in a circle. Klik broadcast a bright light on them, making them gleam like a Pervect's wildest dreams of avarice. Calypsa sat behind Ersatz, at a respectful remove in the shadows.

"What is going on?"

"A conference of war," Chin-Hwag said.

"What for?"

"We do not care for your strategy, and we are discussing our own."

"WHAT?"

"Sweetie-baby," Buirnie said, placatingly, "we just don't dig your idea. It's not really us, if you know what I mean. I mean, Aahz! You can't just hand us over to an evil wizard like a collection of..."

"Artifacts," Payge said, in his gentle voice.

"Why the hell not? Give me one good reason why?"

"With only two days remaining to Calypso's execution, we have no time to lose," Asti said. "I would expect even a mortal with your recalcitrant character to understand. Now, please sit down so we can get on with our strategy."

"We are not yet a full complement," Chin-Hwag reminded them.

"Who's missing, again?" Buirnie asked.

"The Ring," Ersatz said at once. "He is the only member of our coterie we have not yet located."

"I must have it, or my grandfather will never be freed," Calypsa said, wringing her hands. "Please, we have little time to lose. Barrik will lose patience with me!"

"What about it?" I asked Kelsa. "Where is the Ring?"

Kelsa looked apologetic. "I am so sorry," she said. "I have tried time and time again to locate him, but he must be in the midst of some very powerful magik. I have received the same sounds, and nothing more. Here, I'll let you hear them. Perhaps you can gain some clue from them?"

The Crystal Ball turned entirely black. Someone was humming tunelessly, drowned out by rushing sounds like a stream flowing. I could hear the clank of metal-on-metal. Nothing else.

We all concentrated on the image.

"Looks like a black cat sleeping in a coal bin," I said. "No good, Kelsa. Can you bring it in a little clearer?"

"I'm not a television set! This is the best I can do!"

"How about you?" I asked Payge.

"Alas, no. Nothing is written within me about the finding of Bozebos yet. You can go over the possible scenarios."

"How many?"

"Five thousand."

"Forget it. You people aren't much help. Maybe we can do a little detective work. We can go to the Bazaar and a few other places who know where choice jewelry and magik items are being traded around the dimensions. I'll need a description. What's he look like?"

The face under the turban began its eye-bulging antics again, then vanished. An image started to coalesce in its place inside the globe. "Here is the ring Bozebos, great circle of eternity. Its golden band was mined from the same seam that produced the rest of us. We are brothers and sisters in the metal. The wizard Prumdar fashioned it in his workshop under a year's worth of full moons. The gems adorning it are of equal quality, all precious beyond compare. Behold, the Diamond of Justice! The Sapphire of Purity! The Spinel of Curiosity. The Cubic Zirconia of Economy..."

"Gaudy, ain't it," I observed.

"That could not possibly be the Ring," Calypsa said, gawking at it.

"Why not?" I asked. "It looks like the mother of all magikal rings. In fact, it looks like several put together. Liberace would have loved it."

"Who's Liberace?" Calypsa asked. For a moment I thought about Skeeve, and how he never got my cultural references, either.

"Never mind," I said. "WHY can't this be the Ring?"

"It cannot possibly be great Bozebos, because it is a piece of junk jewelry that my grandfather got from his mother, who received it from her father's mother. He wears it when he does his Dance of Lights."

Tananda and I looked at each other. I raised an eyebrow.

"There is no way that Barrik didn't know that," she said. "I'd bet the last pair of panties in my underwear drawer."

"If we didn't think this was all a trap before, I'm sure of it now," I said. "Kid, Barrik has no intention of freeing your grandfather once you bring the Golden Hoard to him. In fact, if you do it, you'll be lucky to escape with your life."

"That is the rede of what I have been seeking to convince her," Ersatz said. "We need an approach that will upset the wizard's plans."

"Grandfather has the last of the treasures!" Calypsa said, absorbing at last what we'd just spent the last several minutes telling her. "Then we must take the rest to Barrik immediately."

"No way."

"But, Aahz! You have been saying all along…"

I cut her off.

"I changed my mind. We can't do it."

"Tananda!" The girl pleaded. "We must go."

Tananda shook her head. "I agree with Aahz. It's a trap. You can't walk in there and expect a fair deal. You'll hand the Hoard to him, and he'll have his minions take them away so that he doesn't have to pay off on his promise. He wants to keep the old man locked up forever, probably to discourage any other Walts from thumbing their noses, er, beaks at him."

"Then, what shall I do?" Calypsa asked, piteously.

"You have us. We have the power between us to break any stronghold," Ersatz assured her. "And with your promise as a swordswoman and me in your hand, none shall harm you."

"You're thinking of setting her, one inexperienced girl, alone against a castleful of minions?" I asked disbelievingly.

"I believe that she will not be ALONE," as you suggest so insultingly, friend Aahz. We will be with her. We shall under-take this rescue ourselves. Pardon me for my forwardness, Calypsa, but you are inexperienced in these matters. We will take the lead, if you do not mind."

"Thank you," she said, looking at the Sword with an ex-pression of admiration and trust.

"Tananda and I have plenty of experience at rescues and dealing with enemy wizards," I said.

"Perhaps," Payge said, vaguely. "Do you mind not intrud-ing? My colleagues and I are conferring. All right, sharpie, what is it *you* think we should do?"

"Hey!" I protested. "What am I, chopped liver?"

"Silence, Pervect," Asti said. "This is none of your concern."

I goggled at her. Ersatz's eyes turned pensive.

"A direct assault is the best way, the Sword said, ignoring the Book's insult. "With me in her hand, I will guide her to defeat the forces of the stronghold. She can win through to the sanctuary of the tyrant. He will not be able to stand against us! He must surrender, in fear of his life."

"To an army of one?" Buirnie asked, with heavy sarcasm. He twinkled at Calypsa. "No, it would be far better if you and I went in there together, sweetheart! With your dancing and my singing, we could waltz in there, excuse the pun, and waltz out again before he knew what we were doing. We'll get your grandfather out of his jail cell, and 23-skidoo!"

Calypsa let out a wail of sorrow.

"My poor grandfather! That the house of Calypso suffers so!"

"There, there, child," Ersatz said. "I promise, I will assist you to free him."

"We all will," Asti assured her.

"And just how do you think you're going to do that?" I asked. The Hoard ignored me.

Payge rustled importantly. "The fact of the old Walt's very captivity could mean that Bozebos is no longer in his possession."

"Barrik has him!" Buirnie said. "That must be why the villain has demanded the rest of us. He's decided he wants the entire set! Well, what's not to like? It has happened in the past, by the masters of Valhal who first assembled us in one place."

"I have foretold it will happen again before the world's end," Kelsa said. "More than once. This may be one of the times. In fact, it could cause the end of the world. Again, it might not."

"How frivolous of you," Payge said. "Calypsa, if Bozebos is in the possession of your grandfather, then he has no need of rescue, child. Bozebos is a most powerful magik ring, the most versatile of all rings ever made. I am surprised that you have never seen a demonstration of his talents, since he has belonged to your grandfather for so long. The Ring is not shy about his talent. If he were there, he would have protected your grandfather. With Bozebos's help, Calypso could have destroyed the castle, let alone set himself free. Are you certain he *is* in the dungeon?"

Calypsa looked bewildered. "Why would Barrik lie to me?"

"He *was* taken prisoner, Payge," Kelsa assured him. A picture appeared in her depths of a Walt who looked like an elderly, male version of Calypsa, chains on his wrists and ankles, being rushed through the gates of a solid-black castle by a whole troop of long-snouted reptiles in black capes. "After that, I couldn't say. The spell is blocking me."

"I can counter the spell, with a little research," Payge said. "I am the one you need to bring with you, Calypsa of Walt. With me in your hand, you will be as great a wizard as any other that walks the dimensions. Barrik will not hold your grandfather prisoner for long."

"I've seen those critters before," Buirnie said, studying the reptilian guards flanking Calypso. "They're from Dilando. The Dile has very sensitive hearing. I can defeat them with music. They are vulnerable to my Compulsory Dance music. Mixed with a little of their own war songs, they won't know what hit them. Zildie, a one, a two, a three!"

He started to blatt out kazoo music. In spite of myself I found my feet moving. Tananda and I got up and boogied around the room. Calypsa rose to her feet and started twirling in helpless circles.

"Stop that!" I demanded. He paid no attention to me, but Ersatz bellowed.

"You are making my protégé bounce up and down. It is most disconcerting."

"Whine, whine, whine," Buirnie said, but the kazoo music died away. "It's the answer, I tell you. Calypsa, carry me to the gate of the castle. I promise that they will be helpless before us."

"That won't unlock the prison cell, you pennywhistle," Asti said. "We need to take over their minds, and the bodies will follow. I have a potion, if poured into the well that serves the castle, will make them your willing slaves. All of them, including their master, will obey your every command."

"What if he doesn't drink water?" Ersatz said. "No, you must confront him, Calypsa. With me in your hand you cannot fail. Kill him, and your grandfather's freedom is assured."

"A bribe will do better," Chin-Hwag said. "I will determine if the henchmen are corruptible. Gold will do more to undermine any blood oaths that they have taken, I promise you. I have seldom met any creatures who, when acting with free will, would not take the money if they were certain that they wouldn't be caught."

"Oh, bosh," Kelsa said. "I know where the sewers open up, Calypsa, dear. I can guide you through to the dungeons. It is the simplest thing."

"I thought you said you could not see through the walls," Payge reminded her. "I have spells to undo Barrik's obfuscation. All I need is time to search through my memory. I can counter anything that he can throw. I will render them into your language, and you shall cast them. Have you ever done magik before, Calypsa?"

"No…"

"Hold hard, friend!" Ersatz said. "She cannot carry us all!"

"No, I fear she cannot. Therefore she must use the object with the greatest range of usefulness. That would be me."

"How now? You would attempt to suborn MY apprentice?"

I put my fingers in my mouth and whistled.

"Hold it! Hold it!"

The Hoard turned to look at me. Ersatz's eyes fastened upon mine. They were as sharp as his blade.

"What say you, friend Aahz? We are very busy."

"Busy? You're beating your chops! This doesn't sound like a coherent strategy. The idea's to break Calypso out of the dungeon, right? You each have your own plan! There's no co-operation. You're all talking, and no one is listening. Look, if you tried…"

"Enough," Ersatz said. "This does not concern you, friend Aahz. Pray let us continue uninterrupted."

They all turned back to their argument.

"I predict victory," Kelsa said. "But, only if you use my talents, Calypsa, dear. Don't pay attention to the others. I will be able to foresee your enemy's movements…"

"You cannot even see into the castle!" Ersatz boomed. "I will be your key and your guide, Calypsa. Follow my instructions. We will succeed!"

"It might be better," Asti said, "if along with you she had something to protect her weak side."

"If only the Shield still existed," Kelsa said.

"He doesn't?" Buirnie asked, his mouth hole round. "I didn't know. That's terrible!"

"He fell bravely defending a warrior maiden," Payge said. "I have the whole tale in section…"

"Never mind," Asti said. "I can brew you a potion that will harden your skin, girl. It may interfere with your suppleness, but you can't have everything."

"No one is going to impair MY PROTÉGÉ'S natural gifts!" Ersatz exclaimed.

I couldn't stand it any longer. "You're going to get this kid locked up or killed! And you call yourselves the greatest magikal items ever made? I'm NOT impressed."

Asti eyed me then turned to Calypsa.

"Perhaps you should tell your hired help that we do not need his assistance in order to conquer one small castle and one ordinary mortal wizard," she said, her voice dripping with icicles.

"Just what do you mean by that?" I snarled.

"Why, that you should take a seat and let us work out what to do. Calypsa will decide, then she will tell you what tasks you will undertake. Under our direction, of course."

"You're out of your collective minds!"

"Give them a chance to work out a plan," Calypsa said, pleadingly. "They have so much experience."

"But not at working together," Tananda said. "At least, not in centuries, if the story they told us before is accurate. *We're* used to working together. We combined our talents. As a result, we accomplished some truly amazing things. Why not listen to us for a moment?"

"You're not going to try and tell me again that you mortals had a company greater than OURS, are you?" Asti said. "We are legends!"

I leaned over them. "Did you ever think for a minute that we were legends of a different kind? Ask anyone! M.Y.T.H., Inc. solved some pretty knotty problems, and we did it by working together. You're each trying to convince Calypsa that she ought to take you, and the others can play backup. That's not the way to handle a situation like this. You're all vice presidents with no middle managers."

"If you are afraid you will not receive your reward, Pervect," Payge said, "rest assured we pay our debts. Once this matter is settled we will find a way to give you what was promised. Now, if you will, shhh!"

"DON'T YOU TELL ME TO SHHH!"

"Now, as for storming the castle," Ersatz began.

"It's a dumb idea, excuse my being blunt," Buirnie said. "Now, my plan…"

"I can show you precedents where spells read by an amateur succeeded…," Payge put in.

"Potions," Asti said. "Potions are the only real answer."

Kelsa rolled her eyes. "Oh, dear, no! Anticipation. That's what is needed here."

"Appeal to their baser natures," Chin-Hwag said. "All of you are foolish to think anything else…"

Tananda made a throat-cutting gesture to me. The power was building up in the room. Even I could feel the floor starting to shake. Two disasters were brewing, one present and one future, and the Hoard wasn't paying attention to either one.

"THAT'S ENOUGH!" I bellowed.

The eyes all turned to look at me.

"I won't take the rewards," I said. "As of this minute, I'm releasing all claims."

"You don't mean that, Aahz," Tananda said.

"I mean it," I snarled at her, more harshly than I intended. "Don't make this harder than it's gonna be."

Tananda was an old friend. She understood at once without having to have a long, painful explanation.

"You do not need to refuse repayment, my Pervect companion," Ersatz said kindly. "You are more than worthy of your hire. When we find Bozebos, then he will surely be able to restore your powers."

"I don't want them back that way," I said, flatly. "You're all experts in your own field, but you're not presenting a coherent strategy. As long as I am beholden to you for what you promised me, you aren't paying any attention to me. Well, I am fed up with the way you bicker between yourselves. It's not getting us anywhere. You don't even know when you're about to cause a major cataclysm. I'm tired of you treating me and Tananda like minions. We're professionals, seasoned professionals. Calypsa doesn't know anything. You're confusing her. She doesn't know what to do, and she's going to get hurt because she trusts you. Calypso has very little time left. Someone has to take charge, and that someone is ME."

"What are you saying, friend?" Ersatz asked.

I took a deep breath. "I'm relinquishing it, money, powers, everything. We're all fighting for the same thing, now, setting Calypsa's grandfather free and getting the Ring away from Barrik. I don't want any legendary treasures left in that castle. In fact, I want the place vacated completely. He'll just have to find a timeshare somewhere else."

"Well." For the very first time, Asti regarded me with a measure of respect. "This selflessness isn't like you, Aahz."

"Yes, it is," Tananda said. I turned to glare. She put her hands on her hips and stared me straight in the eye.

Ersatz made an 'ahem!' noise. It wasn't exactly throat-clearing, since he had no throat, but it got our attention. We broke the stare-down.

"I beg your pardon for interrupting this modesty fest," he said, "but this makes us equals in interest. We have a grandfather to rescue and a Ring to retrieve. Pray, Aahz, tell us your plan."

Chapter 22

RECONNOITER, WAS MY first order, so we *bamfed* into Walt to scope out the situation. The sky over the scenic and hilly landscape had a faint purplish cast, and in the distance I could hear the sound of music.

Back on her home turf, Calypsa twirled for joy. "Let us go and see my parents! I know they have been worried. Oh, they will be thrilled at our adventures! I want them to meet all of you, and see Ersatz, and Buirnie, and Asti..."

"Barrik's men will be watching to see if you come back," I said. "It's what I would do, and he's proven to be pretty savvy so far. We're not just going to hand the treasures over to him first thing."

Calypsa's face fell. "But they will be worried."

Kelsa's Walt-face disappeared and was replaced by a couple of the locals, a male with dark plumage and a female who was a slightly older version of Calypsa.

"Yes, they are, dear. They're worried about you and your grandfather. And your younger brother. Did you know he had a still in the caves down by the river?"

I waved my hand for the Crystal Ball's attention.

"Can you see inside Barrik's castle?"

The two faces disappeared in a cloud and were replaced by lines of static, then a test pattern.

"He is blocking me, she said. My goodness, that's a strong interference spell! It is even stronger here than I thought it would be."

"So, you're saying we have to go in blind?" Tananda asked. "I've tried that already, and I have to tell you, it's impossible."

"Well, no," Kelsa said. "Look, here!" We gazed into her depths at the image of the castle walls. Down at the base, three figures were slipping around the silhouette of a tower.

"So that proves that we *will* get information. I will just have to work on getting past his spell."

"You don't need to," Payge said. "I have a floor plan."

Surrounded by an illusion of a hazel copse overlooking the black castle, we watched guards go in and out for a few hours and studied the illuminated elevation on page 846 of Payge's section on Famous Buildings of Evil Overlords and Wizards. We propped up the Golden Hoard so they could look it over with us.

"A fairly traditional layout, with defensive positions well designed." Ersatz said.

I turned over to Figure 3b, which showed a lot of colored arrows lying over the castle.

Tananda whistled. "No wonder Barrik can have magikal protection like he has. There are four major lines of force intersecting above and below the castle, not to mention about six smaller ones. It's a major nexus point."

So, friend Aahz, what is our plan?" Ersatz asked.

"Plan?" I asked blandly, turning to meet him eye to eye. "There's no plan. Calypsa here asked us to help assemble the Golden Hoard to trade for her grandfather with this wizard Barrik. That's what we're going to do."

"What?" he asked, outraged. "I have heard you say so over these many days, but I still cannot believe that is your sole plan. Having assembled us all, you have no intent on making use of our talents?"

"Why not?" I asked coolly. "You all decided you could ignore mine, and for what I think is the most petty of reasons. As far as I am concerned, you're just a bunch of hot trade goods."

"You are justified in your anger, friend Aahz," Ersatz said, after a moment's reflection. "It is hubris as that which we have shown that caused the fall of Valhal. We will not follow in its wake. We were created to serve mortals in their aims. It would appear that we are acting in our own interests, whether for ego's sake or not. That is inexcusable. You have proven your merit again and again. It was wrong of Asti to complain of your wish to be reimbursed, since it was I who persuaded you to incur the debt. Otherwise I might not yet have regained my freedom, and found such a worthy apprentice to teach." His eyes swiveled to Calypsa, whose eyes were fixed on him in adoration.

"You're right, Ersatz," I said, with a grin. "He has no way to expect your talents. What's your best guess on penetrating the castle?"

The eyes narrowed slightly, but with humor showing. "Why, Calypsa will be expected, but you must be admitted. And if all goes ill you will require a diversion to get out, as well."

"We have one." I turned to Kelsa. "Buirnie said you're no better than a snow globe for predicting the future."

"What?" Kelsa said. She turned to the Fife, whose mouth gaped open. "You said that! I can see it now! How dare you!"

"I told you that in confidence," he protested to me.

"He's not that original a songwriter, you know," Payge said. "I can show you at least a dozen references where Buirnie played music that he claimed he wrote himself, but they date back hundreds of years before. Turn to page 1,047, if you don't believe me."

"You comic book!" Buirnie exploded, loosing a whistle that pierced both of my ears to the center of my skull. "How dare you claim to be the greatest historical archive of all time! Ersatz said you missed out completely on a dozen of his battles. He says you ignored them out of jealousy!"

"That is not true," Ersatz protested. "I said he might have downplayed my role in the wars out of deference to the mortals involved. But I should have been mentioned where I took a part!"

"Your ego is not the point of my documents," Payge said. "It is for the ages."

Tananda grabbed my arm. "It's starting again."

The ground started to shake underneath our feet.

"Make them stop, Aahz!" Calypsa begged me.

"No," I said, with satisfaction. "This is just what we want."

"Hah!" Asti exclaimed. "You provoked that on purpose!"

"Sure did," I said with satisfaction. "You all go up like balloons right on cue. Works pretty well, I think."

Ersatz's dark blue eyes were summing. "Friend Aahz, you are not only an excellent judge of character, but a clever captain of resources."

I grinned. "I bet you say that to all the Pervects. Now, here's what I've got in mind. We're going to give Barrik what he wants. Calypsa's going to go home and visit her parents."

"What?" Calypsa said, after she had finished a spontaneous dance for joy. "I thought you said that it would be too perilous for me and my family if I did."

"Simple," I said. "We want Barrik to think we don't suspect anything. Before her mother's broken out the baklava, Barrik will know that Calypsa is home. Nothing travels faster in a small town than gossip. They'll be talking about the fabulous treasures she's carrying. What they won't be able to tell him is whether they're real or not."

"But of course we are real, dear Aahz," Kelsa said, patiently.

"*You* are," I said. "But the goodies that Calypsa will be bringing to Barrik aren't."

"Should he not meet us?" Ersatz demanded. "Will we not bring our full force to bear upon this caitiff? He has insulted her family and cast her honored ancestor into durance vile"

"Sure he will meet you," I said, not able to keep myself from grinning. "Just not in the way that he expects to."

We went into a huddle.

Calypsa looked like a baby chick whose mother hen had abandoned it on the doorstep as she stood with her bag full of pseudo-Hoard swag, waiting for the portcullis of the black castle to rise. I didn't like the glee of the Dile henchmen as they marched out and surrounded her. They were plenty rough as they towed her inside. Her parents hung back on the other side of the moat with the rest of the townsfolk, clutching one another in fear. Calypsa kept her back straight.

"That's the girl," I said in a low voice. I felt pretty confident as long as she had Ersatz with her.

Even if she had no opportunity to draw him, he could talk her spirits up. The other real treasure she had with her was Chin-Hwag. I did not like the idea of the Purse falling into the clutches of the Dile wizard, but she was right about the thoughts of endless streams of gold keeping anyone from looking too closely at the fake treasures.

Tananda had done us proud. She had bounced back to Deva to shop for the fakes. I thought the substitute Asti was the best, a deconsecrated chalice from a cult that had gotten shut down by the authorities on Como for tax fraud, bedizened with a wealth of glass gems. The others were pretty good, too, though I hoped Barrik set Calypso free before he opened up the fake Payge. The scam book was a complete collection of "Danger Whelf" comics for the last fifty years, bound in genuine iron pyrite embossed covers.

"I cannot follow her now that the gate is closed," Kelsa said. "My goodness, I'm not used to feeling so helpless!"

"Read my Breaking Updates section," Payge advised us.

As directed, I turned to the header. Beneath it was a series of illustrations, quick-drawn as though they had been jotted by a court reporter. The first showed Calypsa, a tragic expression on her face, in the midst of the guards. The second was a broad image of a courtyard, huge, but with every detail suggested by quick pen strokes.

"Nice work," I commented.

"Thank you," Payge said.

"That's Barrik?" Tananda asked, pointing to a skinny figure in a cloak.

"Not very impressive," I agreed.

The evil wizard, who had moved in and taken over the town, kidnapped at least one of its most prominent citizens, and had set up a ring of spells that defeated even some of the most powerful magik items I'd ever come across, was a skinny, green-scaled geek with an overbite and poor taste in hats.

"Fedoras like that are even out of style on Imper," Tananda said.

"Wait," Payge said, groaning at the strain. "Here come some captions."

A surprised Barrik confronted Calypsa on the steps of a shining black stone dais. "I did not expect you to return... so soon."

"I want my grandfather returned to me," the girl replied, her chin held proudly high.

"In time." Barrik rubbed his hands together. "Let me see them! I want the Hoard!"

Two henchmen ran forward with the bag Calypsa had brought with her.

The next frame merely read, CLUNK!

The one after that was a pair of reptilian eyes, narrowed greedily. "Beautiful. Beautiful. I wish to see a demonstration of their powers."

"When will I see my grandfather?" Calypsa asked.

The eyes again, looking perturbed. "When I am satisfied. Now, show me!"

I heard the sound of plodding hoofbeats, and glanced up.

The ruminant-drawn cart full of vegetables groaned up the hill with one of the Walt townsfolk at the reins. I wouldn't have thought of his tunic with the fancy ruffled sleeves or the patterned silk bandanna tightly tied around his brow as go-to-market clothes, but Calypsa had assured me that Walts loved to dress up no matter what the occasion.

"Our ride's here. Come on. Let's go invade a castle."

Tananda and I lay on the bottom of the cart while the driver piled sacks of potatoes and a few sides of raw meat on top of us.

"I can keep up a verbal narration if you like," Payge said. "I do very good descriptions."

"Just the dialogue," I said. "And keep it low."

"Meanwhile," Payge said, "the brave Calypsa's companions hid themselves in a cart full of food being delivered to the castle."

"Skip the parts about us!" I hissed. "We know what's happening here. Tell me what Calypsa's doing."

"Forgive me. 'She stands bravely before the slavering Dile and reaches for the first of the treasures. "What is that?" Barrik askes. "A chamois? I don't remember a sponge as one of the Golden Hoard."

"'O Barrik," Calypsa says. "This is Chin-Hwag, the Purse of Endless Money. She gives forth gold coins upon request.'"

'Barrik slaveres greedily. "Give me gold. Give me lots of gold!'"

Chin-Hwag frowned. "Scaly j…" Er, Aahz, do I need to repeat the invective of my fellow Hoarders?"

"Not if it has no relation to the action," I said. "What's she doing?"

"Er, she spits a gold coin into the air, a Meringuian solidus. Barrik leaps to catch it. He seems disappointed. He wants more, a stream of gold. Calypsa asks Chin-Hwag to give him more coins. She is producing them, albeit one at a time. There goes a Devan spite. I don't believe they have minted those in six hundred years."

"Perfect," I said. "She'll keep him too busy to notice us."

"Meanwhile," Kelsa said, "we are here, and the guards intend to search the cart. Our driver will put them off successfully, but only if we do not attract attention."

"A guard produces a spear," Payge whispered. "He prods the produce. Aagh!"

"Shh!" I hissed.

"He dogeared one of my pages!"

"Shut up!" I growled.

"What's in there?" a rough voice demanded.

"Cheese curds," the amiable voice of the farmer replied. "So fresh, they squeak!"

"Let's see 'em," the guard said.

"I must not unwrap them; they'll get stale."

"Get 'em out here!"

"If I cannot make you happy any other way," the carter said, reluctantly.

We heard things start to shift. There were only two layers of sacks over me. If the guards decided to help, we'd be uncovered in a second.

Tananda's eyes were close enough to me that I could see the alarm in them.

"Someone do something!" she whispered.

Someone did. A terrible smell wafted up and surrounded us all in the miasma.

"Aahz!"

"It's not me. It's Asti."

"What the hell's that stench?" one of the guards demanded.

"I TOLD you, it is the cheese curds!"

"Yeeaagh! You go right on in there to the kitchen, pal. The cook'll cut you to pieces and serve you for dessert when he smells that!"

More grumbling as the sacks of root vegetables that had been removed thudded back on top of me. I waited until the guards' voices receded, and the heavy cart started lumbering forward again.

"We're out of sight," the carter whispered.

"I can't stand it any more," I said. "Turn off the stink!"

"It's not me, Aahz," the Cup protested.

I flexed my muscles, and the sacks slid off my back. I helped unearth Tananda. She brushed powdered dirt off her clothes. I looked around to discover that we were behind the midden heap.

"I stand corrected," I said. The three of us dug the Hoard out. They were all disguised in worn burlap bags. Buirnie and his backup were piled into one carrier together.

"Ah, that's better!" Kelsa crowed, as I pulled her loose. "I can see everything now!"

I dumped the Hoard out of their sacks. Zildie jumped to its feet and shook its drum head until it rattled.

Kelsa's face spun around her globe in delight. "Barrik is very clever about his shield spell. It's most economical, I see that now that I am inside the barricade. He has made a shell of a spell—I mean a spell shell. It is embedded in the walls, probably enchanted mortar."

"Binding spells, see page 10,582," Payge intoned.

"Yes! I couldn't see a thing until we were inside, but now I can see everything!"

"Keep it down," I growled, as Tananda tied Buirnie to Zildie's side. "Let's not attract the attention..."

"Who goes there?" a voice demanded. "Hands up!"

I turned, a big smile on my face. Three long-snouted guards came toward us with their spears pointed in our direction.

"Well, hello, there!" I said. "We got a little lost on the tour. Can you direct us to the gift shop?"

"Guardsmen, ho! We've got a big, ugly one here!" the first guard yelled.

"Who are you calling ugly?" I yelled back. "You look like your mother stuck your nose in a vise!"

The guard captain poked me in the ribs with the spear.

"OW!"

"No talking!"

In a moment, we were surrounded by at least twenty men-at-arms. Their heads were draped in chainmail coifs, out of which their long, pointed faces grinned toothily.

"I can blast their ears off," Buirnie declared.

"I have just the spell," Payge said. "If you repeat after me..."

"Potions, anyone?" Asti asked.

"Which treasure is Calypsa on?" I asked.

"Still on Chin-Hwag," Kelsa said, gaily. "My goodness, how Barrik dances with impatience. It's almost elegant for a creature like him. I didn't think Diles had any sense of rhythm."

"No talking!" the guard barked, prodding me with a spear.

"Have we got enough time to get into the dungeons and out again?"

"Oh, you're going to the dungeons, all right," the chief guard hissed, as more of the contingent appeared and surrounded us. "You're just not getting out again."

"How cliché," Payge sighed.

"That's all right," I said. "We want to go to the dungeons."

"It's very convenient," Tananda said, flirting her eyelashes at him. "It saves us asking directions."

"I could give you directions," Kelsa said, sounding hurt.

"You must be crazy," the guard captain said, his snout bobbing. He waved his free hand at the Hoard. "Confiscate those...things!"

"We're not 'things,'" Asti said, peevishly.

The captain turned to me. "Make them shut up,"

"Buddy," I sighed, "If you can get them to shut up, you're doing better than I am."

"Now, move it! March!"

"May I give you an update on conditions in the audience chamber?" Payge asked.

"Just the dialogue, okay?"

"Certainly. Chin-Hwag emitted a noise that sounded like "Ptoo." "Beautiful, beautiful," said Barrik, wizard and conqueror of Walt."

"Save the editorializations," I growled.

"It is like that in the archives," the Book said, sounding hurt.

"Well, save it." I turned to the guards. "Can we get a move on? We're running on a schedule, here!"

"They are crazy," one of the guards commented. "His Enchantedness is going to want to know about them as soon as possible."

"Go report," the captain said.

"Stay here!" I ordered. "We're too dangerous for a reduced squad to handle."

"What?"

Tananda wound herself around the guard and fondled the toothy jaw with a finger. "Look, I'm escaping."

"Back in line, stranger!" the captain commanded.

"That's no way to talk to a lady," she said. She stiff-armed the guard in his long snout, knocking him backwards off his feet.

The whole contingent surrounded us, prodding us with the point of their spears.

Tananda lifted her hands in surrender. "Easy, easy! I don't mind playing rough, but I do draw the line at toys."

If the Dile guards could have blushed, they would have.

"March," the guard captain said, more hoarsely than before.

"Calypsa had better stay on schedule," I said.

Chapter 23

THE DUNGEONS WERE about what I would have expected from someone who had read the Tyrant's Guide to Oppression, or Despotism For Dummies. A heavy iron door with a grate the size of my hand creaked open onto a downward spiral stairway so narrow that we could only walk down it single file. The guards at the front and rear lit torches, which smoked like five-pack-a-day addicts, and shed just enough light that you couldn't really tell the difference between shadows and solid objects. The place smelled of blood, fear, eau de unwashed prisoner, rotten food and rat droppings. Considering we were nowhere near the dimension where rats had originated, I took a moment to marvel at the ubiquitousness of the vermin species.

My thoughts took my attention away momentarily from Payge's nonstop commentary.

"His efforts to spur Chin-Hwag to greater speed in producing money have failed. He has threatened Calypsa's life, but the Purse is pretending she can't hear him. He's assigned a flunky to catch the coins when she spits one out.

"Let me know when he runs out of legitimate items, willya?" I asked.

"Silence in the ranks!" the captain's voice echoed up to us.

At the bottom of the staircase, they pushed me and Tananda up against the wall. The jailor grinned at us, showing gaps in the rows of hundreds of stunted, yellow teeth.

"Guess the lack of dental hygiene among cell-keepers is pretty universal dimensionwide," I commented.

"Silence!"

Payge broke it. "The wizard eyes the Sword. He signs to the Walt maiden to hand it to him. She is reluctant. "If you do not give it to me, your grandfather will die a long, slow, terrible death," he said."

"Will you pay attention to your cases?" Kelsa said peevishly. "You keep jumping in between present and past tense."

"Forgive me. I am not accustomed to reporting something so recently recorded into the archives. The tenses change."

"What do we do with the gold?" one of the guards asked his captain.

"What do you think? We save them for His Enchantedness! He knows everything that goes on around here."

"Not everything," Kelsa said. "Why, he doesn't know that you have made up a song about him. It goes, 'Barrik is a squint-eyed boob, his nose is like a spiky tube...'"

"Say, that's snappy!" Buirnie exclaimed. "Give me the rhythm, Zildie!"

RAT-TAT! RAT-TAT!

"Silence!"

Ba-dum. The drum dipped its head in disappointment.

"You really know how to hurt an artist," Buirnie complained.

"Knock it off," I told him. "You'll have plenty of opportunity in a minute."

"Can I dose them now?" Asti asked me. "They are getting on my nerves almost as much as you do."

"Not yet," I said.

"Against her will," Payge continued, "the Walt maiden holds out the Sword. The wizard Barrik snatches it from her. 'Will you serve me?' he asks the Sword. Ersatz looks at him. 'You have a very poor grip. You would lose me the first time you swung me.' The wizard becomes enraged. 'Ptoo!' says Chin-Hwag. Barrik is distracted as his servant leaps to catch the coin...'"

"Chain them to the wall in cell 47," the captain said.

"I ain't cleaned it up yet. That other guy who died in there, he's still there!"

"No matter," the captain said, leering at me. "Perverts don't mind a little rotten flesh, do you?"

"Now, Aahz?" Asti asked.

"Not yet," I growled, as the guards steered us at spearpoint toward a low, soot-darkened door. I could see that the hasp for the lock was on the bottom third of the door, well away from the gloating-hole. Even Tananda would have trouble reaching that, even assuming we could undo the promised chains.

"Aahz," she said.

"I know! Kelsa, what's going on?"

"Well, he just tossed Ersatz aside. Calypsa almost fainted when he hit the ground. He started to pick up the Book."

"I am the Book," Payge said, offended.

"Yes, I know you are, dear, but you're not the one that Calypsa is trying to pass off as you, you see."

"What's going on??" I interrupted her.

"Oh, well, Chin-Hwag waited until he started to pick it up, then spat out another coin. She's just stringing him along so beautifully, you would think she's done this before!"

"She has done this before," Payge said.

"Barrik frowned," Kelsa said, her Pervect face wide-eyed. "He's counting. Oh, he's upset! Listen!"

A tinny voice came through the crystal loud and clear. It had to be Barrik.

"But there are only six of the Hoard here. Where is the great Ring, Bozebos?"

"That's His Enchantedness," the captain burst out, terrified. "How are you doing that? Can he hear us?"

"Oh, dear, no," Kelsa said. "I'm a receiving set, not a broadcaster. For that you would have wanted to talk to…"

"Shut up," I said. "I'm listening."

Calypsa's voice followed. She sounded defiant, even though I know she was scared half to death. "I will produce the Ring when you bring my grandfather up here and let me see that he is all right."

"What makes you think you have room to bargain? He stays in the dungeon, and unless you want to join him, you will turn your treasures over to me now!"

"I am going to find him."

"That's not in the script," I groaned.

I heard the sounds of a scuffle.

"Get your filthy, scaly hands off me!" I had to say Calypsa was magnificent in her indignation, though I didn't like her choice of insults. The outcry was followed by a slap that was audible to everyone in the dungeon.

"How dare you touch me! You shall pay! I will do the Dance of Death!"

Tananda and I exchanged glances.

"That's really not in the script," I said.

Barrik's voice was higher than usual.

"Guards! Guards! ALL my guards, seize this wench!"

"We've got to go," the captain said, signing to the jailor. "Lock these two up. Everyone, get ready to move out!"

They shoved us toward the yawning black hole that lay behind the low door. I braced my feet on the floor, trying to slow them down. Tananda grabbed hold of a wall sconce. The Diles peeled her fingers away one by one and dragged her, an inch at a time, into the cell.

"NOW, Aahz?"

"Be my guest," I said, holding Asti right in the captain's face. "Hey, pal, look at the pretty cup!"

Asti overflowed, not with the milk of golden kindness, but an olive-drab oil slick that would have done a double-ought agent proud. The captain made a grab for me, but his feet whisked out from under him.

CLANK!

He knocked over the next man in line, who dominoed into the third one.

"Omaniee balundarie straterumie brigunderie..."

Payge started reciting spells. The guard holding him stiffened into stone. A couple more Diles reached for the Book.

"Whiskerie sposorie toppirie zing!"

They began to spin in place like tops.

"St-o-o-o-op!" they moaned.

The Book flapped his covers and floated up toward the staircase like a giant golden butterfly.

"See you in the audience chamber," his soft voice called.

"Well, that's my cue, too," Buirnie said. "Come on, Zildie, Klik! On the beat. A one, a two…"

Buirnie, accompanied by his drummer, set up a deafening barrage of martial kazoo music that would have had the henchmen on their knees with their fingers in their ears, if it wasn't compelling them to dance their brains out. Those on dry land dipped and twisted, with a shuffle-off-to-Buffalo for good measure. The rest kicked and hopped. One guard went over backwards. He fell into his companions. They went down like dominoes. The whole troop ended up on their backs in the oil slick. Their legs were still moving. They were begging for mercy by the time I sauntered past them, my feet protected by a nonslip lotion Asti had brewed up earlier that also protected us from Buirnie's compulsory dance spell.

"Father and I went down to camp, along with High General Mikwuk Trimbuli. There we saw the Imps and Mumps as red as pasta fagioli!" Buirnie sang, accompanied by the nasal buzz. The henchmen kept time with the drum, beating their limbs on the ground. "Let's go, boys."

The snare drum, with the Fife on board trotted over the oil slick, lit by Klik's beam. The prone Diles kept on dancing.

"Help me, Pervert," the captain begged. He rocked back and forth.

"That's Pervect," I said. I located the jitterbugging jailor and relieved him of his ring of keys. "Thanks, pal."

"I had better get up there ASAP," Tananda said. I handed her Asti, who continued to spew oil, though carefully missing Tananda's feet.

"Move it. I'll get up there as soon as I can."

She nodded and ran away on tiptoe.

"Light it up," I told Kelsa.

"Light? Right!" Kelsa said. She burst into hysterical giggles. "I made a rhyme!"

But the globe started glowing brightly, until we were surrounded by a golden nimbus. I held her out in front of me and started looking in the cells.

I saw no reason why Barrik should get to keep any of his prisoners. I opened all of the doors I came to along the way. The Walts seemed to have a natural immunity to Buirnie's music. They stepped out of the cells with dignity. Some of them even bowed their thanks as they sashayed past me and bounded out of the cavern.

"Look out for the oil..." I called, but I didn't need to have bothered. When they hit the slick, they just glided over it. I went back to my search.

The corridor was no short passage cut into a natural fissure in the rock. It went on for blocks. I was impressed that the old boy had managed to build such a sizable dungeon in the short time that he had been on Walt. The ceiling got lower and lower as we moved further into the depths underneath the mountain. By the time we got to the last cell, I was stooped over. I unlimbered the last key, a huge piece of iron with a dozen complicated wards at the end of the barrel. I looked into the tiny window. A stooped figure looked up from where it sat. Feathered arms rested on its knees.

"Calypso?" I asked.

The head snapped up, and the Walt's posture went as erect as anyone's could in a half-height cell. "Who wishes to know?" he demanded regally.

"Name's Aahz," I said. "Your granddaughter sent me."

The aged eyes popped wide open.

"Calypsa! Where is she?"

"Upstairs," I said. "She's doing something called the Dance of Death."

The old man sprang up. He fluttered his arms.

"What? That is most serious! If she has begun that, either she or her foe must die before the dance is finished. We must go to her aid!"

"Hold it," I said. "First, where's the ring you've been carrying around?"

He put a hand on his thin middle.

"I swallowed it," he said. "That terrible Barrik must never possess the treasure of the Calypsos!"

"Ah!" Kelsa said. "That would explain the noises I was hearing. It's not good for you to have that much heavy metal in your diet, dear."

"Can we get it out of him?"

"Asti can prepare an emetic," Kelsa said.

Suddenly, a multicolored glitter joined the golden light. A brilliant cluster of jewels bobbed at face level. It was the ring in Kelsa's vision. My heart beat hard with avarice, even as I acknowledged the thing was a product of the Totally-Over-TheTopSchool-ofDesign. A small face like that of an annoyed leprechaun appeared in the top gem, a diamond as big as my eyeball.

"Bozebos does not need help getting out of tight places," the Ring said.

"It can talk!" Calypso said. "A treasure of the Calypsos, talking!"

"What is so unusual about that?" Kelsa asked. "There are thousands of magikal rings in the universe. Most of them talk."

"Kelsa? Is that you?" the Ring asked, turning its little face to her. "What are you doing here?"

"We're all here, dear."

"That appalling din—is that Buirnie?"

Kelsa's face appeared in the gleaming sphere. She beamed at him. "Yes! Sometimes it's been a trial having him around constantly for the last several days, but I have to say that it has been MOST interesting, you know. I haven't seen any of you in, my goodness, centuries! That is, in person. I've seen all of you in my visions, of course..."

"But *why now*?"

"We had to, dear. It was necessary to get together to save the life of this Walt here."

The hovering Ring seemed to shake with fury. "You should all leave at once! This is MY dimension! I am the One Ring."

The elderly Walt stared in amazement.

"I thought it was costume jewelry. Why did it not speak before?"

"Your family is so talented you never needed my help," Bozebos said. "But you were nice to live with for a while. I will have to move on soon. Others need me." He looked at Kelsa distastefully. "I would not stay in any case if the rest of the Hoard is here. It *already* feels too crowded."

"My goodness, don't be such a prima donna!" Kelsa said. "Oh, speaking of such things, you should have seen the pirouette Calypsa just did! She rose about eight feet in the air, and came down with her sword almost at Barrik's throat! It made him mad, I must say. He's not nearly as good with a sword as she is, and she has only been taking lessons for a few..."

"Why can you not stop talking trivia?" Bozebos said. "It is enough that you are here, ruining my privacy."

"Hey!" I bellowed. I captured the Ring in one hand and glared at it. "Calypsa needs us pronto! Let's go."

Chapter 24

FOLLOWING KELSA'S INSTRUCTIONS, I led Calypso to
a different set of steep stone stairs. He looked at the spiral
leading up well past the beam of the Crystal Ball's light and
swallowed deeply, but he gamely started climbing. Within a
few steps I could tell he wasn't going to make it.

"Wait a minute," I said. I addressed the Ring. "You're such
a big-time magik item. Help him up the stairs."

The little face turned up its retroussé nose haughtily. "I
can do better than that, Pervert!"

Before I could finish saying, "That's Per-VECT," a blue
light blinded me. When it cleared, I found myself in an immense chamber with a soaring frescoed ceiling, facing a set of
double doors. The blatting sound of a kazoo was faint in the
distance, but Buirnie's magik was potent enough that Barrik's
employees, courtiers, servers, drudges, were jumping, twisting and swaying to the piped tune. The guards that should
have been facing us to defend the doors were arm in arm,
doing a grapevine step up and back.

"Halt!" the guard on the end demanded, as he did a fancy
step-kick-dip-step. "Who goes there?"

"Forget about them," Tananda said, coming from behind a pillar. "They can't stop moving long enough to lay a hand on you."

"Why aren't you in there looking after Calypsa?"

"I can't get inside," she said. "I told you this place was
proof against thieves."

I tugged on the door handle, an iron ring the size of my
head. "Nothing."

"It will be an effort, but I can blast it," Bozebos said. "Stand
back."

"The interesting thing, you know," Kelsa said, "is that everyone always enchants the *doors*, but no one ever bothers with
the *keyholes*."

"Hah!" the Ring exclaimed. He lanced a crimson beam toward the oblong hole. "You are right! Together, now."

Gold and glitter focused in one beam. The hole got larger and larger until I barely had to duck to get through it.

Inside, the Dile henchmen stood in rows, all gazing at something happening beyond them.

"They're not dancing." I said. "How's he doing that?"

"Barrik is a powerful magician, dear," Kelsa said. "The child really has bitten off more than she can chew, not that Walts really bite or chew, so to speak…"

"What my babbling associate means, is that Barrik controls all that goes on within that chamber," Bozebos said. "It will take more than one of us to defeat him utterly."

"It's a good thing there's more than one of you, then," I said.

"Hurry!" Calypso said. "My granddaughter needs me!"

The guards who should have challenged us had their attention on something going on in the center. We pushed our way through the crowd to see.

In the center of a wide circle left by the henchmen, Calypsa and the reptilian-looking Barrik circled one another. He, in his cape and little feathered hat, bobbed low. She, in her tightly-laced dancing shoes, circled him, her arms held high. It looked like some kind of wild National Geographic mating ritual. The only difference between this and a pasa doble was the huge sword Calypsa was wielding. The Dile wizard made a point of keeping out of her range. On the floor was a heap of gold, the discarded fake treasures, with Chin-Hwag on the top. Once in a while, she spat a coin into the air. With all eyes on the duel, the gold clanked to the floor unnoticed.

At one side of the room, Tananda leaned against a pillar.

"You must be Calypso," she said, taking him warmly by one wing. "Glad to see you're out of there. I'm Tananda."

"Why are you not doing anything to help my granddaughter?" Calypso demanded.

"She doesn't need me," Tananda said. "She's doing fine. Watch."

The young Walt female stepped grandly around the green-scaled Dile. He seemed to be the one who was at a disadvantage. He must not be used to threats from a teenaged dancer, and it was throwing him off. Instead of taking action, he was responding. Calypsa tossed her free hand, stamped her feet and whirled. Ersatz's blued steel whistled as it cut the air.

"Granddaughter, stop!" Calypso shouted. "You should not be doing the Dance of Death! Your whole life is before you!"

The two combatants on the floor turned to see who was yelling. Both their mouths dropped open.

"Who let that old fool out?" Barrik snarled.

"Calypsa! Be careful!"

"Grandfather!" Calypsa shrieked with joy. Then she regained her poise. She sneered at Barrik. "You villain! You, who would keep the great Calypso in durance vile! You tried to disgrace our family! You sought to trick me! You shall die!"

"I will kill *you*, wench," Barrik exclaimed.

"One shall live, and one shall die," Calypsa countered, sounding melodramatic. They kept circling one another, looking for openings.

"What's the significance of the Dance of Death?" I asked the old man. "Isn't it just a dance, like all the others?"

Calypso straightened his thin back. "Sir! All our dances have meaning! The death dance is a challenge and a geas. Once it is begun, it can be interrupted, but never ends until one of the participants is dead!"

"Ayieee!" Calypsa shrilled. She held Ersatz horizontally over her head, the point aiming at Barrik. "Honor must be satisfied!"

She charged him. The Dile wizard leaped away. He felt in his cape pockets, his hands tangling in the thick velvet.

Calypsa advanced upon him. Just before she got in slashing range, he whipped a wand out of a pocket and leveled it at her.

"Parry four!" Ersatz yelled. Calypsa brought the sword down in a twinkling and twisted the blade up and to the left.

Barrik withdrew in surprise and attempted to riposte. "Parry six! Now, fleche!"

Calypsa rose on her toes and bounded toward the startled wizard. She swung Ersatz up and across. The wand went flying.

"Attagirl!" I shouted. Gleefully, I slapped the nearest henchman on the back. "What do you think of that?"

"Ten silver pieces on the wench," the henchman said promptly.

"What?" I demanded. "You think I'm going to bet against my own contender?"

"I will take your action," a large, ochre-skinned reptile said. "Fifteen says she can't touch him. He is the great enchanter!"

"Fifteen says she guts him," the first henchman said.

"I will take both of you!" the big guy insisted.

"You can't wager on whether he'll kill her or not!" Tananda said. She looked shocked.

"Who says?" I stood gleefully collecting bets. "I'm going to win."

Calypsa thrust the huge weapon, then recovered onto one long foot. Barrik backed up, clapping his hand to his chest. He looked at it for blood, but Calypsa had missed him by a scale. He had been taken by surprise once, but it would take some work to pull that off again. He held out his hand and the wand jumped back into it. Calypsa narrowed her eyes.

Suddenly, the Dile jumped toward her, pointing the wand. A bolt of lightning jumped from its tip. Almost of its own volition, Ersatz dipped in front of her body, deflecting it.

The bolt cracked off the blued steel and rebounded. Barrik threw himself to the floor as it blasted over his head. It hit a huge ceramic vase on a pedestal, which exploded.

"Now, press your advantage, child," Ersatz said. "He is off guard. Ballestra!"

Calypsa leaped and lunged. She would have gutted Barrik, but he rolled bonelessly to his feet. He aimed the wand at Calypsa again.

"No!" Calypso cried. He tried to break away from my side to help her.

"Stay back," I said. "We've got this under control."

"But she is just a girl."

"She's your granddaughter," Tananda said. "Believe in her. She'll make you proud, I promise."

"Yes," the old man said, his eyes gleaming. "She is my grand-daughter."

The two combatants circled each other. Barrik was start-ing to wheeze. He didn't have the stamina to keep up with a trained dancer. I knew sooner or later he would start to play dirty tricks.

I left Tananda guarding Calypso. The old man was gazing at the action. I headed to the opposite end of the audience chamber. With henchmen pressing coins into my hands I was still collecting bets.

I spotted Chin-Hwag on the floor. The Purse coughed up one more coin. She gave me a fishy embroidered eye. I signed toward Barrik. She nodded. If there was anything she could do to help, she was ready.

I had no idea what I could do against a powerful magician when the time came, but I could direct operations. A rattling sound attracted my attention to the rafters, where Payge flut-tered in and balanced on a fancy carved boss.

Barrik started muttering. Tananda sent me a high sign. She was feeling a drain on the lines of force passing through the castle.

"Penny-ante, cheap, showboating legerdemain!" Bozebos muttered darkly. I opened my hand and looked at the face in the gem.

"What's he doing?" I asked.

"Oh, calling up a whirlwind," the Ring said. "That sort of thing went out with séances and disembodied floating faces outside the window."

"What?" I sputtered.

I dove for a spot behind a heavy pillar as a gray funnel cloud dropped out of the ceiling and joined Calypsa on the dance floor. The henchmen backed up, giving the miniature tornado plenty of room.

She tossed her head. She had no trouble staying out of its way. The pasa doble became a troika, with Barrik trying to avoid Calypsa and his own creation. He snarled and whipped a hand. The whirlwind got larger.

"Can you tie a knot in that windbag?" I asked the Ring.

"No trouble," he said. The sapphire next to the base glowed, and the funnel cloud constricted. It squeaked like a deflating balloon, and vanished. Barrik looked perturbed.

"Who dares to interfere with me?" he demanded, glaring around him. He leveled the wand, and green flame spurted out in a ring. The henchmen wailed and ducked to avoid their master's spell. I kept low. Fire is one of the few things that can hurt my thick Pervect hide.

"Exterie vaunterie bellerie," came Payge's soft voice from the rafters. Barrik's flames went out. He started to look frightened.

"Who is doing that?" he asked, his voice an octave higher than before. He turned to Calypso. "YOU must be responsible for this! I knew the dancing was some kind of front! You are both magicians! Confess!"

He whipped up the wand. Waves of green light radiated toward the old man. I held up the Ring, but Tananda had Asti in her hands. From the bowl of the Cup arose a cloud of pink smoke. Green met pink and burst outward.

BLAM!

Half the henchmen in the vicinity were knocked off their feet. Barrik sprang to his feet, fuming. He faced Calypso.

The old man held himself proudly, pushing aside the wand.

"You don't scare me, tyrant. The Calypsos will withstand anything you can throw at them."

Barrik eyed him keenly. He looked like a guy who knew his way around lines of force. I wasn't wrong. He glared.

"The magik isn't coming from you! It is the Hoard that defends you! I shall destroy them!"

Magnificently, Barrik turned and aimed his wand at the heap of golden treasure on the floor.

"A load of magikal junk is no match for Barrik the Enchanter!" he declared. A blaze of white light shot out of the wand, landed on the pile and exploded, sending shards of white-hot metal flying.

Calypsa threw herself toward him, but too late. Even at that distance I could recognize a thermite grenade. Barrik must have some high-tech weaponry around to supplement force-line based magik.

"Chin-Hwag was in there," I groaned.

"No, she isn't," Bozebos corrected me. "Check your belt."

I looked down. The woven Purse looked up at me, perturbed.

"You could have come to get me," she said.

I was relieved, but I wasn't going to let her make me look incompetent.

"Why?" I asked casually. "The Ring was on the job."

"Perverts! You are all so lazy. You wait for others to do your work."

"That's a big fat lie," I snarled. "I'm just waiting for the right moment to step in."

Kazoo music loomed nearer and nearer. Zildie, the drum, raised its three little feet over the threshold of the enlarged keyhole. Buirnie gleamed brilliantly in the light from Klik, his personal spotlight.

"Say, everyone, did you miss me?" Buirnie asked. "Hey, you're not dancing! Everyone should be dancing!"

He struck up a livelier tone.

Now that he was inside the audience chamber, Barrik's barrier spell was useless. The henchmen broke into a shuffle. They looked at each other uneasily, as their feet started moving unwittingly. In a moment they had started doing a mass hora around the room. Barrik stared at them in horror.

The penny dropped.

"Those were fakes!" he shouted.

"It only took you a minute to figure that out," I said, stepping forward. "Congratulations. I heard Diles weren't completely stupid. Just most of them."

"You! You Pervert!" Barrik said, his toothy face focusing on me. "I knew it couldn't be the child or her senile old grandfather who came up with such a scheme."

"Senile?" Calypso said, his back as straight as a die. "The Calypsos never become senile!"

"Per-VECT!" I corrected Barrik. "And one smart enough to realize that you were too greedy to tell you weren't dealing with the real thing. Here they are," I said, waving at the golden treasures, hanging from the rafters, floating in the air, or waving dangerously close to his long, pointy nose. "The Golden Hoard. Legends. You can't blow *them* up like Hill 59. They're more than a match for you." I waved a lazy hand. "Get 'em, guys."

Kelsa started the ball rolling, so to speak. The window of her little case became the focus for a laserlike beam of hot gold light. It struck Barrik in the belly and left a rectangular scorch mark.

"Ow! Curses!" he yelped.

"I didn't know you could do that," I remarked.

"Oh, I developed that to deal with Stygian darkness," Kelsa said, cheerfully, swiping another beam past the Dile, who leaped over it. The tail of his cloak caught fire, and he beat it out with an angry fist. "Styg is a nice place, but so much particulate matter in the air that one can barely tell when the sun is up…"

Barrik aimed the wand at us. I backpedaled into the conga line, trying to get out of his way.

"My turn!" Buirnie called. The kazoo music got faster and faster. The henchmen were doing shuffle-ball-change-shuffle so fast that their feet were flashing. Barrik's face concentrated. I could tell he was doing everything he could to keep from dancing, but the music was irresistible. Even I was starting to feel it, and I had been inoculated. Barrik fired bolt after bolt at the Fife, trying to silence him. His feet broke into a jig. He hopped and skipped. I almost applauded.

Calypsa, as usual, was unaffected by Buirnie. She continued to circle Barrik.

"We are not finished with our duel," she said.

"It's not fair," Barrik whined. "You're using Ersatz!"

"You have your wand," she countered. "Throw it away, and I will surrender the Sword!"

"He has no honor, child," Ersatz chided her. "Do not believe him."

"I will disarm if he will," she said. "We will settle this like civilized beings."

Barrik faked as if to throw his magik stick away. Calypsa followed him, move for move. On the third flick, he actually cast down the wand. Calypsa followed suit. Ersatz went spinning across the floor. I caught him.

"Fool!" Barrik grinned. He opened his hand, and the wand went flying back.

"Return me, friend Aahz," Ersatz pleaded, his dark eyes blazing.

"Calypsa!" I called. She glanced at me. I tossed Ersatz, hilt downward. She dove for it and caught it just above the floor. Barrik aimed a beam of purple light at her.

"Look out," Tananda yelled. Calypsa rolled. The floor where she had been just a moment before blew up in a burst of mosaic tiles. She sprang up, the sword in her hand

Asti threw in her two coppers. From her bowl, a yellow liquid overflowed and began to cover the floor. Barrik, backing away from Calypsa, didn't see it until he stepped in it. He tried to raise one foot. It didn't move. He tried to pick up the other. It was stuck, too. He aimed the wand at his feet.

"Silelie benifie usteckie," Payge chanted. The Book flapped his way down from the rafters. Buirnie ordered Zildie to trot him over to join the circle.

Barrik started throwing spells. The Hoard countered him, tossing visible waves of force in his direction. The

"Take me there, Pervect," Chin-Hwag said. "I must join my fellows."

I brandished her, Bozebos and Kelsa at the trapped wizard, who cowered from them as if I'd been leveling a live dragon. Tananda held out Asti, who looked like she was thinking up another potion to evoke.

"You wanted us all here," Ersatz boomed. "I do not care for what nefarious purpose, but you have us now. He who invokes the Hoard must stand the consequences."

"Leave him alone!" Calypsa demanded. She came toward him with Ersatz covered in blue fire. "Now, we will face one another in the Dance of Death, evil Barrik! When Asti releases you, it will be to the finish!"

Barrik's beady eyes went wide with terror.

"Noooo!" he whimpered. He whisked the wand over his own head.

BAMF!!!

One second later, there was no one in the middle of the circle. Nothing remained but the impressions of his feet in the hardened yellow glue. Calypsa realized she was confronting open air. She sagged. I put out an arm to support her, but she waved me away. Her grandfather came over to embrace her.

"You do the family of Calypso great honor," he told her. "Thank you, child. Thank you."

"Oh, grandfather!" she said. The two of them embraced.

"Oh, cut it out," I said. "You people can't really be like this, day after day. It'd be like living in a soap opera."

"Oh, Aahz," Tananda said, punching me hard in the arm. "You just can't stand it when someone's happy."

"Now, do you see how well I did that?" Asti said. "My glue is proof against even your noise, Buirnie."

"But I am holding thousands of Diles in thrall!" the Fife protested. "They must dance to my music!"

"It is interfering with my ability to direct a clean battle," Ersatz said, sternly. "What if one unwittingly pranced into the midst when Calypsa was directing a strike? I do not attack noncombatants!"

"Oh, I suppose you would let them live just because they tell you they were only following orders?" Bozebos said, offensively.

The ground started to shake.

"Knock it off or I'll have to separate you!" I bellowed. "It's over. You won."

"We did?" Kelsa asked. "Oh, yes. We did. Of course we did!"

"The archives," Payge said, with a gentle noise like a throat clearing, "will say that Calypsa won. We were but tools to aid in the victory. Adjuncts."

"Oh, well," Buirnie said. The kazoo music died away at last. I wiggled a finger in my ear in relief. "At least I'll get royalties on the dance music I wrote!"

"He's gone!" one of the guards said. "His Enchantedness is gone!"

"Oh, yes," Bozebos said, looking around at the sound of the voice. His eyes fixed on the Diles huddled around the big room. "Them."

A thin rope of power looped out from the Ring and penetrated right through the walls of the audience chamber. After a few moments, the loop started to contract. With it came the entire contingent of the black castle, Diles in armor, in uniform, in livery, in cook's whites, in chambermaid costumes, all looking panicked as the blue thread gathered them in.

"We should slay them all," Ersatz said.

"Mercy," squeaked a Dile henchman, falling to his knobbly knees.

"Mercy!"

"You must not kill them," Calypsa said. She made a grand, sweeping gesture. "Send them home. Send them away from our fair dimension, back to whatever dread place that spawned them."

"It's not really so bad," one henchman muttered.

"Did she give you permission to speak?" I bellowed.

"No, sir," he said, gulping.

"That is a fair solution," Ersatz said.

"And then," Calypso said, looking around the grand room, "the Walts will take possession of this fine castle. It will make a grand dance hall. So many nice floors!"

Chapter 25

SINCE BARRIK WAS no longer maintaining the spells, the castle already seemed less oppressive. Suddenly, I could hear birds singing. Sun shone in the courtyard. The Diles cast a last wistful look at the black castle before they were banished by a spell from Payge.

With the Golden Hoard still bickering over whom was going to get what mention in the history books, I had Tananda airlift us over the juddering ground to the castle gates. The prisoners I had freed were already among them. Calypsa's mother and father were at the forefront of the crowd, their hands clasped with worry. When they saw their daughter and their father, they started swaying and raising their hands in a celebratory dance. I just shook my head. Pervects would never be so undignified.

We sailed out of the building and right over the moat. Tanda set us down in the midst of the townsfolk.

"It is a miracle!" Calypsa's mother said, embracing her daughter and her father at once. "Come, we will feast and dance! And sing and dance! And drink and…"

"Dance," I finished. "I get it."

"You will be our honored guests," Calypso said. "You will sit at my own right hand and enjoy the hospitality of the Walts!"

"Thanks, pal, but no thanks," I said.

"I do not know how I can ever thank you enough," Calypsa said, embracing me and Tananda.

"Just part of the job," I said. "Look, kid, I don't think I'm going to stick around for the celebration."

"But why not?" the girl asked. "It will be a great event."

I shook my head. "I'm done with what I promised. Now I'd just like to go back to where I left off on my vacation. I hope you and Ersatz live happily ever after."

"You are still cross that you gave up your reward," Asti said. "Don't be. It was noble. I will always remember how unselfish you were."

I winced. "Don't you let THAT get around."

"Oh, come on, Aahz," Tananda said. "Let's party. I wouldn't mind a chance to let my hair down after all that."

The Walts were nearly as good as the Bonhomies at throwing a shindig. Wine and hooch flowed liberally. The food was spicy, and there was enough even to satisfy my long-thwarted appetite. Asti added her own brew to the punch bowl, and everyone got pretty silly. The dancing went on and on. And on. And on. The Walts really knew how to pound the floor. I understood why they were famous for their native art form.

Calypso got up in front of the crowd and did his own interpretation of his capture, imprisonment and rescue. In spite of myself I got interested in his performance. Calypsa had a right to be proud of him. He was every bit as good as she claimed he was. The guy elevated dance to a level I had never known it could have. Still, the kid was no slouch herself. I was beginning to wonder if I'd been smart to let Ersatz take her on as an apprentice instead of taking her myself. She had the promise to do anything she wanted to.

Nah.

After the fourth or fifth gallon of booze, I let go of my snit. After all, I was part of history. The Walts were thrilled to be in the presence of the Golden Hoard, who were admired and passed around the entire village. The praise and attention kept them from getting into any more arguments, but I knew the next one couldn't be far away. If they really got going, it could spell catastrophe, and the Walts had just finished with the last major disaster. Tananda warned me from time to time when she felt tremors in the lines of force so I could defuse minor spats. Barrik had chosen one heck of a location for his castle, in the nexus of so much magikal energy. I felt like I was sitting on top of a volcano.

About three o'clock in the morning of the second or third day of the party (I had lost track of time), Calypsa, dressed in her travel clothes, brought Ersatz to where

Tananda and I were sitting, at a table on the edge of the town square. Two or three couples were swaying to the tune of a melancholy guitarist.

"Hey, there," I said. I gestured to a spare stool. "Take a load off."

"Aahz, we must go now," Ersatz said.

"Go?" I asked, blankly. "Go where?"

"The Hoard cannot occupy a single dimension together. Kelsa just informed us that she foresees trouble should we not absent ourselves from this place, and soon."

"Very soon," the Crystal Ball said, from her bag, which was slung over Calypsa's shoulder.

That sobered me up in a flash. I got to my feet. "What do we have to do?"

"Bring all of us to one place," Ersatz said. "One in which it will be safe to let the energy build. Nature will take care of the dispersal."

It took some doing to find where all the treasures had gotten to in the course of a three day party. I found Payge telling stories to a group of solemn old men in the tavern. He had a coffee ring on one of his pages, but he seemed happy. He wasn't surprised when I picked him up.

"Thank you, Aahz," he said. "This reduces the number of potential outcomes of this evening to thirty-seven."

Bozebos, along with a bundle of authentic cheap costume jewelry, was being used for dress-up by a gang of little girls who were pretending they were the latest hero on the block, their very own Calypsa, hero of the Walts. He seemed grateful to be rescued.

Buirnie was downright glum.

"This place is a natural for me!" he wailed.

"Maybe you'll come back on your own," I said. "In the meantime, I don't want anything else to happen to these people. They've had enough trouble without needing an egomaniacal Fife hanging around."

"Oh, well, on to our next triumph," the Fife declared.

Asti was in a different tavern, mixing drinks. Her sapphire eyes turned to me as I came in.

"Sorry, boys, last orders," she said.

"Ay! You cannot leave us!" one of the males declared, touching her foot passionately. "What will we do without you? You are matchless at bartending."

The engraving on her side tilted upward in a wry smile. "Just drink a toast to me once in a while."

Chin-Hwag had never left my belt. We had not said a thing to one another since Barrik's defeat.

"How about the castle courtyard?" Tananda suggested, as we carried the Hoard up the hill. "It's still deserted, and there's no ceiling to fall down on us."

"Good idea," I said. "If it gets knocked down, who cares?"

"Have you said your farewells to your parents?" Ersatz said to Calypsa.

"I did," she said. She sighed. "We have done the Dance of Farewell."

"Why?" I asked. "Where's she going?"

The blue eyes slewed to me. "Calypsa has to finish her mission. She started the Dance of Death, and it must be completed. I will assist her. But that may not be the first task we undertake. As always, we will go where the winds of fate take us. She is my new wielder, as I am her teacher."

"And you are on board with this crazy idea?" I asked, turning to the girl.

"Oh, yes," Calypsa said. She eyed the Sword adoringly. "I knew that the task was perilous when I undertook it. I know that with Ersatz at my side I cannot fail."

"How can you argue with that?" Tananda asked.

We got to the castle. The moon shone down on the empty enclosure. Kelsa's glow provided the only light.

"What do you want us to do?" I asked.

"Arrange us in a cluster in the center," Ersatz said. "We need a good deal of room. This could be dangerous. This is the first time we have attempted such a dispersal since the first time it happened. It has never been done since."

"We do not know if it will be safe," Payge explained.

"But there were twenty of us, then," Bozebos said.

"Alas," Ersatz said. "I had not realized until now how few we had become. Perhaps the time HAS come to recruit some new members to the Hoard."

"Why not?" Buirnie asked. "I've heard of an artifact or two that might be worthy."

"As if YOU are a good judge of who belongs in the Hoard," Asti said.

"You are not even an original member," Chin-Hwag pointed out.

I felt the floor start to shift under my feet.

Tananda looked alarmed. "Save the argument until we're ready," she said.

"One thing we wish to say before we depart," Ersatz said. "We have not met your like before. Perhaps this M.Y.T.H., Inc. was as great a fellowship as you say. We depart to be at the side of heroes, but allow me to state that you are of that number as well. I for one am proud to have served with you."

I felt embarrassed. "Get outta here before I melt you down into spoons," I growled. Secretly, though, I was pleased.

"Now you must scatter us to the winds of fate, dear," Kelsa said.

"How?"

"Just move us close together. Then back away."

"Just one thing," I said, pausing. "You've fought in battles for thousands of years. You could have waltzed around me at any time with what you know about strategy. Why didn't you?"

Ersatz's eyes were amused. "Because our heroes must take a hand in their own fates," he said. "Otherwise we are their masters, and not their servants. Besides, you did a creditable job. Asti was never fair to you, but she was challenging you in her own way."

"Yeah, remind me to thank her for that some time."

"You're not so bad after all," Asti said, grudgingly. "For a Pervect."

Ersatz laughed. "You are my most worthy friend, and I am at your service at any time when you find yourself facing an epic challenge. *We* will help you." He looked fondly at Calypsa, who looked very modest.

"Yeah, well, thanks, but I can handle myself."

"I do believe that," the Sword said.

Calypsa left the middle of the circle one more time to embrace Tananda.

"I nearly forgot," she said. She handed Tanda a small purse. "It is not enough for all you have done for me, but it is what we agreed." The bag jingled modestly.

"Thanks, honey," Tananda said, hugging her back affectionately. "I'd almost forgotten."

"I didn't," Calypsa said, beaming. "And I never will. Goodbye."

She raced back into the midst of the Hoard.

"Just out of curiosity...?" I began.

"Ten silver coins," Tananda whispered.

"You're kidding!"

"SHHH! Just wave goodbye to the nice artifacts," she said, firmly taking my wrist and flapping my hand at the Hoard.

Calypsa pulled the Hoard closer to her and Ersatz. Buirnie and his entourage huddled in tight, whistling and thumping to make room. Bozebos glittered like a disco ball in Kelsa's light. The girl pulled Asti and Chin-Hwag close to her, and she sat down on Payge. When the items were all touching one another, the gleam surrounded all of them. Calypsa's big dark eyes picked up the glow, and her feathers seemed to turn gold. She was one of them now.

I didn't need a tour guide or a nuclear scientist to tell me when the Hoard energy hit critical mass. The ground heaved up and down, throwing us both backwards. Tananda grabbed my hand and put up as much of a protective magik shield as she could. I threw one arm over her and the other over my head.

BOOM!

When the blast came, it was practically a nuclear explosion. I hung on as the floor bucked and shimmied. It took a long time to calm down. When I could hear again, the only noise was musical clinking. Hard little objects rained down on me. I opened my eyes to see us and the floor covered by a heap of shiny yellow coins.

"What the...?" I said, brushing gold out of my ears.

"I think," Tananda said with a grin, "that this is the Hoard's parting gift for you. You earned it."

I hesitated for about a microsecond then began shoveling the money into my poke.

"Darned right I did. Where'd Calypsa go?"

"Wherever Ersatz was needed, I guess," Tananda said. "She's riding on his ticket, now. She's going to be a legendary swordswoman. We did a lot more than help her save her grandfather. All the things she went through, like learning all the languages in the universe, make her an extraordinary person, not that she wasn't one to start with. It takes something special for a girl from a backwater dimension to break out of the mold like that. Keep your eyes open for coming epics."

"We seem to specialize in that," I agreed. "She had some great stuff in her, that girl."

"Is that a tear, Aahz?" Tananda cooed. "You, sentimental?"

I snorted.

"Nah, just a little dust. I like to see a legend get launched with a bang." I jingled my refilled purse. I felt better. The Hoard wasn't such a bunch of cranks after all. "I think I'll even go back to the party for a while." I stuck out an elbow. "May I have the next dance?"

Tananda curled herself around my arm. "Right with you, hero."

ADULT BELIEVING

Peter Ball

ADULT BELIEVING

A Guide to the Christian Initiation of Adults

Peter Ball

PAULIST PRESS
NEW YORK & MAHWAH

First published 1988
by A.R. Mowbray & Co. Ltd,
Saint Thomas House, Becket Street,
Oxford, OX1 1SJ

Library of Congress Cataloging-in-Publication Data

Ball, Peter.
    Adult, believing.

    Bibliography: p.
    1. Ghurch membership.   2. Christian education of
adults.   3. Catechumens.   4. Initiation rites—Religious
aspects—Christianity.   5. Christian life—Anglican
authors.   I. Title.
BV820.B35   1988   268'.434   88-25474
ISBN 0-8091-3053-X (pbk.)

Published by Paulist Press
997 Macarthur Blvd.
Mahwah, N.J. 07430

Printed and bound in the United States of America

Contents

Preface

This book is written to be read by clergy and lay people who
are concerned with the Church's ministry of presenting the
Gospel as an adult faith for adults. In the first place it is meant
to help them to develop appropriate ways of accompanying
men and women towards Christian faith and commitment in
preparation for baptism, confirmation and life as a communi-
cant within the Church. I hope it may stimulate both action
and reaction. Action, in that people will be encouraged to
undertake what is for them a new and fuller way of working
with enquirers and candidates for Christian initiation. Reaction, in that people who are either excited or dismayed by
what happens as a result, will respond to me and take part
with a growing number of men and women who are trying to
meet the questions and the needs which newcomers present
to the Church in a serious and open way.

Most of what follows is about the early stages of the
journey of faith, though Christians further along their journey
may find it good to be reminded of the importance of their
own first steps. There are also some parts which will be useful
as guides for church members of some experience who recognize that they are called to deeper understanding of their faith
and to deeper commitment to its implications in their lives.

There is nothing secret about all this and enquirers about
the faith and the life of the Christian church are welcome to
read my book and judge whether it could be for them. What
really matters, though, is meeting and talking with the local
Christian community. Books can only go so far; they can
describe, but they can't live.

Acknowledgements

I make no claims that the material to be found in these pages is original. Over the years I have learned a great deal from many people, professional and lay, in the field of helping adults into faith. In particular I recognize the influence of the Adult Catechumenate in France and other countries on the continent of Europe and mention especially the help of Henri Bourgeois and Gérard Reniers. In Britain, apart from all I have learned in association with people at St. Nicholas, Shepperton, I recognize a debt to the Roman Catholics working with the Rite of Christian Initiation of Adults in England, not least among them to Patrick Purnell, Céline Murphy and Michael Fewell. Several Americans have helped a great deal, in particular James Dunning, Karen Hinman Powell, John Westerhoff and James Fowler. No doubt all these people will recognize their ideas and their influence in what I have written, but I have to bear full responsibility for the whole. They are not to blame for errors and omissions!

I thank the authors and publishers who have given permission for extended quotation from their work. The details of the books and other publications are in the Notes.

1

Introducing the Themes

I start from the conviction that Christianity is an adult religion for adults. Even deciding to follow the direction of Jesus that we should become like little children to enter the Kingdom takes a mature decision. He was a fully grown man when he taught, ministered and was crucified. We know his close companions were adult men and women and certainly the proclamation of the Gospel by the first church preachers brought about the conversion of mature people.

It is clear from the statistics of people confirmed in the Church of England that adults still respond. Indeed the proportion of adults to teenagers grows steadily, as does their actual number. What has perhaps not changed is the way in which they are prepared for Christian initiation. Much work has been done to develop the approaches and methods of adult education in the secular world. Some of the new thinking is now affecting the Church. Alongside this there has been a shift in attitudes among Christians, most notably in the Roman Catholic Church since the Second Vatican Council. This shift, which has slightly different expressions in different denominations, is seen in liturgical revision, in changed expectations of the ministry of lay and ordained people, and in a new (or renewed) awareness of the role of Christian communities in the mission of the Gospel to the world.

Within this range of movements is the renewal of a way to prepare men and women for the sacraments of baptism, confirmation and the eucharist which has come to be known as the Adult Catechumenate or Rite of Christian Initiation of Adults. (There is a note about the language, including the word 'Catechumenate' on page 6). It offers an alternative outline for what has been known for a long time as 'The Adult Confirmation Class'.

The background from which I write is that of the Rector of the Parish of St. Nicholas, Shepperton and more recently as a Canon at St. Paul's Cathedral. This means that I write as an Anglican from an Anglican base, but for nearly twenty years I have been involved in close co-operation with members of other churches in the work of adult initiation. In particular I have been an active member of the European Conference on the Adult Catechumenate and worked closely with the North American Forum on the Catechumenate. So, although most of this book is couched in the language and practice of the Church of England, it is based on the conviction that the adult journey into Christian faith and commitment is not a denominational matter. I hope that readers who are not Anglicans will be able to translate easily enough into their own language where necessary.

Marion's Story

'Since childhood I'd wanted to get to know the mysterious person you never see but who understands everything, is concerned about everything and who above all loves everything and everyone. When I grew up I trained as a nurse and found that the faith of sick people affected me deeply. Like everyone else I had my troubles and upsets but I recognize that these were leading me towards my Creator. Then, when my baby Andrew was born, I decided to ask to join the Church. I felt I needed help in bringing him up the right way.

'I was in a group with the Curate, Barbara, Stephen and Gillian who were church members. We had deep discussions on many subjects; human life, God who made us, all that Jesus did for us. What stood out for me was how open I could be, thanks to the welcome which made me feel at home. Living through the course was like being born again, starting all over again – a kind of apprenticeship leading to meeting with Jesus Christ. His teaching is a wonderful school.

'Although nothing much seems to have altered – my life is

just the same – there are all different vibes inside me. It's as though by preparing to be baptized, I've started a whole new adventure. I've found a new life, very strange but truly pointing towards God and towards other people through Jesus.

'I'd like to add my very warm thanks to all the people who have helped me to know Jesus. Some of them have done it consciously and some without ever realising it.'

The person I have in mind as I write is the man or woman, ordained or lay, who has accepted the responsibility of acting as guide to someone like Marion on their journey from unbelief or little belief in Jesus to that point where they can make their profession of faith and be baptized or confirmed and accept their call to be a Christian in the Church. My book is not meant as a detailed how-to-do-it guide like a car owner's workshop manual. It gives some answers but certainly suggests no techniques which are guaranteed universally successful. Rather it is a base on which people can build their own way of working. What I hope for is that a group of people in a Church community will with their clergy work together to see how best the Church in their place is to fulfil the injunction of Jesus, 'Go forth therefore and make all nations my disciples; baptize people everywhere in the name of the Father and the Son and the Holy Spirit, and teach them to observe all that I have commanded you'. (Matt. 28.19f).

There's a powerful note in the Introduction to the Roman Catholic *Rite of Christian Initiation of Adults* which expresses that Gospel spirit of mission which I hope underlies all this book stands for:

The people of God, as represented by the local Church, should understand and show by their concern that the initiation of adults is the responsibility of all the baptized. Therefore the community must always be fully prepared in the pursuit of its apostolic vocation to give help to those who are searching for Christ. In the various circumstances of daily life, even as in the apostolate, all the followers of Christ have the obligation of spreading the faith according to their abilities.[1]

The Roots

The idea of the adult catechumenate, as it is expressed in the *Rite of Christian Initiation of Adults* and similar Rites in churches like the Episcopal Church of the U.S.A. and the Anglican Church in South Africa, has its roots in the church of the first three centuries after Jesus. Until the Christian religion became established in the Roman Empire under the Emperor Constantine with his edict of Milan in 313AD, the Christian community was for much of its life a persecuted minority. Membership was something both valuable and dangerous. It mattered a great deal that enquirers and con-verts should be carefully prepared and also carefully ex-amined before they were admitted to the fellowship. It would have been important to make sure that they were not police spies. On the other hand it was only right that if they were liable to be arrested themselves and brought to court for their Christian allegiance, they should be well aware of the com-mitment they were making. This resulted in the development of a preparation lasting two or three years for those under instruction before they came to be baptized.

Recent years have seen the principles that lay behind the early Church's catechumenate re-expressed in many parts of the world where the church is in mission to a non-christian society.

For people to whom the whole concept is new I have written a summary of what the modern adult catechumenate is at the end of this chapter. It is easily skipped by those who already have experienced it.

Help Needed

It is to help people who are involved in the task of accom-panying enquirers along their road to baptism that I am writing this book. There are many different ways in which you can help someone else to know Jesus. I suspect that our trouble in the Church of England (and Anglicans are by no means alone in this!) is that we have tended to become one-sided in our attitudes of instruction. We look to books and to courses which emphasize the need to understand. We explain Christian doctrine. Manuals for adult confirmation classes tend to be designed like simplified courses for students in theology. Of course there is more to it than that, but with this as the general approach it is natural that the main (often the only) person responsible for the preparation should be the person who has had that sort of theological education.

I am pleading for balance to be restored and for much more weight to be given to individuals with the questions and the experience they bring. I am pleading for much more weight to be given to those other aspects of what it means to be human. Certainly intellectual understanding is important. But we also need to work with our awareness; our feelings; our artistic imaginations, perceptions and creativity; our relationships and our belonging to a community. With all that we, of course, need to enter into the whole realm of what we call the spiritual.

To set out to work in this way from experience rather than from a laid out pattern of doctrinal beliefs can be frightening for some people, even threatening. But I believe it is more in accord with the truth of most people's spiritual journey than leading from the head. In everyday life we experience first; then we reflect upon our experience to make sense of it for ourselves. We do not start with an analysis and then have experiences to fit in with that!

From this approach follow two suggestions. The first is that it is often a handicap to rely on a previous theological education, unless of course it has been so worked into and through that it is part and parcel of personal experience. Often the person who has reflected deeply (and theologically) on their own experience of life and community and the world is a better guide for an enquirer than a person who has spent years in the study of the doctrines of the Church. The second is that this thinking, reflective but not 'theologically educated' Christian is, in today's Church climate, going to feel that they

are quite inadequate to the task of guiding anyone else to
Christ because they 'don't know enough'. It is one of my
intentions in this book to help that person to see it is not a
question of being ashamed of the knowledge they do not
have. It is a matter of being reassured and confident in those
real gifts with which God has endowed them in order to share
them with others. There is strong encouragement to move
away from syllabus-based instruction in the direction of the
journey accompanying the enquirer along the road of conversion. This, as we shall see, involves change in all aspects of a
man's or woman's life and personality. Conversion concerns
their attitudes, their understanding and knowledge, their spirituality and their relationships and moral choices.

Language

One of the difficulties anyone has in trying to write or speak
about the catechumenate is the words. Many of the terms
used come directly from the first centuries of the Church and
are Greek or Latin. This means that anyone coming new to
the subject is likely to be confused or put off by being faced
with a new language, even though the topics, activities and
relationships are really very straightforward and easy to enter
into. The trouble is that, once you have learned the special
words, it is so much quicker and easier to use them – despite
the dangers of upsetting other people. I have tried to keep
their use to a minimum, but some are inescapable, like
'catechumenate' itself.

The family of words beginning 'catech-' comes from the
Greek and has the common thread of teaching or instructing,
especially in the specific sense of giving instruction to people
preparing for baptism. The name for a person being instructed is 'catechumen' and the process of instructing someone in the faith is 'catechesis'. A catechism is a summary of a
church's teaching and catechetics is the study of how the
teaching is done. (This book is an exercise in catechetics.)

The main advantage of using this cluster of words is that it avoids long phrases about 'people who are in the process of preparing for baptism' if you simply call them 'catechumens'. But I generally prefer the extra words for the sake of avoiding unnecessary mystification. Other authors and trainers in the catechumenate are prepared to expect people to learn a new glossary of words to accompany a new outlook on the whole scene of initiation.

The Outline

The plan of the book is as follows. Chapter 2 is about the journey taken by someone towards Christian faith, commitment and initiation into the Church. It enters into some of the consequences of thinking in terms of personal journey rather than dogmatic syllabus.

Chapter 3 is about what is taught and learned. In technical terms it is about catechesis for adults, how people learn and mature in coming to Christian faith and how those already in the Church can help them. It includes suggested ways of developing the dialogue between people's lives and the gospel, which for me is the main task of theology.

Chapter 4 is largely about praying. Its purpose is to provide the Christian companion with a brief survey of the ways people can find and express their friendship with God so that they can have some confidence in talking openly about spirituality.

Chapter 5 enters into the topic of conversion and tries to show both the vital importance of change in the catechumenal journey and the many varied ways in which it takes place.

In Chapter 6 the idea of conversion is brought forward to include the new Christian's part in the Church's mission to and ministry in the world.

Practical suggestions about the training and support of leaders in the different ministries of the Catechumenate come in Chapter 7. An Appendix of books and other resource material and groups closes the book.

A NOTE

What is the Catechumenate?

It depends which part of the world you live in and what
Church you belong to whether you talk about *The Rite of
Christian Initiation* (*R.C.I.A.* for short) or *The Catechumenate* (or perhaps *The Adult Catechumenate*). The titles refer to
exactly the same thing. There is a stream of experience over
fifty years of Christian missions in Africa and elsewhere and
of the work of the Church in France and other countries in
Europe and French-speaking Canada. This stream tends to
talk of 'the Catechumenate'. Following the directive of the
Second Vatican Council the Roman Catholic Church produced the official *Rite of Christian Initiation of Adults*, first
published in English in 1976. Roman Catholics in Britain, for
example, speak regularly of *The R.C.I.A.* Anglicans in South
Africa and the U.S.A. have also produced texts along the same
lines for the admission to a period of preparation beforehand
of people asking for baptism.

   The Catechumenate—R.C.I.A., marks a distinct change
from the past in the way people are prepared for initiation. It
involves a new set of attitudes on the part of the Christian
community; it introduces new ministries for people in the
Church and it presents a series of liturgical events in which the
Church and the new Christians celebrate the stages of their
journey into faith.

The Main Points

It will be helpful for people who are new to the idea of the
catechumenate if I outline the key notes.

WELCOME

The way in which the Church and its members and ministers
receive an enquirer is of the very greatest importance.
Warmth matters. Respect matters. Acceptance matters. These

aspects of welcome are vital at the start of anyone's journey towards a commitment to Christ within his Church. Clergy and people need continually to be aware of this and to review how they behave. People notice how the vicarage phone is answered, whether there is a smile at the church door for people venturing in for the first time to hear their Banns of Marriage read, or what kind of response is given to a request to have their new baby christened.

Welcome is extended to people as they are and for what they are. Many, perhaps virtually all, churches have some sort of preconditions they consciously or unconsciously put as turnstiles at the entrance. One of the most damning remarks is 'They're not the kind of people you'd expect to come to church'. Behind it lie all kinds of expectations, social class, dress, age or personal behaviour. Few congregations are free of them. What is needed is an openness and a valuing of people with all they bring with them. The example we need to follow is in the ministry of Jesus described in the Gospels.

Lay men and women are often more likely to be effective welcomers than the clergy. After all they are not paid to be nice to people! In the catechumenate it is lay members of the Church who have the prime responsibility of acting as sponsors, welcoming friends and guides to new people.

FAITH-SHARING

At the heart of the catechumenate is a person's conversion to a living, committed faith in Jesus Christ; expressed in a life guided by his teaching and in active membership of his Church. One of the routes to this is through open sharing of belief between the Christian friend and the enquirer.

This is a two-way process and, again, involves that respect for the enquirer and his or her faith which is part of welcome. People begin where they are and where they are needs to be celebrated as true for them. They need to express their own faith whatever it may be and however inadequate the Christian may feel it is. The dialogue has to be a genuine meeting of two people, not a cloak for indoctrination.

Later in the book there is a chapter on the content and possible methods of this faith-sharing. Suffice it here to say that although head knowledge of the Christian faith is an important part of faith, far more important is to help people into a personal awareness of God and to accompany them through the stages of their own experience of conversion.

AN ACCOMPANIED JOURNEY

The language used in the catechumenate is often journey language. It is about movement and change of direction. It is also about travelling companions.

The journey is one which is personal to the individual. There are recognized stages which most people go through, but speeds vary, strengths and weaknesses vary, and perhaps most significant, length of time varies.

Notice that generally in the catechumenate the duration of a person's journey from start to baptism or confirmation is considerably longer than is often reckoned to be needed in 'Adult Instruction Classes'. A year is normal, eighteen months nothing unusual. This is because what is at issue is not whether the candidate has attended all the items in the course of church teaching, but whether he has matured as a Christian to that point where baptism is appropriate, whether he shows signs of the changes in life which are evidence of a personal conversion to faith in Christ. These things are to do with development, a kind of organic or dynamic change and growth which of their nature take their own time and need to be given that time. The measure of the catechumenate is not the syllabus nor the calendar – nor even the priest's need for a successful new member rate! – but the truth of the candidate's journey.

They do not take the journey alone. They have as companions and guides members of the Christian community. Sponsors, catechists, leaders, friends and guides, however they are described, have the ministry of welcoming, sharing faith, pastoring, instructing and helping the enquirer on the journey. The image is of a coach rather than a teacher, someone who runs alongside an athlete, a guide who shares knowledge of a route they have travelled already, who journeys with a newcomer.

Journeys pass landmarks and the catechumenate journey has certain recognized stages which are marked by celebration. These are the Rites of the R.C.I.A. Here let me emphasize that there is far, far more to the R.C.I.A. than a series of good, interesting and impressive services. The Rites or Liturgies which celebrate the stages along the journey are effective signs of what is happening spiritually and personally to the people who are on their way. They are signs to them and to the congregation of what it means to become a Christian.

There is first a time of enquiry, the 'Pre-catechumenate', during which someone meets the church, tests out what it has to say to them; whether the people are friendly or not; if it is worth persevering with. It is a time of initial encounter, of getting to know, of telling and listening to stories.

Those who want to go further express this desire at the celebration of Entry into the Catechumenate or Admission of Catechumens, in which they are formally welcomed by the congregation and signed with the cross as people who have made their first step into the household of faith.

There follows the time of learning, growing and maturing which is the period of the catechumenate proper. It takes as long as it needs. General experience seems to point to an average time of nine to twelve months.

At the close of this period comes the Call of the people to be baptized. In the classic pattern Easter is the time for initiation at the Vigil and the Solemn Call (The Rite of Election or the Rite of Inscription or Enrolling of Names) takes place at the beginning of Lent. At it the Church in the person of the Bishop or his nominee examines the people who are to be baptized, calls them to prepare for their baptism and invites them to sign their names on the roll of those so called. The people who have accompanied them and the whole congregation are responsible for sponsoring them and giving evidence of their fitness for the Sacrament.

Lent or the equivalent period leading up to the Baptism is
the time of Enlightenment, a spiritual preparation, often
marked by special celebrations of prayer (the Scrutinies) and
the symbolic presentations to the candidates of the Creed and
the Lord's Prayer.

The centre of the whole journey is, of course, the Celebration of Baptism, Confirmation and the Eucharist, at which the
whole congregation should celebrate the entry of new
brothers and sisters into the death and new life of the Risen
Christ.

There follows (again classically from Easter to Pentecost)
the time of Mystagogia when the newly baptised enter into
the meaning of the sacrament and have the chance to witness
to the congregation of what has happened to them.

Evidence from many parts of the world and from people of
different churches and cultures shows how much value has
been found in the liturgical expression of these turning points.
Candidates have spoken of the strengthening they have received and members of congregations have been moved to
reflect deeply on what their own Christian commitment
means for them.

CHRISTIAN COMMUNITY

'In the catechumenate we don't talk about Church; we make
Church.' The aim is to provide an opportunity for the enquirer to experience what it means to be part of a community
where the love of God is expressed by love of the neighbour.
To this end in this book I propose the basic unit of the
catechumenate is a group of about ten people where this
experience of life in the Body of Christ is possible. The life of
the whole congregation is too large and a one-to-one relationship of enquirer and catechist or priest too restricted.
What is needed is a human-scale group where it is possible to
know and be known; to be accepted and learn to forgive; to
pray together and to support and be supported by one
another.

In another sense the catechumenate is essentially concerned

with Christian community. It is the work of the whole community, people and priest together. Each baptized member of the Church has a ministry in it. Some have the ministry of intercession, of participation in the liturgical celebration, of being the welcoming, supporting community. Others have more specific roles as sponsors and catechists, or as spiritual directors and helpers, or again as leaders and trainers of leaders.

In an age where 'every member ministry' is a catchphrase in many parts of the Church, the Catechumenate is a field where the phrase finds 'lively' practical expression which seems to put it into effect in a natural and proper way.

2

A Journey Shared

Essential Topics

Language reflects attitudes and beliefs. In this book my beliefs
about what is important for the man or woman coming to the
Christian faith, personal commitment and initiation into the
Church are reflected by the use of language to do with
journeying, with growth into maturity and with search. I am
writing about a process which is concerned to help someone
discover and become what God has it in his plan for them to
be. This concerns the whole of a person. It affects their
understanding, their attitudes, their spirituality, their relationships with other people and the choices they make in life.
It is affected by their character, by their experience of living
from birth to the present day, by their friends and by the
society and communities to which they belong. I aim to
present a holistic approach to the work of adult catechesis. It
is something very wide, as wide as life itself.

Journeys always have to begin somewhere. It is important
that people responsible for accompanying others recognize
where their starting point is. Begin where they are. My own
experience in common, I suspect, with most other Church
leaders in parishes and chaplaincies is that by far the greatest
number of people who come to us for baptism or confirmation or for help in their search for a meaning in life have at
some time previously come into contact with Christianity in
some way.

I write in the second half of the 1980s. It may well be that
the movement of Britain away from organized Christianity

and from exposure to Christian teaching and influence will accelerate. It may mean that in a relatively short time there will be fewer and fewer people who will have received even a nominal amount of Christian education or contact with the Church. Even today there will, of course, be people who begin with no understanding from their past about Christianity and there will be people from other faiths. But most will have some idea of their own what Christianity is about.

Faith

The journey is about faith. John Shea has a telling remark: 'The right question is not, "Do you have faith?", but, "What is your faith?" '[1] The point where people start their journey is in fact a point of faith, their own faith. Even if it is not what is generally recognized as religious, there is something in everyone which gives them (or fails to give them) a sense of purpose or meaning or simply a sense of who they are. It is their attitude towards life, how they lean into life.

Faith in this sense may seem a much reduced idea to someone who is used to talking about the Christian Faith. It can be both a strong, positive, creative attitude to life or an empty, negative and painful attitude. There is no need here to go into the psychological explanations of how we come by the sort of personalities we have. It is enough simply to ask you to think about, say, six people you know, the first six or so who come to mind, and to ask yourself what you know about their faith, what, deep down is important to them. The possibilities are infinite. Among them you may well recognise the importance of family with the loving or less than loving relationship of parents and children; the sense of being given worth by someone who loves you; a pride in skills and achievements, your own or those of someone you admire – 'My dad was regimental heavyweight champion'. There are people whose lives seem to be governed by status or money and people who have almost given up making choices in life because of a kind of apathy which sees everything as 'Fate'.

The faith, in this wide sense, which has brought someone towards the Church may well be one of questioning. People become dissatisfied with attitudes which no longer meet their needs. Something may have happened in their life to cause them to reassess the principles by which they live.

That is a rather analytical way of describing the sort of thing which happens to a young man when his wife gives birth to their first baby, or to a middle-aged woman when the mother she has nursed through her long final illness at last dies. Or the kind of challenges to making sense of life that are presented by unemployment to the school-leaver in a derelict steel town, or to the car worker whose settled habits of regular work are shattered by the closure of the factory. Questions about who I am, where I am going and why, are raised in a fresh way and with a different urgency.

What adult catechesis is concerned with is recognizing those questions and accepting their importance for this woman or that man. Christians who are accompanying enquirers will want to help them to understand their own questions and will work with them to see what answers are to be found in all that comes under the label of Christianity. In Chapter 3 I shall be looking in more detail at ways in which this can be done. For the moment let me simply say that the task is to help forward growth, change and development. It is the movement from the faith which the enquirer brings towards a mature Christian faith. Catechesis of this kind takes the person seriously; it listens to and respects the story of their life; it presents to them the story of God's love and helps them to meet the challenge of God's story to their own.

Choices

The use of 'journey language' implies that real choices are there to be made and that the choices belong to the person making the journey. The responses to God's challenge and initiative can only be made by them. They will be lived out in changes made in real life. It is the whole man or the whole woman we are dealing with and they have the right to expect that the Church should respect their God-given adulthood and humanity.

Sooner or later the question of conscience will come up. Right and wrong are important to everyone, though not everyone will have the same judgement on what is right and what is wrong. For many Christianity is really about good behaviour, living by 'Christian Principles', 'following the Sermon on the Mount' – or even simply 'not doing anyone any harm'. Part of the work of the journey towards Christian maturity is the working out in practical terms what these 'Christian Principles' are and how they are to be applied in everyday life.

Journey language also implies that there are by no means always easy answers, nor is there any guarantee of success – whatever 'success' may mean in this enterprise. Certainly there are some people whose way into Christian belief and whose life as Christians look easy and happily God-given. For others the journey is harder; it calls for patience and an understanding of yourself and of other people. As falling in love is a painful process for some individuals, so can conversion be.

Accompanying

The other aspect of journey language is that it carries with it the image of companions sharing the journey, rather than the image of teachers passing on information. This accompanying is essential. The Christian community as a whole is responsible for the welcome and nurture of enquirers and new Christians. The duty is primarily discharged by those who have immediate contact with them, their friends and sponsors and their catechists, the people who are charged with their formation as Christians, whether they are professional ministers and clergy or, more probably, lay people.

Later in the book I deal with ways of training and continuing help for the people who are responsible. Sufficient at
this point to say the best way to learn how to accompany
others on a journey of faith is to enter yourself into the
experience of being open about your own faith with someone
else. It is worth quoting James Dunning's maxim, 'Thou shalt
not do unto others What thou hast not done for thyself'.

What I hope you will do as you read this book is check out
what I write or suggest by talking it through with a friend.
Make time to discuss at quite a deep level the things that
really matter to you. The best resource a Christian communi-
cator has is their own experience of God and what they
themselves have made of that experience in their private
reflections and in the way they live their life. That is what they
have been given to share with other people. Yours may not
seem very much compared with St Paul's conversion on the
road to Damascus, or even compared with the obvious holi-
ness of the backs of necks in the rows in front of you in
Church on a Sunday morning, but it is what you have been
given and for you it matters. It is your first-hand evidence and
carries far more weight than your being trained to repeat
correct Church teaching. So, try it out with your friend!

Formation

It is worth making a distinction between the ideas which go
along with the word education and those which are to do with
the word formation. For me education speaks of school and
learning about subjects. Although other things are involved,
(there is 'Physical Education' after all) it is largely intellectual, about retaining and using facts and concepts. It is
training the mind. Instruction plays a large part in it. For most
people education means being taught by a teacher.

Formation on the other hand is giving form to something,
shaping it. In formation the concern is, certainly, to some
extent with understanding subjects but it is far wider. Forma-

tion is about helping a person to develop into shape for which God has given them the potential. In Christian formation the first aim is not to impart doctrines about God but rather to encourage someone in their search for God, in their meeting with him and in letting their whole life be moulded and changed by that experience. Christian formation is about being transformed into the pattern of Christ.

Using formation rather than instruction as a model gives a great weight to the importance of story. As a later chapter will show, this is both letting the gospel story and the stories of our Christian tradition do their work simply as stories. That, after all, is what they are before they become transmuted into doctrines and dogmas. It also means valuing the individual personal stories of the people with whom we are travelling as important for themselves and as the scene within which God is at work in his world.

To work with story is to enter into people's experience, to invite them to reflect upon what happens to them and upon what their own actions and reactions have been in the light of the story of the Gospel. From this relating real life and God's revelation comes the challenge to change in the present and the future.

Relationship with God

The journey we are on ourselves and the journey of the people we are accompanying is a journey of faith, a journey in God and to God. The work of clergy, catechists and sponsors is not primarily to teach about the Christian religion. It is to open eyes, minds, hearts and souls to God and his love, power, goodness, truth and justice seen in the person and the work of Jesus. Our first aim is not understanding but faith. It is conversion to Christ. It is helping people to the place where, like the Ethiopian in some readings of Acts 8.37, they can say, 'I believe that Jesus Christ is Lord'. The many different aspects of the process of conversion are the subject of another

part of this book. Here simply let me say that if the Church is
not working for change in people's lives in response to the
Gospel, it is failing in its commission from God.

Spirituality

One very important part of Christian formation is prayer and
the development of spirituality. The world of the 1980s in
England shows many signs of a thirst for things of the spirit. It
is remarkable how many people in their search for meaning in
life turn to spiritual practices like yoga or meditation, following eastern religions like Hinduism or Buddhism – or at least
borrowing from their habits of spirituality. This is to say
nothing of the people who look to the more modern ways of
self-discovery through psychoanalysis or the deep personal
conversions which lie in the heart of Alcoholics Anonymous.
The occult, too, in all its manifestations, offers a sense of
meaning and purpose as an answer to some people's spiritual
search.

What I find sad and worrying is that, for all its centuries of
devotion to things of the spirit, the Christian church (or the
Christian churches, to be more accurate) are not resources to
which enquirers naturally turn for help in their quest. I
suspect that one reason for this among several is that Christians are not themselves confident that they have anything to
give to other people. For a very large number of Church
people prayer is an important part of life, but in my experience only a few feel strong enough to talk openly about it.
There is a hidden conspiracy about to say that prayer is for
experts to teach, rather than for 'ordinary people' to chat
about. Of course there are people who are acknowledged
leaders; they give retreats, write books and help individuals to
grow in spirituality. But there is a real danger of a 'guru-
culture' which while exalting the guru, perhaps too much, at
the same time devalues the ordinary practitioner of prayer,
the man and woman in the pew.

So, once again, here is an area in Christian life where the

catechumenate method encourages lay men and women to share their own experiences with other people. This accompanying others in spiritual matters also encourages the Christian to grow, to explore for himself or herself. The chapter on 'Friendship with God' is meant to whet the appetite. Clergy, members of religious communities and lay people need to be sufficiently at home in the world of prayer to help beginners. Once they discover that it is possible to dare to talk openly about an intimate relationship with God; once they experience that in a caring dialogue people can grow in their awareness of God and the ways he wants them to develop, then they may want to acquire the understanding and learn the skills that belong to spiritual direction.

Worship

Private devotion is not the Christian's only way of expressing their relationship with God. At several points in this book we return to what for many English people Christianity is mainly about – 'going to Church'. The Christian community meets for worship. Apart from the actual work of worshipping God, this also provides a shop window display of the Church. It is where the fact of Church is made manifest in the town or city or the suburb or the village. It is often where men and women come, shyly perhaps, to test whether this group of people or this priest can help them in their search for meaning.

Common worship moulds those who take part in it. It too is part of the formation of the new Christian. Therefore it needs to be both attractive and true to all that Christian discipleship means.

Christian Tradition

My emphasis on formation rather than instruction does not mean that I ignore the inheritance of belief and practice which is to be found in Church and Bible. To talk about leading people to faith in God, does not wipe out talk about 'The Faith', it simply puts it in a different place.

As people come to faith in Christ they have to face the fact of the Church. Their route to faith will almost certainly be marked by their encounters at different times of their life with members of the Church, official or lay who have either hindered them or helped them forward on their journey. For some the fact of the Church as they have met it or as they imagine it is a barrier. Jesus may attract them but they are put off by his people or by the organisation which represents him in today's world. On the other hand there are men and women who find an attraction in the life of the Church and look for friendship among the people who belong to it.

I have a vivid memory of asking a candidate for baptism and confirmation what made her take the step of asking for it. She had first approached the Church to have her baby christened and she replied, 'The lady who came round from the Church to talk about the christening had got something and I wanted it too'.

The Church is often seen quite simply as a place to find friends, somewhere to go if you are lonely. It is an institution which is thought to be in the business of offering help, of offering healing to people who are hurt.

Sacraments

If the journey towards faith in God through Jesus Christ is also a journey towards the sacraments of Christian initiation, then it is a journey towards joining the Church. Christian baptism, as well as being baptism into the one, holy, catholic and apostolic Church is also baptism into the local manifestation of that wonderful body – the Church where you and I worship, where we are members and where we are called to exercise our ministry. People who are on their journey towards baptism will need to get to know the people and the life of that Church. They will take part in its worship and in the social events and neighbourhood service which the community offers.

The Local Church

The trouble is that they will meet, not some ideal Christian community, but the strange mixture of people and the even stranger set of habits, attitudes and cross-currents of emotion which mark the congregation at the Parish Church in the High Street.

This faces the local Church fairly and squarely with the need to ask itself whether the story it has to tell and which its life displays is a true reflection of the gospel story. Can the newcomer see a line of continuity between the Jesus he or she meets in the New Testament and the Church of Jesus which meets in the Parish Church? There is a whole range of qualities which a community could well take note of. Is the Church welcoming or cold? I mean the people even more than the building! Are they open or closed? What about the unity of the Church? Is it cliquey and do people cherish factions and resentments? Where is the attention of the community focussed, on self-preservation or concern for people outside the fellowship? Is there a sense of a desire for God, his worship and his service which runs deep or is there a suspicion of superficiality? What sort of people belong? Is there a sense of selection or of preconditions for entry?

In this kind of self-examination members of the Church need to look both at what is public, the worship, the activities, the organizations and the involvement in society and also at the more private assumptions about patterns of responsibility and authority and about the different layers of needs met and help offered by the Church. I mention all this as Christian tradition because it is the tradition which the enquirer sees. The established lay person and even more the trained and educated minister may well think of the tradition of beliefs and liturgy, of culture, history and doctrine which are part of the inheritance to be shared with the newcomers of this generation. These are all important, they are part of the story we have to tell. As someone goes through the process of joining the community they need to get to know at least some part of the story and to make it their own. However what an enquirer looks for is some kind of agreement and harmony in the Christian community between the behaviour of that community and its gospel. It is against this practical testing that those who are accompanying enquirers have to share their faith, helping them to enter into the inheritance of what it means to be a Christian and a member of the Church.

There is a Christian inheritance, a living tradition of revelation which seeks in every generation to present the story of God's dealing with his creation to the people of that generation in a way which is both true to the tradition and relevant and challenging to contemporary people. The catechist or the sponsor needs to be enough at home within the tradition to be able to hear and feel the relevance of the Christian story to their own lives and to the life of the society in which they live. They need to have enough confidence and sensitive perception to relate the tradition-story with the story told them by the person they are accompanying. This is, I believe, the work of practical, local theology. It is open to clergy and lay alike.

3

Faith and Believing

'It is Jesus Christ I believe in most. He lived like us; he knew poverty and want; he experienced what is true for people, what it means to be a person. Jesus didn't bother about the noise the crowd was making – he only heard the blind man. He was strong; not weak like us. He died having fulfilled what he had to fulfil, still with his strength and his faith. I want to have this strength, which I haven't yet got.

'Jesus is not dead. For me it's not finished. I hope when I die to be with him. For me he is always there.

'It's Jesus who makes God real for us.

'I always wanted to go to Church as a girl, but my family was against it. I found the opportunity when I came to ask for my babies to be christened. I have been helped by a priest and this group of friends.

'My mother's death helped me towards faith. I'm sure I will meet her.

It was in Northern France that I sat in on an evening session with the small group of people accompanying a young mother of two children. She worked as a bank clerk. Her baptism was in a few weeks and together they were preparing her 'Profession of Faith'. At Epiphany as she stood before the water she would be asked to affirm her belief in her own words, along the lines of those notes which I took at the time.

Faith is what being a Christian is about, but like so many

vitally important things in life people are uncertain about exactly what it means. They build up all sorts of different personal and shared images about it. We are concerned with the work of accompanying people to that place on their journey where they can make their own commitment to the faith of the community they desire to join.

The work of adult catechesis is to be found in the process of welcome, conversion and nurture. It depends both on the method and the material content used in that process. I put method first because it is essential to recognise that the approach is concerned with people; programme or syllabus come second. We are not dealing with a course of instruction; it is journeys, each individual person making their own. The method has to model this.

The task of the Christian guide and friend is to foster and provide for dialogue, meeting, creative confrontation between the person, who comes with his or her own story of life, events and relationships, and the Church's story of God's revelation of himself in the created world, in the life, death and resurrection of Jesus Christ and the continuing life of his people. Later in this chapter I shall suggest some methods by which this can be achieved. For the moment I simply point out that there is an infinite variety of ways of helping people meet God and be changed by him. They involve every side of human personality. Sometimes it is through one-to-one conversation; sometimes it is through meeting God's people as a community. It could be the experience of worship or the healing brought by forgiveness and acceptance. The dialogue is between individuals with their own story, their gifts and their requests and the Gospel as told by and lived in the Church. There is a place for wonder and awe, for the excitement of new discoveries of meaning and relationship, for falling in love with Jesus, for letting God's love, truth and justice challenge and reshape the attitudes and responses of everyday life.

More than teaching people about the Christian faith so that

they understand it, what we are about is a process of learning, growing and changing which involves the whole person and which affects every aspect of their life, private and public. Of course in this life it never can achieve its fulfilment. Here in the preparation of people for baptism and confirmation we are dealing with the opening stages. However we are right to expect it to make a difference in people. Indeed one of the areas of enquiry to see if people are ready for initiation is around the question whether their life and behaviour shows signs of Christian commitment. I have a vivid memory of a man with his own small engineering company who said to me, 'Peter, I don't know if I ought to be confirmed. I'm not sure what difference it will make to the way I run my business.'

Faith

There is a family connection between the words and phrases we use: 'A meaning to life', 'A purpose in life', 'A faith' or 'The Faith'. They all have to do with our making sense of ourselves and people and things around us: or, indeed, being unable to come to terms. They are about 'The way you lean into life'. It is presenting to ourselves what really matters to us. Turn all or any of these into areas of human search, questioning, pain or fear and you find the roots of most of the requests for help which people bring to the Church, its members or its ministers.

The Christian response is to invite the enquirer in one way or another to share in the Christian faith. I say 'in one way or another' because there is a wide variety of personalities and a wide range of life-stories. Both will influence someone in their perception of what matters for them in the cluster of meanings around the nucleus of the Christian faith. This is one of those occasions when I wish the following pages could be accompanied by a videotape of animated graphics. Faith is dynamic and relational rather than analytical and static. So please bear that in mind as you read on.

'Belief that . . .'

When Philip the deacon baptized the Ethiopian eunuch the condition 'If you believe that Jesus Christ is Lord' looks like the earliest form of test for Christian initiation. From it developed the Creeds as we have them, the Apostles' Creed growing from the baptismal creed of the Church in Rome and the Nicene Creed developing through the processes of Ecumenical Councils of Bishops in the Church to define the Orthodox Catholic Faith in the face of different heresies.

For some people the Christian faith consists of their ability to recite the Creed and mean it wholeheartedly. Among a certain range of members of the Church of England there is a feeling of standing to attention during the saying of the Creed in Church, not far removed from the feeling of the National Anthem or the Last Post on Remembrance Sunday at the two minutes' silence. The words matter. They express the truth and demand assent. Here are a series of beliefs about God and Jesus expressed in summary form as the essentials of the faith.

'Relationship with . . .'

Not so much 'believing that . . .' as 'trusting in . . .' is another approach to faith with a different emphasis. Jesus endorsed the two short summaries of the Jewish Law, 'Love God with all your heart and mind and strength', and 'Love your neighbour as yourself'. Christian faith is seen not so much in the intellectual assent to doctrine as in the commitment of the will to respond to the love of God by loving him in return, following the example of the Jesus seen in the Gospels and entering into a relationship with the Father through him and in his spirit.

This relationship with God overflows and finds its practical expression in a life lived in obedience to the teachings of Jesus. Christian faith implies Christian living. The Gospels are full of the insistence of Jesus that, unlike the Pharisees, his disciples were to live out their belief in God's love by sharing love with others. There is an essential practicality about being a Christian. Belief in the incarnation, that God took human flesh, demands that it is in the choices and relationships of human life and human society that faith is to be realised.

Belonging

Christian faith is the faith of the Christian community. The gospels record the story told by that community; the Creeds are its summaries and its existence bears witness to a desire to live obedient to the command to love one's neighbour.

Whether it is seen from a 'high' belief in the Church as the Body of Christ or a 'low' belief in the Church as a community of believers, Christian history shows that the faith is essentially a community experience. Jesus did not leave behind a set of rules or a code of doctrine; he left a group of people. What gives this group and its successors meaning and cohesion is the story we tell. The story of the Good News is in our books, summarised in our Creeds and is the ideal by which we try to live our own lives as a community and as individuals.

Many Christians naturally define themselves as Christians not by the beliefs they hold but by their church allegiance, either to a denomination or to a particular local congregation 'I'm a Methodist' or 'I go to St. John's'. Belonging matters. Faith is a corporate event in their lives and is as intimately connected with friendships and group loyalties as with belief or behaviour.

Balanced Faith

Clearly none of these aspects, intellectual assent, relationship with God and its overflowing into lifestyle and community, are mutually exclusive. It is not a question of either/or. Far from it; a balanced Christian faith contains them all and each gives shape to or expresses the others. At different stages of development and in different types of person one or other aspect of faith will predominate. When one aspect grows out of all proportion and swamps the others, there is a distortion.

Among Anglicans there has, I suspect, long been a heavy reliance on assent to the written statements of belief and a comparative neglect of the other two. An emphasis on books and reading; churchgoers who feel lost if they cannot follow the Service for themselves from the page in front of them; and a certain mystique of the priest as one who has studied theology – all these tend to result in a down-grading of faith as relationship and belonging.

I am concerned to restore the lost balance and to give full weight to the non-verbal, non-intellectual side of Christian faith experience. The process followed in formation of adult Christians matters as much as the content. People learn by example and by experience as much as (or more than) by persuasion or explanation. The method used in adult catechesis should reflect and incarnate the belief that God cares for and gives infinite value to each man and woman.

Norbert Mette writing on *The Christian Community's Task in the Process of Religious Education* describes six aspects:
'(a) Learning the faith is a total process of learning that involves the whole man or woman. The invitation to discipleship and the challenge to conversion cannot be compartmentalized, but affects all spheres of life. The aim of learning the faith is becoming a responsible agent, is man's or woman's "integral liberation". This rules out every form of compulsion and manipulation.
'(b) Learning the faith is a process that lasts as long as life itself. It follows the course of human development and encourages it by continually challenging one to become personally aware of and appropriate the fullness of life with the promise it offers.
'(c) Learning the faith is a process that transcends the generations and a mutual process in which those involved learn from each other . . .
'(d) Learning the faith is a process of learning in solidarity. It takes place when faith and life are shared among each other and interpreted jointly in the light of the biblical message.

'(e) Learning the faith is a committed process of learning. Learning to grasp the possibilities of life given by God makes one sensitive to everyone deprived of the elementary rights of living and bringing one's life to fulfilment.

'(f) Learning the faith is an innovatory process of learning. It does not simply limit itself to instruction in current values and norms. Rather it arouses at the same time the ability to examine them to see whether they make human life possible and in certain cases to change them.'[1]

Process and Content

In ordinary everyday relationships and conversation the actual words we say to one another form only a part of the interchange between people. The content, the message carried by words is reinforced or denied by many other facets of communication. Gesture, facial expression, tone of voice, social accent, even clothes, each carry their own strong message. We may hear and understand what someone says, but what we remember is the kind of person they showed themselves to be and the overall impression they made on us. We look for answers to questions such as, 'Do I trust her?'; 'Does he like me?'; 'Am I safe here?'; 'Is he listening to what I have to say?'.

Communicating Christian faith is no different. Certainly there are people who have met Christ and been changed as people through the printed word alone, but I suspect they are few and far between. The normal way to learn and grow, the way to conversion is by way of meeting with other people and being open to their influence.

This is why I believe that the way adult formation takes place is as important as the content of the teaching which is given. Throughout this book I have in mind the model of working with a group of people, probably no more than eight or ten. It is small enough for a certain intimacy and large enough to give some variety of experience and attitudes. I suggest there will be either one or two leaders who have some ability to work in and with a group and who are mature enough in their own faith and knowledge to help others with some confidence (though not, I hope, with overweening self-assurance!). Some members of the group are Christian helpers, already partway along the journey and the rest are those for whom the group has come into being, the enquirers and people on their way towards Christian commitment, faith and initiation. The kind of life experienced in this group has as much effect as the content of the syllabus. As simple evidence for this I merely ask you to look back over your own life, reflect upon times of learning in church and ask what stands out in your memory, what has had the most influence. I should be surprised if it is not more the people and their attitude or events and feelings about them rather than items of knowledge or insight into doctrines which come strongly to mind.

In the church as anywhere else there is always a danger that good ideas get over-used or misused and strong words end up as jargon buzz-words. I worry about the words 'share' and 'story'. They could be facing this danger, but I want to use them and to enter quite deeply into their meanings and connections.

I envisage the enquirer learning about God and finding faith in him through his or her encounter and developing a relationship with the people of Jesus. For this to happen there must be a situation where they can actually be welcomed, be met as individuals and be accepted. It is most unlikely that this can be found in church services or in large gatherings. It does happen in individual encounters; one-to-one conversations and friendships are very much part of most people's maturing as Christians. They involve to a greater or lesser extent each person in openness about themselves and accepting the other for what they are. 'Sharing' is the shorthand for what happens when people talk in that way. It involves being willing to speak about one's life, one's experiences, feelings, insights and expectations within an assurance of a proper confidentiality and a trust in the other's sincerity.

The same conditions apply to the sharing within a group.

Trust is essential and it has to be earned or merited. People must not be forced into confidences they are not ready to share or burdened with other people's problems they are not willing to carry. On the other hand it is part of the natural bonding between individuals that they are willing to expose their lives, their personalities – even their names to one another.

In a Christian group journeying towards faith and commitment this bonding counts for more than a simple exercise in inter-personal dynamics. It is an experience of and a witness to God's love in accepting and forgiving men and women. It involves leaders and members in all the human skills of tact, delicacy and friendship. It also calls for the exercise of prayer and a continual desire to be open to the leading of the Holy Spirit in the work of his Church.

'Story' is shorthand for talk about someone's life with its events and relationships. It means listening to what they see as their high and low points; what matters most to them; what their interests and concerns are. Story in this sense is what gives to each person their meaning and identity. Part of it is narrative – the story told – and part is in the weight of feeling and personal investment given to different incidents or relationships or hopes and fears. It stands for this woman or this man as the person they are with all they have and bring with them into an encounter with someone else. It could be a long life-history. It could be an intense single experience which at the time is all important.

Part of the work of the group is to give value to each member's story. Apart from the natural building of friendship and trust, this valuing is essential in a Christian group for two reasons. It is again, evidence that each individual has infinite value to God and so to his Church. 'I need to know by experiencing it that I matter.' It is also a vital part in the work of Christian formation to recognise God at work in the ordinary, everyday life of each person. God can be seen at work in very ordinary situations and events.

There are two streets in North London, parallel turnings off a suburban High Street. The houses were very much the same, built as part of a 1920s development, but one was a friendly, neighbourhood street and the other was cold. When I asked why the difference, the people in the friendly street told me about a woman who'd lived there some years before. Whenever a new person or family moved in she went round with a bunch of flowers. Although she had died, the neighbours kept up the habit.

Gerry told me his story. His wife had left him for a man at the firm she worked for. He had taken it hard, got very depressed and drank too much. He'd thought of suicide. His boss was complaining about him. What changed all this was a friend who just asked him if he would like to go fishing the next weekend. He felt someone had noticed – and he enjoyed sitting peacefully by the canal beginning to sort himself out.

The Jewish-Christian vision is of a God who is Creator and Judge responsible for and active in the life of people and communities in his world; a God who in Jesus Christ has entered fully into all that it means to be human to redeem humanity. So it is right to give high importance to individual lives as the place where vocation is at work, the process of God's call and human response in and through the events of childhood and youth, work and leisure, marriage or single-ness, maturity and old age, birth and bereavement.

The third of the elements in the process of Christian formation as I see it, along with the life and dynamics of the group itself and the sharing of the stories of the members, is the Gospel, the Bible story or the Church's story. It is what we as followers of Jesus have to tell about him and what he shows us of God. Here is where we enter the realm of the books of instruction about the Christian faith, the beginners' guides to the teachings of the Church. But, once again, I want to plead for narrative rather than analysis.

John Westerhoff writes: 'Our identity is dependent on having a story that tells us who we are. Our understanding of life's meaning and purpose is dependent on having a story that tells us what the world is like and where we are going. To be a community of faith we must be a people with a story, a common memory and vision, common rituals and symbols expressive of our community's memory and vision and a common life together that manifests our community's memory and vision. The Church is a story-formed community.'[2]

To put it over-simply: What gives the Jewish faith of the Old Testament its strength is the covenant story (or stories) with the continuing account of God's involvement in the history of his people. It reaches its peak in the saving event of the Exodus, combined with the demand that his people respond by life lived in accordance with his Law.

What the New Testament calls for is a faith-response to the story of Jesus, seen as God's Messiah, crucified and raised from death. His story includes, of course, stories of his Ministry, teaching, parables, signs and miracles as well as the continuing story of his followers in the letters and the Acts of the Apostles. It is retold and re-experienced in each successive generation of the Christian Church.

One particular way the Church tells its story is in the keeping of the Christian year. The church calendar acts out the Gospel and the Sunday readings in the different cycles in use in the churches provide a resource of material to base the work of a group on.

Story-Gospel Dialogue

'Our first task in approaching another people, another culture, another religion is to take off our shoes, for the place we are approaching is holy; else we might find ourselves treading on another's dream. More serious still, we may forget that God was there before us.' I saw these words in a wall poster at a centre preparing volunteer missionaries for service in the Third World. They are as true for the ministry of the Christian accompanying someone into faith along the lines we are dealing with here. The dialogue between the Church and the enquirer, between the Gospel and the person's story begins with the Church listening to the enquirer. The leader helps the newcomer to tell their story and tries to listen and discern with love and attention both to the man or woman speaking and to God who is and has been active in their history.

Listening

It is not difficult to listen to someone else's story. To do it well may take a bit of practice, because it is not something everyone is good at. Most people seem to find it easier to talk than to listen! In fact once you set yourself to listen and help the other person tell their story simply by giving your attention, you will find it intensely interesting. This is usually a surprise to the story-teller because he or she thinks their own life dull and ordinary!

It will be clear by now that what I mean by 'Story' is rather wider than a simple recounting of events. It covers what is important to the person; what he would like me to know about himself; what she has weighing on her mind this evening.

If you invite someone, 'Tell me a little about yourself', expect all sorts of answers. 'I was born in Pontyprydd and my parents moved up to Streatham when I was three because my father lost his job in South Wales and came up to London to find work.' 'My husband and I have got three children at school so I don't go out to work any more.' 'I am a stewardess on short-haul flights. It's all right but you get very tired in the summer'. 'I don't know, life seems rather a mess at the moment. Since we split up, nothing's going right. I get very anxious and depressed.' 'I've got a job at Robinson's, in the paint shop. There's my two brothers in the firm. It's where the family's always worked.'

Just five possible answers are an indication. As you read you can think of scores of others. How do you answer a question like that yourself? What do your close friends say? Can you think of recent conversations with people you have met? As you reflect on the answers I suggest you may begin to ask what they show about the speaker's sense of and meaning in life. What matters to them? What are their deeper questions? The description people give to their own story or the tone in which they tell it may well point to how they judge the meaning and purpose in their life at that moment. The value they give to their own past, their childhood, parents and grandparents. The value they put on themselves – 'I'm afraid I'm only a housewife'.

Status in life is important for most people. It is about the image we have of ourselves. Many factors go to a sense of status. From within there is a personal sense of worth, of being someone; or of lostness, being unwanted. Externally there are different sorts of achievement, at work, in family life, among friends. There are the indicators which mark social status; size of house and the class of neighbourhood speak volumes to other people.

The work of a good leader of a group or a friend accompanying an enquirer towards faith begins with these stories. There is common ground there. Maybe the events and the personalities are not common to everyone – it would be surprising if they were. But what is common is the living of life and the being affected by the relationships and events of life. It is vital to be able to listen well. The leader needs to encourage and reassure and reinforce without telling too much of their own story. A danger is in the natural desire to swop excitements and to cap the other person's tale with one of our own. Resist this urge! It may sometimes be suitable, but only rarely. What is called for is the ability to give attention and to draw out what really matters for each person in the group. Beyond that and deeper into the heart of the process is a need for discernment, first in order to see the high points and the depths in someone's telling of their story, and then to be able to suggest where in the story God is to be encountered, who is the meaning of life.

Stories of Faith

As people tell their story they may well talk about their beliefs and their awareness of God for themselves. Many will have a 'pre-history' of contact with the Church, perhaps as a child in

Sunday School or through a family funeral or a wedding.
They will have faced situations in their lives when they have
asked deep questions or have been moved by experiences they
cannot quite explain.

Leaders need not only to encourage, listen and discuss.
They also need to respond appropriately with the Christian
story. At times and probably more often as the journey moves
forward towards deeper commitment and awareness on the
part of the enquirers, the group sessions will begin from
Gospel and move towards life story, rather than the other
way. Whichever direction the dialogue takes it does call for a
degree of knowledge of the Christian tradition and a certain
agility on the part of the leader to move about the material
and select what is suitable.

Joan is a single woman. She lives at home and cares for her
mother who is an invalid. She goes out to work at an office
job which is safe but dull. She dislikes it, but can't face the
thought of moving to a new firm. Anyway she might not find
one. She feels stuck and flat – and not a little angry. Her life
seems less than it could be.

The group leader asks what the Gospel has to say to Joan in
this particular time. Who did Jesus meet who felt like Joan?
What story seems appropriate? As you read, you might like
for a moment to put the book down and ask yourself those
questions.

You may well come up with something quite different from
me. I simply suggest that there is something in Joan's story
about being blocked, paralysed. I think it would be suitable to
read or tell the story of the four friends who brought the
paralysed man to Jesus and let him down into the house
through the roof. The conversation could go on to the echoes
and meanings which the story of the healing brings to Joan;
where she can hear a connection between forgiveness and
release from paralysis; what is the part played by these friends
in the group; and what response she finds proper to make to
the word she hears.

The range of stories and concerns is infinite from intimate

personal worries and pleasures to the military use of space. I hesitate to give too many examples. I would much rather that people who either are already working with adults or are preparing to accompany others on a faith journey used this as an opportunity to reflect on what they have heard from other people and also what they know about themselves. Let the reflection enter into underlying causes and trends and see what needs for healing, forgiveness, salvation come to the surface. Ask yourself what in your understanding of the Gospel story speaks to those needs. As well, spend some time reflecting on the story of your own journey in faith. What parts of the Gospel, the story told by the Church or lived in the Church, have been bright and alive for you, a source of saving or healing or insight.

In this I am asking people to use their skills and abilities of perception. Words like 'see', 'hear', 'realize' are more important at this point than 'think', 'analyse', 'give reasons'. That throws us back to the purpose of the exercise. What I am not talking about is a Bible Study Group, working through, say, the Gospel according to Luke with a commentary. Still less am I talking about a session on the Bible as part of a 'Bishop's Certificate' course. These, of course, have their proper place and I would hope that they formed part of the preparation of group leaders. No, here we are seeking to provide an opportunity for a meeting between God and a person, for an opening or a deepening of the person's awareness of what the Good News is for them. For this to happen we need to let the telling and listening to stories do their own work.

A friend of mine was working with a group of Cambodian refugees now settled in the U.S.A. She told the story of the people of Israel in bondage in Egypt and their escape in the Exodus. As she spoke and as one of them translated into Cambodian, their faces lit up and they became more and more excited. 'But that's our story', they said, 'We have been oppressed and persecuted. We have seen people we love killed or tortured. Now we have escaped across the water into a new country.'

We try to let the story speak and then to discuss and develop what people hear in the story. God speaks through his word and people can be helped to listen.

The Gospel is the story which gives the Church its meaning. So there is a parallel reason for story telling. It is that people who want to join the Church need to be part of that story and the identity it brings. They need to be able to sing the community songs and recognize the names of the community heroes.

As I said above, the Church year with its seasons and its festivals tells of the suffering, death and resurrection of Jesus at Easter. It tells of the empowering of his disciples to become the Church with a world-wide commission to proclaim the Gospel and baptise at Pentecost. It looks back to the Jewish Church's story of Creation and Fall, of Abraham and Moses and David, of covenant between God and man, of God who communicates in judgement and hope, punishment and forgiveness with his people. It looks forward from the story of Jesus the man, his birth and his Ministry, to the story of the Body of Christ. It commemorates the heroes of the Church of the New Testament and of the Christian centuries since. It proclaims the Christian hope for the Kingdom of God now and in the infinite future.

This is the story which the Church has to tell and to which the enquirer is invited to respond. This is the story which the enquirer rightly challenges to give meaning to his or her own life. In the telling and the hearing of this story a man or woman has every right to ask, 'Does the God who acts like this, does this Jesus who says, performs and suffers these things, speak to me in my own life? Where do my story and this story meet?'

Probably it is not going to be for most people the broad sweep of the story in the Christian year which provides the revelation and excites the wonder. Rather than the *Story* it will be the *stories* which connect. The Old and the New Testament are filled with good stories with human interest, whether it is of the journey in faith which Abraham took to an

unknown country or David's shameful adultery with Bathshe-
ba and his murder of her husband; or the call of Isaiah; or
Jeremiah's proclamation of God's judgement on his own nation and his persecution because of it. In the Gospels there are
the parables which Jesus told, there are the stories of his
miracles, his encounters with people and the stories of his
birth and of his passion, death and resurrection. They are
often good stories, simply in themselves, but their purpose
and their use is to engage the hearers and to draw them into
relationship with God as the central character. There is a
danger in working from the individual person's story that the
conversation can become over-subjective. The Bible points to
the wider reference, it roots human events within God's plan
for his world, it sets up an external set of values to judge our
reactions by.

Pictures and metaphors are a kind of miniature story. The
words and images the Church uses for God are part of its
story – or at any rate the language of its story. They are well
worth entering into. God as Creator, Father, Redeemer. God
as love, light, wind and fire. God as rock, depth, warrior.
Read the hymns and hear what echoes resound in your
imagination at the language without the music. Listen to
Isaiah, Hosea and St. Paul. Listen to the evangelical revival
preachers. Listen to the words of the liturgy and let the names
of God work on your deep needs or highest aspirations and
those of the people you are accompanying. Which names sing
for you and which are empty?

Starting from the Gospel

There is no one right way to help people to hear God speaking
to their lives through the Bible. In this Section what I offer is
simply ideas on which each leader will base their own group
sessions, always leaving room for adaptation in response both
to what they hear themselves in their reading and to what the
members of their group ask for.

Preparation is vital. I am indebted to Karen Hinman Powell

of the North American Forum on the Catechumenate for her stages of preparation, designed for a Sunday morning catechetical session following the Ministry of the Word and here slightly edited for more general use. The leader is encouraged to follow these steps. No one can guide anyone else unless they have been there themselves before! If leaders are working in pairs, then this preparation should ideally be done together, allowing plenty of time for individual silent reflection as well as time for sharing insights and practical planning:

1. Find the readings. If you are following the pattern of the Sunday Cycle, this means reading through all three readings slowly and thoughtfully at least three times. Underline words or phrases that strike you as significant. Make a note of connections between the different readings. Get to know what is there in them.

2. Now enter into the Gospel. Read it over slowly and deliberately again. Picture it in your mind or imagination. Where does it take place? What time of day? What season of the year? Does place or time make a difference to the story? Who are the characters in the story? What are their names? Who do you find you identify with?

Who is the principal person in the Gospel story? What is their problem or their interest? Find in the text a phrase which expresses this from their perspective. (It is imperative to discover all this from *within* the Gospel.)

What is Jesus' response? How does he meet the interest or deal with the problem? (Again, find the answer in the text.) How do the other characters respond to the situation.

In all this try to place yourself in the text, experience it through the senses of your imagination – touch, sight, smell, hearing.

3. Once you have finished this visualizing and entering into the text and not before, read commentaries on the passage and let your mind work on it. How do the commentator's notes enlarge your understanding or challenge your perception of the Gospel?

4. Then leave all the reading, visualizing and thinking with

commentaries on one side and come before God to pray in and with this Gospel. You may find yourself listening for answers to questions like, What do these readings mean to you in your life? What do you hear Jesus saying to you (perhaps in your identification with one of the characters)? Are there strong echoes in your memory of incidents or people in your own life and experience? If there are, recall them carefully before God in the light of the Gospel. What are the connections? How do you respond? What does all this tell you about God, about Jesus, about yourself?

5. With all you have so far gathered, ask what questions are raised about the Christian tradition, the teachings of the Church and the life of the Christian community to which you belong.

6. Then design the outline of your group session and get together any materials that will be needed. Think which texts you are going to use. Work out a basic timetable. Design the layout of the room you will be in with any pictures or objects you want as a focus for prayer or reflection.

Three Models

These three patterns which follow are a resource to draw from. They have been designed with an awareness of the way adults learn and mature; they are specifically aimed at relating life and Gospel and they have been tested over a long time of experience.

An African Model

1 Opening prayer to gather the members together and focus the session.

2 Read the Gospel aloud slowly and deliberately. Ask people to listen for a word or phrase that stands out or speaks for them.

3 One minute of silence.

4 Invite everyone simply to say the word or phrase that touched them. Do not discuss!

5 Read the Gospel again.

6 Tell the group you will give them five minutes of silence to be with the Gospel (or three minutes if they are new to it). Be quiet for that time.

7 Invite them to note down what they hear in their heart, what the passage says that touches their life.

8 Divide into groups of not more than four or five, perhaps twos or threes, to speak of what they have got from the Gospel. It is very important that they use the word 'I' and own their personal experience and insight, rather than say what others believe. It is not a time for discussing or preaching or solving the problems of other people.

9 Read the Gospel again.

10 Ask people to consider what, in the light of the meeting so far, they believe God wants from them this week. How is he inviting them to change? What are they taking home with them this week? Specific answers are important, rather than responses like 'God wants me to be good for ever and ever'!

11 Again in little groups share these answers.

12 Gather the group together for a closing prayer with perhaps one of the readings, open prayer, silence or singing.

13 Give details of the next meeting and the passages to be read.

St Augustine's Church, Washington DC

Raymond Kemp suggests the following pattern.

1 Opening prayer, to include a reading of the Gospel.

2 Invite people to write their responses to the following questions:

(i) What did you hear? Write three thoughts, ideas, phrases, images that grabbed you in the reading.

(ii) What does it mean? Why did these words or images grab you today? What do they mean for your life? Can you recall a time in your life (past or present) which you experienced something similar to the event in today's reading? How does the reading enlighten or challenge that experience?

Write three questions that today's reading raises for you about your life, about your faith, about Church . . .

(iii) What does it cost you to live this message?

Note one concrete way you feel called to live this message this week.

What will help you to live this? What will be the obstacles?

3 Divide into small groups for members to share their reflections with each other.

4 All together in one group share insights learned and any questions left unresolved.

5 Closing Prayer.

6 Arrangements for next meeting.

Karen Hinman Powell's Model

1 Opening Prayer to include reading of the Gospel.

2 Reflections on the Gospel. Ask people to make notes:

(i) List three or four ideas, images or thoughts that struck them in today's reading.

(ii) Describe a time in the past week when they were called to live out one of these ideas. How did they respond?

(iii) Write down two questions the reading raises for them about being a Christian.

3 Share these reflections in small groups of four to six people.

4 In the large group feed back the experiences in small groups. In particular ask what similarities and differences they found; what questions do they have as a

group about the Christian tradition and the Church
(list these questions on a board).

5 (Optional) A short input by the leader on one or more
of these issues, either a spontaneous response or prepared beforehand.

6 Discussion on the input.

7 Quiet reflection. Ask people to name one concrete way
in which they feel challenged to live differently this
week. Let the changes start small, definite and limited.

8 Share this with one or two people.

9 Closing prayer.

10 Arrangements for next time.[3]

The Context

In some places the catechumenal session takes place on Sunday at the time of the main eucharist. Following the ancient
pattern the people who are preparing for initiation take part
in the Ministry of the Word, the reading and the sermon and
then withdraw for their 'Breaking of the Word' while the rest
of the Church goes on to the Breaking of the Bread. Where
this happens, there is further material for people to work on
from the sermon in the Service and preacher and the leaders of
the session on the Gospel may well want to prepare, if not
actually together, at least with some reference to one another.

Group Life

It is not my intention in this section to train people to lead
groups. That simply is not possible in a book. The skills and
attitudes needed in a good group leader have to be acquired or
developed in practice and with personal guidance, teaching
and review. As with so much else in what I am putting
forward, it is as much a matter of experience and talking over
actual events and relationships as of learning the principles
and techniques beforehand.

Along with most of the things in life, working in small

groups has its pluses and its minuses so it is worth noting some of them and underlining a few of the points already made.

The Positive

A group of up to, say, a dozen people provides what a congregation often cannot, a human-sized community. It is small enough for members to get to know each other well, large enough to provide both a variety of characters and temperaments and also space for individuals to relax and rest. It is where people can find human relationships within the Church. Rather than be taught about Christian love, they can actually experience it. Anne, after a year or so in a group leading on to confirmation, said, 'I very much valued being taken seriously, being properly listened to, not being ridiculed'. There is a sense of safety, of the support which is given and received by people who have begun to care for and about one another.

In the group as an experience of what it means to be Church there is fellowship which includes two essential elements in the Christian life. One is forgiveness. Sometimes it may be a very clear expression of repentance for a wrong done and the assurance of God's love and the love of the members of the group. Sometimes it is the less formal but no less real experience of being accepted for oneself with one's faults and difficulties, of being given value as someone loved by God.

With all this a small group can be the place to foster growth into Christian maturity. Debbie wrote, 'In our group over eighteen months, I believe we have all grown in patience with each other, especially the men for the women. We are more inclined to listen to each other and try to make helpful suggestions about personal problems. This is where comparison with the Gospel has been drawn. One of the men said he'd grown in confidence since coming to the group. He has, and it shows.' People are able to be open to others and to them-

selves. They can be seen to develop towards achieving their
own potential. 'I know how much I have grown since becoming confirmed. It is lovely to watch others who go through
these groups becoming more mature as Christian people
within the Church and in the community.'

The Negative

There are dangers too, both within the working of the group
itself and in its relationship with the wider Christian community. Small groups are open to several forms of manipulation. A leader can exercise power over members for good or
ill. It is possible to restrict and distort and so to reduce the
freedom of people to grow in their own way. The imposition
of standards and expectations, proper though this is in an
institution which does have standards and expectations, needs
very careful watching to make sure it does not tend towards
some kind of tyranny. Individual members can manipulate
too. There may be people with crying needs for recognition or
obsessive hobby-horses who can disrupt the relationships and
the work of the group as they hog the time and the attention
of the people they are with.

A person's privacy needs to be respected. There are people
for whom it is not natural to expose their all among comparative strangers. There are those who are hurt or vulnerable;
they have the right to be silent or to withdraw. Others may
rightly or wrongly not trust the confidentiality of the people in
the group and be unwilling to talk about intimate matters for
fear of gossip.

Group pressure is a force to be reckoned with among adults
almost as much as among children and adolescents. There is
an urge among many to conform. I remember one group of
men who realized the danger of this when it came to decisions
about whether or not two members should in fact go forward
to confirmation with the others. They both had reservations
and everyone in the group gave assurances that nobody was
to feel pressured or a failure if they decided against and that

they would all support each other's choices. In the event the two did decide to wait and were confirmed nine months later. But it showed how much care needs to be taken.

Although I spoke of the group as the place for growth into maturity, it is also possible for it to be the place where people can be kept in immature dependence, whether as followers of a strong leader or as companions in a tightly dependent group that dare not finish or divide up.

As far as the wider life of the congregation is concerned, I doubt whether any Church person, let alone any Vicar, is unaware of the danger of cliques. It is not uncommon for a particular group to be regarded as arrogant and exclusive by other people. Nor is it unknown for members of that group to feel that they are in fact the real Christians because of the specialness of their fellowship. Obviously this needs watching in any church. All I can offer is that over twelve years working in this way in a parish there was little sign of it, I think for two reasons. The first was that the Church was not in the habit of tolerating cliques in any case. But secondly there was no doubt that the groups had their special purpose in welcoming and preparing adult confirmation candidates and this aim was generally recognized and accepted. They were not a threat.

The groups of the sort we are describing need leaders. I suggest that it is better to have a couple of people as leaders, but that is just my suggestion. In any case leaders have a responsibility to help the group and its members to function well.

The diagram of three interlocking circles has stood the test of time. Any group leader needs to be aware of the three things to which he or she has to give attention. The group has a task to achieve. In our case it is the accompaniment of people to Christian faith and initiation. Each individual in the group is important and the leader is concerned for them, to ensure their comfort, their opportunities to put their point of view, whether they are people who need encouragement or restraint. The maintenance of the group is the third concern.

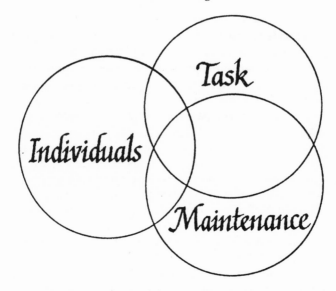

The leader needs to be aware of the relationships and the
pressures within the group as well as the practical factors
which will help or impede. It matters how chairs are set,
whether coffee is served before, during or after the main work
of a session and what time of day or day of the week suits
most people.

The Bible – True or False

I have been outlining a responsible ministry for people who
are to lead others along a journey of faith and into a dialogue
with the Word of God met in the Gospel. They will recognize
their own need to grow in faith and to develop their understanding of the Christian tradition. Bishop's Certificate
Courses, lay training, Christian Institutes and similar agencies
and events are available to meet this need in many places
around the country.

   What many people who undertake study of their Christian
origins will discover is that the Bible is not as simple a source

as they once thought. Someone said to me, 'I'm worried about what all this learning about the Gospels and their make-up is doing to my Jesus'. Once people enter into the world of Biblical criticism they begin to discover that it is possible to ask questions about whether the events in the Gospel happened as they are described or not, finding discrepancies between different Gospels, and the whole range of new ideas which face a student of the Bible. There is a real dilemma for many in how to present stories from the Bible for new enquirers.

Literalism has its followers in every generation. It amazes me that there should in the twentieth century be any problem over the Genesis creation stories, but I find that I have regularly to work through the different ways of expressing what is true about the world we live in. That it is the result (probably) of a big bang; that it belongs to a small solar system which is a little part of an expanding universe; that it is God's world; that it is unfair and in a mess; and that God loves us. Even so Adam and Eve are easier to deal with than questions about the Virgin Birth or Jesus walking on water.

What always needs to be remembered is that the intention of the writers, compilers, editors and users of the stories in the Bible was and is to convey truth. The means they use may be factual reporting, poetry, myth or just a good tale. God can meet us in our story through all of these. Certainly for some people it matters intensely that their search should be an intellectually responsible journey. They will rightly want to test evidence. For others story will speak to story in a way which engages quite different faculties.

In the Church of today we have rather lost faith in the power of Bible stories to do their work as stories. We are so given to analysing, explaining and cross-referring. There is ancient precedent for this, as you can see in the way in which Jesus' parable of the sower, a good story in itself, is explained a few verses later.

No, what I am suggesting is that you tell one of the parables, say the Labourers in the Vineyard or the Prodigal

Son, and simply let people respond with what the story says to them and where it leads them on to. There may well be a good deal of resentment about being unfairly treated or expressions of jealousy. Rejection bites deep into people, as does being forgiven. There are widely differing feelings about fathers and fatherhood, just as there are about employers and workers and the job market. Any of these and many other ideas may come in answer to those two stories and provide more than enough for a group to work on.

Often silence is more valuable than talk. People need space to do the hard and deep personal work of reflecting and accepting challenge of the Gospel story. The wise friend will always make further space for people who need to share their discoveries to offer their insights or to express their fear, pain or joy. It is not my intention to teach leaders how to run groups. The skills of a group leader cannot be learned from a book. No more can the kind of sensitivity and awareness which I am suggesting are needed in this work of accompanying another on a journey into faith. At the risk of being repetitive I urge that people who are invited to take up this ministry use every opportunity to experience this kind of story-dialogue for themselves. Let it be something which finds its place in a prayer group or in conversation between friends where reflection and open sharing are possible. Again, listen not only to the front part of your mind, the part which asks questions and gives answers and explanations; listen to the feelings and echoes and memories; let them have their proper important place.

Church Habits

Experts use words like 'socialization' or 'enculturation' to describe one aspect of education. It means being trained, encouraged or led to adopt and be at home in the manners, attitudes and habits of a society or a group. It is part of anyone's life in virtually any context, whether it is to do with what clothes to wear on this particular golf course; how not to feel out of place when you go to tea with the girl friend's parents; keeping to your position in the bus queue; or not using that kind of language in this office! The content of adult growth into Christian faith and commitment will naturally include a certain amount of learning about the community ways of the Church and learning to conform to its expectations. This can be about the little things of Church worship, the candles, the names for people and things, sitting or kneeling and how to find your place in the right service book. It may be much deeper about community attitudes, about Church as representing a certain class or about whether gay couples are welcome in church or the relationship between our Church and the R.Cs. on the opposite corner.

Learning how to fit into the way a Christian community behaves is quite a subtle business. Sometimes you can ask straight questions if you feel lost and get clear answers from people. Sometimes it is more difficult because the habits of a community build up over a long time, often without their causes being obvious. This needs to be recognized, as I said earlier, because people who are looking to the Church for help in finding a purpose and meaning in their lives have a right to expect that the life of the Church should reflect the Gospel it professes.

It is not all one-way, of course. New people joining a community bring their own gifts and insights. Their presence and their questions may well challenge or change some of those habits and attitudes.

4

Friendship with God

'Spiritual Direction' is what happens when one Christian is helping another to grow in their discipleship. I want to use the title in the widest possible way. Used narrowly it can mean a formalized relationship between a spiritual guide, often very skilled, and someone well advanced on the Christian journey. But in this chapter I hope it will become clear that the work of spiritual direction at an appropriate level is something which many people can do and ought to be expected to take on as part of their ministry. It is certainly work which lay people ought to expect their ministers to be capable of. As well as the clergy, sponsors, friends, group leaders, catechists and other Christians who accept the responsibility of accompanying men and women on their journey into faith will also be engaged in a certain amount of spiritual direction.

The task sounds frightening because it seems to imply responsibility for someone else's soul. Certainly there should be training; there are things to learn and there are skills and attitudes to acquire. Some of them this section covers. Others can only be learned from other people, in dialogue and relationship. In some places there are courses available on Spiritual Direction for people with different experience ranging from beginners to fairly advanced practitioners. There are books, again varying in intensity. What there also needs to be is some kind of support, review and continuing development for people who are in this ministry. It is not for everyone, but it is for far more people than are at present engaged in it.

People are shy about matters of faith. They are reluctant to talk about spiritual experience and practice. You may well pray and your prayer may play an important part in your life but it is hard to be open about it. You feel it is private; perhaps you also feel it is inadequate, not good enough. This combination of not wanting to parade something which is intimate and not wanting to expose a weakness means that, while many people may be able to talk about their belief in God, they recoil from speaking about their friendship with him. It follows that they also feel chary about opening up the subject of how others pray.

For balanced growth into Christian maturity a developing friendship with God is essential; it is at the very centre of all that we are about. People usually need some help in cultivating that friendship. They need someone who will walk with them along their journey in this just as in the other aspects of their way to faith and commitment. This is the work of Spiritual Direction.

Praying

Prayer is the work of the Church, the Body of Christ. As the Christian community we, ordinary human men and women, are intimately caught up in the eternal relationship of love between Jesus and the Father in the Holy Spirit. This is what provides the basis for all our activity of praying. The worship which is part of the life of the Church comes first; it is one of the givens. During his lifetime the prayer of Jesus was the open offering of himself to the will of the Father. The Church's worship continues this prayer and is caught up in the eternal relationship of Father and Son in the Holy Spirit. Each Christian has their place and their part in it.

This theological belief about prayer finds practical expression in what goes on in the local church on a Sunday and in the wonderfully varied ways in which men and women give their attention to God either privately on their own or together with other people.

I want to stress the idea of variety. I am writing what I hope will help you if you are acting as a guide to someone on their spiritual journey. I also hope it may help you to reflect on your own journey, because that is needed before you can help anyone else. But your way of praying is probably different from theirs. Just as your face and figure and character are different. Once again it is vital to start where people are, not where you'd like them to be or imagine they are.

So it is useful when you are listening to someone to have some simple headings in your mind as a guide in discerning where they are and how, if at all, you can respond.

'Public' Prayer

I hinted to one pair of headings just now. You can sort prayer into 'Public' and 'Private'. Public Prayer is the common worship of the Church. Its form will depend on the type of Church. It happens when the community meets as the people who belong to Christ in that place to offer praise, thanks, penitence and prayer. Almost always they will follow a pattern, often a formal liturgy. Most often the common worship will be the Eucharist.

For some newcomers and enquirers and also for some established church members this joining in public worship may be their main, even their only way of praying. It stands rather like an oasis of refreshment in the week, when they can concentrate on their relationship with God.

Music is an important part of common prayer for a great many people. Hymns in Church are for many the only occasion for singing with other people. They engage emotions and memories in worship and are often the most meaningful part of a Church Service for certain people.

Common prayer is the prayer of the community. It has an ongoing quality about it, its own life and validity. I take part in it. I also take my part in it. That comes first. It may also be an occasion when I say my own prayers, bring my own needs to God and offer my own gratitude. But, in theory at least, this opportunity for private devotion comes second. The first thing about public liturgy is that it is corporate; it expresses the truth that Christians belong together in the Body of Christ.

'Private' Prayer

Praying on your own or with one or two other people is different from common worship. I want to spend most of this chapter discussing the ways in which people pray individually and how individuals vary. I have in mind the map on page 58 as a help in sorting out the different faculties and parts of ourselves that we bring into praying. It is not complete. You may well find it does not answer every situation, but I offer it and these notes as somewhere for you to start from.

People vary in prayer by the weight they give to these different aspects, which I have called 'Words and Systems', 'Thoughts', 'Images and Feelings' and 'Attitudes'.

Words and Systems

For some it is words that are the main vehicle of their praying. They like books of prayers written by other people to use as their own prayers; sometimes they write their own or make up their own set forms. Church services mean a lot to them, especially services with a fixed form and shape. They are people who like order and system in their relations with God. Daily prayers follow a pattern, perhaps for example working through 'A.C.T.S.' – adoration, confession, thanksgiving and supplication (asking) – or some other simple formula. Lists are helpful; lists of people to pray for, booklets of causes and institutions which ask for intercessions.

'Chatting with my friend God' is how one person described her prayer, going through the day and referring things to him which happen, decisions that have to be made, problems and worries encountered. For her and for a great many people prayer is a conversation, sometimes actually spoken aloud, more often voiced silently in the heart, with a God who cares

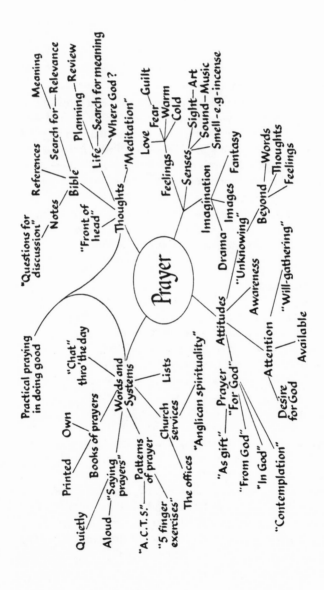

The Pattern of Prayer

and listens and from time to time is recognized as responding in some way.

Thoughts

Thinking about God, using the front of your mind to get in touch with him, to try to understand who he is or what he is about – that is how some people pray. For them the search for a meaning in life is about how to explain things, how to make sense. They are people whose intellect is important in their praying. For them the kind of Bible Study notes that are most helpful are the ones which end with 'questions for discussion'. They may find it easy and helpful to use a Bible with cross-references to other passages to compare what different writers have to say.

Faced with a problem, someone praying in this way may well think it through, worry it out with God in their prayers.

A friend of mine had been seriously ill. He could have died. He spoke to me afterwards about how he had been, as he said, unable to pray. He knew he was very seriously ill. He was facing the prospect of eternity and he found that he spent a great deal of time in his illness trying to think what eternity would mean and where God came into it. Normally, he was someone whose prayer was quite different, a mixture of set prayers and a feeling of warmth towards God. He found it hard to recognize that during his illness it was not that he had been unable to pray. He may not have been able to pray in the way he had before, but he was using another part of himself, his thinking mind, to pray with instead.

For another of my friends there are all the 'why' questions that spring out of the injustice and horror of famine and natural disasters. How is she to come to terms with a relationship with a loving God who is responsible for a created world where things like that happen?

Someone for whom this way of prayer is strongest is likely to find themselves more at home in a discussion group than in a prayer group. Their road to faith may well be along the way of reason and argument rather than through music or dramatic worship.

Images and Feelings

I was not sure whether to head this Section with the word 'Images' or the word 'Imagination'; because both are true of another way people pray. It is not primarily using words, nor is it using the thinking part of your mind. It is using perceptions and faculties which are, to use rather high words, affective rather than intellectual. Praying in pictures, entering into stories, living out dramas, carried by music, expressing your relationship with God in song.

To return to the use of the Bible in praying: for people praying in this way the Gospels are not a quarry for texts to relate to other texts nor for evidence to support this or that belief. The Gospels contain stories to be entered into. They present people to be met in the imagination.

Prayer, the expressing of a relationship with God, has for thousands of years been sung or prayed on a musical instrument. For someone who has appreciated Handel's 'Messiah' it is almost impossible to read the Bible texts on which that work is based without hearing the music to which they are set echoing in the mind. I find that when in my prayers I want to express praise to God it is often the tune of a well known hymn of worship that means more than its words.

Imagination has to do with images, of course, but to use the imagination in prayer is more than simply creating images. It is letting the non-rational, non-intellectual side of your personality have its place in your journey into God. People spend time happily fantasizing about all sorts of things, success at work, sexual encounters, what to do if you win the Pools. Not to mention the darker side of fantasy, the fears and distresses which arise to scare and disturb you awake as well as dreaming. Fears of the death or injury of someone you love in an accident. Even the simple fear of not putting the fire out when you left home. Notice what happens inside you when you see an ambulance answering an emergency call and are startled by the siren.

The prayer of images and imagination enters this area and opens this side of a person to God. Rather than thinking about incidents in life or incidents in the Gospels, the person praying this way enters into them in their imagination to experience their meaning.

Emotions play a large part in human life and they have their proper place in praying. For some people feelings are the heart of their prayer; for others just an aspect of it. Feelings of warmth or distance, of love or shame or the fear of the Lord of which the Bible speaks; being moved to prayer by anxiety about someone you love or by being afraid for yourself; enjoying a sense of comfort, reassurance and being in tune with God, which is how some people some of the time describe their praying. In these and many other ways the affective side of our nature is either a way into prayer, or a way of praying or a way of experiencing its affects.

Attitudes

Feelings can be a bridge leading into this fourth kind of prayer. Warmth, excitement, fear, anticipation, desire – all these focussed on God can be a way towards what I call the Prayer of Attitudes. In this you direct your whole self towards God in love or openness. This prayer of attitudes, though, is more than simply praying with feelings or with a feeling. It may have an emotional content, but what distinguishes it is that it is primarily a prayer of your attention; you may have arrived by way of conversation with God, by way of thinking or by way of imagination or feelings, but in this way of prayer you simply make yourself available to contemplate God as he is, open to be aware of him, waiting in his presence.

It is a way of prayer which, because of its nature, is very hard to describe in words. Even pictures are little help. The title of a mediaeval book about it, *The Cloud of Unknowing*, emphasises that it is not a prayer of the intellect. It is not a

way in which there is much activity. You pray more by
waiting, by being available. My image is of a she-cat hunting
by long grass. She does not prowl dramatically about looking
eager or menacing. She sits, at once alert and relaxed, and she
listens. Her hunting consists largely of being aware of every
sound in the long grass and discerning the distinct rustle made
by a mouse or a vole.

This way of prayer more than any other illustrates what I
believe to be the truest purpose of prayer. It is for God. This
prayer of the will, of attitudes, points away from the person,
their thoughts, feelings or concerns and dwells entirely on
God as he is. God is recognisably both the source of the
prayer and its aim.

The Body

People are not only souls or intelligence or feelings. We have
bodies. Prayer is concerned with and affected by physical
things in many different ways. Yoga has taught western men
and women the importance of posture, exercise and breathing
in a search for well-being and a balanced life. They are
important aspects of Christian prayer too. Kneeling is one
attitude for prayer and expresses humility. It is not the only
way. Standing, sitting or lying are others. They each express
something different about the relationship with God. Dance
and movement can have their place in prayer either as a
preparation or as a way of praying or as a form of response to
God.

Spiritual Companionship

This very short survey of human spirituality is clearly only a
rough guide. Libraries of books have been written about the
subject and there are many living spiritual guides who can go
deeper into it. However I feel it is important that it should
appear in this book to give people accompanying others on

their faith-journey an idea of the breadth of spiritual experience and of the resources for spirituality that lie in a human being.

I would expect anyone reading these brief classifications to recognise something of their own experience in several, perhaps all of them. I would also expect them to settle on one or two which most nearly fit their own present way of praying. All are perfectly right and valid ways of praying for any Christian. What is important is that a Christian friend can recognize and reinforce someone else in their growing friendship with God by helping them to develop on lines which are true for them. These lines may be quite other than the sponsor's own way of prayer. Spirituality varies. What suits one person may be quite improper for another.

When it comes to books of prayer or about prayer, be careful! You may have had it happen to you. A friend recommends a book, 'You must read it, it's marvellous. A lovely book.' When you try it, you find it dull, meaningless and not in the least helpful. It says nothing to you and you feel both guilty, because you've let your friend down, and also a failure because you are clearly not a good Christian if you can't enjoy and benefit from such a fine book. (The same thing happens with commending preachers and sermons.) Accept the truth that God has made people different and that he has given to each their own proper way to himself. Always remember that what is good for one may very well be no good for the next. Be prepared to pick and choose what suits you.

The work of accompanying demands a gift of discernment, an ability to listen and a certain degree of background knowledge. It requires both enough confidence and enough humility. The confidence comes from having accepted that it is part of the accompanying ministry to be a coach in spiritual matters and from having sufficient understanding of the basic principles of spirituality. It is also important to have proper backing and help from somebody else who is acting as your own guide. The humility comes from the recognition that the person you are accompanying has their own true spirituality and that your work is one of helping them under God's guiding to grow into what he has planned for them to become. The spiritual director is to be God's instrument, using their own gifts of perception, discernment and intelligence, certainly, but all for God and the other person.

John Westerhoff writes: 'The best guide on a spiritual journey is one who does not need to be helpful or needed, one who does not try to bear the responsibility for another life, but who can leave others in the hands of God – and get a good night's sleep. It is to take responsibility for one's own spiritual growth and be with others as they do likewise.'[1]

The Givenness of Prayer

Prayer is a dialogue. It is something which is a gift from God. He makes it possible for someone to pray. He is the inspiration. Without him there would be nothing. On the other hand prayer is a human work. It requires an effort on our part; it requires that we choose to put aside some time for it. We have to make ourselves available. We have continually to be recalling our wandering attention from all sorts of other thoughts, day-dreams and interests to the business of seeking God.

The most common danger at all stages along the road to prayer seems to be the danger of over-worrying and guilt at being a failure. Prayer is gift and our part in it is response to gift.

In the four-way analysis of prayer earlier in this chapter I was aware of a gap. The Charismatic Renewal sweeping through Churches of all denominations speaks strongly of prayer as gift from God, prayer as meeting a God who is spirit, who is the giver of life and relationship and power in prayer and in the human response to his call. This emphasis on the grace, the gift or, in religious technical language, the charism of praying should be recognized as a firm counterbalance to the common feeling that we need to work harder and harder to achieve and to succeed in spirituality.

Variations and Change

People who have prayed over a length of time, several months perhaps, several years certainly, will know that the temperature of their praying varies considerably. There are times when it feels warm and meaningful to pray; God is real and near. It is quite easy. However there are times when all that disappears. Praying is a cold, dull and lonely activity. It becomes difficult to persuade yourself that there is anything in it. God seems totally absent, if he exists at all.

Any spiritual director has to be aware of these variations. After all they are common enough to all praying Christians. Probably they are the source of most conversations about spirituality. 'I used to be able to pray. I used to enjoy it. But now I can't, it doesn't work any more for me.'

Putting it simply, probably far too simply, there are two possible reasons lying behind this experience of the emptiness of prayer and one which is commonly given but, I find, very often mistaken.

The reason which is usually false is the one which the person experiencing the emptiness is most likely to offer. It is that they are not trying hard enough; they think they ought to pray harder and they feel guilty about not doing so. This is a perfectly natural reaction but in my experience it is usually wrong. It falls into the danger of seeing prayer as only a human activity. It forgets the givenness.

What is far more likely is that the underlying cause is the regular dynamic of prayer. Like most human growth it develops in phases. Periods of brightness are followed by duller periods. There are alternately times of encouragement and help and times for developing our spiritual muscles. Dryness in prayer is a time for being faithful and staying with God; it is when the Christian learns to live by hope and faith and love for that which is not seen.

The skill of discernment and awareness of the spiritual director comes into play here, because the kind of boredom, guilt and anxiety someone feels in one of these times of dryness can also be a sign that the way they are trying to pray is in fact the wrong way for them. It may be that they have set out to follow a model which does not suit them or it may be that they have changed within themselves and are growing into a new way of prayer.

The four ways of praying I described earlier in this chapter can be different stages in one person's spiritual development. It is not uncommon to begin with simple prayer in words, using a defined pattern of prayer. Later you may find the system too tight and move to a more open, less wordy approach to God through the imagination or feelings or the will. The work of spiritual direction needs the sensitivity to notice the signs when someone ought to change and develop new ways of praying, or to support them as they come to terms with a time of dryness.

Practicalities

I am aware that what I have written so far will not be appropriate for everybody. To develop a pattern of prayer along the lines I have suggested may well be easier for people who can find the space for privacy in their lives and who are able to devote time in the day to it. It is not that you cannot pray unless you have leisure; rather it is that prayer has to be appropriate to the possibilities of life's demands.

For instance, the demands on a mother of a baby or small children or on someone caring for an invalid at home may well mean that prayer is a matter of a few scattered moments of turning attention to God rather than keeping a daily pattern of time offered as God's time.

Busy people and people whose life and work ask a lot from them may well see their prayer as offered in the things they do. It is a prayer of action, doing a job well for God's sake or consciously offering the care given to someone in need as a kind of intercession.

The Practice of the Presence of God is a short book by a lay brother in a monastery whose work was in the kitchens. In it he describes a way of prayer which is real to very many people whose lives are full of activity and little space. It is the way of carrying God with you all the time, working as if consciously in his presence, being aware of the spiritual within the everyday.

Pattern and Rhythm

I am someone who has been greatly helped by having what many Christians call a 'Rule of Life'. This is a way of describing the pattern of praying and other aspects of discipleship which are the basis of a person's spirituality. It could include how much time is given to prayer daily or weekly, the pattern of Bible reading and of Church worship, the proportion of money given away, time for family or for relaxation and other aspects of self-discipline which are appropriate. A rule of life like this is something to be worked out in discussion with someone else. The pattern should be sensible, possible to keep and not wildly beyond their ability! There is no point in setting such high standards that they can never be achieved. That just compounds feelings of guilt. Moreover there are people who feel strongly that for them what seems a rigid structure would reduce the spontaneity of their relationship with God.

Praying with the Bible

The stories in the Bible are a central resource for someone who is trying to pray and to grow in prayer. But the Bible is a very hard volume for anyone to find their way round. Anyone who is acting as a spiritual friend to a new Christian needs to be able to guide them into a creative use of the scriptures. This means, first of all, selection. Short passages, incidents, stories and sayings are the best material to work on in prayer. Slow, repetitive reading to draw out meanings is often more valuable than covering a lot of ground. So it is useful to have a system to select by. There are the Sunday readings; there are

booklets of selections and notes published by the Bible Reading Fellowship, the Scripture Union and many other organizations. These cover a range of approaches to the Bible and are
written for a range of different ages, abilities and interests.

Praying with other People

I began this section on praying with the central importance of
the common prayer of the Church both theologically and as
part of a Christian's personal spirituality. We need to meet
with the community, to take our place in the prayers, the
hearing of God's word read and taught, and to share in the
breaking of bread in the Eucharist.

A different kind of praying with other people is group
prayer. It is not the formal prayer of Church liturgy, nor is it
private prayer taking place in company. It is important for
people making their journey into faith to have some experience of it. In particular I suggest that groups accompanying
people for baptism and confirmation should be sure to make
time for prayer together. It should be more than a formal
opening or closing with a prayer. There should be a space for
perhaps a Bible passage, some comment, some sharing of
ideas, reactions and concerns from people in the group; a time
of silence and a time for open prayer, spoken or silent by the
members.

Prayer groups are not without their dangers and may often
need careful and experienced leadership. Before people can be
open with each other before God there has to be a certain
sense of confidence and a secure confidentiality within the
group. But, given them, prayer groups offer their own particular dimension of praying, alongside the public worship of
Church services and private prayer.

It can be a source of strength and fulfilment to join in
prayer with one other person. Many married couples pray
together as part of their pattern of family life.

5

Conversion

Central to all that this book is about and central to the work of accompanying people on a journey into the Christian faith is conversion. The word itself is a highly respectable, ancient Christian word. Maybe the way it is used in certain church circles has become so narrow that people from other church circles view it with suspicion. At its root, conversion is about turning, changing direction and this makes it a very suitable metaphor to use as part of the overall picture of a journey. So I intend to use it.

Before going any further, though, it would be as well to defuse some of the strange reactions some people have in the area of conversion. I trust that as you read on you will realize that I am talking about conversion in all sorts of different ways and over varying time scales. Certainly I shall notice the kind of experience which can be described as conversion in the narrow sense, often over a short length of time, accompanied by an onrush of fervour and emotion, but I am more broadly concerned with a great many different ways in which a man or a woman comes to a personal life-commitment to faith in and obedience to God as revealed in Jesus Christ.

New Testament Conversion

Different writers in the New Testament use their own pictures to describe the idea of conversion. Luke in the Acts of the Apostles has what for some people is the classic picture of Saul struck to the ground and blinded by the light on the road to Damascus, dramatically switched from persecutor to missionary preacher.

In Paul's own writings there is the image of pagans turning away from idols to serve the true and living God in 1 Thessalonians 1.9–10. He has the image of conversion as being altered into a new shape as in Romans 12.2 'Let God transform you inwardly by a complete change of your mind' (TEV). In 2 Corinthians 5.17 he has the lovely image, 'When anyone is joined to Christ, they are a new being; the old is gone, the new has come'.

However the most usual word, often translated 'repentance' or 'repent' is the one used by John the Baptist (Mark 1.4) and taken up by Jesus and his followers. It is about changing your mind or heart; being changed in the depths of your being.

Change is at the centre of the response evoked by hearing the Gospel. Some words and images are active; they indicate choices I have to make in order for change to come about. It is I who have to turn away from the old way to the new. Other words and images are passive; the changes happen to me as a result of my hearing the Gospel or of my being called into relationship with Jesus; I am reshaped and redirected. Both are true to human religious experience. In journey language there are corners and bends which are simply followed by the traveller and there are junctions and forks where the traveller has to make definite personal choices of the direction to go.

We often describe the start of this faith-journey as the expression of a need for an answer to questions about the meaning of life. This is not simply an intellectual question. It is about the shape and direction of mind and heart, about personality and purpose affecting the whole of life. It is to do with the inwardness of a person, how they see themselves, and with all their relationships, with other people, with things, with events, with the world around them and with God.

Terry was in his early thirties when his Mother and Father, taking their first-ever holiday abroad, were killed in a plane crash. 'I was shattered because I was close to my parents', he said. 'I couldn't make any sense of it. It seemed so unfair. I'd never had much time for religion or anything like that but I thought, "If anyone's supposed to have the answers, it ought to be the Church". So one Sunday I went to our local church. I'd never been in before and it was awful. Cold and dull and the Vicar's sermon made me think he'd never even asked any questions, let alone find any answers. But I didn't give up. I went to another church nearby the next Sunday and found it quite different. The people were friendly and welcomed me and the service felt alive. I went back for a few weeks and began to feel part of the place. I joined a housegroup. I had a long talk with the Vicar. It wasn't that I found answers to all my questions. I still don't know why it had to be Mum and Dad. I still think it's hard to have a God of love and all the suffering. The difference is I now reckon that there is a God like that and if he's like that then he knows the answer even if I don't. It all began to open out for me in the first few times in that friendly church. People there seemed to be concerned about me. They couldn't solve my problems but they didn't run away from them.'

Once it is recognized that conversion is all-embracing, it becomes clear that it cannot be a once-for-all happening. Conversion is a process. Certainly within that process there are likely to be high peak events – and also troughs and valleys. Bunyan's *Pilgrim's Progress* is only one of many classic portraits of the conversion journey, with his description of the long struggle to get to the goal. He pictures the dangers on the way from enemies on the road or the treacherous nature of the path itself and we are left with the strong impression that Christian at the end of his journey has achieved a maturity which has been won through life's encounters.

Certainly there will be for some people, but by no means for everyone, incidents, times and places, conversations or experiences which they remember as sharp turning points when they recognise that God can be seen to have acted decisively or which they know were moments when they made a definite choice for change.

In a world where the prevailing mood of people is increasingly non-religious, the process of conversion is often a lengthy and by no means easy one. People brought up and living in today's secular culture have attitudes very different from Christian values and often a deep ignorance of what Christianity is. The change which conversion involves is neither easy nor cheap. It may well be demanding. I hope that nothing I write will leave you with the idea that simply by following an offered formula you will be assured of success! It is not like that. We live in the world of real people and each one will follow their own route of conversion, or, it may be, of resistance to the changes which conversion initiates.

Points of Conversion

In describing different ways in which people come to conversion I have to offer a fairly arbitrary set of headings. There are many sorts of choices about change of direction in life, both active, chosen changes and passive, imposed changes. Different people will use different ways of analysing them and presenting them.

I find it simplest to use four headings. They are true to my experience of people and they are a handy guide to accompanying men and women on their journey. These headings work both when we look at how conversion comes about and also as we look at the changes which it results in.

They are the realm of feelings and emotions;

The realm of faith in the broad sense of attitude to life;

The realm of the intellect and understanding;

The realm of behaviour, how a person makes choices and decisions in their everyday living.

I have no desire to dissect human personality in such a way as to leave someone in different, separate heaps on slab. The whole tenor of this book is to say that people are whole and individual. My picture of the journey into Christian faith is of a journey which is towards coherence and a sense of being together. But experience shows that people's conversion and their routes to it are varied. Some people lead with their feelings, others with their spiritual search for purpose and meaning, others with their questions and arguments and others with the practical choices of living life. All these aspects are essential to what it means to be a human person. Genuine conversion, however much it may centre on one or other of these divisions, makes changes in them all.

It was the experience of giving her life to God at a Mission to London evening which led Maureen to our catechumenate group. She had been clearly moved by the music and by the speaker. She was in love with Jesus. However unbalanced some members of the group may have thought her reaction was, it was very clear that they all accepted the reality of her conversion. Over the weeks that followed they talked through its implications for her. There were strained relationships with two people at work which she felt badly about. She knew she had to apologize and do what she could to improve the situation. Prayer was a new country for her and she looked for help in developing it. Perhaps hardest for her was the need to come to terms with the very mixed nature of the church, that not everyone shared her experience and that in the parish congregation and even among the eight people who met every Tuesday in her group there were tensions and conflicts.

Conversion is both a continuous process, the process of being transformed by God and by conscious personal decisions into Christian maturity, and it is also a moment or series of moments at which sharp changes of direction can be recognized.

We are here dealing specifically with Christian conversion, about what happens when a person is taken by the Gospel, when God's story draws them into some participation or a degree of commitment. Or put it the other way, when a person takes God's story and makes it their own story, letting their life be moulded by what they perceive of God.

Evangelization is a word which can be used in two senses.

One, the sense usually found in Anglican circles, is the work of the evangelist, the missionary. It is proclaiming the Gospel where it has not been heard or accepted. The other sense is more to do with the Gospel having its effect upon someone. To be evangelized in this sense is not simply to be preached at, but to take hold of the good news of the Gospel or to be convinced and changed by it. It is a daily event and a life-long movement of change. Both the present, where we are now, and the future, what we may become, are important. They are the field for developing evangelization. There is a continuing tension between the two. We are forever faced with the challenge of turning from where we are now and turning to where we may go in the future. The Gospel is about hope and about movement.

Ancient Jewish prophets and New Testament writers spoke of turning from idols to the one true God, from the false to the real. Although there may not actually be idols on every British street corner, there are certainly plenty of idolatrous attitudes to be turned away from in contemporary life. The three temptations offered to Jesus in Luke 4 are still there for twentieth century men and women to turn away from in order to worship and serve the living God. Materialism, money and acquisition of things: – the power of Mammon is strong; appetites are there to be satisfied. Popularity, being admired, being successful are attractive. (How many advertisements play on the idolatrous worship of admiration?) Power, influence and prestige matter, both to those who wield them and to the powerless. Having power is a mark of the successful human being. To be powerless is to be a failure. Turning from these attitudes to Christian values is not easy. We live in an idolatrous culture. Faith, hope and love are principles which run counter to the prevailing direction. The transformation from self-centred to self-giving is a radical change.

Models of Conversion

As I have talked with people about the movement of conversion in their own lives and the changes which they recognize are connected with it, I have found there is a general trend towards a greater openness. It is not universal by any means, but as these people look back over their lives and as I look back over my own we find that with deepening commitment comes a deeper sense of freedom. There is less dependence on systems and regulations, less timidity, more willingness to change, more acceptance of being vulnerable to other people and giving room to ideas that are foreign. Trusting God leads to trusting generally. To be open to God means to be open to life.

In the section which follows I am aware of the danger of giving the impression that there is a hierarchy of importance, because one aspect heads the list and another only comes half-way down, or that there ought to be a progression from one to another for orderly development. No, it is a whole complex person and a whole complex of responses and relationships we are dealing with – all interconnected and all relating to and affecting each other.

Feelings

I put the emotional area first for two reasons. One is because I suspect that the majority of people come first to conversion through their feelings; it has many parallels with falling in love. The other is because of the important fact that we do not generally create emotions; we are affected by them: they happen to us. Dealing with feelings first is a kind of reminder that the initiative in conversion comes from outside a person's willing choice. It comes from God. The person's willing choice is in the nature of a response to God's stimulus.

Five minutes' walk away from where I live and work at St. Paul's Cathedral is Aldersgate Street. In May 1738 John Wesley had been to Evensong at the Cathedral and at a religious meeting in a house in Aldersgate later that evening he 'felt his heart strangely warmed'. From that occasion the whole direction of his life was changed.

Evangelistic mission preachers are well aware of the importance and power of the affective side of human nature.

Feelings of shame and guilt and the desire for love and acceptance provide a powerful stimulus for turning to the God who forgives.

Changes which take place in this area are changes from coldness to warmth, from being inhibited to openly expressing feelings, from fear to trust. It can be thought of as a change from resistance against God to a love for him and a desire to know and be close to him. Not that it all becomes plain sailing. Paradoxically one of the signs of deepening conversion is a sense of the need to deal continually with resistance, with excuses and 'good sensible reasons' for not going deeper.

It's an idea to work out for yourself the kind of characteristics, attitudes, feelings which you would look for in yourself or in someone else as signs of conversion to Christ. They may include a sense of gratitude, awareness of gift leading to expressing thanks to God. Or there may be a sense of the justice and truth or the majesty of God, a feeling of fear or awe, an awareness of guilt which is expressed in a confession of sins and repentance. Joy and pain may be there, sometimes at the same time. People may long to share their experiences by telling someone else or by engaging in some kind of practical action to make their world a better place.

Religious Faith

If conversion comes in and through the feelings for many people, it is the area of change in religious stance that is essential. I mean the change in attitudes to meaning, vision and purpose of life. James Dunning has described the basic movement in religious conversion as that from seeing life as a problem, as one damn thing after another, to seeing life as mystery, one gift after another, and responding with surprise and wonder. It is a movement to the recognition of grace and God as gracious.

For some people the movement is from religion in the head to religion as life. Patrick Purnell describes his youthful religion: 'You know the phrase 'religious dimension of life', meaning life divided into watertight compartments. Well, that in a nutshell is where the weakness lies. My religion was a dimension of life – a compartment of my life . . . I learnt that "God made me to know Him, love Him and serve Him in this world and be happy with Him for ever in the next'; that 'God is a Supreme Being who alone exists of Himself and is infinite in all perfections".

I could easily understand the need to go to Church to worship such a God, to make every effort to obey this God under whose all-seeing eye I spent every moment of my life, and the need I had to beg God's pardon when I broke one of the divine laws; and I was ready to accept that God would reward me for being good and punish me for being bad. All this I could understand: it was all so logical. What I could not grasp was how such a God could be part and parcel of my everyday life; I could not make this God part of my feeling life . . . In fact I wanted to keep this God at arm's length.'[1]

It is movement from believing *about* to believing *in*. For some it may come in a change from worrying about how Jesus did miracles to recognising the miracle which he works in them personally through giving them hope or joy or endurance. It may be the move from intense mathematical speculation about God as Holy Trinity to accepting that we live in and by the love of a God who gives to us our existence and who reconciles us, however rebellious we may be, with himself through Jesus our friend.

The Intellect

When I was dealing with ways of praying I made it clear that talking about the intellectual side of human nature does not necessarily imply that we are talking about what we loosely call intellectual people, academics, scholars and people who earn their living through their minds. We are talking about that ability which everyone has to work things out, to ask questions and to argue their way towards answers.

Some parts of the Church give very high value to the understanding. Faith can be seen as giving assent to statements

about God. For people whose way to conversion is
through the mind the actual step which marks conversion is
more often than not one which is not rational or logical. The
willingness to change is often shown by the willingness to take
not an ordered step but a leap in the dark. It is to jump over
from one set of mental attitudes, one system for ordering life
without God as a factor in it, into a different system which
relies on God existing, creating and redeeming. Conversion in
this sense can be described as my coming to make sense of my
life only if God is part of that sense. Among the many living
images in St. John's Gospel is that of Jesus bringing truth to
people and 'the truth shall make you free'.

The danger for the intellectual is that things of the mind can
simply stay in the mind. The way of conversion is for thought
about God and Jesus, analysis and acceptance of religious
statements, to change into an acceptance of this truth which is
God as the one central meaning of life.

Tony Bridge, formerly Dean of Guildford, has described his
journey from an atheism which was his reaction as a young
man to the distorted Christianity offered to him as a boy.
Through study of philosophy he came to see 'that it was much
more rational to believe in God than not to believe. There was
far better reason in the end to believe that there's some kind of
ultimate spirit, reality . . . but the mere fact that that was so,
didn't make me believe at all. Which shows how really limited
the intellect is. I find it fascinating, but it didn't make me
believe. All this process came to a head when I woke up one
summer morning and discovered to my absolute horror that
something had happened in my head, so to speak. There'd
been a slight shift of angle of viewpoint and I knew that I
believed something. So I came to believe that there must be
some kind of ultimate spirit beyond, just to make sense of
anything, including myself and you and everyone else.'[2]

Behaviour

So conversion is about changes which come through and are
effective in someone's emotions; it is about a radical shift in

their deep personal attitude to life's meaning and purpose and it concerns the way they think and find answers to the questions life puts to them. The way these changes show is in the things they do and say. How a person lives is a sign of the values that motivate them.

Sometimes these may be sharp, clear changes demanded by the Gospel. It is part of some preachers' stock-in-trade to have a repertoire of loose living, drug taking, dishonest, worldly people who were claimed by Christ and are now reformed characters. But most people seem to live without that sort of high drama. 'Conversion of morals' is often a slow business of questioning the way I live and trying to measure it against the way of Christ as I see it. It is the difficult business of recognizing how much the way I live is simply a reflection of the way people around me live. I pick up my sense of right and wrong from my family and friends. Standards of honesty, the importance of solidarity with other people, the importance of independence and achievement can all vary according to my social class. There are grey areas, for instance, between what is accepted as 'middle class morality' and what is Christian morality.

Rarely is it possible to look to the New Testament for specific answers to moral questions. Our society and our world are so different from the first century. What we can look for is principles upon which to base our own decisions. St. Paul's conversion from living by Law to living in response to God's grace can find a parallel in the way for many people the movement of conversion is away from a dependence on rules or the external pressures of their own society towards accepting a responsibility for themselves and for their own choices and decisions as they come to give more value to the principles of self-giving love and of the infinite worth of the other person.

Conversion and Church

Two other dimensions of conversion need mentioning before I turn to think of the ministry of accompanying people in their conversion. The first of these is conversion in relationship to the institution of the Church, discovery of the living reality of Christ present in his body, to put it in rather high blown theological words.

For people who have had some relationship with Church, people who, while not necessarily claiming membership, would say they went to services, the movement is from formality to a living faith. Such men and women are likely to accept the attitudes of the community. They recognize that their adherence to the Church implies some agreement with its beliefs. But their faith is 'of the Church' rather than deeply, consciously their own. For them the movement is towards personalizing faith, expressing their individual awareness of God and their own commitment. It is to take consciously for themselves the living centre of the community's belief in the move from formal to experienced relationship with God.

There is a mirror image to this. For people who come to faith from a non-church background, whose journey began in the world of secular culture and belief, it is often the attraction of Jesus and the friendship of a few Christians which supports and encourages them. Their conversion may be strongly through their feelings or their intellect and have little sense of the wider church. There is a sense in which they need also 'conversion to the church'; recognizing that relationship with God implies relationship with brothers and sisters in his community.

I am aware that that sounds very fine, but I can hear, if not protests, at least anxieties about the kind of church I am expecting people to be converted to. Once I accept that it is important that the Christian finds his or her place in the church, I am faced with questions about whether they are likely, as I said just now, to find 'the living reality of Christ present in his body'. The need to accept, welcome and accompany new Christians should force the members of the local church to ask searching questions about their community life. Is it something worth converting to?

The World and the Kingdom of God

Turning from the inward outwards does not stop with developing a full life as a Christian within the community of the church. Jesus did not come to found a club for friends but to herald the Kingdom of God. The church is commissioned to forward his work, to proclaim the Good News of Jesus and to be an agent of that Kingdom in our own generation. As a community and as individuals Christians are to work for God's will to be achieved in the lives of individuals, societies and nations. God transforms us as we answer his call to conversion not so that we may feel better but so that we may accept his work of mission.

Conversion to mission involves a man or a woman in the same way as it involves the church community in a three-fold work of evangelism, being a witness to the Gospel; of service to the needs of others whether that is personal help of individuals or working on and through the structures of society; and of building up the church with the support and continuing formation which that calls for.

'Stewardship' is a current cult word but I believe it is closely linked with this aspect of conversion to the world. Stewardship is a perception of our own place in the world and our responsibility to and for people and things in the world. It is a change from an attitude of ownership, from domination and exploitation to one of management, service and loving respect.

Within Stewardship, of course, comes the proper use of money. One aspect of conversion is the conversion of the pocket. This can be a very hard area for attitudes to change.

Accompanying Conversion

Conversion, as we have seen, is a movement of change in which both the person and God are active. It also involves other people. In this section I want to offer some ideas to help people to recognise and be sensitive to what may be happening with those they are accompanying. I remind you that this is not a how-to-do it manual and that everyone is different.

You will know from your own experience how much the movement of conversion owes to the intervention of other people in your life. You might find it helpful to stop reading for a moment and just make a list of those who have helped you to where you at present stand in your own journey of faith.

You may well remember something a friend said which met a particular need at the time. It could be the example of a known Christian's behaviour at work; the warmth of welcome at a mother and toddler group, or the words of a powerful preacher.

I have found and there is plenty of evidence from other people that in the way men and women come to conversion there is usually someone in the church or in the Christian group who acts as a link, a bridge of welcome and friendship. Quite often it may be a fiancé, a husband or wife or a close friend or relative, through whom somebody is introduced to the life of a Christian community. Sometimes there is simply a welcoming person to greet a newcomer. In any case the role which a sponsor plays is vital. Support and encouragement are also part of the work done by a group of people. I have many vivid memories of the powerful help given by leaders and members to one another in the often difficult searching and discovery of meaning and purpose in the hard situations in which life had put them.

Delicacy is needed to avoid the danger of indoctrination, over-pressuring. The relationship of the enquirer or the new Christian with sponsor or catechist or the welcoming group which accompanies them is ideally one where the friendship and support provides help but allows freedom. It is adult Christian maturity which is the goal, not slavish conformity. People have to be respected and to be given the full right to choose. They have to follow their own way to God, not some pattern predetermined by the tradition of the particular

Church or the personal experience and vision of the individuals who accompany them.

Above all the key words which mark this work are sensitivity and discernment. Another person's conversion is not forwarded by giving a great deal of information, even less by full instructions on how to do it. What is needed is a willingness to engage in clear and open dialogue in which the other is enabled to listen to God and to make their own decisions.

For this ministry to be fruitful there needs to be an environment of trust and acceptance. My experience has been that the groups of established church people and newcomers provide this. Obviously there is the need to watch the effect of the group processes. The ideal balance is to provide for the atmosphere of loving, tolerant support for each person to grow without the love turning to demand or the toleration breaking into anarchy. In the first there is a danger that people will be forced at a pace or in a direction which is wrong for them, in the second people can be badly hurt if their confidences and their openness are abused or betrayed.

A final reminder as I close this section. The ministry of a sponsor or a catechist is one which demands courtesy. It is the person you are helping who matters. The journey and the changes, the discoveries and the blockages all take time. Sometimes there will be moments of hope, excitement even. Sometimes there will be periods of struggle and difficulty. This first stage in the Christian pilgrimage is only a beginning. The rest of life lies ahead as the time for growth and further discovery of the meaning of what it means to be a disciple. Conversion is not only an initial turning. It is a continued and continual awareness of our need to be changed more and more into the likeness of Christ. There may be occasional glimpses of what it means to achieve a small step but always there is the future hope of true fulfilment.

6

The Church Community and the World Community

If the journey into Christian faith is to be complete it needs to include initiation into the Christian community by Baptism or Confirmation. It cannot be a lone journey ending simply in a deeper personal self-awareness. Other people are involved. So is the whole apparatus of the Church with its systems and its relationships. But the movement is two-way: it is not enough to see how the newcomer is to be introduced into the fold. The presence of the newcomer with all that he or she brings with them is in itself a challenge to and a change in the community. We need to look both at the effect on the new Christian's journey of the fact of the Church and at the effect of the new Christian's joining on the Church he or she joins.

The Church somebody joins is an actual group of people. It consists of a core of dedicated people with leaders and helpers; there are the regular worshippers who make up the committed membership and there is an outer fringe of adherents, well wishers, nominal members and friends. For many of the people about whom this book is written the journey will be from the outer edge of the Church into the more dedicated centre. That move is one external aspect of their conversion.

To enter more deeply into the life of the Church means getting used to the ways of the Church. Partly this is a matter simply of becoming at home in the community but partly, I would hope, it is a matter of testing for oneself the values and relevance of those ways.

There is plenty to learn and plenty to test. Sponsors and

catechists need to be aware of how new and strange many of the Church things they have taken for granted will seem to a newcomer. Churches have their own smell. There is the attitude of respect for the past, for tradition, for what has been inherited, whether this is a set of doctrinal statements or a decaying piece of embroidery. There are rituals to be learned, whether these are the events of liturgical worship or the importance of jumble sales, beetle drives and Friday evenings in the Social Club. There are special languages to be learned, again both in worship and in the business and fellowship life of the Church. There are some attitudes which are generally recognized as acceptable in each particular community, some which are seen to be open to debate and others which are excluded.

The question of Church disunity has to be faced squarely. Although the journey into Christian faith is a journey into relationship with God, the journey of conversion, it is also one which is accompanied by Christians of a particular denomination and issues in the sacraments of initiation as practised by a particular denomination in a particular local fellowship within one broken Church.

The scandal of the divisions within the Church is one of the challenges brought by new Christians to the Church as they find it. There are, of course, many others. If we look at the story of the Church as told to an enquirer we find it a mixed one. There are high points, glories even. There are also times, incidents and attitudes of which as members we are ashamed. Having to retell them faces the Christians accompanying a newcomer with need to come to terms with the history of their own Church and with the present state of it. Doing this may well urge them towards a commitment to working for change to put things right in their Church where they can.

At different points in this book I have mentioned things about the local Church which either help or hinder people in their search for God. At the risk of repetition I want to bring some of them together here.

Unity and disunity between Christians and between churches

are continuing features of church life. A local church where you can sense the warm quality of friendship and unity is attractive. Spitefulness and self-seeking repel. It matters how a Christian community deals with disputes and friction between people and groups. Newcomers will soon notice if there are cliques or mistrust. I have in mind the parable of Christian love given by a church hall kitchen with shelves of locked boxes, each containing the private tea cups of a different church organisation!

I keep stressing welcome, because it matters. It needs to be as unconditional as possible. There is a real danger of churches degenerating into clubs with a closed membership for people of a similar sort and this needs to be faced honestly. How much part does social class play in the life of St. Jude's? Do you have to fit in before you can be welcome? Flexibility comes into this too. With every new member who joins something alters because they bring in a new element. If a community is strongly traditionalist, this can be felt as a threat. 'We don't want new people changing things in our church.' It is fine if someone is looking for the security which that set kind of attitude can offer and is willing to accept its rules. But for the encouragement of the journey of discovery you need a community which is more open to experiment and willing to be changed and developed.

The process is one of dialogue. Two partners are involved and each is open to giving and receiving. Both are likely to be changed. In the small accompanying group this is most obvious, because each member there affects and is affected by the others. The same thing happens with the wider congregation. I have seen churches in which the working of the catechumenate has brought a new life and vision, with a strongly increased sense that lay Christians have their own valid ministry in the worship, the mission and the service of the local community. The Rite of Christian Initiation of Adults celebrated publicly enacts the deepening stages of the enquirers' commitment. Simply by their presence and by the involvement of the congregation in their journey the people who are coming to faith and the sacraments of initiation influence the life of the church they are joining and challenge people in it to look to their own commitment and understanding of faith.

Wider Vision

I am vividly aware of the danger which faces Christians, in England at any rate, of treating their church as a refuge from the hardships and difficulties of the world. It is a temptation which is very attractive to clergymen and congregations are often happy to follow them into a kind of ghetto. In the way I have structured this book I can see that I have let myself be seduced into a collusion with the people who expect a book about the Christian journey to be mainly about life in the Church.

But the Church cannot be seen in isolation from the world, just as no person can be isolated from other people or from society. It is not possible to live simply for yourself or by yourself. The Church was founded to be for the world and to work for God's rule in the world. It can only be true to its nature if it is open in its mission to the world within which it lives.

The trouble is that in most churches the available energy is devoted to maintaining the structure, whether this means repairing the buildings or propping up the organization. The effect is that the task of equipping Christians to be agents for mission in their own milieu does not come high on the list of priorities. Yet it is an integral part of anyone's journey in faith that they arrive at an understanding, at values and attitudes which give shape to their relationship with and their place in society and in their world. The local church's task is to enable this to happen.

I see a real danger of the initiation of adults into church membership stopping dead just at that point. Men and women are not encouraged to move onwards to engagement as Christians with the world in which they live. Of course it is more comfortable to stay within the walls of the church and to limit Christian commitment to things of churchy interest. But it is a sad travesty of conversion.

Mission is many-sided. Conversion to Christ carries with it involvement in his mission. Both for the individual and for the church community I see it as three main interlocking activities.

Evangelism is the presentation of good news to other people whether this is by word of mouth in conversation or from a pulpit of some kind in public proclamation. Personal and community witness are an essential part of it. How people live and how groups behave sometimes give as forceful a testimony as actual words.

Service of the needs of others is the practical side of mission. To feed the hungry, bring health to the sick and liberation to the oppressed are only a few instances of it. They call for both time and effort from men and women and involve political and social action both from individuals and the community.

Body-building is the development of the skills and gifts of the mature member of the Body of Christ as well as of the community itself. Mission here involves prayer and training and education.

The issues which have to be considered are not easy because the claims of the Kingdom of God often run counter to what each of us would prefer. There is also the scale of issues, which easily leaves people baffled. Peace and justice are ways of identifying that Shalom, the rightness of things with God, which is part of what we mean by the Kingdom. But does the idea of peace and justice stop at where I can do something about it? I can make up the quarrel with my neighbour about the broken fence; I can speak up at a Union branch meeting and support someone against unfair treatment; I can use my vote as carefully as I can in the Council or Parliamentary Elections. But what about world peace, America and Russia, the arms race and the North-South divide between the rich and the poor nations?

Even on the intimate, personal scale of events, relationships and choices where an individual is involved and can see some effect from how they act, it is often hard to see what bearing Christian faith has on the way things are. At one level I have heard the problem presented clearly by a financier in the City of London, 'I am a rich man and I am a Christian. I read the parable about the judgement of the sheep and the goats on whether or not people have helped those in need.

'As a wealthy person who is a Christian, I do my best to give generously in support of the needs of other people. What is very much harder is to see how I, as a Christian in a senior position in my firm, can make sure that our business decisions are influenced by the same principles.'

In another area of work I recognize the cost to a man in a factory trying to stand out against the racial discrimination against black workers and sexual harrassment of women coming on to the floor which are part and parcel of the place.

The story of the development of Industrial Mission in Britain and Western Europe provides a parable which has a bearing on this conversion to the world. Since World War II there have been three phases. In the first the church in the shape of its ministers recognized that while it exercised some ministry to families at home, men at work were missed out. Industrial Chaplains and missioners therefore visited factories to meet and 'pastor' those who worked in them.

It became obvious that it was not possible to 'pastor' or evangelize individuals without some reference to the conditions in which they worked. Industrial Mission developed from being mission simply to people at work to being also mission to the structures within which they worked, seeking to understand the way firms and industries behaved and how they were organised and to look at them from the Christian standpoint.

The third phase is the present position where it is recognised that industry is part of the wider society, subject to the forces of world economics and having effects upon all parts of human community. Industrial Mission is involved in bringing

Christian insights to bear on such things as the multinational companies, unemployment, and inner urban decay.

Faced with the world and its life, I find it sad when the 'Time and Talents' aspects of a Christian stewardship programme seems to limit offerings to those given for the service of the church, when a plumber is encouraged to see his Christian commitment as largely fulfilled by maintaining the church heating system rather than in the way in which he does his weekday work on a building site; or when a bank worker is snapped up as a church treasurer rather than encouraged in his idea of standing for election as a local councillor.

None of this is easy. Nor are there any generally accepted guidelines, let alone any correct answers. What I hope that the process I am talking about provides is the means to encourage and equip people for their ministry as lay men and women living out their faith in the world in which they have their work and their homes and their leisure interests. I hope too that the kind of groups I describe will be a forum in which they will be enabled to explore the meaning and the practical expression of that ministry with other people for whom it is a real issue.

7

Equipped for Ministry

It is not possible to write a manual for the ministry of accompanying someone else into faith. In this chapter I can simply point to the equipment people need for this work – the skills, the knowledge and the attitudes. But they have to set about acquiring that equipment themselves. All through this book I have described the process of the formation of new Christians as being one of dialogue. It is about relating with others and in groups. The same is true of the formation of men and women in the ministries of sponsors or catechists. You cannot learn it from a book. You need to learn from experience, by practice and by reflection on that practice.

In what I suggest as ways in which church communities and their leaders can work together to develop these ministries, I bring together much that has already appeared in earlier chapters. It is in no sense a blueprint to be followed slavishly. The right model for any church to adopt is one which grows naturally out of the life of that church and which makes sense to the people who are active in it. Although there should be elements which are common to all, the way one church follows will almost certainly vary from that used by a neighbouring church.

The first of the common elements in the training of leaders is that everyone who exercises a ministry in the accompaniment of others into faith should have their own personal experience of speaking and listening openly about their life and faith. This includes the clergy. It calls for the kind of environment in which priest and lay leaders can be honest together and accompany one another's journey. Each has gifts to offer and each needs to be respected. There is no way in which the professional ordained minister can be thought of as having concluded their journey. Priests, deacons and members of religious communities travel the same road as the newest enquirer. Certainly they may have travelled farther, acquired more knowledge and skills, but they still have to do exactly the same personal work of growing in awareness of God and in the light of his love reviewing their own lives. It is all too easy for the professional to say 'The Church teaches that God is . . .'. What is far more demanding is to say, 'For *me* God is . . .'. Many people who hold authority within the Church find this difficult, because their own personal faith seems far less well formed and less sharply defined than the teaching they have come to accept as Church doctrine.

Group Training Example

Let me suggest some ideas for a session with people who are starting in this sort of ministry. There will be several men and women in a group, say between six and ten, perhaps fewer. The purpose is to help them reflect on God's purpose for them through reflecting on their lives and the gospel in company with others.

The first phase is to talk about what is important at the moment to each of the people in the group; working in twos or threes is suitable here. It involves talking about something that really matters. It also involves the hearers in listening as well as they can. What is happening is that people are putting into words part of their own life-story and their companions are giving their attention, entering into the experience of someone else.

The second phase moves from concentrating on the story offered to looking at the Christian story, some aspect of the Church's inheritance which has some bearing on it. It may be a Bible passage, it may be something about church life or a personal experience of the Christian life. Narrative is likely to be more useful than doctrine. People need to be helped to engage with different faculties, their feelings, sympathies and imagination as well as with their intellect. Story-telling does this better than exposition of dogma.

In the third phase the stories are brought together in conversation within the group. Life and Gospel meet and each person is asked to see what consequences follow from that dialogue. What does it mean in these particular circumstances to say, 'I am a Christian'? Where do I go from here?

In this book I envisage the main work of Christian formation taking place in small groups, rarely more than eight or ten, often in pairs, threes or fours. There is a need to recognize each journey as individual and personal. It is something intimate which needs to be respected. I suggest that the formation of leaders should show the same characteristics. If we hope that catechists and sponsors will be good listeners and be able to discern sensitively, then these skills are to be developed in their formation and in the support and review which is part of their continuing in-service training.

Leading groups is in itself a skill which needs to be developed and the principles and practice of how to help groups and group members should be part of the preparation and support of catechists.

It will be clear that what I have in mind is a team, perhaps only a small one, in which priest and lay people work openly together, each exercising their own vital and distinct ministry. There is a mixture of relationships; there is the relationship of colleagues sharing in an enterprise and there is the relationship of leader and led, helper and helped. Let it be recognised very clearly that it is not always the priest who is the leader or the helper! Often, of course, that will be so. There is the responsibility the priest has as the pastor of the flock, the responsibility as the one charged to guard and hand on the tradition of the church and the responsibility of presiding in worship. But these responsibilities do not prevent the priest from accepting help or guidance from other people.

The Church of England report *All are Called* warns of the danger of the 'Shepherd/Sheep Syndrome' by which a priest hardly ever learns even from very committed lay people and lay people retreat into a superficially respectful but resigned or cynical attitude to their 'Father in God'.[1]

Theology

For many people theology is a frightening word. They think it means being able to recite the whole of Christian doctrine. No, theology is an activity in which people take part. It is the work of men and women thinking about God and his relationship to themselves and their world. Seen in this sense, virtually the whole of this book is theology. There is a proper lay theology which is exemplified in the work I describe. I do not want to deny the value of academic theology. The Church's tradition of belief and scholarship needs to be continually reviewed and its presentation renewed in each generation and for each change in circumstances. Indeed the kind of lay theology I mean can only work if there is a living tradition of thought and study of the Christian inheritance in universities, colleges and schools.

There must be some element of education in the formation of catechists and sponsors. If they are to be able to tell the Gospel story and to represent the church tradition, they have got to know enough about them to handle them honestly and effectively. For many established church people this knowledge will have come over the years of membership. They will have acquired a familiarity with Bible stories and ideas from church services, from sermons and from their own Bible reading. They will be familiar with the pattern of the Church's year and the Creed it pictures. They may well have given time to Lent Courses, Parish Weekends and Retreats. Many districts have study programmes in Christian subjects leading to qualifications in some kind of lay ministry. Some of these will be predominantly educational and concerned with the content of belief and study of it. Others may include training in the skills of ministry.

What I would hope from any programme in the area of lay

theological education would be that it should give to people
engaged in it firstly the opportunity to acquire knowledge of
the Christian tradition, its content and the documents it uses;
then some facility in the use of those resources and in making
judgements about them and, thirdly – for me essentially – the
ability and the interest to think theologically about matters of
importance in life. By this third I mean that I hope people will
be enabled to relate the first and second parts of their education to the events and choices of real life. I have a horror of
students being left with an enclosed capsule of religious
knowledge which does not connect with anything outside its
own narrow historical, biblical or ecclesiastical field.

Fears

I recognise that much of this book will cause people to feel
afraid. There is the lay person's fear that he or she is inadequate to undertake the responsibilities I suggest they should
accept; they feel they do not know enough; they are not good
enough; they see themselves as less than the fully committed,
praying Christians they imagine are really needed to do the
job. To which I answer. 'Fine. O.K. That may be true, but
who else is there? And if you don't start from where you are,
you'll never start at all'. Accepting responsibility for a ministry, exercising a ministry and growing in competence as a
minister all go hand-in-hand.

The fear is a natural one and has to be met by providing the
kind of formation I have outlined and also by the provision of
really adequate team support and on-going formation all the
time.

I recognise two clerical fears. One is the fear that the new
Christians, the enquirers, will be taught less than adequately.
The question I am asked goes something like, 'How can you
be sure your confirmation candidates have been properly
instructed if you don't do it yourself?' I hope that if you have
read through my book as far as this, you will have some idea
of my answer to that one. It is that while I recognise the

questioner's anxiety, I am less concerned to see that the whole dogmatic syllabus is covered than to know the person has moved to that point along the journey of conversion where they can truly say, 'Jesus is Lord'. It is not essential for me as a priest to accompany that journey. Often indeed having a priest as the companion only complicates matters.

The other fear is a personal one. It is about loss of status and purpose, a fear that the priest's responsibility will be diminished if lay people take over some of the pastor's teaching role. I meet it by showing how there is a rather different ministry to be found, one which is both more demanding and more exciting. The priest is the one who supports, informs and leads the ministry of the people who make up the Church in the place.

Wolfgang Bartholomäus writes, 'In the long run, self-determined Christians will only feel at home in communities which promote mutual self-determination ... Self-determining communities live, not exclusively, yet in part from the inspiring power of the priest.'[2]

The Church is not priests: it is the whole people of God, only a handful of whom are deacons or priests or bishops. There is a genuine professional joy to be found in helping others to discover and develop their vocation as mature Christians in ministry to others.

Speaking for myself I have found that this helping and leading the church in the place to fulfil its ministry is a more valid expression of priesthood than simply doing the job myself. On the other hand I recognise the danger that it is often quicker and less trouble to do just that – to try to do it all myself. In that way less and less gets done and the priest becomes increasingly more tired and less effective.

8

Resources

There is a considerable body of experience and understanding of the Adult Catechumenate for individuals and churches to draw on. It is to be found both in books and periodicals and also in the meetings, training events and contacts offered by different networks and groupings. All are there to be used. If you want to find out more, please make use of them.

Networks

Roman Catholic

The North American Forum on the Catechumenate offers comprehensive training institutes for different levels of experience in the catechumenate, publishes a newsletter and is a mail order book seller. Address: 5510 Columbia Pike, Suite 310, Arlington, VA 22204, (703) 671-0330.

Episcopal

The Evangelism Ministries Office of the Episcopal Church Center conducted a pilot project in the Diocese of Milwaukee. The project, "Living Our Baptismal Covenant," sought to apply the catechumenal process to adults entering congregations through baptism, reaffirmation, reception or confirmation. Information and resources are available from Rev. A. Wayne Schwab, Episcopal Church Center, 815 Second Ave., New York, NY 10017, (800) 334-7626.

Associated Parishes is an unofficial network of Episcopalians and other Christians interested in liturgical renewal. Resources are available on the theology and practice of Christian baptism. Membership is $20.00 per year. Contact Co-ordinator, Associated Parishes, 3606 Mt. Vernon Ave., Alexandria, VA 22305, (703) 548-6611.

Association of Diocescan Liturgy and Music Commissions. Contact Rev. Clay Morris, St. Mark's Episcopal Church, 600 Colorado Ave., Palo Alto, CA 94306, (415) 326-3800.

Lutheran

The Academy for Evangelists is a national network for the promotion of evangelization and Christian initiation. Contact Rev. James M. Capers or Rev. Paul H. Pallmeyer for a listing of members or further information. Address: Evangelical Lutheran Church in America, 8765 West Higgins Rd. Chicago, IL 60631-4188, (800) NET-ELCA.

Official Texts

The Rite of Christian Initiation of Adults, 1988. This edition of the rite was mandated for use in the Roman Catholic dioceses of the U.S. as of September 1, 1988. It contains all of the various rites for the catechumenate, the sacraments of initiation, and the post-baptismal period of mystagogy. It is available from the U.S. Catholic Conference and from a number of other publishers.

The Book of Occasional Services (The Church Hymnal Corporation, New York, 1979). This contains an official Anglican Rite of Christian Initiation of Adults produced by the Episcopal Church's Standing Liturgical Commission.

Books

Becoming Adult, Becoming Christian, James Fowler (New York: Harper and Row, 1985). A study of adult human development and the stages of growth in faith.

Breaking Open the Word of God, Karen Hinman Powell and Joseph P. Sinwell (Mahwah, NJ: Paulist Press, 1986, 1987, 1988). A three volume set of resources for using the Lectionary in catechesis.

Building God's People, John Westerhoff III (Seabury: New York, 1983). A detailed and compelling account of the work of catechesis, covering all aspects of the Christian life.

Celebrating Our Faith, Robert E. Webber (San Francisco: Harper and Row, 1986). An introduction of the catechumenate tradition to the Protestant Church showing how adaptable it can be to all denominations as a means of contemporary evangelism.

Conversion and Community, Thomas P. Ivory (Mahwah, NJ: Paulist Press, 1988). Explores how the catechumenate can serve as a model for total parish formation.

Conversion and the Catechumenate, ed. Robert Duggan (Mahwah, NJ: Paulist Press, 1984). A full, practical treatment of conversion and the ministry of accompanying new Christians.

How To Form a Catechumenate Team, Karen Hinman Powell (Chicago: Liturgy Training Publications, 1986). A guide for pastors, catechists, sponsors, welcomers, and catechumenate directors.

The RCIA: Transforming the Church, Thomas Morris (Mahwah, NJ: Paulist Press, 1989). A complete guide for the pastoral implementation of the rite.

Stories of Faith, John Shea (Chicago: The Thomas More Press, 1980). A full development of the use of stories in the growth of faith and the sharing of faith.

Welcoming the New Catholic and *Guide for Sponsors,* Ronald Lewinski (Chicago: Liturgy Training Publications, revised

1987). Two short, very practical handbooks for use by clergy and lay teams in the parish.

Journals and Newsletters

Catechumenate. A Journal of Christian Initiation. Published bimonthly by Liturgy Training Publications, 1800 North Hermitage Avenue, Chicago, IL 60622.

Catholic Evangelization in the United States of America. Published bimonthly by the Paulist National Catholic Evangelization Association, 3031 Fourth Street, N.E., Washington, D.C. 20017.

Forum. Monthly newsletter published by the North American Forum on the Catechumenate, 5510 Columbia Pike, Suite 310, Arlington, VA 22204.

Fire and Water. A quarterly newsletter for the catechumenate published at St. James Episcopal Church, P.O. Box 4463, Jackson, MS 39216, (601) 982-4880. $15.00 per year.

Notes

Chapter 1

1   *Rite of Christian Initiation of Adults*, Geoffrey Chapman, a division of Cassell Publishers Ltd., London, 1987, p.5. Copyright ICEL.

Chapter 2

1   John Shea, *Stories of Faith*, Thomas Moore Press, Chicago, 1980, p.43.

Chapter 3

1   Norbert Mette, *The Christian Community's Task in the Process of Religious Education.* Concilium 174. *The Transmission of the Faith to the Next Generation.* T. & T. Clark Ltd. Edinburgh, 1984. p.73.
2   John Westerhoff III, *A Pilgrim People*, Seabury Press, Minneapolis, 1984, p.1.
3   Karen Hinman Powell, *Beginnings Institute* Conference Papers, North American Forum on the Catechumenate, 1986.

Chapter 4

1   John Westerhoff III, *Building God's People*, Seabury Press, New York, 1983, p.117.

Chapter 5

1   A. Patrick Purnell, S.J., *Our Faith Story*, Collins, London, 1985, p.28.
2   Tony Bridge, *Road to Damascus*, Thames TV Broadcast, 1986.

Chapter 7

1   *All are Called*, Church House, Publishing, London, 1986. p.8.
2   Wolfgang Bartholomäus, *Being a Christian in the Church and the World of Tomorrow* Concilium 174 *The Transmission of the Faith to the Next Generation*, T. (T. Clark Ltd., Edinburgh, 1984. p.83.